OLONGAPO EARP

J.E. Park

Mailing List Sign Up for Newsletter and New Release Info: http//:jeparkbooks.wpcomstaging.com

Follow me on Facebook at
https://www.facebook.com/JE-Park-100409961692113

Twitter handle: @JEPark94519501

Email at: jeparkauthor@gmail.com

Cover design done by DAMONZA.COM

ISBN: 978-1-7350940-2-1 (ebk)
ISBN: 978-1-7350940-3-8 (pbk)

Table of Contents

CHAPTER 1

Master Chief Darrow lit a cigarette, taking one deep drag off of it before passing it through the bars of my cell. The brig of the *USS Belleau Wood* was supposed to be a non-smoking space, but few men were willing to correct the master chief's behavior. They did not want him correcting theirs in return.

I thanked Darrow for the Marlboro while blowing smoke out of my mouth, relishing the flavor. It helped dull the edge of both my hangover and the discomfort I still felt from the barrage of body blows I had endured the night before. "So, how bad do you think this is going to be?"

"To be frank," my master chief started, shaking his head. "I think it's going to take a miracle to get you out of this one. Seriously, Doyle. What on earth was going through your head? You trying to catch up with Macklemore in Pearl Harbor's holding company so the two of you can get thrown out of the Navy together?"

There was nothing funny about the situation I was in, but I chuckled. "You know, the lieutenant blames me for Mack popping Crowley in the kisser in front of all those news cameras when we left San Diego."

The master chief frowned. "Well, if it wasn't for you, he wouldn't have had the balls to stick up for his girlfriend like that. He would've just taken it."

"Yeah, that's how the lieutenant sees it. He's still pissed. He says it made him look bad in front of the captain. You know, Krause chewed my ass again yesterday for the whole thing. He swore all it would take was one more screw-up, one more teeny lapse in judgment, and he would toss my ass right out of the fleet."

I took another drag off of my cigarette. After casting my gaze toward the deck to avoid making eye contact with my master chief, I said, "I know he meant it as a threat, but once I'd killed half a bottle of tequila, it seemed more like an opportunity."

"Seriously?" Darrow asked, sounding quite surprised. "You want out of the Navy?"

I shrugged. "I did last night."

"And now?"

I tore my eyes off of the deck and looked back at Darrow. "Does it matter?"

My master chief let out a long sigh and leaned back against the bars of the cell opposite mine. "Probably not. You got a plan?"

I shook my head. "Not really. I've got fifty grand stashed in a Panamanian bank account thanks to some morally ambiguous Tijuana police officers, though. I guess I could start there. Remember that Green Beret I told you about that was with me in El Salvador? Finn? He was based out of Panama. He knew it pretty well. He told me about a place he liked on the Caribbean, near the border with Costa Rica. Bocas del Toro. He said it's got great diving, some decent surfing, and awesome fishing. Maybe I'll use the money to get a boat and start chartering scuba tours out that way. I could moonlight dropping lines for grouper."

Darrow pursed his lips together as he considered my idea. "Sounds nice, but I'm not sure that money will go half as far as you think it might."

I suspected as much. "It probably won't, but when you think about it, how many twenty-two-year-olds get out of the Navy with that much cash? The way I see it, I'm ahead."

Darrow grinned. "Yeah, when you put it that way, I guess you are."

OLONGAPO EARP

The two of us finished our cigarettes in silence. After I stubbed mine out, Darrow took it from me. "Why do you want out of the Navy now?" he asked, dropping my butt into an empty soda can that he was using as an ashtray. "We're on our way to Japan, finally doing everything you told me you joined the Navy to do. You getting thrown out now means you put up with all the bullshit the military had to throw at you without reaping any of the rewards."

I sighed. "Master Chief, I was in a bad place last night. The weight of everything we've been through the past few months just became a bit much. Hannah breaking off our engagement. All that effort I put into straightening Macklemore out, only to have him blow it by ringing Crowley's bell in public…"

Darrow was shaking his head in disbelief. "In public? Christ, he did it on TV!"

I grinned. "Yeah, he sure did. I hope someone kept that tape." They did. I had no way of knowing it then, but I would see it replayed on national news a few months later.

Shaking my head, I said, "What a waste. Macklemore was the one thing I thought I salvaged from what went down with Hulagu. Well, besides the money, of course."

"Does that bother you?" Darrow asked. "I can't imagine watching those guys murder that prick is helping with all the shit you got going on in your head."

A few weeks before, I watched a Mexican police officer kick Sergeant Francisco Martinez into the Pacific Ocean. He was weighed down with enough towing chains to ensure his body never surfaced. The cops tortured and mutilated the man, leaving him a bloody mess, before pushing him overboard. Martinez was a monster who earned his fate, but his killing had still been a gruesome sight to behold. It should have joined the parade of horrors that often tortured my psyche, but it was conspicuously absent.

Shrugging, I told the master chief, "Hulagu's not what keeps me up at night. It might even be canceling out episodes I should be having of when that son-of-a-bitch tried to blow my brains out."

"So, you're not having your flashbacks anymore?"

Sighing again, I said, "I'm having them more than ever. They're just not about Martinez. I relive the classics. My dad murdering my family. The girl

3

I got killed in El Salvador. What I did to Randy Green. I don't sleep much anymore. I'm exhausted. And now that Hannah left me…"

I had to pause to keep my voice from cracking. "Well, now that she's gone, I'm kind of lost, you know? I've never had a family. I thought that I'd finally get that with her, someone who's actually waiting for me to come back somewhere. We could have made ourselves a home, a place I could go to get away from all the booze and the fighting around here. I'm tired of it."

"You're tired of it?" Darrow laughed. "Is that why you decided to get piss drunk and take on three guys off of Waikiki Beach?"

"Yeah, that worked out a little weird." I grinned. "You know, I was actually on those guys' side in the beginning. I was planning on pounding on that little shit-head even before they got to him."

A look of confusion flashed across Darrow's face. "Wait a minute…start from the beginning. What exactly happened?"

I sat down on my bunk and leaned back against the bulkhead to get comfortable. "There was this guy who walked into the Pineapple Broiler with his girlfriend. He was a really pompous prick. He reminded me of the frat douche who got Mack arrested in Tijuana…"

"The guy you messed up in Ocean Beach?"

I nodded. "Yeah, that one. Anyway, I'm in the bar, and I'd already decided to kick someone's ass to earn my discharge. I was struggling to find a target, though. It's Hawaii. Everyone's here to have a good time, and I could tell most of the people around me were on a once-in-a-lifetime trip. I couldn't bring myself to ruin their vacation. Then this prima donna rolled in and started treating the staff like trash to play the big shot in front of his girl. I figured it'd be fun to knock him down a few pegs."

"But you didn't?"

I shook my head. "I never got the chance. This guy left to use the bathroom and within thirty seconds, another dude swooped in and started talking to his date."

"She hot?"

"She was cute enough, sure. Not drop-dead gorgeous, but pretty. She kind of looked familiar though, like I had seen her around somewhere. Anyway, she wasn't interested in this other guy and blew him off. It was cool, though. The dude was a gentleman about it. He was just turning to leave when the chick's boyfriend gets back. Now, the boyfriend didn't take too kindly to another man giving his girl attention, so he starts making a scene about it. Long story short, this pansy-ass and his girlfriend get tossed from the bar, along with the guy he's jawing at. Two of the other guy's friends settle the bill and leave with him."

I paused to take a breath. "So, the prick with the girlfriend is really being obnoxious, talking shit all the way out the door. The other three guys are trying to be Christian about everything though, and for the most part, they're ignoring him. I followed them out, still planning on kicking the loser's teeth in if given the opportunity. Once they all got outside, this dufus sucker-punches one of the other three guys right in the back of the head. After that, they all turned on the dude and started whipping his ass."

Darrow looked perplexed. "What'd you do? Jump in to help him out because he was outnumbered?"

"Naw," I answered. "At first, I just watched. The punk had it coming, so I was enjoying the show. When it became obvious they were really hurting this kid, though, his girl jumped in. She got on the back of the biggest guy there, dug her nails into his face, and scratched him right across the eye. It must've hurt like hell. The big guy screamed bloody murder, then started wailing on her…"

I did not have to say much more. Darrow knew I grew up watching my old man beat my mother bloody. He was aware that there was no quicker way to set me off than to see a man strike a woman. "How bad did you hurt them?"

"Hurt *them*?" I laughed. "It was three against one, Master Chief. They hurt *me*."

Darrow looked relieved. He knew what I was capable of. As far as the Navy was concerned, though, I was still screwed. After I almost got Macklemore and myself killed in Mexico, the captain was clear that he would show no mercy if I was ever involved in another liberty incident. On the civilian side, though, I was only facing a drunk and disorderly charge, if anything at all. It was no more serious than a traffic ticket.

"You know, Master Chief," I said. "I was trying to keep a girl from getting herself hurt. The captain's a good man. He'll understand that. You think he'd consider…"

"You changing your mind about wanting to get out of the Navy?" Darrow asked.

I grimaced. "Well, let's say I might not have thought things through yesterday."

Darrow crossed his arms and glared at me. "You need to start thinking things through, Doyle! You'd best begin working yourself up a solid sense of self-restraint! You crippled Randy Green because you couldn't control yourself. Then we have you springing Macklemore from the back of a Mexican police car. That little stunt went from Mack spending a night in jail to facing years in prison for escaping custody."

"I got him back, though."

"And nearly got the two of you murdered for it! Not to mention you sparked off a drug war between two Tijuana police agencies in the process. Doyle, the captain's not going to see you as some gallant savior of damsels in distress here. He's going to see you as the epicenter of every major shit-show that's landed on his desk recently. The days of your liberty antics being mildly amusing passed the minute Green started convulsing on the deck of the winch room. You're becoming a real liability here. This one's going to hurt you."

Hanging my head, I asked, "So there's nothing you can do?"

Darrow stood before me in thought for a couple of moments before answering. "I'll do what I can, but you're going to need to temper your expectations. I expect the captain to throw you out of the Navy for this. You've consistently shown an inability to control yourself. That can prove risky overseas. Especially where we're headed. You get picked up by the local dicks in Sasebo, and they're going to lock your ass up. Especially if you get into it with one of the locals. I don't think the old man wants to risk you pulling another Mexico caper in a place like Japan. I'll talk to him, though."

I stood up to show my gratitude. "Thank you so much, Master Chief. Thank you."

Darrow waved me back down. "Don't go thanking me just yet. Like I said before, it's going to take a miracle to get you out of this one."

*****

OLONGAPO EARP

Lieutenant Junior Grade Andrew Krause repeated Master Chief Darrow's words, though in a completely different context and with an obscene amount of exuberance. "It's going to take a miracle to get you out of this one."

I replied with a tone of voice designed to convey how disinterested I was in the lieutenant's take on the situation. "So I've heard, sir."

LTJG Krause ripped the shades off his face to respond, making it the first time I had seen his eyes in months. Before saying anything, though, he squinted at the "No Smoking" sign posted above my cell. That threw him off. Inhaling a deep breath through his nose, he looked up to see the haze around the brig's lights. He then turned toward Master Chief Darrow. "Have you been smoking in here?"

"Yeah," Darrow answered, subtly challenging the lieutenant to do something about it.

Declining, Krause turned his attention back to me. "You realize you've had this coming, right? Sooner or later, these things catch up with you. The unauthorized corporal punishments you guys have been dishing out, undermining my authority to make me look stupid…"

The master chief and I exchanged quizzical expressions. We never undermined the lieutenant. We did not have to. The most efficient way to embarrass our division officer was to do exactly what he told us. We proved this time after time by carrying out his orders to the letter and without hesitation. We called it "malicious obedience."

"…the drinking, the whoring, the fighting…you guys aren't going to get away with that forever. We're going to make an example out of you, Murphy. We're going to show the crew that the *USS Belleau Wood* isn't some floating fraternity house."

"Sir," I asked, taking a step forward to get closer to the bars. Krause instinctively took a step back to avoid being within my reach. "Can I ask you something?"

"What?" the lieutenant snapped.

"My radar repair shop consistently has one of the highest readiness rates on the ship. Our gear rarely malfunctions but when it does, we get it fixed quickly. Our spaces are spotless, our uniforms sharp, and my men show up to quarters every day on time. Why are you so eager to revel in one of us finding ourselves in trouble?"

Krause looked at Master Chief Darrow and then back at me. A victorious smile curled up at the corners of his mouth. "Because you're thugs, Petty Officer Murphy. You, that psycho Dixon, Metaire, and you, Master Chief. You're all thugs. You're also drunks. And lechers. Whoremongers. You all lack any semblance of a moral compass. You're a stain on the tradition of the United States Navy and an affront to God…"

I knew where the lieutenant was going. I had seen it before. He was about to go ranting about our poor, heathen souls. He was going to lament how our country was lost, entrusting its defense to those of us who, according to Krause, lived in Satan's service. He was offended that he never saw any of my men in church and appalled that I possessed a security clearance despite my dog tags labeling me an atheist. To our division officer, that made me a Communist as well. Before he could get going, though, the ring tone of the IC line sounded off.

Darrow answered the call and identified himself. He then muttered a couple of "okays" before hanging up. Looking at me, he said, "That was the master-at-arms. One of his men is escorting the captain down here right now. They'll be here any second."

I swallowed hard. Krause did not concern me much, but Captain Stephen Fleming did. I had a great deal of respect for the captain and genuinely cared what the man thought about me. He also wielded an immense amount of power and could ruin my life in an instant if he wanted to. I stiffened to the position of attention and saw my master chief doing the same.

Lieutenant Junior Grade Krause did not. He was so excited that he could hardly stand still.

Now, I had spent the first thirteen years of my life praying for the Almighty to rescue me from my father's abuse. Only when I grew to the point where I could finally fight back did the cosmos intervene. It ended my torment by allowing my old man to murder my entire family before getting himself blown away by the police. At that point, I figured out that there was no god. If there was, it was not an entity I had a lot of affection for. That said, I have been party to things, such as inconceivable coincidences, that I am at a loss to explain without invoking divine intervention. One of those occurred when the ship's captain stepped into the brig of the *USS Belleau Wood* that day.

OLONGAPO EARP

I tried to call out, "Attention on deck!" when the skipper came through the door, but he cut me off with a curt "At ease!" In civilian clothes, he marched right up to my cell without acknowledging either the master chief or Krause. He then stuck a photograph up to the bars of my cell. "Do you recognize this girl, Petty Officer Murphy?" he asked, showing me a picture of what a miracle looked like.

The photograph was taken in a local hotel room. It was of a cute, blonde-haired young woman with her left eye blackened and swollen shut. Seeing the girl's face in a Polaroid so close to the captain's revealed why she had looked so familiar before. It was a familial resemblance. My heart started racing, and it took a Herculean effort to keep myself from smiling. "Yes, sir. That's the girl I saw being beaten up in Waikiki, sir."

Captain Fleming nodded his head and lowered the picture. "That's my daughter, Murphy."

I did not mean to, but I could not help smirking at Krause when the captain ordered me to be let out of my cage. The EMO went from unbridled glee to looking like a little boy watching his brand-new puppy getting raped to death by a herd of rutting wildebeests. Suspecting that I remained on very thin ice though, I wiped the smile from my face before I could be accused of gloating.

The captain shook my hand as I emerged from the cell. Still, he looked me in the eye and asked, "What did I tell you about fighting, Murphy?"

"Sir, that was not exactly a fight. I mean, I was doing the best I could, but those gorillas beat the shit out of me."

"Did you think you were going to win a fight against three men?"

Actually, it had only been a few weeks since I whipped five bad enough for my fiancée to break off our engagement. To be fair, though, those guys were not exactly varsity material. I was not inclined to brag about it. Seeing how I got away with that one, I was not going to cop to it while still standing in the brig, either. "No, sir," I told the captain. "But I figured if those guys were busy beating on me, they wouldn't be hurting the girl."

Darrow was standing behind the captain, so Fleming did not catch the look on my boss's face when I said that. My master chief saw right through my bullshit and was trying to keep from busting out in laughter. He managed to keep it all inside, though. Instead, he flashed me an expression that broadcast precisely what he was thinking. *Niiiiiiice!*

"Petty Officer Murphy," the captain said. "Cindy told me what happened. Her version of it anyway. I just have one question for you."

"Sir?"

"Why didn't you step in and help while my daughter's boyfriend was getting his clock cleaned by those guys? Why'd you wait until one of them struck her?"

I was hesitant to answer. "Sir, I need to level with you; I'm torn between trying to be truthful and being diplomatic."

"Don't jerk me around, Murphy."

I nodded. "Okay. Your daughter's boyfriend is a dick. I didn't jump in because from where I stood, it looked like he was getting what was coming to him."

Krause's jaw dropped to the floor. My master chief put his palm over his face. Even the duty master-at-arms looked away. It was clear they all thought I should have opted for diplomacy.

The captain did not. After shaking off my blunt assessment, he reached out and patted me on the shoulder. "Yeah, that's kind of what I figured. I don't like that little prick much either. I heard he cried like a little girl the entire time he was in the ambulance. You're free to go, Murphy. Get some rest, take a shower, and go enjoy yourself. You surf, don't you?"

"A little."

"Then give the booze a rest and go catch some waves. There's a hurricane churning southeast of us whipping up some good surfing on the bottom of the island."

"A hurricane?" Master Chief Darrow sounded surprised. "My wife's flying into Honolulu a few hours from now. I didn't hear anything about a hurricane heading for Hawaii."

The captain shrugged. "It's far enough away that it's not expected to affect us much. Go pick up your wife, Master Chief. Murphy, grab your board and hit the beach."

"Thank you, sir. I'm on duty today, though."

The captain stopped. "You're on duty? You know what? As a reward for standing up for my daughter, I'm granting you special liberty until we pull out on Monday. Krause!"

"Yessir?"

"Write up Murphy's special liberty chit for me. Get it to my office in thirty minutes so I can sign it before I leave."

It sounded like all the moisture got sucked out of my lieutenant's mouth. "Yes, sir."

"Murphy, I'll have the lieutenant leave it on the quarterdeck for you. Understood?"

"Aye aye, sir."

"Good." The captain patted my shoulder and shook my hand once more. He then shook hands with everyone else before departing the brig with Krause in tow.

Once they were out of earshot, Master Chief Darrow slid up beside me and leaned his arm on my shoulder. "I have no idea what just happened there."

"I do," I told him. "A goddamn miracle."

Darrow nodded, but I could tell the two of us had different interpretations of what miracle had transpired. For him, it was the coincidence of me picking a fight on behalf of a girl who turned out to be the captain's daughter. It saved what was left of my career.

For me, it was something else entirely. Had those three brutes not started kicking the piss out of that young lady's boyfriend, I would have. It would have been *my* back she jumped on to help him. It would have been *my* face she dug her nails into. She could have ended up hurt as I tried getting her off of me. Had that happened, it would have been far more than my career at risk. It would have been my freedom.

If I hurt the captain's little girl, even accidentally, I doubted the skipper would have been satisfied just sending me to captain's mast and tossing me out of the Navy. He would have had me court-martialed. Jailed. Discharged under other than honorable conditions. With what amounted to a felony pinned to my record, my life would have become even more of a ruin than it already was.

As I let that sink in, I was intensely grateful to the three men who kept me from clobbering that prissy little prick. Those guys saved my life as I knew it. At least for a little while, anyway.

*****

CHAPTER 2

I was no stranger to Hawaii. When I first reported aboard the *USS Belleau Wood*, the vessel was the Third Fleet's temporary flagship. That meant we were practically living in Pearl Harbor until the *USS Blue Ridge* finished its overhaul. At the time, I was underage, so I could not join my shipmates at the bars. It was there I started to dabble in scuba diving to keep myself from going stir-crazy.

After the captain cut me loose for the rest of the week, I attempted to pursue my old pastimes. I dove Hanauma Bay, then tried some south side surfing per the captain's recommendation. It was not as good as he had heard. Attempting to better test my skills, I grabbed my board and headed to the North Shore to ride the bad boy breaks instead.

I damned near killed myself. Flattened on my first ride in an epic wipeout, I got slammed against the ocean floor so hard it knocked the wind out of me. This is not something you want happening while you're underwater. I made it to the surface to expel some of the sea from my lungs, but before I could take another breath, I got blasted by a second psycho swell. That one sent me ass over elbows through the churning surf, but at least I was able to get my feet on the ground.

OLONGAPO EARP

OLONGAPO EARP

I staggered toward the shore, vomiting and coughing to clear my airway. While still waist-deep in water, the ocean tried to finish me off. A third monster break took me from behind, pounded me into the sand, then dragged me along the bottom. As it passed over me, it used the surfboard I still had tethered to my leg to peel me off the bottom. My legs bent over my head, cracking every vertebra in my spine as the Pacific tried to fold me in half.

As if that were not bad enough, Nā-maka-o-Kahaʻi, Hawaii's goddess of the sea, tried to pants me, too. The wave that nearly broke my back also ripped my swimming trunks off. It pulled them down my legs and off of my feet before I could even begin to react. Had it not been for the tether around my ankle, that bitch would have had them. Denied her swimwear sacrifice, Nā-maka retaliated by pulling my board back as far as its leash would allow. She then took aim and released it, sending it hurtling at me as if it were fired from a slingshot. My Ron Jon somehow smashed into my face and crotch at the same time, dropping me naked and dazed back into the water.

A couple of visiting Australians saw the whole thing. While laughing hysterically, they managed to pull me from the water and drag me back to the beach, likely saving my life. Unfortunately, my dignity did not make it. Mourning its loss, I decided to go back to drinking.

*****

It started with a few rounds of drinks to thank the Australians for saving me from drowning. And for getting my pants back on before I ended up on the Hawaiian offender registry's hall of fame. There are few people more enjoyable to drink with than folk from Down Under. Unfortunately, it had only been a week since my Australian fiancée broke off our engagement, and the accents of my new friends kept reminding me of that. Before I realized it, I was no longer drinking for fun. I was numbing my loneliness.

I stuck it out with the Aussies for as long as I could. Eventually, though, it became too much and I started wandering. Before long, I fell in with a group of local entrepreneurs on the outskirts of Waimea. They were peddling a vile home-brewed pineapple spirit imbued with mind-bending potency. I spent the next couple of days transcending time and space on that horrible stuff. When I finally got off of it, I found a shower, bought new clothes, and made my way back to Honolulu *sans* surfboard. I lost it somewhere along the way.

When I got off the bus in Waikiki, I immediately saw something was up. The place was empty. The ever-present sun was gone, the wind picked up, and the sky had turned gray. Waikiki's serene bay had grown tempestuous and its waves lashed the beach with uncharacteristic anger. It took a while for me to find an open tavern. When I finally did, I asked the bartender what was going on.

Looking at me as if he was wondering what rock I had been hiding beneath, he asked, "You haven't heard about the hurricane? Iniki? It's heading right for us."

"No shit?" I said. "Last I heard, it was passing way south."

"It took an unexpected turn a couple of days ago."

That concerned me. I figured I had been blackout drunk for a while, but the bartender's news left me wondering for exactly how long. I prayed it was not enough to have missed ship's movement. Seeing a newspaper lying on the bar, I checked the date. It was only September 10th, and I let out a long sigh of relief. The ship was not supposed to leave until the fourteenth. I was good. "You alright?" the bartender asked.

I nodded. "Yeah, I am now. For a second, I was worried I might have missed my boat."

"Are you in the Navy? If you are, yeah, you did."

"What?!?" I asked, now horrified.

"The fleet's gone," the bartender told me. "They can't ride out a hurricane in port. They had to ship out."

I could not believe it. I avoided getting busted out of the Navy for assault, only to end up in danger of losing a chevron for letting the ship leave without me. That was a big deal. I was screwed. Not to mention, I had to find someplace to ride out the storm. "Damn, I should probably put some effort into getting a room, eh? You think anything's open around here?"

The bartender shook his head. "There wasn't enough time for people to get off the island. Rooms are pretty booked. It's going to be tough."

"Shit," I said. "How long are you planning on staying open?"

The bartender shrugged. "I'm kind of a storm junkie. I'll stay here as long as we have customers."

OLONGAPO EARP

Our tender was a trooper. Besides myself, there were only a pair of women in the bar, seated a couple of stools down from me. Both seemed to be in their forties and far too pale to have been in Hawaii long.

The woman seated closest to me had bright blue eyes and short jet-black hair. She was at least twenty years my senior, but still very pretty and only now starting to show her age. That was something she also noticed, and she was not taking her freshly found crow's feet well. It was the reason she was in Hawaii. Her name was Darlene Gabriel. When she heard the bartender say he would stay open as long as we were there, she raised her glass. "That's what makes this man so bitchin'."

Darlene's friend was Abbie Tindall. Abbie was younger than Darlene but still considerably older than me. If I had to guess, I would say she had just turned forty or was very close to it. She was shorter than Darlene, standing up to my shoulders, with red hair and green eyes. Though by no means overweight, she had a fuller figure than her companion. Abbie also had an adorably high-pitched voice that made her sound like Betty Boop. "His name is Bob too!" Abbie squeaked. "He's 'Bitchin' Bob.'" Turning to me, she asked, "Have you met Bitchin' Bob?"

I shook my head and held out my hand. "No, we haven't been formally introduced. I'm damned glad to meet you, Bitchin' Bob. I'm Doyle Murphy. World traveler. Teller of tales. Seeker of truth. Defender of freedom. Tequila aficionado, and sexual dynamo."

Bitchin' Bob shook my hand as the two ladies erupted into laughter. "Bob Monroe. The pleasure's mine," he said.

I threw a twenty-dollar bill on the bar and told Bob to get the ladies whatever they were drinking. They introduced themselves, then got up to take seats on either side of me so we could talk.

Both were school teachers from Fishers, Indiana, and it was their first time in Hawaii. Having been there several times myself, I gave them tips on what to see and do. I told them that they had to visit the *USS Arizona* memorial and try snorkeling in Hanauma Bay. I also suggested the North Shore, where I had just been. I recommended they avoid homemade pineapple spirits, though.

"What about the nightlife?" Darlene asked. "What're the best clubs around here to meet people?"

J.E. PARK

I laughed a little. "Truth be told, the last time I was here, I was underage. I couldn't drink out in town. Hell, I once got thrown out of a place in Honolulu with a couple of guys from the Australian Navy. They were cool and invited me back to the bar they had on their ship, though. I got so tanked on the *HMAS Swan* that they made me spend the night. I freaked out when I woke up the next morning. I thought I got so drunk that I got press-ganged into the wrong country's Navy."

"What about this time?" Abbie asked while ordering us all another drink. "You look like you've had time to find your way around."

I shrugged. "I don't know. I haven't been looking to meet anybody. I've been drinking with the singular sense of purpose of staying fucked up."

"Why's that?" Darlene wondered aloud.

I shrugged and told the ladies how I got dumped on the pier in San Diego via a letter delivered to me by a shipmate. "Aw, I'm so sorry to hear that," Darlene said as she put her arm around me. "There's a lot of that going around. Isn't there, Abbie?"

Darlene's friend frowned a bit and cast her eyes down at the bar. "There sure is. I was married for almost twenty years. Got hitched right out of high school. I did everything I was supposed to do. I held a job, raised kids, loved my husband, took care of my family, kept a clean house, and stroked his ego every day. The son-of-a-bitch left me for our babysitter. At least you found out it wasn't going to work before you invested the best years of your life into her."

I raised my glass and clinked it against Abbie's. "You win. Unless Darlene has a worse tale to tell."

Caught mid-drink, Darlene needed to swallow before she could answer. "No, I had no real tragedies like you two — just a long pathetic string of poor decisions that kept me single. So here I am, pushing fifty without ever being married or having children. Now it's looking like it may be too late."

"You've never married?" I found that hard to believe. Darlene looked great now. She must have been stunning in her twenties.

"Well, it's not like I never had offers. They were just from men that weren't perfect enough to meet my impossible standards. Looking back, though, all but one of them turned out to be great guys. It was me that was screwed up. So here I am, with my fellow wreck, cruising Hawaii looking to take the edge off a mid-life crisis. We were looking forward to some reckless behavior but ended up thwarted by a goddamn hurricane. Cheers!"

"Cheers!" Abbie and I answered. Looking back at it, I should have known what was going to happen, but at that point, I was utterly without a clue. The three of us kept toasting our screwed-up lives, only interrupting our drinking to peek at the weather outside.

After we returned from one of those trips to the back patio, Bob ran in from the front of the building. He took my drinks from me, placing them out of sight. "You need to hide somewhere! Now!" He grabbed a piece of paper and a marker, writing "Out of Order" on the sheet in bold black letters. He then stuck two pieces of masking tape on it. "Go into the bathroom and go to the last stall. Attach this to the door, then get inside. Make sure you lock it. Stand on the seat so they don't see your feet."

"They?" I asked. "Who the hell is 'they?'"

"The Shore Patrol."

"Shore Patrol!" I exclaimed. "Shit! What are they doing here?"

"Looking for sailors. They're sweeping the bars and picking up stragglers to ride out the storm on base."

Without another word, I grabbed Bob's paper and ran to the bathroom to do what he told me.

I spent an eternity in that stall. I could not hear anything going on out front, only what was going on outside. I listened to the debris swirling about beyond the walls and wondered how safe it was to get so smashed so close to an enraged ocean.

Eventually, the bathroom door opened, and I heard Darlene tell me the coast was clear. I dropped from my perch and waddled out of the stall, my legs made wobbly by booze and bad circulation. "What did the shore patrol say?" I asked as I approached her.

"Nothing much," Darlene said. "They asked us if we'd seen anyone in the Navy. They warned us the police would be following shortly to clear everybody out. Things are getting bad out there. They said we shouldn't wait for the cops to shut us down."

Without any warning, Darlene reached out and grabbed me behind the head, pulling me in close, kissing me. Her other hand made its way between my legs.

I responded by backing her up against the wall, slipping my hands down the back of her panties. We then went at each other, feeling our bodies all over, both above and below our clothing. I attempted to take her right there, but she pulled back. Out of breath, she said, "We should get back to our room. I need to use the bathroom first, though. Wait for me at the bar."

Panting and euphoric, I left the restroom and awkwardly walked back to the front. Taking my seat next to Abbie, I turned to ask her how she was doing. Before I could say anything, she grabbed me too, sticking her tongue into my mouth and guiding my hand to her breast. "D...Duh...Dar...Darrr..." I tried to spit out.

Pulling her face away from mine for a second, Abbie asked, "Darlene? Did she tell you we should be getting back to our room soon?"

It was only then that the moribund machinations of my muddled mind finally came together. My jaw dropped open, my eyes went wide, and I felt myself getting dizzy. That was likely due to the blood rushing out of my head to feed other parts of my body. Fearful of hyperventilating, I lit a cigarette to calm myself down.

Abbie laughed as she saw my hands shake, trying to work my lighter. She started massaging me between my legs to make it worse. "Mmmmmmmm. You've never done this, have you?"

My first reaction was to lie, but it was obvious that I had never been involved in a threesome before. I shook my head.

"Neither have we," Abbie giggled. "This is going to be new for all of us."

I could not even talk. My mouth went dry and my throat constricted like I was experiencing some sort of anaphylactic episode. Unable to say anything, I leaned in and began kissing Abbie again.

"Are we ready?" Darlene asked as she came back from the ladies' room.

I smiled wide and hoarsely whispered, "Oh yeah. I'm ready." The truth was I was a little *too* ready. A couple of months before, I watched one of my guys climax in his clothes as a prostitute led him out of a Tijuana strip club. I was terrified that might happen to me. As each of the ladies took one of my arms and led me toward the door, I struggled to fill my head with the most horrifying visual imagery I could to keep from meeting the fate of Steve Kent.

Decomposing manatees.

OLONGAPO EARP

Eyeballs pierced with darts.
Richard Nixon naked blowing bloody liquid farts.

As we emerged outside, Darlene leaned in close and asked, "Do you have any protection?"

I nodded. "I got a rubber in my wallet."

Abbie giggled. "I don't think that's going to be enough."

At the time, I thought she meant I was going to need more than one condom. In hindsight, I now think she meant I was going to need something more along the lines of a bicycle helmet.

*****

The moment we closed the door behind us, we surrendered to our urges. Darlene pushed me up against the wall of their hotel room. She then ripped my shirt open, sending buttons flying through the air. One of them landed on the nightstand, next to a clock that read 6:42. She then undid the top button of my shorts and pulled everything down to my ankles, taking me inside her mouth. Abbie danced toward the bed, letting her skirt fall to the floor while stripping away her top and bra. She then peeled away her leopard skin panties and fell back upon the bed, exposing herself to me. It was too much, too fast.

Decomposing manatees.
Eyeballs pierced with darts.
Richard Nixon naked blowing bloody liquid farts.

I tried to take a step toward the bed, but Darlene did something with her tongue that made it impossible for me to move. The muscles in my legs tensed up rock hard and the noises coming out of my mouth sounded suspiciously like whimpers.

Decomposing manatees. Eyeballs pierced with darts. Richard Nixon naked blowing bloody liquid farts.

Darlene's teeth got into the action while Abbie started to feel herself.

Decomposingmanateeseyeballspiercedwithdartsrichardnixonnakedblowi ngbloodyliquidfarts.

Darlene then went deep, running her hand up the inside of my thigh. Abbie moaned in a way I never heard outside of the porn Palazzo was always watching in the shop. It was more than I could take.

J.E. PARK

Nixon pierced manatees...bloody something...fart darts...JESUS CHRIST...Aaaaagh! Don't do it! Don't do it! Dontdoitdontdoitdontdoit! Aaugh! Shit! God DAMN it!

I exploded. And when I say exploded, I mean I came so hard that my ears rang. Darlene leapt up and ran for the bathroom. Abbie sat up and stared at me, wondering if I had anything left for her. For a moment, I just stood there, befuddled and embarrassed. It was my first, and quite likely, my only threesome. When my eyes glanced at the nightstand, I saw the clock turn to 6:43. If I had to guess, I lasted about twenty-eight seconds.

Oops.

But I was only twenty-two years old and still aroused. Tripping over the shorts wrapped around my ankles, I rushed to the bed and slipped myself into Abbie before I went flaccid. I went at her hard and furious, knowing I had time before I could release again. As Darlene emerged from the bathroom, undressed and ready to go, Abbie rolled me over. While on top, she worked me even harder. When Darlene joined us, she positioned herself over my face so I could do to her what she had done to me.

Between the alcohol and my prior ejaculation, I was able to last forever the second time. Abbie dismounted after she was satisfied and allowed Darlene to take her place. While I was being ridden anew, Abbie worked her way up and down my body, kissing, licking, and biting me in random places, driving me wild. Once she knew Darlene climaxed, she went crazy on me until I came again. The three of us then took a shower and collapsed back upon the bed for some rest.

The situation outside deteriorated. It was getting to the point that the wind noise was forcing us to speak up to hear ourselves above the din. It was not enough to keep us from falling asleep to recharge, though. At 9:30, I was awakened by the two women taking turns stimulating me orally. Still half asleep, I wanted to push them away, but Darlene produced two pairs of pink furry handcuffs. Before I knew it, I was shackled to the headboard, unable to defend myself from intense, if mildly involuntary, sexual gratification.

During this third session, things got insane. The wind began to sound like a locomotive, and there were times we felt the hotel itself shake. The power went out around ten. Shortly afterward, we started hearing things, rather big things, striking the building. One of these collisions was close enough that Abbie got off me and tried to see what was going on outside. When she returned to bed, she left the curtains open. After that, our room was lit only by lightning strike, giving us the effect of making love beneath a strobe light.

The third time I came was messy, and I expected the girls to un-cuff me so that we could all clean up. To my surprise, however, Darlene and Abbie seemed to revel in the stickiness. They started licking themselves until their naked bodies fell back on top of me.

Watching this, I found myself having a bit of a spiritual crisis. I was questioning my atheism for the second time in a single port visit. I felt that maybe God was finally trying to make up for all the shit He spent the last two decades doing to me. If that entire building collapsed and sent us plunging to a watery death at that very moment, I would have considered myself and the Almighty even.

Between the storm, the cries of passion coming from the girls, and the stuff swirling about inside my head, I could not hear anything from the hallway. It was not until the security guard pounded on the door next to ours that I realized someone else might be in the hotel. I tried to get the girls to quiet down so I could hear better, but they were too into each other to pay any attention to me. It was not until the woman started pounding on our door that Darlene and Abbie stopped what they were doing. They both stared at me in terror.

"Is there anybody in there?" the security guard called out in a raspy voice. She sounded like a large woman who enjoyed chain-smoking and gargling with battery acid.

"No!" I screamed. "There's not!" The girls turned to look at me as if I had lost my mind.

"Sir!" the guard yelled through the door. "You can't be in there! We have to get all our guests into a safer area of the building!"

"Will we have our own rooms?" I yelled back.

"No! It's in the banquet center!"

"Then we're good! We appreciate your concern!"

"Sir!" the guard shouted, sounding like she was losing patience. "This isn't a request! You have to come down with us to the first floor!"

"Fuck that! If things go sideways, that's where all the water will go first! We'll take our chances up here!"

The guard was insistent. "We're not getting much of a surge, sir! It's the wind and flying objects! If something breaks your window, you're going to be trapped in a room with a thousand pieces of broken glass twirling around you at a hundred miles an hour! You need to come with me!"

"I'd rather bleed to death than drown!" I countered. "What if we agreed to stay in the bathroom?"

"Sir! This is not negotiable! I'm coming in!"

"DON'T COME IN! DON'T COME IN!" As I screamed this, I felt both women get into a sort of sprinter's stance.

"Why not?" the security guard asked.

"I'm not decent!"

When the door opened, Darlene and Abbie jumped off of me, running to lock themselves in the bathroom. It was dark, so Abbie, who was closest to my head when she took off, had no idea where to put her feet as she ran across the bed. As luck would have it, she stomped one of her heels down upon my testicles. That set me off screaming and writhing about the bed in agony. I wanted to rub the pain out of them but couldn't while still handcuffed to the bed. When the security guard came in, she shined her flashlight on me and gasped, "Sir! Are you alright?"

When I could catch my breath, I called out, "Yes! I'm fine! I'm kind of into this sort of thing!"

"Are you here by yourself?" she asked, sounding both shocked and surprised.

"No," I answered. I wondered how often she encountered people that got naked and cuffed themselves to their own beds.

"Do you need help getting out?"

I shook my head. "No! I need help staying here!"

At this, Darlene and Abbie opened up the bathroom door and peeked outside. The security guard shone her light on them. Startled, she called out, "Ladies! Are you okay?"

"Yes!" yelled Darlene over the noise.

The security guard shook her head in disgust and made the sign of the cross. A flash of lightning showed us the look on her face. It suggested she felt sexual deviants like us deserved to die in hurricanes. "I'll pray for you," she said as she walked back toward the door.

"Well, I guess that wouldn't hurt, would it?" I mused.

OLONGAPO EARP

Once she was gone, Abbie ran to see if I was all right. Darlene rushed to her bag, trying to rummage through it to find the keys to the handcuffs. I told her to go ahead and leave them. Abbie and Darlene both smiled, then got back to what they were doing, taking care to avoid my testicles. With a little care and tenderness, I broke my personal record and completed an act of lovemaking for the fourth time in one night.

After that, the girls un-cuffed me, and the three of us finally fell asleep. We woke with the sunrise, discovering that the hurricane passed while we slumbered. Despite feeling something awfully strange in my nether regions, we made love for a fifth time. After a bath, we even attempted a sixth. We stopped when I felt a strange pop at the top of my scrotum and knew something had gone wrong.

We were done, and the discomfort I was experiencing suggested that I needed to see a doctor. I kissed the girls good-bye, got dressed, and limped back to the ship. The pain between my legs increased exponentially during my journey home. I feared that I might have overdone things, pushing my genitals way past their natural limits. On the other hand, I also felt as if I had achieved some sort of significant milestone. It was the first time I ever had sex so intense that I required medical attention.

*****

J.E. PARK

CHAPTER 3

When the *Belleau Wood* pulled back into Pearl Harbor, it was a beautiful day. The sun was out once again. The sky had returned to hues of blue and the hills surrounding us were what one would expect in Hawaii, verdant and lush. The birds returned and were singing beautifully while a gentle breeze rolled in off the Pacific and took the edge off the tropical heat. As bad as I thought it had been, Hurricane Iniki only glanced the island of Oahu. There was still a big mess to clean up, but all things considered, we got off easy. The neighboring island of Kauai was not so lucky. It took a direct hit and ended up ravaged. Much like I was.

I was waiting on the pier for the ship with about fifty other men who got left behind. Among them was the ship's Executive Officer and Master Chief Darrow. Sitting against one of the pier's bollards, I was in miserable shape. My stomach was killing me, feeling as if I had done five hundred sit-ups. The muscles of my lower back were screaming from a level of exertion they had not seen even in boot camp. One of Abbie's stray nails had scratched a sizeable gouge across my face. As if that were not enough, I also had hickeys and bite marks running from my neck to regions well below my belt line.

OLONGAPO EARP

The worst pain was radiating from between my legs, though. My scrotum had swollen to a point where it felt like it was getting ready to burst through my underwear. It was excruciating and I could not even stand up straight.

"Jesus Christ," Darrow said once he saw me on the bollard. "What the hell did you get into?"

"A couple of lonely school teachers from Fishers, Indiana," I said, smiling wide. I then showed Darrow the shirt I was wearing. It bore the mascot of the school where Darlene worked. She usually wore it as a nightgown. "Go, Tigers!"

"Are you kidding me?"

"I most certainly am not." I then pulled down the neckline of my tee-shirt to reveal all the marks Abbie and Darlene had put on my chest.

"Good lord, Doyle!" my master chief gasped. "It looks like they put up a hell of a fight! I hope for your sake all this stuff was consensual!"

I held out my hands to show off the bruises around my wrists. "It wasn't, but I'm not pressing charges."

Darrow laughed without needing an explanation. He served multiple tours with the Armed Forces Police Department in the Philippines. The man was well aware of the types of bruises handcuffs made when they were on too tight. "So that's your excuse to the old man? You missed ship's movement because you got cuffed to a bed in Honolulu?"

"Do you have a better one?" After Darrow told me he did not, I asked, "So, how much trouble do you think we're in?"

The master chief shrugged. "I don't know. The storm struck quickly. In the morning, we were all clear. By evening, we were already getting hit by that monster. It's hard to say. Hell, the XO couldn't even get back in time. The captain may make an example out of a couple of his more notorious troublemakers…"

"Like me?"

"Like you?" Darrow asked. "Jesus, after he lays his eyes on you, I have a feeling you're in the running for a purple heart."

Darrow and I talked until the gangplank was in place and the men on the pier began filing aboard. Once the line shortened, Master Chief turned to me and said, "We'd better go face the music."

"I need you to help me up," I told him.

"Are you serious?"

I nodded. I was sweating profusely now, and not from the heat. "Yeah, Master Chief, I am. If you can't pull me up the gangplank, I'm going to need a couple of stretcher-bearers from Medical to come down and get me."

Shaking his head, Darrow grinned. "Taking the expression 'busting a nut' to a whole new level, eh?"

*****

Officially, Navy medics were called "Hospital Corpsmen." Due to the time spent treating their shipmates for venereal disease, though, they were usually referred to as "Pecker Checkers." HM1 Dylan Bateman was the lucky man tasked with checking mine.

Bateman was a nice enough guy, but he was one of the most effeminate men I had ever met. Most of the crew was sure he was a homosexual, which in 1992 was a condition that would get you thrown out of the Navy quicker than damn near anything else. Bateman was also a decorated combat medic, though. He had been wounded in action. If someone tried to question his masculinity to get him thrown out of the service, he would need video evidence to do it. Since Bateman did not seem like the kind of man with a flair for making gay porn, his job in the Navy was reasonably secure.

For obvious reasons, the man was not my first choice to be handling my privates. On the other hand, though, I tended to trust Bateman's medical opinion more than I did that of the ship's doctor, who generally just slipped you a couple of Motrin and ordered you to get back to work. Besides, it was not like I was there for a prostate exam.

"ET2 Doyle Murphy, to what do I owe the pleasure of this visit today?" the corpsman asked as he pranced through the dozen other people in sickbay. Most of them were waiting to get a shot for what we affectionately christened the "Liberty Drip."

"I think my balls are about to explode, HM1," I groaned.

"I doubt they're going to do that," Bateman mused. "What happened?"

When I explained my last sixteen hours, I left out the lascivious details that I would include when I told my friends later. At one point, I did let it slip that there was more than one girl involved when I was injured, however. After hearing this, Bateman pulled the bed curtain closed for extra privacy. "Did you say you went to bed with two women last night?"

I reached over and pulled the privacy curtain back open, so everyone in the waiting room could hear. "That's right, Doc. There were two girls."

Sickbay exploded into a round of applause. Even Lieutenant Booker, the ship's chaplain, poked his head around the curtain and gave me a thumbs up. "Right on!"

As I thanked my audience, Bateman pulled the curtain closed again. "Petty Officer Murphy, we're going to have to take a look at what's going on down there. Can you get your shorts down, or do we have to cut them?"

"If you let me do it myself, I think I can get them off." I unbuttoned my shorts, pulled down the zipper, and gingerly started working them down my legs. Once I got the top of them halfway to my knees, I let Bateman take it the rest of the way.

Before I had the chance to work on my underwear, the corpsman gasped. He lifted my shirt and revealed all the marks on my stomach. "You let them do this to you? Are those teeth marks?"

The waiting room lit up with more raucous cheers and clapping. Petty Officer Bateman found it less than amusing, though. "Murphy, do you have any idea how nasty a person's mouth is? I'd rather be bitten by a vulture than another human being. You're not leaving here until we clean and disinfect all that. How did these girls do this without you smacking them? That had to have hurt!"

"It did, but there wasn't a lot I could do about it," I said while showing him my wrists. "I was handcuffed to the bed."

That earned me a standing ovation from the waiting room. The chaplain quipped, "This isn't confession, Murphy! It's exhibitionism!"

"Okay, petty officer, we need to get your underwear off now. Do you need help?"

"Not yet..." I said, taking a deep breath and holding it while working my briefs off in much the same way as I did my cargo shorts.

Bateman was a professional, but as soon as my privates were exposed, I saw him turn his head while his sweat pores opened up. He kept his cool much better than I did once I saw what happened to me, though. My scrotum was wildly discolored and swollen so much that my penis disappeared somewhere within it. It looked like a hairy, tie-died water balloon that was ready to pop. "Sweet baby Jesus!" I cried, my voice registering instant panic. "Where'd my fuckin' dick go!"

HM1 Bateman stood up and backed away. "I'm going to go get the doctor." He left the examination area so quickly that he forgot to close the curtain. After he departed, three other patients stepped up to see my junk for themselves. They immediately wished they hadn't. Another corpsman ran up and told them to get lost, closing the curtain and calling them all faggots.

LCDR Terrance Broward, the ship's doctor, soon barged into my exam area. He not only kept his composure but even allowed himself to laugh at my expense. "So, a woman did this to you?"

"Actually, there were two of them," Bateman added.

"So I heard."

"Doc, what the hell's going on?" I was now having a hard time breathing.

"You tell me. How did this happen?"

"A chick stepped on my balls!"

"Stepped? Are you sure she didn't stomp on them?" Broward asked, cocking his head to the side to get a better look.

"Yeah. She stepped. The power went out, and she couldn't see where she was going. Did she break them?"

The doctor shook his head and poked my inflated scrotum with his index finger. It was horribly painful. "No, I don't think she broke anything. In fact, if this is what I think, it looks and feels a lot worse than it actually is."

"Then what do you think it is?" I asked.

"A scrotal hematoma," Broward asked, poking it again. It looks like you might have broken a blood vessel somewhere in your groin area that flooded your ball sack. We'll drain it and see if there's any sustained fluid flow from the wound. If there isn't, we'll close everything back up and send you on your way."

"So, I need surgery?"

Doc Broward shook his head. "I wouldn't call it surgery, but it is a procedure, yes. We can do it right here. Petty Officer Bateman, bring me a prep kit and go get a camera."

"Camera?" I asked.

OLONGAPO EARP

"Oh yeah. If you can't be a role model, I'm going to make you a cautionary tale."

As the doctor had said, the procedure was not that bad. The worst thing about it was the shaving. As much as my hematoma hurt, my scrotum was still as ticklish as it always was, and I had a hard time lying still. After a small incision, a lot of draining, and a few minutes of observation, they stitched me back up. I was then lectured about safe sex practices and sent back to work, feeling almost as if nothing happened.

When American ships approach exotic ports, the crew is often required to watch a slide show detailing all the damage that sexually transmitted diseases can do to a man's reproductive organs. It's pretty graphic, filled with images depicting everything from syphilis sores to herpes rashes. They include injuries, too. One particularly hideous shot shows why one should never masturbate behind a piece of running machinery in heavy seas.

Sometime after September 11th, 1992, that training aid added a gruesome new slide. It now shows an image displaying the disfiguring effects of a scrotal hematoma. In reality, the condition is not that severe, but the visuals pack some serious fear factor. Even though they cropped out the part showing me giving Broward two thumbs up as he snapped the photo, the testicles on display in that presentation are mine.

*****

CHAPTER 4

Word tends to spread quickly aboard a ship. By the time I left sickbay, put my dungarees on, and climbed up the island structure to my shop, everyone knew what had happened to me. Radar Repair was full of men waiting to hear the account of what I did to myself. All five of my people were present as was our LPO, ET1 Tony Bard, and Airman Marty Pruitt, an aerographer's mate that worked next door.

Knowing nothing would get done until I spun my tale of wild monkey loving gone awry, I did not even bother to resist. As I spoke, I discovered each of the men were interested in different aspects of the story. My best friend Kevin Dixon, my star radar technician Rick Hammond, and Tony Bard were most interested in how I seduced two women at the same time. ET2 John Palazzo, an insufferable pervert, wanted the details to add to his pornography-addled fantasies. That boy had serious issues. Stephen Kent, our new guy, hung on every word, looking like he wanted to take notes. As far as we could tell, Kent only had a single brush with actual intercourse. That was when he blew that load in his shorts before he had even seen his hooker naked. Tragically, that happened right in front of us and was why we now called him "Speedy."

ET3 Claude Metaire was the shop's resident lady killer. Threesomes were not particularly novel to him, so he was most interested in how I hurt myself. Airman Pruitt was fixated on my treatment in sickbay. "You actually let that faggot Bateman touch your shit?" he asked. He made no attempt to conceal his disgust.

I grinned, knowing how uncomfortable Pruitt was with this stuff. "Marty, I would have let that man tongue-check my prostate if it'd made the pain in my nuts go away."

The airman recoiled. "Fuck that! There is no *way* that I'd let that homo anywhere near me while I didn't have my pants on. I'd beat his fairy ass!"

That was not idle bluster. Marty was a brawler. He had some sort of Zen thing going on with the art of inflicting pain. Because of my reputation of being able to hold my own in a bar fight, he believed us to be kindred spirits, but he was mistaken. When I fought, I had a reason to, no matter how misguided it might be. Pruitt fought because he enjoyed it. He particularly reveled in abusing homosexuals. There was a story about how Marty stepped into a gay bar by mistake one night and tried to take on everyone in it by himself after discovering what it was. He got his ass kicked, but he took a lot of men down with him.

"Well, Marty," I told him. "If you think you'd get away with punching Bateman for doing his job, you've got another thing coming. You'd better be prepared for a lengthy stay in the brig for assaulting a senior petty officer."

Pruitt huffed. "I'd rather do time than get molested by some fucking cock-gobbler. You guys telling me you wouldn't?"

"Eet eez not molestation eef you enjoy being touched by a man weeth eyes so dreamy." Metaire joked. The rest of us agreed with him and pretended to swoon to watch Pruitt squirm.

"Jesus Christ," Marty said as he got up. "Screw all you faggots."

As Pruitt opened the door to leave the shop, Lieutenant Junior Grade Krause walked in. Besides his ever-present sunglasses, the lieutenant wore a skin tone that looked like the side-effect of too much Hawaiian sun. It was more likely the result of having me within his field of vision, however. The man turned red every time he saw me anymore. He tried to write me up for nearly getting Warren Macklemore and me killed in Mexico. Our department head realized that demoting me would mean putting Palazzo back in charge of Radar Repair, though. Having already been through that situation, the Combat Systems Officer declined to pass my chit up the chain. The lieutenant had my number ever since. Poking his thumb toward the exit, Lieutenant Krause ordered everyone out of the space except for me.

No sooner had the door closed behind Bard than my division officer lost his composure. He slammed his hand down upon my desk so hard it sounded like a shotgun blast. This was a signature move. I knew he would do it and made sure that I did not give him the satisfaction of seeing me flinch. That infuriated him even more. "YOU MISSED SHIP'S MOVEMENT!" he bellowed.

I nodded. "I did, sir. So did Master Chief Darrow. And the XO..."

"I KNOW THAT!" Krause brought his hand down on my desk a second time. And then a third. This was not meant to intimidate me. It was the lieutenant venting his frustration. "Neither one of them came back with a vulgar story to corrupt my men, though. Are you proud of what you did out there, Murphy?"

I did not even try to suppress my grin. "Actually, I kind of am. I take it that you've never..."

Krause got so angry he started to shake. "For heaven's sake! No! I've never even..."

"Well, sir, if you don't mind my saying so, you should consider it. I mean, handling two women in bed at the same time is a lot of work, but you know, it's great at relieving stress. I mean, after everything I've been through recently, I feel like a new man! Now, just looking at you, I can see you're under a lot of pressure, so..."

Krause flipped out his index finger and stuck it in my face. "Watch your filthy mouth, son. You're too young to realize you're not invincible, but let me tell you something; you're not bulletproof. You keep pushing these boundaries, and sooner or later, you're going to step over the line. And when you do, I'm going to be waiting there to make sure all your chickens come home to roost."

I stood up from my seat. Looking down at my division officer now, I let out a sigh. "Sir, when I was eleven or twelve, my friends and I came across a few dozen eggs in a grocery store dumpster. We took them to this railroad bridge built over a busy road and started tossing them at cars passing by. Now, I'm not going to lie to you; it was a lot of fun. It was a blast right up until my neighbor caught us doing it. He stopped his car, got out, and started yelling at us, letting us know that he was going to tell our fathers."

The fact that Krause was letting me say so much surprised me. He usually had difficulty listening to more than a dozen syllables spoken by anyone other than himself. Taking advantage of having his full attention, I continued with my story. "My friends all stopped throwing eggs right there. We all knew we were in big trouble. A couple of them even started crying and walking back. Not me, though. I went right back to making Chevy omelets. Why? Because my old man beat my ass damn near every night. For the most part, he did it without having any reason to. At least that time, I earned it. If I was getting beat for chucking eggs at cars, I was getting as much enjoyment out of it as I could."

I never could see Krause's eyes behind his glasses, but I could tell by the rest of his face that he was squinting at me. "And how is that relevant to what we're talking about here?"

How is it not relevant? I sighed again, realizing I had to spell it out for the man. "Sir, if you're looking to bust me no matter what I do, I'm going to do my best to have as much fun as I can before you succeed. Look, I'm not going to antagonize you. I'm not trying to bait you, and I'm not happy being perpetually on your bad side but, I'll be honest. I'm not worried about you much. I'm a good technician. I run a damn good shop and I have the confidence of my chain of command all the way up to the captain. You don't."

I struck a nerve. The color rushed into Krause's face and he clenched his teeth. "Why, you insolent little…"

"Sir," I interrupted. "I don't know what imagined slight you think I committed to spark this vendetta you have against me. I don't think your little crusade is going to work out the way you think it is, though. I recently saved the captain's daughter from serious harm. His tour commanding the *USS Belleau Wood* is not scheduled to be up until December 1994. My enlistment is up six months before that. That means for the rest of my time here, I've got a pretty powerful patron looking over me. Sir, you're wasting a lot of energy and effort trying to bring me down. You're not going to be able to hurt what's left of my career here. Hell, at this point, you can't even hurt my feelings."

"If you think the captain is going to let you get away with bloody murder just because you…"

"Sir, I did the math," I told him.

"What?"

"I did the math," I repeated. "You were commissioned four years ago, right?"

The look on Krause's face betrayed that he knew where I was going with this. "Yeah, so?"

"Promotion from O-1 to O-2 is pretty much automatic. That means you've been a lieutenant junior grade for three and a half years. You're pushing the limit for how long the Navy will let you serve as an O-2 before they deem you unpromotable. If you don't advance by the end of next year, you're going to be forced out."

Krause swallowed hard. I could see in his face that he was painfully aware of that situation. It looked as if the prospect of being pushed from the service weighed heavily upon him. "You trying to say something, Murphy?"

I shook my head and shrugged. "Only that you should focus on fixing your career instead of trying to wreck mine. If you don't, you're going to end up kicked off this ship long before I will."

*****

Hurricane Iniki destroyed the Hawaiian island of Kauai. The death toll was freakishly low for a natural disaster of such magnitude, but the storm still left thousands of people without shelter, food, fresh water, or access to medical care. Fortunately, the *USS Belleau Wood* was perfectly positioned to help. We spent our last several days within the territory of the United States providing relief to those affected by the catastrophe.

We were scheduled to pull out of Hawaii on Monday, September 14th. Because of the hurricane, though, we spent several extra days there supporting Kauai's relief efforts. When we finally did get back underway, we were exhausted, but satisfied with ourselves.

OLONGAPO EARP

At that point, it was over a month since I had last laid eyes on Hannah Baxter. It was more than three weeks since she removed all uncertainty over the status of our relationship. That was when she returned her engagement ring to me via Warren Macklemore. Once the islands of Hawaii passed over the horizon, the pain of losing her finally began to subside.

It might have been all the steam I had blown off during my drunken tear through the North Shore. It could have been the fight I got into in Waikiki. Maybe it was the shock of how close I came to doing something the captain would have court-martialed me for. Or the satisfaction of making Lieutenant Krause realize that he was powerless to do anything to me anymore. My night with Abbie and Darlene probably had a large part to play in it, too. Whatever it was, once we put Pearl Harbor behind us, I accepted the finality that Hannah was no longer going to be a part of my life. I was not at peace with it yet, but I reached a point where I could move on.

Not long after leaving Hawaii, the air conditioning in the crew's berthing area went out. Located right above the ship's boiler, it was not long before it got unbearably hot and made sleeping impossible. Since the air conditioning was more reliable in the SPN-35 radar dome, I strung my hammock up and crashed there. Cool and comfortable, I immediately dropped into a state of deep sleep the instant I closed my eyes. That was something I had not done for a long time.

My dreams were still of Hannah. We were in Bali, the place we planned to start a surf shop catering to Australian tourists. She was radiant and beautiful, cooking over an open fire on some secluded tropical beach. She laughed, and I remembered looking at her, knowing that I would never be happier than I was at that moment. Then I heard the shotgun blast.

Hannah's head split in half, splattering everything inside of it all over me. I ran to her to try to put her back together but knew it was no use. So instead, I rose up to exact revenge upon the man who killed her, knowing it had to be my father, Liam Lyle Murphy. It always was.

Unfortunately, my old man was far from finished. Before I could get to him, he pulled the trigger again and killed my mother for the thousandth time. Then he killed my baby brother in his crib before turning the gun on my older sister. I almost got to him there, but he ran. He bolted from our house in Detroit and fled into the El Salvadoran rain forest. My father had been dead for several years before I landed in Central America. Still, in my dreams, it was he who tracked down the Salvadoran girl that haunted me. I watched my father kill her too, now wearing the uniform of the *Atlacatl* Battalion that her actual killers had.

I knew which flashback came next. It was the one where I saved Rafaela Green and her son from her husband. Even though they both begged me not to, I beat Randy to the brink of death. Then I sent Rafaela and Manny back to the Philippines, where they would be safe. That was when the bogeyman of my episodes transformed from my father to Randy Green. It was he who stalked the jungle with my father's shotgun, looking for his wife and stepson. He screamed as he searched for them, firing his weapon often but never running out of ammunition.

When Green gave up looking for his family, he sought out people that I cared about. Eventually, he found them all: Hannah, my mother, my siblings, and my friends. Raising his shotgun, he pulled the trigger time after time, intent on killing every one of them. As he fired, he laughed maniacally, turning toward me to show how much he enjoyed the carnage. This time the dream was a little different, though. When he showed his face, I realized that it was not Randy Green or my father slaughtering everyone I ever loved.

It was me.

In my dream that night and during the episode that followed, it was I who killed my family, not Randy or my old man. It was I that executed that girl in El Salvador. It was I who was now responsible for the misfortunes of Rafaela Green and her son. Until that moment, I blamed my father for most of the misery that landed upon my shoulders. It hit me that night that Liam Murphy had been dead for a very long time. He was no longer a threat to the people I loved.

I was. Falling to pieces on the floor of my radar dome, I was convinced that I would eventually destroy anyone I ever came to care about.

*****

OLONGAPO EARP

When I opened my eyes, I was no longer in my hammock. I was on the deck covered in sweat, out of breath, and with tears streaming down my cheeks. Dixie was on the ground with me, holding me from behind, struggling to keep my arms pinned to my sides. "Come on, Doyle!" he begged. "Come on, man! It's time to come back to us! Come on back, Doyle!"

I was trying to claw my way back to reality but was not quite there yet. I knew I was in the SPN-35 radar dome and that Dixie was there with me. I was still prepared to confront an apparition of myself holding that shotgun, though. "Oh fuck! Oh, f…It's…it's my fault, Dixie! It's my fault!"

"Jesus Christ!" Kevin grunted as he tried to hold tighter. "What's your fault?"

"Everything! That girl in El Salvador…"

"What?" If word got back to the US that Salvadoran soldiers held female prisoners as sex slaves, it would have devastated American efforts there. That was why my benign training mission ended up classified. For that reason, I never told Dixie about it. He had no idea what I was talking about.

"…and Randy Green…"

"Fuck Randy Green!" Kevin shot back. "He would have killed that woman and her kid if we hadn't stopped him!"

"…and my family…I don't know how, and I don't know why, but I somehow got them killed too."

"Goddammit!" Dixie let go and pushed me away from him. "What else did you do? Are you responsible for the JFK assassination? The AIDS epidemic? How about *Wham!*?"

I was almost back. I felt safe again but disoriented. Looking at Dixie, I asked, "What are you doing here?"

"It's too hot to sleep in the berthing area. I thought I'd check the dome to see if the AC was working and found you in here losing your fucking mind! Jesus Christ, Doyle! Put you in any kind of high-pressure situation, and you're the coolest cat I know. Leave you alone with your own thoughts for any more than fifteen minutes, though, and you completely fall apart! Is this ever going to end?"

I shook my head. "I don't know, Dixie. It's been bad ever since we left San Diego. I thought I got it out of my system in Hawaii, but obviously, I didn't."

"I'll say." Dixie took a pack of cigarettes out of his pocket and threw them at me, hitting me in the face. Without apologizing, he then asked, "I thought you needed a trigger for these things."

"I did too." I pulled a cigarette out of the pack with shaking hands, then tossed it back. "It looks like they're taking on a life of their own now."

Kevin cursed. "Doyle, if people find out about this, you're gone."

"You know, everyone keeps saying I'm going to get thrown out of the service," I replied, pausing to light my smoke. "Yet somehow, I'm still here. It sure doesn't seem like it from my perspective lately, but I'm one lucky guy."

"Whatever," Dixie said. "I've seen luckier. I don't usually count people whose entire family got murdered as particularly blessed."

I dropped my head into my hands. "Yeah, me neither. I miss her, Kevin."

"Who? Hannah?"

"Yeah, her too, but I was talking about my mother. Man, the things she did for me. You would not believe how much pain that woman would take to save me from it. My old man would come after me, and she would jump in his way and pop him in the jaw as hard as she could. She knew what would happen to her after that. She knew she couldn't hurt him. But she did it anyway. Just so that my old man would take his demons out on her instead of me."

Dixie looked mad. "Is that why you think her murder was your fault now?"

I shrugged. "He never hurt her unless she was trying to protect me. That never occurred to me until now. He never hurt my sister, well, not until the night he blew her brains out. He doted on my baby brother until he shot him too. And even though he hurt her so badly, I could tell he loved my mother. He seemed hurt by her more than anything, hurt that she defended me from him all the time. Hurt that she always chose me over him. It was me that man hated, not my mother. Not my sister. Not my brother. Me."

I was trying to keep my composure but failing. My voice cracked as I tried to explain to Kevin what I was finally figuring out. "Dixie, if I had never been born, they could have been happy. If it had not been for me, they would all still be alive. Christ, if I had been there instead of running the streets with my friends, he probably would have killed me instead of them. They would…"

"That's bullshit, Doyle! It's survivor's guilt!" Kevin sounded exasperated. "There's only one person responsible for what happened to your family, and it's your old man. Look, I've never lost anyone close to me. I'm no idiot, though. This path you're trying to take yourself down right now? It isn't helpful. It ain't going to lead to anything but trouble. You need to figure out a way to get this shit put behind you. Now!"

From an intellectual perspective, everything Dixie said was right. On an intuitive level, though, I knew what the truth was. There was something about me, and only me, that fueled my father's rages. I might not have pulled the trigger, but I could feel that my family's death was still a sin I needed to atone for one day.

*****

CHAPTER 5

They say time heals all wounds. It took twenty-one days for the *USS Belleau Wood* to cover the distance between Hawaii and Japan. I would not claim all that ailed me worked itself out during that time, but at least I stopped hemorrhaging my sanity.

The trick was to keep busy. I spent our journey working at an almost manic pace all day. Then, after everyone went to bed, I studied Japanese most of the night. If I stayed awake, I could not have any nightmares. With fewer nightmares came fewer episodes.

I learned to get by on only a few hours of sleep a night until it all caught up with me about a week before we made landfall. Spent and exhausted, I collapsed in my rack instead of in my radar dome and slept the whole night through. I did it again the next night, and then the night after that. Normalcy became routine once again, and my episodes were kept at bay.

Hannah was still on my mind a lot, but so was the exhilaration of starting over in Japan. This was what I signed on to do, to travel the world, to see exotic new places. I had reached a tipping point. The excitement of this new adventure canceled out my mourning over what I had left behind.

OLONGAPO EARP

It was not only me, either. The entire crew was electric with anticipation. I could tell by the banter I heard around me on our final day at sea.

For once, nobody was complaining about having to man the rails as we changed into our dress whites. We all wanted to be the first to see the land of the rising sun emerge from over the horizon. There was a lot of speculation about what Japan was going to look like. We wondered how the food was going to taste and how pretty the girls were going to be. We were full of optimism, which lasted right up until we were topside and saw what was blocking our way into port.

To be fair, there were Americans who received far worse welcomes while approaching Japan. The one that Joint Expeditionary Force TF 51 received off the coast of Okinawa in 1945 comes to mind. Taking that into consideration, we did not have a lot of room to complain. Judging by the flotilla of protest vessels blocking our approach to Sasebo, though, we were only slightly less unpopular than the leathernecks who landed at Hagushi during World War II.

The protest boats blared Japanese nationalist music. They waved long flags and shouted angry speeches our way that few of us could understand. I had been studying Japanese from the moment I found out we were going there but had no one to practice it on. I spoke it poorly. I understood it even worse. At first, I thought all those boats were there to welcome us. I did not realize my mistake until I heard someone with a bull horn screaming, "YANKEE GO HOME!!!"

It looked like the boats blocking our way into Sasebo Bay were on a suicide mission and had no intention of moving. Displacing something in the neighborhood of 40,000 tons, the *USS Belleau Wood* was a slave to its own inertia. We could not change course to avoid a collision even if we wanted to and to be honest, we didn't want to. It would have set a bad precedent.

Our ship blasted the whistle three times to let the protesters know that we were coming through. Not thinking there was any real danger of actually hitting them, though, the captain kept us on the rails. He turned out to be right.

No sooner had the ship's whistle stopped than the wail of several sirens rose from the group of protest boats. Vessels from the Japanese harbor patrol emerged from the mob and started herding watercraft out of our way.

I saw some of the protesters make angry displays of defiance toward the authorities, but the Japanese generally did what they were told. As we passed through the protesters, I noticed that they all wore *uwagi* tops. These looked like the jacket of a karate uniform, except they were blue and covered with *kanji* script. Their headbands were of similar design.

Along the rail, I was standing next to an OS seaman apprentice, Nick Budd, who was half-Japanese. His mother was from Nagasaki, which was not very far from Sasebo. "Can you understand any of this?" I asked him.

Budd shook his head. "Dude," he answered. "You speak more Japanese than I do."

Our new home was a facility that we shared with the Japanese Navy. We had half of the pier, which we split with another American ship, the *USS Dubuque*. Behind us, separated by a chain-link fence, were two cruisers of Japan's Maritime Defense Force. We were still at the rails as we docked, and a small army of Japanese civilians ran out to secure our mooring lines. Though none of them were military, they could have fooled us. They all had the same haircuts, wore the same coveralls, and moved with more precision than we did during basic training.

"Shit!" I heard Budd exclaim as he took in the scene below us.

"What?" I asked.

"We Japanese people really do all look alike."

*****

Typically, the captain excused us from manning the rails shortly after the ship was moored. This time, we had to sit through the welcoming ceremony and several speeches from government officials. Once cut loose, though, seven hundred men who had not had a drink in three weeks were unleashed upon the town.

Being electronics technicians with nothing to lock down, we were some of the first men off the ship. We rushed toward the city but paused at the main gate, confronted by an angry mob dressed the same way as the protesters we had seen at sea. A dozen police officers in full riot gear kept them at bay, but they seemed wholly inadequate for the task. They were ridiculously outnumbered. If that angry mass of humanity wanted to tear us limb from limb as it appeared they wanted to, there was little the cops would have been able to do about it.

The Japanese gate guard sensed our hesitation and smiled at us, looking embarrassed by the situation. In halting English, he said, "Is okay. No hurt. You go. *Irassharimase*."

I understood *irassharimase*. It meant welcome. *"Domo arigato,"* I answered, thanking him. Then Dixie, Metaire, and Tony Bard walked through the gate with me.

The protesters looked *pissed*. They shook their fists, hurled insults at us, and pressed against the riot shields of the police officers holding them back. I sensed it was all for show, though. No one threw anything. No one spit at us, and there was no real effort to get past the cops, which they could have done by just walking around them. As it was, we strolled past the chaos without incident and tried to figure out where to go next.

The military base in Sasebo is not directly connected to the town. Once you exit the main gate, you have to cross Nimitz Park, a stretch of space maintained by the US military but available to the Japanese. It encouraged American interaction with the locals. It was a beautiful park, very green and open. It also boasted a baseball diamond and a field suitable for both American football or soccer, depending on who was using it. The park was also popular because it possessed a set of restrooms one could use without feeling obliged to buy anything.

From the park, you had to cross the Albuquerque Bridge to get to town. This was a pedestrian walkway over a small river, named after Sasebo's sister city in New Mexico. After you reached the eastern bank, you were at the beginning of Alba Kaki Street. A block from there, it intersected with Sakaemachi to form the place the Americans called "Four Corners."

Speaking in generalities, Sasebo was not a city that catered to visitors. Once you got away from the vicinity of the base, it was common to see plaques outside of establishments reading, "No Foreigners Allowed." This was something not found at Four Corners, where the bars catered to American service members. Unfortunately, the taverns were small and quickly overwhelmed. Despite being among the first groups of people to leave the ship, we could barely fit into any of these places. Getting served was even more challenging.

We ended up at Shooters, a bar owned by an American expatriate named Steve Morgan. He was a former sailor who had landed in Sasebo a couple of decades before and just never got around to leaving. His tavern was a local landmark, and Steve himself an institution among the 7th Fleet. We would not get to meet him that day, however. His place was so packed that we could not even get to the bar.

After colliding with several locals and excusing myself with a curt, "*Sumimasen!*" one of the hostesses ask me if I spoke Japanese. I told her I knew a little, then had an excruciating conversation about how insane it was to have such a small area overrun with so many sailors at once. After switching to English, she suggested, "You need get away from crowd. Go to *ginza*, up street two blocks. Find department store. Take erevator to roof — that beer garden. You rike. Very nice up there!"

"*Domo arigato*," I said. Thank you very much.

She threw me an adorable smile, bowed, and told me I was welcome. "*Do itachimashita!*"

Back on the street, I marveled at how putting a little effort toward learning the language could open up so much more opportunity. Most of my shipmates were fighting for a position at one of the Four Corners bars. The four of us, however, ended up on the roof of a five-story building, drinking beer for a quarter of the price that everyone else was paying. We were also enjoying an incredible view of our new home.

If I stood in that beer garden and walked due east for six thousand miles, I would have made landfall in the US somewhere between San Diego and Los Angeles. We were on the same line of latitude that we had left. Geographically speaking, though, the two places could not have been more different. Southern California was a desert. Japan was very green. It was not the bright, vibrant green of Hawaii, but more of the deeper hue you would find in the Pacific Northwest. There were few palm trees in Sasebo, but more evergreens than I had seen since leaving Michigan.

By population, Sasebo was less than a quarter of the size of San Diego, but by land area, it was even less so. The city was packed. It was not as bad as Tokyo, but walking through the *ginza*, personal space was pretty hard to come by.

Looking at the people, I had to agree with Nick Budd. For those of us who just arrived, the Japanese did seem to look alike. If you studied their faces, of course, you could tell them apart, but they seemed to put a lot of stock in uniformity. Everyone plodded about in business attire, and there was little personal expression. All the men wore blue suits, white shirts, and solid ties. Women showed a little bit more variation in color, but not in style.

The school kids wore outright uniforms. Girls were in tops that matched our Navy dress blues, though they wore them with skirts instead of trousers. Boys dressed in black tunics and pants that looked like World War I era military uniforms. Even the criminals had their own style. The *yakuza* by the *pachinko* parlors wore suits of dark red or green and covered their eyes with narrow sunglasses.

Japan was an alien place, with new things to discover everywhere we turned. One of those was Japanese beer. We were quite impressed. We also found a delicious noodle dish called *yakisoba*. That was what Metaire was eating when I saw him look at something behind me, drop a mouthful of noodles back into his bowl, and say, "*Merde.*"

Turning around to see what Claude was looking at, I noticed six men wearing the same blue *uwagi* jackets as the protesters at the base's gate. They spotted us, too. Fearing that, through no fault of my own, there was another night in the brig ahead of me, I repeated Claude's phrase, only in English.

"Shit."

*****

CHAPTER
6

The protesters saw us at the same time we saw them. It did not look as if they were expecting foreigners to find their beer garden so soon after arriving. They all started speaking to one another in hushed tones while throwing side-eye glances in our direction. They did not put any effort into hiding the fact that they were talking about us.

After reaching some consensus, two of them stepped out of sight, disappearing toward the bar. The rest marched toward our table. When they got there the men, bearing somber expressions, bowed at the waist and greeted us. "*Konnichi wa.*" Good afternoon.

I stood up and returned the gesture. Following my lead, my friends did the same. I then held out my hand and said, "*Konnichi wa. Watashi wa* Doyle Murphy." My name is Doyle Murphy.

"Do…da…da…?" one of the protesters stammered, reminding me that there was no "l" sound in Japanese. To him, my first name was indecipherable gibberish. Pronouncing the "r" in Murphy was a little tricky too. I should add that it was no picnic for an American to pronounce a Japanese "r," either.

OLONGAPO EARP

To help him out, I tried to katakanize my name. Pointing to myself, I said, "Do-ru Mu-Ru-Fi."

"Ahhhh." Our protester said while taking my hand and shaking it with genuine warmth. "Murufi-*san. Hajimemashita. Watashi wa* Otsuka Hideki."

"*Hajimemashita*," I said. Glad to meet you.

Otsuka-*san* could tell my Japanese was atrocious. He spoke slowly to give me a fighting chance of understanding him. "You speak Japanese?"

"*Sukoshi*," I answered. A little.

"Your friends speak Japanese too?"

I shook my head. "No."

"Then, I wirr try to speak Engrish." Otsuka-*san* turned to our group and straightened his back. He looked like he was going to say something of great importance with a high degree of formality and gravitas. He did, but when it came out, it was entirely unintelligible.

Realizing that we had not understood a word that he had said, Otsuka-*san* prepared to repeat himself. Before he could get another word out of his mouth, however, his friends snuck up from behind. One of them slammed several bottles of Sapporo beer on the table hard enough to startle us. Finding that hilarious, he erupted in laughter. He then slapped Claude Metaire on the shoulder and cackled, "WEHR-COME TO JAPAN!"

*****

I joined the Navy to see the world and to discover cultures different from my own. The moment I learned the *USS Belleau Wood* was moving to Japan, I started reading everything I could about it. I was expecting the unexpected.

Still, I found myself surprised by the hospitality of Japanese protesters. Hours before, they were apoplectic about us trespassing within their country. Now they were buying us drinks in prodigious quantities. Ichiro Kida, the man who spoke the best English, tried to explain the contradiction.

"No, we do not want more American mi-ri-tary peo-po in Japan," he said. "Would you want Chinese army peo-po occupying San Francisco?" If I had to guess, Kida-*san* was in his early thirties. He was a serious-looking man and stockier than most of the other Japanese we saw. He obviously worked out in some fashion and moved with the confidence of someone who knew how to take care of himself.

"No, I guess not." I watched Tony Bard take his chopsticks and stick them into the rice he was eating so that they stood up straight. I reached over, pulled them out, and laid them down across the bowl. Tony looked at me, trying to figure out what I was doing.

"That makes the food an offering for the dead," I explained. "It's bad luck and poor manners. Lay the *hashi* over the edge of the bowl like the Japanese guys are doing."

Kida-*san* watched this and nodded his approval. "That does not mean we do not want you to visit us, to rearn about us or rike us; we just want to have con-tro over our country. The bases ah-so make us a target. We have ar-ready been attacked with nuke-re-ar weapons once. We do not want Russians or Chinese to bomb us again to get to the American Navy."

"*Wakarimasu*," I said. I understand.

Otsuka-*san* was closer to my age. He was a little taller than the other Japanese guys but still shorter than us Americans. Except for Dixie. Otsuka had a more typical build of a Japanese man, thin and wiry. I sensed that he wanted to improve his English skills as much as I wanted to improve my Japanese. He hung close to Kida-*san* and me. "How rong you study Japan ranguage?" he asked.

"One year," I said in Japanese. In the simplest English I could muster, I added, "This is first time I try speaking."

"Aaaaah," They both said. "Is good for first time!" They were lying.

"*Domo arigato*. I still need much more practice."

"Me too." Otsuka-*san* smiled. "With my Engrish."

"You rike Sapporo?" Kazuo Yabuta asked, pointing at the beer we were drinking. Yabuta-*san* was a stereotype breaker. He was a jovial man who laughed without reservation. Yabuta-*san* liked to drink, and more importantly, he enjoyed making the rest of us drink with him. His English was limited to fundamental phrases, but he had a way of communicating that had us in stitches. He spoke in single syllables, pantomime, and hilarious audio effects.

Yabuta-*san* was a very loud man that inadvertently called attention to himself. That tended to make the other Japanese uncomfortable. We

OLONGAPO EARP

Americans ate it up, though. It was impossible not to like the man, and he was the most popular of our new friends. "You rike Sapporo?" he asked again.

"*Hai! Hai!*" Dixie answered, showing that he had at least picked up the Japanese word for "yes." Turning to me afterward, he asked, "Doyle, how do you say it's delicious in Japanese?"

"*Totemo oishii desu.*"

Dixie tried to repeat what I said but slaughtered it. I do not know what he actually articulated, but whatever it was, Yabuta, Takahashi, Koshimizu, and Sasaki found it hilarious. When they finished laughing, Yabuta told him. "Japan good beer! Japan very good beer! Oh-dah Asahi now!"

"We drink Asahi." Claude tried to explain. "Eet ees very good!"

"Oh! Oh!" Yabuta said, having decoded Metaire's French Guianan accent for the first time. "*Wakarimasu!* Oh-dah Kirin! Oh-dah Kirin now!"

By then, waitresses were prowling the beer garden, so I caught one's attention and ordered, "*Kirin o kudasai.*"

She asked how many, but I did not understand her. Otsuka-*san* answered for me. "*Shi-chi*," he said. Seven.

When our beer arrived, Kida-*san* paid for it before I had the chance. Yabuta-*san* showed it off, filling up the glasses of his American guests before sitting back in anticipation. Dixie reached forward to try a drink, but I stopped him.

"Dude. Grab a bottle and fill their glasses first," I told him, giving my guys another cultural lesson. "That's the way it's done here. You never fill your own glass, and you always make sure that none of theirs are empty. When you're done drinking, leave the glass full in front of you."

Again, Kida-*san* noticed this and nodded. He seemed to appreciate that I did my research. With the drinking etiquette established, we went through the Kirin like it was water. Having grown up on weak American beer, we found the Japanese version a pleasant surprise. We drank a lot of it.

At some point, Yabuta-*san* wanted to show off more Japanese booze. "Oh! Oh!" he said. "Oh-dah *saké*! Oh-dah *saké* now!"

I caught the waitress's attention. "*Sumi…sumi..sumimasen. Osaké o kudasai!*" By this point, we had been through all the Japanese beers the garden offered several times. I was starting to forget the little Japanese I knew. After the *saké*, my English was getting sketchy too.

J.E. PARK

"Oh! Oh!" Yabuta-*san* said after the second round of *saké*, the one with the flakes of gold floating in it. "Oh-dah *shochu*! Oh-dah *shochu* now!"

Following Yabuta-*san*'s suggestion, I tried to order seven bottles of *shochu*. The waitress gasped. Our Japanese friends burst out in laughter once again. Otsuka-*san* smiled and corrected my order to one. "*Shochu* is vay-dree strong. One bot-toh fine."

We were now getting into the hard stuff. I asked for seven more beers as chasers. When I turned over my yen to our server, I realized that it was the first time I paid for anything since our new friends arrived.

When we finished the *sho-chu*, a form of Korean vodka, we were all absolutely pie-eyed. I was thinking things were getting ridiculous when Yabuta-*san* suggested we try a popular Japanese cocktail.

"Oh! Oh! Oh-dah *chu-hai*! Oh-dah *chu-hai* now!" A *chu-hai* was *shochu* mixed with tonic water and lime juice. It was tasty, but not what we needed. Dixie was stoned, looking weirdly around the area, trying to keep his head upright. Claude was obliterated. He was a fitness nut, not a drinker. Even Tony's eyes were growing very heavy, and I sensed he would not be conscious long if we did not get him moving.

I needed to figure out a way to put the brakes on our drinking, but my own head was so muddled I had no idea how. Then Yabuta-*san* said, "Oh! Oh! You need drink *omanko jūsu*! Oh-dah *omanko jūsu* now!"

I couldn't. I was wrecked. My friends were wrecked. Still, I felt that we would lose face if we did not at least try *omanko jūsu*. Once again, I got our waitress's attention, and when she arrived, I said, "*Omanko jūsu o kudasai.*"

The waitress blushed and asked me to repeat myself. When I did, she turned even redder. She then said a lot of stuff that I could not even begin to understand before she shuffled away. She looked embarrassed and maybe even offended. Clearly, something had gone wrong.

I turned and looked at our hosts. Kida and Otsuka averted their eyes. Takahashi, Koshimizu, and Sasaki stared at me with very grave expressions. It looked like they disapproved of what I said. Yabuta looked like he was doing everything he could to keep from busting out in laughter. A moment later, an older woman I assumed to be our waitress's boss showed up to ask me what I had ordered. "*Omanko jūsu…?*" I asked.

OLONGAPO EARP

"You know what is *omanko jūsu*?" she asked me. She did not sound amused.

"*Iye*," I sheepishly answered. No.

"Where you rearn '*omanko jūsu*'?"

I turned and looked at Yabuta-*san*, who immediately erupted into a fit of hysterical laughter. So did Takahashi, Koshimizu, and Sasaki. Kida and Otsuka cracked up too, despite making their best effort not to. This set off a very animated exchange between Yabuta-*san* and the beer garden supervisor that got us asked to leave. "What is *omanko jūsu*?" I asked Otsuka-*san* as we stumbled toward the exit.

"You no want know," he answered.

I did, though. If I was getting banned from the beer garden, I had to understand why. "Kida-*san*, what is *omanko jūsu*?"

Kida smiled. "Do you know what *jūsu* means?"

I nodded. "Yes. It means juice."

"*Hai*. It is juice. *Omanko* is a woman's…"

I buried my face in my hand. "Never mind," I told him. "I figured it out."

After staggering out of the department store's elevator and back into the *ginza*, we stood there swaying around each other for a moment. We were trying to keep our balance and figure out what to do next. Of course, it was Yabuta-*san* who made the suggestion. "We eat! Oh! Oh! You need try *odori ebi*! We go *odori ebi* now!"

I do not know where we went next. All I remember was that it was a very long walk, and part of it was through downtown Sasebo. There were flashing lights, sirens, and people yelling into megaphones. Their amplified voices bounced off the buildings, further disorienting us. Beautiful girls dressed as anime characters wove through the crowd on roller skates. They were trying to entice us into the nightclubs, restaurants, or whatever other business it was that they worked for. Near the base, the people we saw seemed pressured to conform. In this part of town, young people seemed perfectly willing to express themselves in ways both delectable and garish.

It took forever to reach our destination, which was good because we needed to walk the alcohol out of our system. By the time we arrived, only Claude Metaire was still hopelessly drunk.

J.E. PARK

Yabuta-*san* had chosen a traditional Japanese eatery for us to dine at. There were no chairs, and the tables were communal and close to the ground. You sat cross-legged on the floor while you ate. Our hosts were used to this. We Americans had a hard time sitting still, having to shift position constantly to keep our legs from falling asleep. We were also squeezed between two other groups of diners, which felt claustrophobic and added to our discomfort.

"*Irassharimase!*" a tiny older woman said as she got us all situated. Once we were seated, she used a set of wooden tongs to pass us each a steaming hot towel to wipe our face and hands on. If there was one Japanese custom that I grew to appreciate, it was that one. It was a refreshing way to rejuvenate oneself before eating.

Yabuta-*san* did all the ordering while Otsuka and I smoked my last two cigarettes. We then did another shot of *shochu*, the ten of us toasting, "*Kampai!*" I then excused myself to buy smokes from a vending machine I spotted on the way in. I returned as our appetizers arrived, three heaping bowls teeming with writhing live shrimp. *Odori ebi.*

I noticed that all eyes were upon me. I was the guy who made the effort to learn Japanese and familiarize myself with the customs of the land. That made me the man who was going to try it first. The Japanese knew I would likely be disgusted by live food but wanted to see how I would react. The Americans were watching me, too, hoping that I knew a graceful way to decline the dish. I didn't.

All I could do was get it over with. Without hesitation, I picked up my *hashi* and went for it. I was proficient with chopsticks, but I discovered that picking up noodles was far easier than trying to grab food that was excitedly trying to get away from me. Our hosts found it hilarious watching me work, but they cheered me on as I sought a victim. When I finally caught one of the bastards, I popped it into my mouth without ceremony. Before I could think about it, I began chewing, washing it down with a long pull of Asahi.

"Aww, man," I heard Claude groan. Metaire turned far more pale than a man of his complexion could reasonably be expected to. He then struggled to get to his feet. Once up, he bolted for the door with his hand over his mouth. Tony Bard followed him to see if he was alright.

OLONGAPO EARP

Our hosts looked concerned, but after they saw Dixie trying to keep from laughing, they busted up too. They then said something between themselves that I missed. After that little discussion, each of them reached into a bowl, grabbed a shrimp, and ate it as I had. Dixie did too, though I caught him gagging as he swallowed.

When they finished, Kida-*san* leaned in and said, "That was very interesting. There is another way to do this, though. Would you like to see?"

My face flushed red, knowing that I messed up. My Japanese friends only ate a writhing live shrimp themselves to save me from embarrassment. It likely disgusted them just as much as it had disgusted me. I watched Kida-*san* grab another shrimp, separate its head from its tail, and shell it. He then used his *hashi* to dip the meat in one of the sauce cups before putting it in his mouth. After that, he stuck his tongue out at me to show the tail was still wriggling before chewing it up and swallowing it. "*Odori ebi*," he said. "Dancing shrimp." I had to admit; his method was far better than mine. Still, I do not think *odori ebi* will become a staple on American appetizer menus anytime soon.

Claude and Tony were never able to see *odori ebi* done the correct way. Ten minutes later, Bard stepped back into the restaurant, looking concerned. He also looked a little relieved to have found a way out of eating live shrimp. "Claude's down, Doyle. He's tossing his guts up into a garbage can outside."

"You need me to help get him back to the ship?" I asked.

Tony shook his head. "No, Doyle. No way. You're in your element here. You stay. You're doing us proud."

"Thanks, man. You know how to get back?"

Our leading petty officer shook his head. "No clue whatsoever. We're going to take a cab."

"Then make sure he's done getting sick before you put him in a car." A few months before, Claude made a Tijuana taxi driver pity-puke all over the inside of his own ride. I was in the front seat and barely escaped taking a direct hit.

Once Bard and Metaire left, plates of chicken *yakitori* came out. And then came *gyoza*. Both were delicious. After that came tuna *yakitori,* which, because I am not particularly fond of fish, was actually more challenging for me to swallow than that first shrimp.

When we finished our feast, our table was an overflowing mess. Our waitress slipped between Takahashi and me to clear our plates. Once her arms were full of dishes, she tried to pull away from the table but looked like she was going to hit me square in the forehead with the saucers. To let her by, I cocked my head to the side. As the mess passed above me, a moist scrap of food fell from one of the bowls and landed right in my ear.

At first, I was just mildly disgusted. I winced and reached for a napkin to clean myself up. Before I could grab one, though, I felt ten tiny legs emerge from that little morsel. In a very arachnid-esque fashion, they then started probing around my ear canal. I panicked. With one fluid motion, I raised my right arm and batted my ear with everything I had. The offending shrimp went flying across the table, where it struck Yabuta-*san* right in the center of his forehead. It then ricocheted, performed several aerial somersaults, and landed just shy of my dinner plate. It sat there staring at me, stunned, but poised and ready to strike again.

Now, shrimp do not look very formidable when all you see is their tails dangling from the side of a margarita glass. Seeing one whole just after you interrupted it from burrowing into your brain is a different matter altogether. They are primeval-looking creatures with appendages tipped with tiny lobster claws. They have long antennae, capable of picking up scents and vibrations deep underwater. Shrimp are also armor-plated and have the same emotionless eyes as any other cold-blooded killing machine. Staring at that little beast, I knew I had the advantage in size and strength, but it had unpredictability on its side. No matter how deep I looked into its little black eyes, I could not figure out what it would do next.

Yabuta-*san* did not wait for a counterstrike. With a yell more appropriate for a karate dojo than an intimate Japanese eatery, he brought his hand down upon the table, crushing the little monster. He also scared half of the restaurant, including me, right out of our seats. After that, Yabuta-*san* rose his hand, showing me a palm covered with pulverized shrimp guts. He then told me, with complete sincerity, "Got it. Save your rife!"

Dixie howled in laughter, and the rest of us followed suit. While in hysterics, Dixie asked, "How do you say 'crazy' in Japanese?"

OLONGAPO EARP

"*Baca,*" I answered, practically crying.

Dixie pointed at Yabuta-*san* while roaring with laughter. "*Baca!* Yabuta-*san baca!*" Then the whole demeanor of the party suddenly changed.

"I NO *BACA!*" Yabuta-*san* yelled, jumping to his feet, his face red and ready to fight. He was beside himself with fury, and Takahashi, Koshimizu, and Sasaki had to restrain him from leaping over the table to break Dixie's nose. Yabuta lacked the English skills to tell Dixie what he wanted to, so he unleashed a flurry of vindictive down upon him in torrential Japanese.

"Why did he say that?" Kida asked me.

"Say what?" I asked, utterly clueless about what Dixie did that was so offensive.

"*Baca!* Why Dikushi-*san* call Yabuta-*san* crazy?"

"Why wouldn't he?" I asked, still not sure what exactly had happened. "Yabuta-*san* is a very funny guy! He is trying to pay him a compliment! In English, crazy means funny! It means he likes to have fun, to drink a lot, to get crazy." Turning to Yabuta, I pled, "*Gomen nasai. Gomen nasai.*" I was telling him we were sorry.

Kida-*san* jumped in and got things calmed down. As a show of remorse for the misunderstanding, Dixie and I picked up Yabuta-*san*'s tab. The conflict got cleared, and everything was explained, but the atmosphere was still tense. Sensing that it was too late to return the party's dynamic to what it had been, Yabuta, Takahashi, Koshimizu, and Sasaki decided to call it a night. Dixie did too and was pointed in the general direction of the base by Kida-*san*. I offered to go with him, but Otsuka-*san* invited us to one more place, and, sensing that I really wanted to go, Kevin told me that he was fine on his own.

That left only three of us to finish out the night.

*****

Kida, Otsuka, and I ended up in a small nightclub somewhere closer to base, but way past the *ginza,* near where the town ended and the mountains began. As we walked in, I noticed one of those "No Foreigners Allowed" signs and pointed it out to my hosts. Kida-*san* shrugged it off. "You okay if you with us. They no want trouble. Foreigners bring trouble with fighting and getting rude with girls. You okay, so if we responsib-oh for you, they ret you in. If you act good and they trust you, you can come yourse'f. They no ret you bring friends, though."

Once inside, I realized that calling the place a nightclub was a bit of an overstatement. It was actually a glorified karaoke bar. Otsuka led us all to the back, where four girls sat waiting for us. Hisako appeared to be Otsuka-san's girlfriend. She kissed him and held his hand once we arrived. Her hair was in pigtails, and she was outfitted in a schoolgirl sailor top with a plaid miniskirt, platform shoes, and knee-high socks. Her English skills were on par with her boyfriend's, and she greeted me with, "Herro. Nice meet you."

Mamiko was older and introduced to Kida-san by Otsuka. She wore typical business attire, which was understandable as she was a bit more mature. Hitomi spoke no English, greeting me with "Hajimamashita." She ignored me after that, seeming much more interested in the match potential of Mamiko and Kida. The last girl was clad in Goth garb, black from neck to foot, and she was positively gorgeous. Her English was perfect too, her accent oddly flavored with a hint of the American south. "Hi, Doyle. I'm Yukiko Fukuyama. It's nice to meet you."

"Wow," I said. "Your English is better than mine. Where did you learn it?"

"I studied English at university. I also spent two different years in the United States as an exchange student. One in San Francisco and another in Tuscaloosa, Alabama." She pumped her fist in the air and said, "Roll Tide."

I laughed and ordered each of us a beer as Yukiko bummed a Marlboro Light from me. After inhaling, she coughed. "Damn. I was hoping this was an American cigarette."

Shrugging my apology, I said, "I ran out hours ago. I had to get these from a vending machine. They do seem a lot harsher for some reason."

Yukiko nodded. "They are. Japanese cigarettes use charcoal filters. They're not the same."

"Next time, I'll make sure I bring more American Marlboros."

Yukiko waved me off. "Don't do it on my account. I smoke one cigarette a month usually."

"I wish I could say that," I told her. "I smoke about once an hour. One every ten minutes if I'm drinking."

"And you're drinking now?"

OLONGAPO EARP

I nodded. "Oh yeah. Taking in the Japanese salaryman culture, I guess."

"Cool." Yukiko exhaled her smoke. "And now here you are, about to ascend to the pinnacle of it: karaoke. Do you sing?"

Shaking my head, I answered, "I wouldn't call what I do singing. I don't think anyone else would either."

"Well, you better get used to it. It's terrible form to refuse karaoke in Japan."

I sighed. "No respectful way out?"

Yukiko shook her head. "None whatsoever. If it comes down to it, they'll hold you at gunpoint until you're up there singing *Girls Just Want to Have Fun*. I suggest you squeeze yourself in your private areas to hit the high notes."

I laughed. It was not that Yukiko's joke was so funny. I just found it amusing how un-Japanese she was. Every local woman I had met to that point was very demure, shy, and seeking approval. This was most evident in how often they ended their sentences with the word "*neh?*" which means, "isn't it?"

Granted, Yukiko was speaking to me in English, but even when she spoke Japanese, the "neh?" was conspicuously absent. As I sat there trying to figure her out, she passed me a book of songs that the club offered. It was written in *katakana*, though, and I could not read it.

"You didn't do your homework before coming to Japan?" she asked, taking the catalog back. "You can't read the script?"

I shook my head. "Yukiko, I studied my ass off before coming here. I did my best to learn the language, but without anybody to practice on, I still suck at it."

"Well, if you really want to learn Japanese, you will. It's very easy to do when you're immersed in it."

"I don't even need immersion," I told her. "Picking up foreign languages is kind of my superpower."

"Really? What do you speak?" she asked as she turned a page in the karaoke catalog.

"French and Spanish," I said. "My Spanish got really good while in San Diego because we spent so much time in Mexico. One of the guys in my shop is from French Guiana, so I keep current in French as well. I also have a working knowledge of Tagalog. I picked that up from working on the mess decks."

"The what?" Yukiko asked, showing the first weak link in her English skills. She was not familiar with nautical terms.

"The ship's kitchen."

"So, you're a cook?"

I shook my head. "No. I'm an electronics technician. I fix radars."

"Then why were you working in the kitchen?" Yukiko asked.

I flashed her a mischievous smile. "I got into a little trouble and ended up down there for ninety days as punishment."

Yukiko grinned back at me. "Oh, so you're a bad boy?"

"A little." First impressions were important, so I kept the rest of my rap sheet to myself.

"How did you learn Tagalog in the kitchen?"

"It's mostly Filipinos working in the mess decks. I was in the wardroom, the officers' mess, so I had a lot of downtime. I learned it from the cook I was teamed up with. We're going to the Philippines at the end of this month, so I'll improve my Tagalog there, I'm sure."

"You live on the base then?"

"Yes."

"I pass by it often," Yukiko told me. "I work near there for Kodak as a translator, in Yamagatacho. I live in Sonodamachi. That probably means nothing to you, does it?"

I shook my head. "Not a thing."

"They're different neighborhoods. The base is between them. When I walk home, I usually go through the park, by the river."

"Cool," I told her. "I hope to see you around then."

"If you're there around seven at night, you probably will."

As Yukiko warned me, my turn eventually came to sing. She helped me pick something I could musically slaughter, settling on *What a Wonderful World* by Louis Armstrong. Doing my best to imitate Armstrong's gravelly voice to conceal the fact that I could not carry a tune, I accidentally nailed it. To my surprise, Satchmo was very popular in Japan, and everyone knew the song. The crowd went nuts, sending me back on stage time after time to sing every Armstrong hit in their collection. By the time the night was over, I could barely speak.

OLONGAPO EARP

Yukiko and I talked a lot about what she missed in the United States and what I should try while I was in Japan. We also spent a lot of time discussing punk rock, which was a shared interest. I told her a story about how I got thrown out of a concert for being underage and spent three hours breaking back in, only to succeed in time to catch the last thirty seconds of the final act. When things wound down at about one in the morning, we shared a cab home.

I thought we had a pretty good time. Because of the confidence that came from ten straight hours of drinking, I leaned in to kiss Yukiko when the taxi parked to let me out at the Albuquerque Bridge. She stopped me by putting her index finger across my lips. "Ah ah ahhhhh. You need to behave." She then held out her hand. "Just friends. Okay?"

I grinned. It was a little much to expect to come away with a Japanese girlfriend on my first night in Sasebo. So, I took her hand, shook it, and said, "Okay. Friends. I hope to see you around."

Yukiko smiled politely, but without any sign of whether she shared the sentiment. She did tell me goodnight as the cab started up to take her home, though.

I waited for Yukiko to drive out of sight before I crossed the bridge into Nimitz Park. Halfway across the path back to the base, I ran into Palazzo, who was with two other sailors walking a beat on Shore Patrol. "So, how was it?" he asked as I passed by.

"How was what?" I asked back.

"Japan."

Looking toward Sasebogawa Street, back into town, I took a moment to think about it. I thought about Japanese beer, *saké*, dancing shrimp, anime girls on roller skates, strobe lights, megaphones, street signs I couldn't read, karaoke, and Yukiko. I then turned back to Spanky Palazzo and told him, "It's eventful if nothing else."

*****

CHAPTER 7

Japan seemed to agree with me. It was a land so different from Detroit that it was like hitting a reset button somewhere deep within my mind. With few things to remind me of home, I had fewer triggers to summon my demons. My nightmares decreased dramatically and I stopped having my episodes altogether.

I had spent a lot of time in stateside bars where it was too easy to cross paths with another drunken hooligan and end up in trouble. That could still happen in Japan if you hung around Four Corners with the other sailors. Because of that, I opted to spend more time with my Japanese friends like Otsuka Hideki. That kept me deeper in town, away from the base, and allowed me to keep my nose clean.

I enjoyed my new friendship with Otsuka. Besides being my age, he was also something of an adrenaline junkie. Instead of bar-brawling his way through Tijuana nightclubs, though, he had healthier ways of getting kicks. When he broke away from his day job as an electrician, Otsuka spent his time in a local *dojo* honing his martial arts skills. When he was not doing that, he would hike the more treacherous trails around the local mountains. When he found out that I was into scuba diving and surfing, he expressed an interest in giving both a try. We planned on researching Kyushu surfing spots when the *Belleau Wood* returned from the Philippines at the end of November.

As much as I enjoyed Otsuka-*san*'s company, I had other motives for spending so much time with him. Otsuka was the person who introduced me to Yukiko Fukuyama the day I arrived in Japan. She had been on my mind ever since. Yukiko was gorgeous. She was also exotic, mysterious, and intelligent, speaking flawless English. I was a long way from being fluent in Japanese. Since landing in Sasebo, I had met other girls, but communicating with them outside of very basic topics proved exhausting.

Yukiko told me she passed by Nimitz Park going to and from work, and if I hung out there, I would see her. I tried that a couple of times a week, but we never came across one another for some reason. It was not until the end of October, a few days before we were to leave for the Philippines, that I finally saw her again.

On my last duty day before setting sail for Subic Bay, I was assigned to serve on Shore Patrol. Unfortunately, the crews of the *Belleau Wood* and the *Dubuque* came to blows in the Enlisted Man's Club and leveled the place the night before. With the best Shore Patrol assignment left in shambles, we were all sent out into town. As an E-5, I ended up in charge of a three-man team ordered to walk Nimitz Park.

BM3 Danny Gibson from the *Belleau Wood*'s Deck Department was with us. That was good because Danny was a huge guy and could de-escalate a situation simply by his size. The downside was that Danny was about as swift as a three-toed sloth in the throes of a savage valium bender. Conversations with him were painful and they tended to make a long night even longer. YN3 Curtis Sorenson was my third man. Luckily, he was smart enough to take the edge off of walking a beat with Gibson.

My chief, ETC Ramirez, was also on Shore Patrol that night, but he was a little closer to the action at Four Corners. Our beats had some overlap and we would periodically meet in the middle of the Albuquerque Bridge. There, he would give me a fresh can of mocha pulled from a heated vending machine, which made a great hand warmer. Sasebo was a lot like San Diego, where the nocturnal breezes coming off the cool ocean waters could cut you right to the bone after the sun went down. It was not bad if you were bouncing from bar to bar like Chief Ramirez was, but if you were walking out in the open like we were, you stayed cold.

For all the excitement of the night before, our watch started off largely uneventful. There was a lot of foot traffic along the path that ran along the river, and I enjoyed it while it lasted. Most of the people passing by were Japanese. I greeted each one with a smile and a *"Kanban wa! Ogenki desu ka?"* Good Evening. How are you?

This drew a warm response from the older folks, who would stop and talk back. They were not used to having a *gaijin* addressing them in their native tongue. None of the pretty Japanese girls I was hoping to talk to stopped, though. They just giggled, returned the greeting, and picked up their pace to get away before I said something else.

When the Japanese traffic decreased, the American exodus away from the base accelerated. I spotted several familiar faces. Sergeant Fordson, ET2 Darius Cleveland, and Claude Metaire stopped to say hello. I also crossed paths with Marty Pruitt from the AG shop next door a little while later. He was hanging with his snipe buddy, Vinnie Decker. It was the person who ran into me that made my night, though.

"Well, well, well! Is that Doyle Murphy?" It was a girl's voice coming up from behind. There were very few young women in Japan that had even heard my name at that point, let alone remembered it. I only knew of one who could pronounce it. Yukiko Fukuyama. "Look at you, Doyle! Why is your government dressing you so funny?"

I was in dress blues but wearing a pea coat that at least covered up the part of our uniform that made us look like Japanese schoolgirls. My coat was cinched at the waist by a white duty belt, from which hung a two-foot-long nightstick. My right bicep was adorned with a black armband emblazoned with the letters "SP" in bright yellow. The bell bottoms of my trousers were wrapped around my calves, then covered with white leggings to keep them in place. With my white Dixie Cup hat cocked a bit to the side of my head, I might have been considered dashing had it been the 1940s.

"Yukiko! How are you?" I called out. She was with two of her friends, so I bowed to them, held out my hand to shake theirs, and said, *"Kanban wa! Watashi no namae wa* Doyle Murphy *desu. Hajimemashita!"*

Yukiko and I both laughed as her friends tried to pronounce my name. We settled on Do-ru, which was where English and Japanese pronunciations seemed to intersect. As I introduced Danny and Sorenson to the young ladies, I saw Pruitt and Decker heading back toward the ship. More importantly, they saw me.

Having heard the account of my sexual adventures in Hawaii, Pruitt gave me an enthusiastic thumbs up and mouthed, "Three?!? Three girls this time?" He had no idea that I had been friend-zoned by Yukiko weeks before, but I felt no need to correct him. I just smiled and waved.

Gibson attempted to make conversation with one of the young women. Instead of trying to speak Japanese, however, Danny just enunciated louder, as if volume was the key to breaking the language barrier. He turned to the girl closest to him and shouted, "Do you like Motley Crue?" It was a line that probably did not work any better with women who actually spoke English.

As the boatswain's mate continued, the rest of us stopped talking and stared at him. Trying to describe his favorite band to the girl, Danny started playing air guitar and serenading the young lady with a horrid rendition of *She's Got the Looks that Kill.* He was so loud that people walking on the other side of the river stopped to gawk at him too. After Petty Officer Gibson brought his hillbilly courtship ritual to an awkward end, I glanced at my watch. Seeing it was 10:30, I looked back at Yukiko and said, "It's a little late to be coming home from work, *neh*?"

"You shouldn't use the word '*neh*,'" Yukiko told me. "It makes you sound like a girl in Japanese. But yeah, we are not coming from work. My friends and I were out for the night. How has Japan been treating you so far?"

I nodded. "Not bad. It's a bit expensive, though. I'm finding that I can't afford to be an alcoholic here, so I'm struggling to find cheaper things to do than drink."

"That's not too hard," Yukiko told me. "There are lots of parks in Sasebo. If you like hiking, there are paths through the mountains."

"You hike?" I asked, mildly surprised. "You don't strike me as a great outdoors type of girl."

Yukiko laughed. "I'm not. I drive into the mountains a lot, though. I like to see the monkeys."

"There're monkeys here?" I asked, betraying my excitement. I had a thing for lesser primates and had always fantasized about having one as a pet when I was younger. I had never seen one in the wild.

Yukiko laughed and pointed due east. "Yes, you can't see it from here, but there's a mountain over that way that has three groups of them. One of the groups contains something like seven hundred animals. It's really neat."

"That's awesome! How do you get there from here? Can you take a bus?"

Yukiko thought for a moment. "I don't know how you get there without a car. I go all the time. I can take you." She then pointed her index finger at me. "If you behave yourself, okay?"

I held my hands up in surrender. "I will behave to see monkeys. If you're taking me, you do have to let me buy you dinner, though. It's the least I can do."

Yukiko pointed at me again. "As friends, though!"

"As friends."

One of Yukiko's companions turned to her and said something in Japanese too fast for me to pick up. When she finished, Yukiko said, "You have to excuse us for a minute. We need to use the washroom."

"No problem," I said. "We'll wait here. It's slow, and we've got nothing better to do."

As the girls turned off the footpath and headed for the restrooms, we heard a commotion rising in the general area they were heading. There was the faint sound of some sort of crash, followed by cheering and singing. It sounded like a couple of sailors were getting rowdy. Since another team of SPs had that quadrant, I assumed that they would handle the situation. They were slow to respond, though, and I saw Yukiko looking back at me with apprehension.

Seeing an opportunity to show off, I puffed out my chest, turned to my partners, and said, "Let's go check it out. Tell them to pipe down. They're intimidating the locals."

"That's not our patrol area," Gibson protested.

"If we can see or hear something going on, it's our patrol area. Besides, I don't see the other team anywhere. I want to make sure they're not sleeping or goofing off."

OLONGAPO EARP

Once the girls spotted us heading their way, they continued on. When we got a little closer, I saw the other group of SPs appear, having heard the same things we had. Since they were closer and led by someone who outranked me, I decided to let them handle it. "Okay. Let's get back to the river," I told my men.

No sooner had we turned our backs when all hell broke loose. The singing stopped, only to be replaced by a lot of yelling and the unmistakable racket of an all-out brawl. "Shit!" I exclaimed as the three of us turned and sprinted toward the bathrooms. The other shore patrol team was from the *Dubuque*. I initially feared that they got jumped by some *Belleau Wood* men in retaliation for what happened the night before at the EM Club. I hoped that we were not going to have to crack the heads of our own guys. There were only a few days left before we set sail for the Philippines. Somebody would be missing out on some epic liberty if they mixed it up with Shore Patrol right before we pulled anchor.

We overtook Yukiko's group and arrived at the restrooms in time to see two men breaking away from a pair of the *Dubuque's* SPs in the distance. They took off north into the trees while the other team went after them. The three of us followed as well, but stopped when we heard one of the girls scream behind us. We did a quick about-face and rushed back to see what was going on.

One of Yukiko's friends was being held by the other. Yukiko herself stood near them with her arms crossed, tears streaming down her cheeks. She was shaking. "You need to help them, Doyle," she told me, pointing toward the men's room.

Stepping into the water closet, to my left, was a bank of three stalls that blocked the view of the urinals from the door. Someone was lying on the deck beneath them, his legs twitching in an almost insect-like manner. A large puddle of blood rolled out from beneath the door of the furthest stall. The third member of the other Shore Patrol team was on his knees next to the injured sailor, whimpering, "Oh, man! Oh, man! Oh, man…" He knew he needed to do something to help but had no idea where to begin.

My first emotion was frustration. We needed to act, and the *Dubuque* puke seemed paralyzed by indecision. Once I rushed up and saw what kind of shape the victim was in, though, I understood. I tossed my radio to Sorenson and screamed at him to call in a man down. I then tried to figure out where all the blood was coming from so I could stop it. Judging by how big the pool was that the guy was lying in, he did not have much more to lose.

I checked the victim's extremities and torso, shocked to find that everything seemed broken. And I mean everything. He did not look like someone on the losing end of a fight. He looked like the victim of a high-speed car accident. There was blood for sure, but I could not find a wound bad enough to produce such a large puddle.

Eventually, I checked the victim's head, something I was reluctant to do because it was so misshapen. I had to force myself to touch it. After some probing, I found that his skull had ruptured in the back. That was where all the blood was spilling from. I also felt something else, something gelatinous and much more distressing protruding from under his hair. It felt like his brains. I looked at the sailor from the *Dubuque* and felt myself starting to panic too. "We've got to move him," I said.

"Are you nuts?!" he screamed at me in response. "If we move him, he's going to fucking die!"

"If we leave him here, he's going to die!" I shouted back. "The ambulance can't get back this far! We've got to get him to the other side of the Albuquerque Bridge, where the street is!" I knew then that it was already too late, but we could not just stand there and watch the man pass. By now, the other two shore patrolmen had returned, both of them out of breath.

"Did you get them?" Danny asked, lacking the attention span to stay focused on the more critical task at hand.

One of the men, a first-class boatswain's mate, shook his head. "No. Motherfuckers got away."

I leapt up and ran to a stall to wrap my mitts with all the toilet paper I could. It did not seem right to try to hold someone's brains inside of their skull with one's bare hands. "I have his head. Danny, BM1, you're both big guys. Grab his mid-section, one on either side. Sorenson, and you, SM3, take an arm." Turning to the guy who was with the victim when I arrived, I asked, "Can you get his legs?" He nodded and moved into position.

We counted to three and lifted the victim. Suddenly, it was like we were pouring out a human pitcher as blood started streaming out of the poor guy's head. I had to have the men try to lift his torso enough to get it

flowing the other way, but it was difficult. The guy was so broken that he just did not move as a normal human should. In fact, the arm that Sorenson was holding was shattered so completely that we could not use it to lift the victim's weight. We feared we would tear it right off.

When we came out of the bathroom, Yukiko's friends screamed again. I was so focused on keeping our man's head together, though, that I did not even see them as we passed. Despite our awkward positions, we sprinted through the park and heard things coming together before us. There were sirens quickly approaching, and once the bridge came into sight, I saw Chief Ramirez running down with his team to help. The Japanese police showed up just as we were starting to cross the river. We were disoriented. The flashing lights, the foreign sirens, and the orders screamed at us in a language we could not understand proved more than we could process.

Once we hit the sidewalk at Sasebogawa Street, we laid the victim down as gently as we could. The other men backed away to let the paramedics do their thing. I stayed in place, trying to keep our man's head together. The toilet paper had disintegrated, so I ended up holding his brains in with my bare hands anyway.

I forced myself to look at the victim's face and knew for sure that he was not going to make it. Shuddering, I wondered how his family was going to recognize him at his funeral. What happened to this kid was so much more than a fight. This young man had bones broken all over his body. His head had been crushed like a grape, his ribs had splintered, and his chest had caved in. Both his arms and his legs were twisted in directions that they should not have been able to turn. I was beside myself, wondering what kind of animal could do something like this.

One of the Japanese paramedics pointed at my hands and said. "*Dozo. Dozo.*" Please. Please. Thinking he needed to look, I let go of the kid's head and stepped away. The paramedic did not bother to check anything, though. There was no need to. The guy was gone. The paramedics stepped back, and the police stepped in. As I backed up, I stole one last look at the body and felt a lump of dread rise up in my throat. I recognized the lizard tattoo on the man's left forearm.

I knew him. He worked next door to me but on the opposite side of the shop that Ben Gott and Marty Pruitt worked. He was a radioman. I did not know him well, but I saw him around enough to remember the tattoo.

Months before, he discovered Warren Macklemore lying still beneath a bank of radio transmitters. Unsure whether Mack had dozed off while working or if he had electrocuted himself, he was the one who reported it to me.

His name was RM3 David Miller.

*****

"Miller?!?" YN3 Sorenson exclaimed. "That's fucking Miller?!? You've got to be kidding me!"

Curt looked at his blood-covered hands, but much in the way that a condemned man would stare at a guillotine, knowing it was about to take his head. You could see his eyes begin to dart around in all different directions as panic set in, as if he were searching for something that could save him. Hysteria eventually took hold. Sorenson began shaking his arms, trying to get the blood off his hands with a renewed sense of urgency. That did not have the effect he was looking for, so he tried wiping them on his soaked uniform. That added more gore than it removed. "Oh, no! Oh, no!" he cried. "We need to get this shit off of us! We gotta get this shit off of us NOW!"

Right there in the street, Sorenson started pulling off his uniform top and sweater. Seeing that his undershirt was soaked through as well, he ripped it off too. Chief Ramirez and I both ordered him to stop undressing, but Curt ignored us. When he saw the bloodstains on his bare chest, he came completely unglued. "Get this off of me! GET THIS SHIT OFF OF ME!"

"Sorenson!" Chief Ramirez yelled. "What the hell's the matter with you! Get your clothes back on!"

"We're gonna get AIDS! We're gonna fuckin' get AIDS!" Curt started ranting. He was inconsolable.

"What are you talking about?" Looking down at my hands, I noticed that I was still holding a few pieces of Miller's gray matter between my fingers. Disgusted, I tried to shake them off.

"He's a fucking faggot, Doyle!"

"What?" Chief Ramirez asked.

OLONGAPO EARP

"He's a homo! Didn't you go to the last captain's mast? He's a fag! He got busted for broadcasting it to the entire Pacific Fleet to support that Clinton guy who's running for president!"

"Seriously?" The gears in my head started to churn, and things began to fall into place. Though I was not as close to hysteria as Sorenson was, I felt a strong desire to clean myself up. I got doused with Miller's blood worse than any of us, but because I was wearing my pea coat, I was not as soaked as Curt was. I grabbed the attention of one of the paramedics. Through a combination of simple Japanese and some universal hand gestures, I got across the point that we needed to clean up. The paramedics were eager to help.

"Jesus Christ!" Sorenson was quaking, as much from fear as from the cold. It got worse after the paramedics started spraying him down with disinfectant. "I just processed his travel paperwork this morning. He was being discharged. He was going home tomorrow!" By now, Sorenson was breaking down into sobs.

A thought occurred to me. "Curt...you said Miller got busted. Was he reduced in rank?"

"Yeah!" Sorenson answered, shaking even worse.

I remembered Marty Pruitt talking about how he would kill HM1 Bateman if he ever touched him because he was sure the corpsman was gay. I remembered how he reacted when we joked about Bateman having dreamy eyes. I remembered Pruitt waving at me as I was talking to Yukiko. I recalled him walking into the park toward the direction of the restrooms.

If Miller had been busted to E-3, he would no longer have outranked Pruitt. If Marty beat up Miller now, it would no longer be an assault on a senior petty officer. It would have just been a fight.

My heart sank. I turned to the BM1, the boatswain's mate from the *Dubuque*. "Hey Boats, the guys you were chasing...was one of them a big guy, a little taller than me?"

"Everything happened pretty fast, but yeah, one was pretty tall."

"Real athletic build?"

The boatswain's mate shrugged. "I have no idea."

"I do," the guy who I first saw with Miller answered. "Fucker punched me in the gut so hard I damn near shit myself. Yeah, the guy's strong as an ox."

"The other guy shorter? A ginger?"

"A redhead, you mean?" asked the BM1. "Yeah."

I turned to Chief Ramirez, shaking my head. "It was one of the AGs that did this. Call it in. Martin Pruitt. The other guy was Vincent Decker."

Ben grabbed his radio. "Are you sure?"

I nodded. "I'm pretty sure. Pruitt's got very little tolerance when it comes to homosexuality, and he loves to fight when he's out drinking. Decker's kind of a stooge of Pruitt's. I saw them both cross the bridge right before this all went down, walking in the direction of the restroom."

The *Dubuque's* BM1 was shaking his head. "When we walked in there, the big guy took a running start to jump up and stomp on that kid's head. It was the sickest thing I've ever seen. My God, what the fuck was going on in that son-of-a-bitch's mind?"

"What about the other one?" I asked.

"The ginger?"

"Yeah."

The boatswain's mate shrugged. "He looked a little sick, like he knew shit had gotten out of control. Once he saw us, though, he bolted first, so he knew they both fucked up."

I saw Yukiko and her friends getting escorted across the bridge by the Japanese police. I moved to get closer to her, and she reached out to me as she passed, grabbing the hand I held out for her. Her face was black with running mascara. "Are you OK?" I asked.

Yukiko looked over and caught a glimpse of Miller's lifeless body. She closed her eyes as tight as she could, sobbing as tears once again began streaming down her cheeks. "No! I'm not! This isn't happening! It can't be!" Her grip tightened around my hand even as the policewoman told her that she needed to let go and keep moving. "Come see me tomorrow? Here?"

"I don't think I'll be able to!" I said, walking with her to keep up as the police herded Yukiko and her friends toward the squad cars. Thanks to my experience with Randy Green, I knew what my immediate future held. "I'm going to be tied up with investigators for the next couple of days! Then we leave for the Philippines! Can you meet me here when we get back?"

Yukiko nodded her head. "Yes! I will!" Her face then twisted up, and before she burst into sobs again, she added, "We'll go see the monkeys!" It was a stupid thing to say at that moment, and she realized it as soon as it left her mouth. She then let go of my hand and bawled as the police led her and her friends across Sasebogawa Street.

We spent the next couple of hours bounced between Japanese police officers with poor English skills and one of the base's duty master-at-arms, a junior petty officer who was way out of his depth. While we were being interrogated, every other man on Shore Patrol was directed to Nimitz Park to search for Decker and Pruitt. Word of what happened spread through the bars and a crowd was beginning to form around us. Some were there because of morbid curiosity, but most were stuck because there was no way to get back to base besides walking over the closed Albuquerque Bridge.

*****

As the shore patrol teams gathered to get their new assignments, a call came over the radio. Decker had been taken into custody while trying to scale the fence to get back on post. He was hoping to gain an alibi, claiming he was already on base when the murder happened. Within an hour, Marty was in custody as well, but Pruitt being Pruitt, he resisted arrest. Japanese police do not have the same restrictions against using force that American police do. Pruitt ended up having to go to the hospital before being locked up.

There was a brief discussion about who had jurisdiction. Technically, it occurred on Japanese territory, so they could have pressed the issue and kept custody of our airman. Since both the victim and the perpetrators of the crime were American, though, they were happy to wash their hands of the affair. They let us deal with it under the Status of Forces Agreement.

Since the six of us who tried to help Miller were deemed walking bio-hazards, we were dismissed. They loaded us into vans and returned us to our ships to be checked out by medical. When I arrived at sickbay, I got HM1 Bateman again, who tried to lighten the mood the best he could. "How're your nuts doing?" he asked me.

"Swell," I answered. I was usually good with witty retorts, but that time I was in shock. It felt like I was still holding pieces of Miller's brains in my hands, no matter how many times I washed them. Now that the adrenaline was dying down, deep inside, I feared that my episodes were coming on, too.

"Are you hurt?"

I shook my head and felt tears threatening to burst out of my eyes. *That poor kid.* What they did to Miller was barbaric. I couldn't wrap my head around it. *Pruitt was singing while he was...*

"Petty Officer Murphy," Bateman said softly, interrupting my thoughts. "I need you to answer me out loud. Are you hurt?"

"I don't think so," I said.

"I need to be a little more certain. Did you get punched? Did you get cut? Did you..."

I looked at my hands, wondering how I could get the sensation of feeling Miller's brains to go away. "There was a lot of blood. Doc, we got a lot of blood on us. Do we have to be worried about HIV or anything?"

Bateman shrugged. "Well, there's not a lot we could do even if you were exposed. It takes a while to incubate, so it's not like running a test right now would do any good. Did it get in your eyes?"

"No."

"Mouth? Nose?"

"No."

"Open wounds that you know of?"

I shook my head. "No."

"Then you shouldn't have anything to worry about," the corpsman told me. "If you want some extra peace of mind, though, I can assure you that David was not HIV-positive."

David. Not Petty Officer Miller. Not even Miller. David. Oh, Christ. Bateman knew him.

HM1 Bateman caught it almost as soon as he said it. He looked up at me after slipping to gauge my reaction, trying to see if I figured out that he and Miller were intimate. I was not in the right frame of mind to put on any sort of poker face. He knew I made the connection the very instant it happened.

Bateman was in a vulnerable position. Back then, being gay was seen as a moral failure, especially in the military. As a product of my times, I essentially thought the same way. Bateman was an exception, though. He saved Randy Green's life after I nearly beat him to death and kept me from spending decades in prison. He was a decorated combat veteran and damn good at his job. Most importantly, the man never wronged me in any way. Bateman was not hurting anybody. I gave him a nod to let him know his secret was safe with me. He was much closer to the victim than I ever was. I did not have it in me to pile onto his pain.

That was a turning point for me on the subject of homosexuality. I came to realize how dangerous being gay was back in 1992. To admit it was to risk being disowned. You could get thrown out of the military for it or even murdered in a public toilet in a land far from home. I began to suspect that it was not a choice, but rather, just how some people were wired. It was the first time I had ever entertained the possibility that we had no more control over who we were attracted to than we did what skin tone we were born with.

*****

I did not sleep that night. In fact, I did not even try. I knew what was coming. There were just too many triggers. I smelled the blood for real this time; I held a man's brains in my hands. Even though I could not pinpoint the exact moment that David Miller expired, I was looking right at him when it happened. I knew this because I could not bring myself to look anywhere else.

This time I was an eye witness to the carnage, and, unlike with my family, I was not imagining what happened. I saw it for myself. I had an episode coming my way—a big one. The moment I made it to my radar dome, my hands started shaking. I then noticed the sweat, and my mind started leading me to places that I did not want to go. There was nothing I could do but surrender to it and resign myself to the fact that for the next several hours, I was going to lose my fucking mind.

And lose it I did.

*****

J.E. PARK

CHAPTER 8

Shortly after getting underway to the Philippines, I got called to the Combat Systems Office by our department head. Lieutenant Commander Barry Winston was the polar opposite of LTJG Krause. Born poor and black and raised in Compton, California, he worked his way up from E-1 to O-4. That was an impressive feat of rising above the circumstances of his youth. Accompanied by Chief Ramirez, I did my best to recall every detail I could about David Miller's death. When I finished, Ben Ramirez was not satisfied with my account, so he added a few details of his own.

"Sir, when I arrived at the scene, Petty Officer Murphy had complete control of the situation," my chief told Winston. "He was not the ranking petty officer on station. There was a first-class boatswain's mate from the *USS Dubuque* there, but there was never any question about who had taken charge. The men were all following Murphy's lead."

LCDR Winston nodded as he looked me in the eye. "Did you make the call to move Miller from the bathroom and take him to the other side of the bridge?"

I swallowed hard. "Yes, sir. I did."

OLONGAPO EARP

"Why? The most fundamental rule of first aid is that you don't risk moving a critically injured man. You wait for the paramedics to arrive and move him on a stretcher. Didn't you know that?"

"I did," I said. "I was pretty sure that Miller was going to die no matter what I did, though. I felt the only chance he had…the only chance at all…was for us to get him medical attention as soon as possible. We had to take him to it. We couldn't wait for it to find us."

"Did anyone contest your call?"

I nodded. "The *Dubuque* man first on the scene did, sir."

"And how did you respond when he challenged you?"

"There was no time for debate, sir. I shut him down."

Winston looked me over for a couple of moments, trying to get a read. "Knowing how things turned out, do you wish you had acted any differently?"

I gave it a few seconds of thought before I started shaking my head. "Not really, sir. I know now that I did everything I could to preserve that man's life. If he'd died while we waited for the paramedics to get there, it would have felt like we wasted the only opportunity we had to save him."

The Combat Systems Officer breathed a heavy sigh. "I wish you hadn't screwed up your opportunity to go to BOOST, Murphy. If you'd just grown up a little, you would've made a terrific officer. I read the reports. That kid was dead no matter what you did. He never had a chance. You never gave up, though, and you made sure everyone around you never gave up, either. That's what leadership is all about."

Chief Ramirez agreed. "When you were running across the park with that kid, all I could hear was you giving orders, Doyle. And every time someone had a question, you were who they turned to for guidance. Even after I arrived, there was never any question about who was in charge. I was the ranking man there, but you were the guy with all the answers. Time is critical in a situation like that, and I knew that I needed to stay out of your way to give that kid a chance. I also knew that you were the best man we could have hoped to have there making things happen. I never felt that I needed to do anything other than what you asked me to."

"Chief Ramirez is putting you in for a Navy Achievement Medal," the CSO said. "I'm going to approve it."

I drew in a deep breath. A Navy Achievement Medal was a big deal. Not one that I thought I deserved, though. "Sir, Miller didn't make it. I'm not sure what I actually achieved. I appreciate the gesture, but…"

"There's no 'but.' I'm not saying that you haven't done your fair share of messing up lately," Winston said. "But when push comes to shove and things get hairy, you always come through. I want that in your record."

"But…"

"I said no 'but,' Murphy." Winston stood up, signaling for the chief and me to do the same. Our meeting was over. He took my hand and shook it. "Obviously, we all wish that things would have worked out better for Miller. That does not negate the fact that your actions last night deserve recognition."

"Yes, sir." After the CSO released my hand, I took my leave, with Chief Ramirez following me from behind.

"Ben," I asked when both of us were out in the passageway. "Do you really think that I did anything out there that deserves a Navy Achievement Medal?"

Ramirez shrugged. "I don't know, Doyle. You do deserve a very detailed description of the look that will flash across Lieutenant Krause's face when that citation lands on his desk, though. Too bad that I can't think of a way to get video of him while he's signing it."

*****

You would not have thought that Lieutenant Krause and LCDR Winston had read the same report about the murder of David Miller. He barged into the radar repair shop, once again ordering everyone out but me. The instant we were alone, he started screaming about how I was directly responsible for the radioman's death. He took particular issue with us moving him over the Albuquerque Bridge instead of waiting for the medics to arrive. This took place less than thirty-five minutes after my conversation with Chief Ramirez and the CSO.

"As far as I'm concerned, that was a gross dereliction of duty!" Krause yelled. He then took issue with me speaking to Yukiko Fukuyama right before the attack happened. "What were you doing talking to a girl when you were supposed to be patrolling the park?"

OLONGAPO EARP

"I was furthering relations between the American military and Japanese civilians by portraying a positive image…"

"Don't give me that crap, Murphy! You were trying to get into her pants, weren't you? You should have been observing your post!"

"My post was fully under observation, Lieutenant. Nothing happened in my area of responsibility. I had to leave my post to render help to the team patrolling…"

"You left your post? That's another dereliction of duty and…"

I was done humoring the EMO. I was done listening to him. I was done looking at him. We already had this conversation when he wanted to write me up after missing ship's movement in Hawaii. The circumstances under which he wanted to place me on report now were even more frivolous than that. It was as if he did not even remember our previous conversation. Standing up, I asked, "You think I was derelict in my duty for trying to save Miller's life? Seriously? Then do something about it."

"Wha…What did you say to me? Are you suggesting that I place you on report?"

"Suggesting? Oh, no," I said, shaking my head. "Sir, I'm daring you to."

The color rushed into Krause's face. I would have loved to have seen the look in his eyes, but his sunglasses were on, per usual. Losing control, he pointed his finger toward the door. "Get down to the EMO office now! On the double!"

I stormed out of my shop, but I was not about to run as Krause ordered. As it was, my gait was so much longer than his that he struggled to keep up. The two of us descended three flights of stairs in silence but bearing expressions so full of rage that everyone stepped out of our way as we passed. Chief Ramirez later said that when I stepped through the door of the EMO office, I looked so pissed that he thought I had come to kill the lieutenant. He was unaware that Krause was a half dozen steps behind me.

"Get to my desk and stand at attention, Petty Officer Murphy!" Krause screamed as he burst into the office, causing Master Chief Darrow to stand up and take notice.

"What's going on?"

Before I had the chance to answer my master chief, Krause cut me off. "Shut your mouth, sailor! Zip it!" Turning back toward Darrow, he continued. "I'm sending this man to mast for dereliction of duty. He was talking to girls out in town instead of patrolling his watch. Had his attention been on his duty instead of on his dick, he might have been able to de-escalate the situation before it got one of our men killed!"

I watched Darrow and Ramirez trade expressions between themselves as if to ask, "What the fuck?"

"He also displayed gross incompetence when he decided to move that man from the bathroom to the other side of the bridge!" Krause had by now brushed past Darrow and was rifling through his desk. "Had it not been for that, Mullins might have been able to make it!" Nobody corrected the lieutenant for getting the murdered radioman's name wrong.

"He even left his post!" Our division officer stopped looking through his drawers to announce that as if it had just occurred to him. "He was supposed to be patrolling the river! But he left his patrol and ran into the park to get himself into another fight! Can you believe that!?!"

Ramirez and Darrow looked at each other again. They could not believe what they were hearing. Nobody was this stupid, not even Krause. They were trying to figure out how an officer with more than twenty years' experience could come to the insane conclusions that he was reaching. I was too. It looked to me like Krause was in the larval stages of a nervous breakdown. He seemed to support my suspicion when he finally stopped tearing apart his desk and screamed, "WHERE ARE THE REPORT CHITS?!?"

"In the overhead shelf above…"

Chief Ramirez tried to answer, but Krause cut him off. Bunching both of his hands into fists, the lieutenant yelled out, "Aaarrggghhhhhh!" That convinced us all that he had officially lost his mind. "Master Chief! Put this man on report!"

Darrow shook his head. "I'm not putting my name on that shit. If you want him written up for doing his job, you're going to have to do it yourself." My master chief then reached into an overhead bin. Pulling out a report chit, he tossed it onto the lieutenant's desk.

Livid, Krause stuck his index finger out at Darrow. "You're getting dangerously close to being insubordinate yourself, Master Chief." From where I stood, Krause was wrong on this. Darrow was being blatantly insubordinate. The lieutenant was just too scared of the man to take him on in a frontal assault. "But, fine! I'll write it myself! I'll add the charges of…"

The lieutenant picked the wrong form up from off of his desk, pausing when he saw my name on it. "Navy Achievement Medal Recommendation," Krause mumbled as he read, allowing us to pick out a few of the words. "Doyle Murphy…RMSN Miller…on the night of…displaying exemplary leadership in a crisis situation." He then glanced over at the Post It note attached to the form in the CSO's handwriting and read that loud enough for us all to hear. "LTJG Krause, please sign and return to me ASAP – LCDR Winston."

Krause dropped the form back down upon his desk. He realized that our department head intended to decorate me for the exact same thing he was hellbent on placing me on report for. Shaking his head in disbelief, he whispered, "goddammit…"

It was barely audible, uttered under his breath, but the lieutenant's curse grabbed our attention. Krause was a devoutly religious man. A fanatic even. Where most of the men in our division used the vilest of obscenities as punctuation marks, Krause was not in the habit of swearing. He was certainly not in the habit of casually blaspheming.

The lieutenant looked at me again. "Goddammit!" he shouted, slamming his hand down upon the desk. Nobody flinched. "GODDAMMIT!" He then punched the desk hard enough that I would not have been surprised had he broken his hand. "OUT OF MY OFFICE! ALL OF YOU! OUT! OUT! OUT!"

The way events panned out, I was never awarded the Navy Achievement Medal, but I was okay with that. I did not believe I did anything to earn it. Chief Ramirez proved prophetic about the look on Krause's face once he discovered my nomination, though. We did not go far after the lieutenant ejected us from the office. We stood in the passageway outside the door and listened to Krause completely melt down for more than twenty minutes. *That* gave me far more personal satisfaction than any trinket pinned upon my chest ever would.

*****

CHAPTER 9

I was atop the ship's island structure as we pulled into the Philippines, looking off the starboard side. We were near the city of Morong, and there was a hillside cemetery there that faced the sea. Hundreds of Filipinos had gathered within it, all reverently walking amongst the tombstones with lit candles in hand. It was a vision that was at once both somber and serene. Despite the macabre pageantry, it was the first time since we left Japan that my thoughts were not consumed with David Miller's gruesome death.

It had been a rough trip. My episodes came back with a vengeance after witnessing Miller's murder, and I was back to sleeping in my radar dome. Dixie and Metaire were there when I crippled Randy Green, so they were intimately familiar with my condition. They both kept a very close eye on me.

To a lesser extent, so did Master Chief Darrow. It was he that interrupted the reverie I had slipped into while watching the procession in the cemetery. "It's beautiful, isn't it?" he said, startling me.

I nodded. "Yeah, it's kind of cool. What are they doing?"

"It's *Araw ng mga Yumao.*"

OLONGAPO EARP

Trying to remember the Tagalog I learned on the mess decks, I asked, "The day of those who died?"

Darrow nodded. "Yeah, something like that. 'Day of the Dead' is the way it's usually translated. It's a Catholic thing."

Shrugging, I said, "I'm not so sure about that. Being as Irish as I am, I was raised Catholic. I never heard of it."

"Not even in Mexico?" my master chief asked. "With all the time you spent in Tijuana? It's an even bigger deal there. They all wear those skull masks and put skeleton decorations out all over the place."

"That's what that was?" I asked. "I always figured that was the way they celebrated Halloween south of the border. I thought they were just so into it that they made it a three-day fiesta."

Darrow laughed. "If I remember right, it only lasts one day here. It's quite a party, though. It's a good day for us to pull in. What're your plans tonight?"

Shaking my head, I told him that I did not have any. "I'm on duty. I've got the twelve to four Petty Officer of the Watch."

"Aw, man," Darrow groaned. "You didn't try to switch with anybody?"

"Why would I? I'm sure there'll still be plenty left to drink when I get out there tomorrow."

"Yeah, but you don't want all the hot girls to be taken before you're free!"

I sighed. "I'm pretty sure we went over this. I don't pay for sex, Master Chief. I never have, never will."

"We all pay for sex, Doyle. It's just a matter of what kind of currency we use." Darrow grinned and leaned over against the rail. Taking in the lush tropical scenery around us, he said, "You know, this is the place sailors are told about from the time they get to boot camp. The debauchery, the drinkin', the fuckin', the fightin', this is where sea stories...no, sea *epics*...are made. There's no place like it on earth, and we're here to shut it down. You telling me that you finally get here, to this sacred land, at a point in history where it is about to all come to an end, and you're going to sit on the sidelines?"

"I'm not sitting on the sidelines of anything," I responded. "I'll be in the thick of it. Trust me. I've got a lot to drink off of my mind. I'm just not going to take advantage of some poor little peasant girl selling her body to keep her belly full."

"So, you'd rather see her starve?"

I gave Darrow the type of look that I usually reserved for Lieutenant Krause. "You trying to tell me I've got some sort of moral obligation to sleep with hookers in Olongapo?"

My master chief shook his head, grinning. "No, I'm telling you that what these girls are doing is not really a 'black and white' kind of thing. They need a way to provide for themselves and their families. They're offering a service…"

"A disgusting service…"

Darrow scowled at me. "Hey. You think you're better than these girls?"

"I didn't say that…"

"I don't care what you said. I care what you meant. If you had a hungry kid at home, would you be willing to rent yourself out to perverts so that your child can eat and go to school?"

"No. Of course not."

My master chief looked cross. "Well, the women working the bars in Olongapo love their children enough to make those kinds of sacrifices. They don't enjoy the work, Murphy. They do appreciate being taken care of, though. If you commit to one of them, can get them out of that life for even just a few weeks, you're doing a good thing."

"Jesus, Master Chief. It sounds like you're trying to push me to sleep with whores out there."

"I ain't forcing you to do shit," Darrow growled. After softening his tone, he said, "Look, son, you've been through a lot lately. That shit that went down in Mexico. The scholarship, Krause, and losing Macklemore. Then there was Hannah leaving you, and this horrible shit with Miller. Man, I just want to see you take it easy for a little while and get your head straight, you know? A woman can do wonders to help with stuff like that."

"Yeah, well, you know, I've always been kind of an over-achiever when it comes to girls, Master Chief. I'm sure I can meet someone here who's not a hooker."

Darrow shook his head. "Don't do that, Doyle."

"Do what?"

OLONGAPO EARP

"Get into some sort of emotional entanglement here. These girls around this area, well, landing an American man is like winning the lottery. Life is uncertain in this part of the world. There's this crushing poverty, violence, and powerlessness that's always hanging over their heads. There's very little security. These girls fall in love with the concept of getting away from here and going someplace where it's not so easy to lose everything you have in the blink of an eye. A place where you have something left after you've bought food and shelter. A place where people with even a little bit of power can't do with you whatever they want with impunity."

Darrow waved his hand toward the shore. "The civilians, the girls not working in the bars, well, they're different. They're not equipped to handle the heartbreak that comes with getting your hopes up that you're going to get a whole new life, only to end up left on the pier.

"The bar girls, though, they know the deal. They've been through it a few times and know what to expect. If you're pursuing a woman in Subic Bay, soften the blow of leaving by making your relationship a business transaction."

I shook my head. "Sorry, Master Chief. I'm not wired that way." Trying to change the subject, I asked, "How about you? What're your plans for tonight?"

Darrow sighed. "Well, I'm not getting mixed up with any bar girls either. I'm on my third marriage and can't afford another divorce this close to retirement. I'm looking up a friend of mine in the Philippine National Police and going apartment hunting. I need to lay low. When I shipped out of here the last time, I kind of left a lot of things unresolved with a girl I was seeing. I really don't want to run into her here. Her and some other people."

"Other people?" I asked. "Like who?"

Darrow shrugged. "I'm Olongapo Earp, remember? I spent the better part of eight years here as a police officer. I'm not a cop this time, though, so I won't be walking the streets with a .45 on my hip. If word gets out to certain people that I'm around and without backup, they may want to settle some old scores."

"That why you're looking up an old cop buddy? For backup?"

My master chief shook his head. "Not really. Sergeant Tejada is just a good friend. He's not my bodyguard. Actually, Doyle, when it comes to backup, you're the guy I'd trust the most."

"Me?" I asked, both surprised and flattered. I counted Darrow among the toughest men I had ever met. It was an honor that he considered me to be in the same league as he was.

"Yeah, you. You know how to handle yourself in a fight. You've got street smarts, and you proved in Mexico that there's nothing you won't do to protect a friend. Doyle, it's not like I'm expecting a specific threat out here in Olongapo, but I'm going to be keeping my head down anyway. I'm getting an apartment out in town and hunkering down. If you ain't going to be out whoring with the rest of the fellas, feel free to hang there with me. I enjoy your company, and to be honest, I'll be more at ease knowing you're watching my back."

*****

After the ship was tied to the pier, the captain required us all to assemble on the flight deck before he would turn us loose in town. Once there, the officers pulled the division in and informally briefed us on what we were, and were not, allowed to do in the Philippines. I say 'informal' because the Navy was not going to come right out and instruct the crew on the correct ways to deal with Filipina prostitutes. They did not want us to get into trouble or hurt out in town either, though. So, there were no hand-outs, there were no pamphlets, and there was no structured training. It was just the men we reported to letting us know what was what.

Krause started with the basic stuff. "This can be a dangerous place, men. Safety is paramount. There will be no multiday liberty passes without special permission. We will muster right here, on the flight deck, every morning at 07:30. Got it?"

"Yeeeeeeesssss, sir," we all groaned.

"Gentlemen, the Philippines is currently fighting three civil actions. Over the past few years, rogue elements of the Philippine army have attempted to overthrow the government of Corazon Aquino multiple times. They all failed. Now they're holed up in the mountains all over the island of Luzon doing all kinds of mischief. If they weren't bad enough, we've got communist guerillas around here too. They're called the New People's Army, or NPA for short. Olongapo's relatively safe, but things can get hairy beyond it. For that reason, the captain has put a twenty-five-mile quarantine around the city. If you get caught more than twenty-five miles from this base without permission, your liberty will be canceled. Any questions?"

Tony Bard raised his hand. "You said the Philippine government was fighting three civil actions. You listed off the NPA and the failed mutineers. What was the third?"

"The Moros down south," Master Chief Darrow answered. "That's a holy war involving the Muslims. That's a long way away from here, though."

"There is a curfew in Olongapo, men." Again, the lieutenant's statement met a chorus of groans, so he spoke up to be heard above them. "You can stay out in town overnight, but you need to be off of the street by zero-one hundred. If you get caught out after curfew, your liberty will be automatically revoked for the rest of our time in port. Master Chief, do you have anything else to tell the men?"

"Oh, do I," Master Chief Darrow answered, rubbing his hands together deviously. "Men, there are plenty of drugs to be found around here in Olongapo. They've got some good stuff here, too. None of it, however, is worth the consequences of doing it. There is no cocaine to speak of in the Philippines, but they will gladly sell you heroin and tell you it's coke. If you do it, you'll die. It's that simple. It's very pure. You may also come across something called *shabu* around here. This is methamphetamine. It's highly addictive and also very powerful. A lot of the girls working the bars here are on this shit. I can hardly blame them. I'd be on something too if I had to sleep with your ugly asses. Especially yours, Palazzo!"

We all laughed. Even Palazzo. "If you catch your girl doing dope, walk away, gentlemen. If you are with a woman who gets busted with it, they'll consider you in possession of it too. You will not survive very long in a Philippine prison, boys."

I had a hard time taking my master chief seriously when it came to the topic of drugs. Especially after he spiked my drink with LSD in Las Vegas. That was probably why he was looking right at me while lecturing us on the subject.

"Now, to the subject of bar girls," Darrow went on. "The main drag outside of the base is Magsaysay Drive. There is bar after bar there filled with more types of women than you could imagine. If you can think it up, you can find it there, boys. Now, there are also men out there that can make themselves up pretty damned good as women. They're called 'Benny Boys' here. Gentlemen, there is only one sure way to tell these guys apart from actual women before it's too late. Does anyone care to enlighten us?"

The crew grinned and turned to Palazzo, the division's resident pervert. He sparked off a riot during our last trip to Tijuana by punching out a transvestite that he had been making out with inside of a whorehouse. "Look for the Adam's apple," John answered, setting off a roar of laughter from the rest of the men.

"That's right, guys. Look for the Adam's apple. Now, I would recommend staying close to base if you're out carousing so that you can get back before curfew. If Magsaysay gets too rowdy or crowded, though, Barrio Barretto is within the 25-mile perimeter. It has everything Magsaysay has, but with a beach too. That's a good time. Now, you may have heard about how Angeles City's nightlife is so much better than Olongapo's, and you'd have heard right. It's much better. It's also off-limits. So is Manila. And Pagsanjan…"

"A word about Pagsanjan," Krause interrupted. "You guys are going to do what you guys are going to do. Whatever. Go to town, get your girls, soil your bodies and damn your immortal souls with sins of the flesh. I don't care. Stay out of Pagsanjan. I mean it. That place is a hotbed of child prostitution. If I catch any one of you there, I promise you that I will have you imprisoned. I am not joking around about this, men. I spent three years stationed at Cubi Point. During that time, I put more men behind bars for using underaged prostitutes in Pagsanjan than the Armed Forces Police Department did. I will *ruin* you if I see you there! Is that clear?"

As the lieutenant warned us away from Pagsanjan, I caught a glimpse of Master Chief Darrow watching Krause as he spoke. He was studying the man as if something had piqued his interest. My master chief had the same look on his face as the two NCIS agents had on theirs when they were interrogating me after my fight with Randy Green. It was a cop look, the look of a predator who had caught the scent of some very tasty prey.

OLONGAPO EARP

Sensing that I was looking at him, Darrow turned his head to me and grinned. He was on the hunt, and though I knew he would not tell me what it was quite yet, he wanted me to know something was up.

*****

CHAPTER 10

I was the Petty Officer of the Watch when the captain finally unleashed the *Belleau Wood*'s crew upon the streets of Olongapo. There were six hundred men in the hangar bay when I declared liberty call, and they were already streaming down the gangplank before I could finish the announcement. Unlike our base in San Diego, where you could walk from Pier 2 to the first bar outside of the main entrance in ten minutes, Subic Bay was immense. It seemed like a fifteen-minute bus ride just to reach the station's perimeter.

By the time I was relieved from watch, the *Wood* was deserted and silent, quieter by seventeen-hundred than it usually was in the dead of night. I remember wondering what it must have sounded like in town right about then. After changing into dungarees and grabbing a quick dinner, I made my way to the EMO to scavenge for office supplies.

When I opened the door and turned on the overhead lamps, I was startled by the agitated shouting of Lieutenant Krause. He was yelling at me to turn off the light as he tried to find his sunglasses. "You have a migraine or something, sir?" I asked.

OLONGAPO EARP

"No, but I will if I don't give my eyes time to adjust!" Krause barked at me. "What are you doing here?"

"I need some pens and grease pencils for the PMS board," I answered, stepping over to get a better look at my division officer. I figured something was going on and wanted to see what it was. "What are you doing here, sir? This is the Navy's last hurrah in Subic Bay. Aren't you going to get out into town and take it all in before it's gone?"

"Good riddance," the lieutenant growled. Now that he was wearing his shades, Krause flipped the switch on the fluorescent lamp over his desk to give us some light. It did not reveal anything out of the ordinary. The bible that he always kept close by was before him on the desk, lying unopened. I suspected that I interrupted him in prayer. "This is a wicked place, Petty Officer Murphy. It's a wicked place besotted to the whims of wicked men, rotten to its core. Olongapo has been damning the souls of American sailors for a century now. I'm rejoicing that the Lord has finally seen fit to remove this stain of evil from the moral fiber of the United States Navy."

"I don't think God had much to do with us pulling out of the Philippines, sir. I think it was Corazon Aquino and President Bush."

"Oh? You think so?" Krause asked. "You think President Aquino and President Bush smote Clark Air Base too, wiping it off of the map as God did to Sodom and Gomorrah?"

I sighed. Sixteen months before, Mount Pinatubo exploded. It was the second most powerful eruption of the twentieth century. Clark suffered extensive damage, but saying that it was wiped off of the map was an overstatement. In fact, my understanding was that it was accessible enough to be looted by the Philippine military before the Americans could return to it. That was one of the reasons the US gave it up. It was too expensive to repair the airfield and to replace all the stuff that had been stolen.

As for all the wickedness Krause was pontificating about, all Pinatubo did was move it. Some of Angeles City's working girls went to the flesh markets of Manila. Others came to Olongapo. The truth was that the eruption drove down the price of tail everywhere on the island of Luzon not covered in seven feet of ash. "Well, sir," I started to say, once again ignoring my better judgment. I knew little good ever came from voicing doubts about where the pious saw their miracles. "Considering all the damage that volcano did, I did not hear of anyone getting turned into pillars of salt."

Krause glowered at me. "You think it's funny to mock God, son?"

I wasn't mocking God, sir. I was mocking you. "I find little humorous about religion, sir."

The lieutenant opened his mouth to say something but reconsidered. He looked tired, like he did not have the energy even to try to rage at me that evening. "Murphy, get what you came in here for and get out. Go catch up with the rest of the whore-mongers out in town."

"I'm not a whore-monger, sir. I don't pay for sex."

Krause cocked an eyebrow at my tone. "You sound offended."

"Well, I am a little bit."

"Wait a second…you're offended when I imply that you're going to go out into town and do what ninety-percent of the crew is doing out there? Yet, you're not even the least bit ashamed of being a godless atheist?"

I shrugged. "Not ashamed at all. I'd be more ashamed believing an idiot like Father Bennigan somehow had all the answers to the cosmos when he couldn't even navigate a clitoris."

That slipped out of my mouth before I had a chance to stop it. I expected Krause to have a conniption, but all he could do was shake his head. "It's your soul, Murphy."

Considering that the end of our conversation, I stepped away to get my office supplies. I was interrupted by an urgent announcement over the 1MC before I could finish, though. "Security Alert! Security Alert! Away the Security Alert Team! Away the Back-up Alert Force! All hands not involved in Security Alert stand fast! Reason for Security Alert: small craft approaching the ship on the starboard side!" There was an urgency to the Petty Officer of the Watch's voice that made me feel like this was not a drill.

As a member of the Combat Systems department, I was a part of the Security Alert Team. I dropped everything and stormed out of the EMO office, running to the Master-at-Arms shack where the weapons were stored.

When I hit the main deck, I ran into DS3 Darren Stovic. An inveterate gambler, I guessed that he had his duty section poker game interrupted. "Is this a drill?" he asked.

OLONGAPO EARP

"I have no idea." I had to duck to avoid cracking my skull on the top of one of the watertight fittings. We had a security alert drill every day for the duty section. They were typically delivered in monotone, though. "Crider sounded a little excited, didn't he?"

Since most of the men responded from the berthing area, which was much closer to the MAA shack, Stovic and I were the last two men on station. MA1 Thompson passed me a 12-gauge shotgun, a belt full of shells, and a flak jacket. Stovic got a .45 automatic. "Go to the catwalk! Take up positions at mid-ship and wait for orders! This is NOT a drill!"

"Catwalk?" I asked, looking at the weapon I was issued. "I'm too far away from the waterline up there for a shotgun to be any good! Give me an M-14!"

Thompson slammed the armory door. "Just do what you're told, Murphy! I'm not looking for accuracy out of you. I'm looking for noise. If I give you the order to fire, you aim for the fish. I'm hoping that hearing the blast of the shotgun will be enough to scare the threat back to shore!"

"Scare? Threat? Wha…?" We did not train to fire warning shots. Thompson's directions went contrary to standard operating procedures. "What do you mean…"

"Goddammit, Murphy! Get going and get on that fucking catwalk! NOW!"

Stovic and I bolted from the shack and ran to take up our positions. Once on the catwalk, we dropped to our bellies then crawled to the edge to spot our target. Neither of us saw anything. We did hear the duty watch officer above us on the flight deck, yelling through a bullhorn. "Attention! You are trespassing on American property! We are ordering you to pull away and return to shore immediately! If you do not comply, you are risking arrest! If you come any closer, we will fire on you to protect the ship!"

"Fire on us!?!" I heard a woman cry out in English, almost directly below me.

They were so close that I had to stick my head over the edge of the walkway to see them. There were three old American ladies in a motorized canoe. The pilot of the craft was one of the locals, a young man about our age who appeared to suffer some minor mental impairment. He had one eye, a severe overbite, and though he looked startled by the duty officer screaming at him from above, his mouth bore a huge smile. It was as if that was the only expression he knew how to give. I grinned as I realized that this was the "threat" that got the duty Master-at-Arms so worked up. I wondered how he would react to a Zodiac craft full of Russian Spetznaz commandos heading our way.

"Please don't shoot!" one of the other women pled in an acute Alabama accent. "We just wanted to see the ship! It's so big!"

"We won't shoot as long as you follow our orders," Lieutenant Commander Bertram told her. "You need to get away from the ship and return to port immediately before someone gets hurt."

"Okay! Okay! We're sorry!" another lady said before telling the pilot something in Tagalog. As the local gunned the motor and started steering them away from our ship, they all waved and called out their apologies. "We didn't mean to cause any trouble!"

The driver made eye contact with me as they left and smiled. "Bye-bye!" he yelled, waving.

I waved back. "Bye-bye!" At 17:30, it was all just a cute misunderstanding. We had another cute misunderstanding about an hour later. It stopped being cute and ended up just being a misunderstanding at about 20:00. Forty-five minutes after that, we had another security alert, and I was pretty pissed to see that the one-eyed canoe guy came back. He was at the ship's bow that time, though. I was near the stern. The distance made it difficult to express my displeasure with him. By 23:00, we had been called to security alert seven times, and we were getting aggravated.

It seemed like everyone with a boat had to motor in to get a better look at our ship that night. The infuriating part of it was that damn near every one of those vessels carried Americans who should have known better. Yet there they were, taking pictures in front of us and trying to get someone's attention so that they could ask questions. It was as if they thought we were tour guides instead of sailors. The foolhardiest of them tried to get close enough to touch the hull. Every expatriate Yankee within a hundred miles had lost their freaking mind and wanted to keep us up all night. Still, the duty officer handled each one of them with professionalism and restraint.

Sometime after midnight, though, even LCDR Bertram's patience started to wear thin. That time Stovic and I were assigned as his escorts. We were standing on the flight deck with him, watching old one-eye coming at us for the fourth time. "For Christ's sake," the duty officer complained. "Is this ever going to stop?"

I shook my head. "Not as long as we're so congenial to the sons-of-bitches."

Bertram scoffed. "What do you want me to do? Start blowing them out of the water?"

"Naw," I told him. "Just put some fear into them."

"How?"

"Let me get a little excited with them. That one-eye fucker likes to get in close and drive them down the length of the ship to the fantail. I've got access to the Nixie Winch Room. There's a fueling station right inside with a hatch that opens up closer to the waterline. From there, I can get personal with the bastards."

Bertram looked at me for a couple of moments. Like everyone else on the ship, he knew what I had done to Randy Green. I could tell he was wondering if I could handle myself with enough restraint to keep someone from getting hurt. "Let me see your weapon."

I passed the lieutenant commander my shotgun, and he checked it to make sure it was unloaded. After passing it back to me, he said, "Give Stovic your shells. Petty Officer Stovic, you keep them on you unless you're fired on, understand? Gentlemen, you are not to touch those people in any way at all. If someone gets hurt, it's your ass, Murphy. Go do your thing."

"Aye-aye, sir!" At that, Stovic and I both took off to make our way to the well deck.

We got to the fueling station just in time, and we could hear the canoe motoring up alongside us. When it sounded like it was passing underneath, I kicked the hatch as hard as I could. It flew wide open until it crashed against the side of the ship with a calamitous clang. Both Captain Cyclops and his American passenger jumped at the racket. I then threw half my body out of the hatch, pointed my shotgun at their heads, and ratcheted back the forestock to make it sound like I was chambering a round. They both dove down and covered their heads with their arms.

"GET YOUR MOTHERFUCKING HANDS UP WHERE I CAN SEE 'EM!" I screamed, mustering as much volume as was humanly possible.

J.E. PARK

"NOW, GODDAMMIT! NOW! GET 'EM UP BEFORE I BLOW YOUR FUCKING HEADS OFF! MOVE IT!"

The American came unglued as he leapt to throw his hands in the air. He did it so quickly that he damn near capsized the canoe and tossed them both into Subic Bay. "Don't shoot! Don't shoot! We're unarmed! We just wanted to…"

"KEEP YOUR MOUTH SHUT AND YOUR HANDS UP!" I pointed my weapon at the canoe's pilot. He was still hunched over with his hands over his ears. "YOU! YOU! GET YOUR FUCKIN' HANDS UP, GODDAMN IT! HANDS UP! ARE YOU LISTENING TO ME OR DO I HAVE TO BLOW A…!"

"Please! Please! Don't do this! He doesn't speak English! He can't understand you!" The American then said something to the young man in Tagalog that convinced him to look up. He was shaking uncontrollably with tears running down both of his cheeks. That goofy-ass mouth full of all those funky teeth was still smiling at me, though. Suddenly, I was not very proud of myself.

"This is the fourth time he's been here!" I shouted at the American. "What's it going to take to get it through his fucking head that this is an American warship and not some goddamn cruise liner?"

His hands still up, the American said, "I'm sorry! It's not his fault! It's ours! He works with our mission, Hope's Children Ministries! We've been paying him and a couple of the other young men to take us out here to see you! Please don't hurt him!"

I let out a sigh. I tended to distrust bible thumpers in general, but the man in the canoe did not appear cut from the same cloth as Lieutenant Krause. I lowered my weapon and looked at the canoe pilot again. He was terrified and openly weeping now. "What's his name?"

"We call him Freddy."

"Freddy!" I called out. "Freddy! *Tingnan mo ako! Ito ay magiging tama. Hindi kita masasaktan.*"

Turning back to the American, I asked, "Did I say that right?"

The missionary nodded. "Good enough to get your point across. You told him everything's going to be OK."

I shook my head in exasperation. "Look, this stuff has to stop. Right now. Do you understand? You're putting this kid at risk and…"

OLONGAPO EARP

"Look, man, he's just trying to earn some money…"

"I don't care. If this keeps up, somebody's going to get hurt. It's probably going to be him. Freddy works for you guys, right?"

The missionary nodded. "Then get him to stop. Get his friends to stop and tell your people to stop hiring these guys. You're trespassing. The next time I catch one of you guys here, I'm going to hold you for whoever's supposed to be patrolling the fucking harbor. Hold on a second."

I scooted back inside the hatch and pulled a twenty-dollar bill out of my wallet. I crumpled it up around a couple of quarters I found in my pocket to give it some weight and tossed it into their canoe. "Give that to Freddy. Tell him if he keeps everyone else a hundred meters from this ship for the rest of the night, I'll give him another twenty if we ever cross paths again."

The missionary grinned and translated what I said. Freddy's tears dried up and he beamed at his newfound fortune. He then bobbed his head up and down, saying, "*Salamat! Salamat!*" Thank you.

The missionary seemed grateful as well. As they pulled away from the ship, he called out, "Thanks! I appreciate you letting us go! When I get back to shore, I'll shut this thing down. Hey, what's your name?"

"I'd rather not say!" I shouted out. "I generally don't introduce myself to people I've recently pointed weapons at!"

The American laughed. "Fair enough! My name's Michael! I hope to meet you again under better circumstances sometime!"

Once Freddy's canoe was gone, we were dismissed from the security alert. We turned in our weapons, crawled into our racks, and were no longer awakened by announcements over the 1MC. Instead, we were kept awake by the steady flow of drunks rolling in just in time to beat the 01:00 curfew. I had to laugh when Palazzo and Kent showed up. Both of them were stupid drunk and covered in hickeys. I was exhausted but listened to the lurid details of what they had done that evening.

I did not get nearly enough sleep before morning muster, but I was still one of the first people to arrive on the flight deck for roll call. Strolling over to where the CSE division formed up, I heard my name called. I looked up and saw Lieutenant Commander Bertram looking over the starboard side. He was very close to where I had left him the night before, beckoning me to join him. "You gotta see this!"

Out in Subic Bay, about a hundred meters away from us, one-eyed Freddy was patrolling the harbor all by himself. He was intercepting any of the other boats that looked like they intended to get too close. "Oh my god," I said. "How long has he been out there?"

"The rovers reported all night. You must have scared the piss out of that poor guy."

I let the duty officer think that, keeping the fact that I bribed the man to myself.

Looking out into the bay, I found myself somewhat befuddled at why so many people wanted to see the *USS Belleau Wood* that night. The Subic Bay Naval Station was an American military base. Ships visited there all the time. The *Wood* was an impressive vessel but dwarfed by the massive supercarriers that pulled in a few times a year. I was at a loss to explain what made us so special.

The historical significance of what we were doing in the Philippines was lost upon me at the time. There were plenty of people around that area who fully understood the ramifications of what was happening, though. Thousands of retired servicemen living in Olongapo realized that we were dismantling their connection to the US. We were taking their grocery stores, movie theaters, and health care facilities with us. They were facing a future of uncertainty now, not knowing if they would be able to maintain their quality of life there anymore.

There were also plenty of businesses that were going to fold once the *Wood* completed its mission. The economic shockwaves were going to be felt throughout the northern part of the country, the part hit hardest by the eruption of Pinatubo. Their livelihoods were simply going to evaporate once we cast off our mooring lines.

Young men in Philippine schools also knew that without the base's lease agreement, the Navy was no longer required to take in Filipino recruits. Another opportunity to provide prosperity to them and their families would soon be out of reach. Young women not able to seek their fortune in American military service were losing their chances for a better life also. There were plenty of them getting forced out of their jobs as nurses, cashiers, waitresses, and domestic help with the closing of the base.

And then there were the ladies working the bars of Magsaysay Drive and Barrio Barretto. They may not have had the skills required to land a job working for the American government, but they had dreams, too. Many of them hoped to be rescued from the bleak situation that they were born into by some young sailor who could whisk them away to a better life in America. For many girls from remote villages with no education or other means of upward mobility, it was their only way out. Their dreams would also be dashed once our ship crossed over the horizon.

The *Belleau Wood* was not only dismantling a military base; it was scrapping a way of life. For better or worse, Subic Bay was the beating heart of Olongapo. Things were going to change after we left. They had to. Everyone in Olongapo knew that, and it scared many of them.

No doubt, there were plenty of people who were elated to see the Americans leave. Still, there were many whose lives were so tied to the US military presence in the Philippines that they could not help but feel powerless in the face of what was happening. They knew what they were losing, and as they cast their eyes upon the *Belleau Wood*, they knew we were taking it away. There was an army of people out there who wanted to see an American warship moored to that pier one last time. They wanted to hear it. They wanted to touch it.

And for the moment, there was only ole' One-Eyed Freddy keeping them all at bay.

*****

J.E. PARK

CHAPTER 11

Master Chief Darrow told me at quarters to meet him in the SPN-35 dome at noon. I took in an early lunch and arrived at 11:45, only to find him already there with a big grin on his face. "What?" I asked as I closed the door behind me. "Did you win the lottery or something?"

"Close," Darrow answered. "You remember the lieutenant's warning yesterday about Pagsanjan? How he said he busted more people there than the Armed Forces Police Department?"

"Yeah…"

"Well, I went to the Shore Patrol station on base yesterday and took a look at some files. He did. He personally got more than two dozen military personnel charged for being with underaged prostitutes when he was stationed here. He made sure they all did time."

I nodded my approval. "Good for him. I'm glad to see he's got at least one redeeming feature."

"You don't see anything wrong with that?" Darrow asked.

I shook my head. "Should I?"

OLONGAPO EARP

"Two dozen people, Doyle. That's a lot. It doesn't make you wonder why he was spending so much time in Pagsanjan himself? Especially considering that he wasn't a cop?"

I started seeing where Darrow was going with this.

"Do you remember the story I told you about the captain's wife and her first husband?"

"Of course." It was not a story I was likely to forget. When Darrow was on the AFPD in the 1970s, he caught a lieutenant commander molesting boys in Pagsanjan. Desperate to keep the cover his marriage provided for his lifestyle, the officer snapped when his wife asked for a divorce. He tried to kill our captain, a young helicopter pilot stationed at Cubi Point that his wife was having an affair with. While defending himself, Fleming killed the lieutenant commander with the man's own gun, which Darrow helped to cover up. It was why my master chief had so much pull on the *Belleau Wood*.

"Well, that dirtbag spent a lot of time in Pagsanjan, too. He also busted a bunch of his men for frequenting the area. He did it to put fear into them, to make sure they stayed away from his playground. He didn't want anybody catching him doing his thing out that way."

"And nobody ever asked that son-of-a-bitch what he was doing out there?"

Darrow shook his head. "Nope. He had a cover. He played the part of a bible thumper. He went out there as part of a Christian outreach group called Hope's Children Ministries."

"No shit?" I gasped. "I crossed paths with one of them yesterday. He was in a canoe that got too close to the boat and sparked a security alert. You saying that's a front for pedophiles?"

"No, no. Not at all," Darrow said while strenuously shaking his head. "They actually do some excellent work out here. Child molesters know how to work a system, though. They know the ministry will give them access to vulnerable kids and cover things up if they get caught. The missionaries aren't complicit in this shit, but they're terrified of the publicity they'll get if one of their guys gets caught molesting kids. Pedophiles know how to exploit the hell out of that shit." Darrow paused, trying to read the look on my face. "You don't look surprised."

I shrugged. "I was raised Catholic. There were a couple of priests my mother made sure to keep me away from. After I got older, I heard some stuff."

Darrow nodded in understanding. "Yeah, well, guess who else spent a lot of time working in Pagsanjan with Hope's Children Ministries? Even at the same time as that prick our captain shot."

"No shit? Krause?" I asked.

"Yep. Krause," Darrow answered.

"Do you honestly think that he's the type of guy that would…"

"The only type of guy that ever gets caught doing shit like that is the type of guy that you would least expect to. Every dirtbag I ever arrested over there was otherwise a model citizen. They were usually married, too, with children of their own. I never had someone come up to me after I popped one of these assholes and say, 'Yeah, I knew there was something off about that dude.' Everyone is always surprised."

I shook my head. I could picture someone like Palazzo, our shop's pornography addict, doing something like that, but not the lieutenant. Darrow spent a long time as a police officer in Olongapo, so I was reluctant to second guess his instincts. From where I stood, however, he was long on suspicion but short on evidence. There was not enough to make an official accusation. As much as I detested Krause, there was no way I was going to try to pin a jacket like that on the man unless I was sure it was true. "So, what are you going to do about this?" I asked.

"I'm going to try to get to the truth of the matter," Darrow told me. "And I'm hoping that you'll help."

"Me?"

Darrow pulled a folded piece of paper out of his shirt pocket and handed it to me. "I could use some backup. The captain heard me out, and he's suspicious enough that he wants me to look into it. He's particularly curious if that cocksucker has any ties to the prick his wife was married to. This is written permission for the two of us to hang out in Pagsanjan and look around. Not just for Krause, either. If we catch any *Belleau Wood* men out there, he wants us to give him what he needs to hang 'em high. He has zero tolerance for that kind of bullshit."

"Seriously? Just the two of us? Are we even authorized to do this kind of thing? This isn't the US."

OLONGAPO EARP

Darrow shook his head. "No, we're not authorized at all. My buddy in the Philippine National Police, Sergeant Tejada, is on board and willing to let us do it, though. He's using it as an excuse to hang out for old times' sake."

I unfolded the piece of paper. It was indeed authorization for us to travel outside of the twenty-five-mile perimeter of Olongapo, signed by Captain Fleming. When I finished reading, my master chief asked, "So, are you in?"

I did not even hesitate. "Hell yeah, I'm in. Man, whoever said the best part of coming to Olongapo was the booze and the broads? They must never have had the captain's permission to ruin the life of their division officer."

*****

It was sixteen hundred before I managed to leave the ship. When I did, it was within an entourage that included Dixie, Metaire, Tony Bard, Rick Hammond, and Master Chief Darrow. Spanky Palazzo was a little ahead of us, but he gave up his place in line to join our group.

It took a while, but we eventually seized spots on one of the buses for the run to the main gate. To pass the time during the ride, I turned to Darrow and asked, "So what's the plan today, Master Chief?"

Darrow grinned. "The plan? The plan is that I'm showing you all where the apartment is that I got yesterday, so you know where to go if you get into trouble. Then I'm going grocery shopping, getting some booze, and laying low."

"You found an apartment?" Dixie asked.

"Yeah. I got a three-bedroom, so if you guys screw up and find yourselves out past curfew, you run to my place for the night."

"You're not going to be out with us?" Dixie asked.

The master chief shook his head. "Guys, I've spent a third of my career stationed in the Philippines. I've done it to death. The last couple of times I was here, I had a steady girlfriend that I should have married, but for whatever reason, didn't. Me and her have a lot of history together. Truth be told, I still think about her all the time. Now, I'm on my third marriage and my final enlistment. I can't afford another divorce. I *cannot* run into this woman while we're here."

J.E. PARK

Dixie laughed. "You mean the infamous 'Olongapo Earp' of the Armed Forces Police Department has to go into hiding to avoid the wrath of a woman scorned? What's this world coming to? How tough is this chick?"

"Oh, she's tough, all right," our master chief told us. "She'll hurt me. The problem is that she'll hurt me in ways that I'm kind of into. Look, I'm not known for my willpower when it comes to women. It's the reason I've never been very successful at marriage. My divorces were both preceded by a trip to the Philippines, boys. One of them ended over this particular girl. I'm telling you, I'm going into hiding. I'm staying off the street."

There were some protests about Darrow keeping a low profile, but they were all good-natured. We even started coming up with ideas for stuff we could do with him that did not involve drinking binges through whore houses. "Hey, Master Chief," Bard asked at one point. "I see they have a canoe trip that you can sign up for on the ship. It's out in Pagsanjan. Isn't that the place the lieutenant ordered us to stay away from?"

The master chief nodded. "Yeah, it is, but you'll be alright on a sanctioned trip. Krause is right, there's some twisted shit in Pagsanjan, but there's plenty of normal girls to meet there, too. Take that trip. The river's a hoot. The last time I went down it, the movie set for Kurtz's castle was still there. It was eerie."

"Kurtz's castle?" Dixie asked. "From the movie *Apocalypse Now*?"

"That would be the one," Darrow answered. "The movie was filmed on the Bumbangan River just outside of Pagsanjan."

"Man, I might need to check that out," Palazzo mused. "Can you still sign up to do that?"

I felt the hair on the back of my neck stand on end. Sexually speaking, ET2 Palazzo had some serious issues. He lost his position as the shop's work center supervisor because he refused to obey the captain's order to get rid of his smut. Triggered by the stress of his demotion, he suffered some sort of psychotic break that compelled him to masturbate incessantly. The man could not keep his hands off of himself. He got caught at it so often that Darrow and I tried to refer him for a psychological examination back in San Diego. Our previous division officer blocked it out of fear of losing our only IFF tech before leaving for Japan.

Having worked with Palazzo for over a year at that point, I knew he had very little interest in war movies. He would have had even less interest in a cerebral war movie like *Apocalypse Now*. He was into mindless stuff like *Star Trek*. If there was something in Pagsanjan that stirred Palazzo's interest, it certainly was not a movie set. Nor was it something adventuresome like white water rafting. That left…

I shuddered as I tried to force that thought out of my mind. All Palazzo said was that he wanted to sign up for a boat ride. It was a massive leap for me to suspect that he wanted to act out on some pedophilic curiosity. All he had done was say something a bit out of character.

Palazzo was oblivious to it, but I caught myself staring at him for the rest of the bus ride. Was he capable of going to Pagsanjan and doing something so vile? Something so irredeemable? I assumed that he would be far more capable of it than Krause would. I did not think Palazzo was into kids, but he had a warped view of morality. If a girl initiated an intimate encounter, I did not believe Palazzo capable of thinking it wrong no matter how young she was.

Stop it! Stop it! Stop it! Palazzo was enjoying himself with the rest of the men. He was even fitting in with us, something he had struggled to do ever since he reported aboard. He was joking around, laughing, and having himself a good time. All he said was, "Man, I might need to check that out." Then he dropped it. He did not dwell on it. He did not even follow up on it. It was a passing comment, and then he moved on. I was making far too much out of it.

When we disembarked from the bus, I lit a cigarette to calm myself down. I was still struggling to get my mind off Palazzo when I caught an awful stench that distracted me. "My god!" I called out. "What the hell is that smell?"

The rest of our group, all of whom had been there the night before, broke out into laughter. Master Chief Darrow put his hand on my shoulder and spun me around to face the bridge on the other side of the main gate. "That, Doyle, is the sweet aroma of the world-famous Shit River."

"Oh, man!" I cried out. "I can taste it!" If the canal that separated the Subic Bay Naval Station from the City of Olongapo had an actual name, no one ever knew what it was. All we knew was that it was the main conduit for carrying excrement away from the shantytown built a half-mile upstream. I eventually found that it did not always smell that bad. For whatever reason, though, that day it was particularly rank.

J.E. PARK

Across the bridge was a bustle of human activity. Jeepneys were rushing in and out to transport people along the standard routes. At the same time, trikes, which are motorcycles with attached sidecars, offered door-to-door service to wherever we wanted to go. There were also food carts lined up along the curb. Most were selling something called "monkey meat," but it tasted more akin to teriyaki chicken than simian flesh. Scattered among the food carts was a mob of trinket vendors. There were also a couple of sketchy tattooed hooligans standing by in case anyone wanted to score dope. Darting in and out of the traffic was a small army of children looking to make a buck any way that they could.

Able to sense a newcomer by the look of bewilderment on my face, the street urchins mobbed me, begging me for money. To get them out of my way, Palazzo reached into his pocket and pulled out some peso coins he had left over from the night before. He whistled at the kids to get their attention, then tossed the change over the fence and into the river. The children left me in a mad dash to the water, throwing themselves into it to be the first to come up with the cash.

"What the fuck?" I stopped dead in my tracks and stared incredulously at Palazzo.

"What?" John asked, clueless about what I was so upset about.

"Did you really just throw coins into a goddamn sewage canal so that kids would dive in after them?"

"Wha...hey...Doyle...It's not like that," Palazzo stammered. "I was trying to help you out and get them away from you. Plus, they get some money too."

"You telling me you were trying to help them? Seriously?" Reaching into my pocket, I pulled out a handful of American change and threw it over the fence also, but I made sure it landed on the bank. That drew a bunch of the kids out of the water to look for coins on dry land. "If you wanted to give money to children to get them out of the way, that's how you do it to keep them from catching cholera, you fucking ass clown. You think that shit's funny, Palazzo?"

John's eyes darted around the other faces of our group, looking for support. None was forthcoming. He had not done anything different than a hundred other men that day, so he did not understand why he was being

104

called out for it. Still, he tried to apologize. "Hey, Doyle, man, I'm sorry…"

"Why are you telling me that you're sorry?" I asked while taking a couple of steps toward him. "Why don't you tell those kids that you're sorry for being such a fucking prick? In fact, how about I chuck your fat ass into the water so that…"

I lunged forward and grabbed Palazzo by the shirt. Before I could follow through with my threat, however, Darrow came up and grabbed me from behind. He put himself between the gate guard and me so that the sentry could not see what was going on. Then he wrapped his arm around my neck and put me into a chokehold to keep me from decking Palazzo.

"Let him go, Doyle," the master chief whispered. He put the squeeze on my throat just enough to make my breathing difficult. "You're not even five minutes into Olongapo liberty, and you're already risking getting restricted to the ship for the whole time you're here. Settle down and back off."

"But…but…" I tried to say as my face started turning red.

"But nothing. Turn him loose. Those kids have been doing this shit since they could walk. They were doing it before we got here; they'll be doing it after we leave. Yeah, it's shitty, but if those boys are going to get sick from this, I doubt that it'll be this dive into the canal that does it. Let him go. Now."

I released my man and watched him stumble backward a bit. Once he regained his footing, Spanky appeared like he was going to say something to me, but Master Chief stopped him before he had the chance. "Get out of here, Palazzo," he snapped. "And if I catch you doing anything like that again, I'm going to be the one that kicks your ass. Got it?"

Spanky stared at us for a moment in disbelief, blindsided by what had happened. And crushed. A chronic outsider, Palazzo made great strides toward becoming an accepted member of the division. Over the last six months, he had received some mentoring from Rick Hammond to improve his technical skills. He embraced the fitness regimen offered by Metaire to get his weight down and took leadership cues from me to gain the respect of the men. All that progress was undone with a literal flip of a coin. With sagging shoulders, Palazzo turned his back on us and walked away, blending into the throng of people on the other side of Columban Road.

J.E. PARK

As I watched Palazzo disappear into the crowd, I began to suspect that I might have overreacted. Had Dixie or Metaire done something like that, I know I would have handled it differently. I would have told them to knock it off and stop acting like idiots. I would not have tried to throw them into Shit River. With my mind still hung up on Palazzo's interest in Pagsanjan, my subconscious was probably looking for an excuse to lash out at him.

Unfortunately, that was a realization I did not come to until my blood was down. By then, Palazzo was long gone and back to being an outcast. The damage had been done.

*****

The apartment Master Chief Darrow had rented was perfect for a man going into hiding. It was about a mile away from the Magsaysay bars and as far northeast as one could get from the main gate and still be living in the city of Olongapo. Located off of Harris Street, the master chief's flat was on the upper floor of a four-unit building divided in half by a shared courtyard. It looked perfectly suited to accommodate fifty drunken *Belleau Wood* men on a regular basis.

One drawback to the master chief's new digs was that it backed up against a hill covered in thick jungle. Because of this, Darrow feared he would have to put up with monkeys getting into his garbage. The residents found that if they secured their waste bins well enough to keep the macaques at bay, the sanitation workers could not get into them either. Another problem was that there were no grocery or beer stores anywhere near the place. To stock up on supplies, the master chief was going to have to go to Magsaysay Drive anyway, the very place he was trying to avoid.

Still, it was a nice apartment, quiet and out of the way. It was precisely the type of place I could have used to straighten out my head for a while. After the way I had handled Palazzo earlier that day, I realized that I was still very much on edge. Considering it was barely a week since I had watched a man die in front of me, that should have been little surprise.

While Darrow and the boys packed into the bathroom to figure out how the shower heater worked without electrocuting the bather, I went outside to get a better look at the courtyard. I stepped out of the apartment and walked down the steps, discovering a beautiful little girl about seven or eight years old. She was drawing chalk pictures on the cement underneath the stairs. When she saw me, she looked apprehensive, but after I smiled and waved, she returned the gesture and said, "*Halo*."

"*Kumusta!*" I answered back. "*Kung ano ikaw?*" How are you?

The little girl's eyes opened wide and she giggled. She was delighted to see a foreigner trying to speak Tagalog and likely found how I was failing at it hilarious. When she stopped laughing, she said, "*Ako ay mabuti*," I'm good. She then said other things that I could not understand, mistaking my Tagalog to be much better than it was.

It was difficult, but I got through to her that I knew just a little of her language, although I was trying to learn. She decided right then that teaching me new words was far more interesting than her chalk. Before I knew it, the girl had me by the hand and was leading me all over the courtyard, telling me the word for everything we came across. She was so chatty that my friends were already coming out of Darrow's apartment before I got the chance to introduce myself. "*Nagagalak akong makilala ka. Ang pangalan ko ay* Doyle Murphy."

"*Ako si Mari!*" Her name was Mari.

As my friends walked up, I thanked Mari for the lesson and told her that I hoped to see her again. I then waved goodbye to her as we left. "*Paalam!*"

"*Paalam*, Doyle," Mari said before she went back to her chalk.

"Jesus Christ," Dixie said as he caught up with me. "Is there any language that you don't speak?"

*****

We took trikes back to Magsaysay and had them drop us off in front of the grocery store that Master Chief Darrow needed to visit. After telling him that we would stop by his place later, we parted company and made our way to a bar called the Captain's Mast. The Mast was a dive, everything you would expect a Third World watering hole to look like. Dark and smoky, the bar had no air conditioning, relying upon a battery of ceiling fans to keep the air circulating. The lighting consisted of strands of Christmas lights run throughout the rafters except for the stage, which used floodlights to show off the girls who stood upon it, swaying unenthusiastically to cheesy pop songs played on an ancient boom box. As lethargic as the stage ladies were, the women on the floor were bubbly and energetic, working hard to win themselves a date for the night. Stepping inside that place was the closest I ever came to knowing what a rock star feels like.

There were thirty women in the Captain's Mast, each one more exotic than the next. Every single girl was a heartbreaker and insanely out of my league, yet they were falling over themselves to capture *my* attention. It was insane. As much as I was disgusted by the thought of paying for sex, I was ill-prepared for how difficult it was to resist. Dixie, who was not even trying to hold back, disappeared with one of the young ladies inside of twenty minutes. Claude Metaire was gone ten minutes after that. Being married, Rick Hammond did not want to deal with the temptation and left to seek other ways of entertaining himself.

I turned to Tony Bard and asked which one of the women he was shacking up with for the evening. He smiled wide and said, "You know, I've been thinking about what we're doing here, and I came to the conclusion that we're playing with fire. If you mess around with a different girl every night, it's only a matter of time before you catch something you can't get rid of. As hot as these chicks are, I'm going back and getting the girl I was with last night. It's safer."

I nodded. "Yeah, I figure it would be. What bar does she work at?"

"Not around here," Tony said after he finished his drink and stood up from his seat. "She works in Barrio Barretto, near Baloy Beach. I'm going to head over that way now."

"Baloy Beach?" I asked as I finished my drink. "Is there any surfing there?" I hoped I could throw myself into riding Philippine waves instead of spending the next month testing my sexual willpower.

Tony shook his head. "I wouldn't think so. It's still Subic Bay, so it's protected from the ocean swells."

I let out a long sigh. "Well, there's got to at least be swimming out there, right? You mind if I tag along?"

Slapping enough money on the bar to cover both of our drinks, Tony said, "No, not at all. Let's go."

We took a jeepney out to Barrio Barretto and as soon as I laid eyes on Baloy Beach, I knew where I was going to be hanging out. Though not as crowded, Baloy reminded me of Ocean Beach back in San Diego. On the saltwater side of Long Beach Road, there was little more than sugar sand and the occasional wooden *casita*. The landward side was loaded with bars, but they bore little resemblance to the gaudy nightclubs of Magsaysay. Baloy watering holes were more like the Sand Flea, my California haunt. They were simple shacks, with seating beneath a palm frond *palabra*.

Like the bars on Magsaysay, these ocean-side taverns were full of willing young women. Fewer servicemen made it out that far though, so the ladies seemed much more plentiful. Tony and I split after a drink at the Piccadilly Well and I spent a couple of therapeutic hours soaking in the water with my clothes on.

Lying in the ocean, I meditated on why I had blown up at Palazzo and thought about how to make it right. When I got thirsty enough, I left the bay to venture into a bar called the Blue Shack. There I was again besieged by hard-bodied vixens even though I was still dripping wet.

"Wha? You no tink I pretty," pouted a stunning mocha-skinned heartbreaker when I rebuffed her advances.

I smiled at her. "Sweetie, you're one of the prettiest girls I've ever seen. I just don't, you know, I've never paid for, well…"

"You don't puck whores," she said.

That was not the way I wanted to phrase it, but her sentiment was spot on. "I don't pay for sex."

"Why no? You tink we dirty girls? We no good enough to…"

"Hey," I interrupted. "I don't think anybody should be told what to do with their own body. I'm not judging you, and if you're happy doing this, then more power to you. It's just not my thing."

The girl cast her eyes down at the bar. "I no happy doing this," she sighed.

I looked at her for a moment and then nodded my head in sympathy. "Is someone forcing you to do it?"

The girl shook her head. "No, but I got not'ing else. I can quit anytime I want, but ip I quit, I no get money. I go hungry."

"Yeah, that's the real reason I don't sleep with bar girls. It feels like I'm taking advantage of some poor woman's misery, you know? That's not exactly a turn-on."

The girl nodded. "I understand. You nice guy."

"Well, I wouldn't go that far," I said. As the girl got up to leave, I stopped her. "You get a commission if I buy you drinks, right?"

"Yes."

"Then what are you drinking?"

"It call a Butterply."

"Butterfly? What's in it?"

The girl smiled. "It just orange juice, but ip you buy it por me, it cost double you pay por you beer."

I raised the bottle of San Miguel I had bought for what equated to seventy-five American cents. "Deal. Let me buy you a drink."

In the end, I bought her four. I learned that her name, well, the one she used while working anyway, was Betty. She was from Iloilo City and was lured to Olongapo by the prospect of finding a job at the base. It had not worked out, and she ended up working in the bars like most of the other women that came there. Though she wished to make a living some other way, she also told me that she was better off now than she had ever been.

We talked at the bar for a couple of hours until we were interrupted by another woman slipping up from behind me. She caught my attention by placing her hand on my shoulder, then running it into my shirt against my bare chest. Whispering in my ear, she said, "*Halo*, Petty Oppicer Murpee."

I recognized the voice. Gasping, I spun around in my seat to face her. The last time I had seen Rafaela Green, she was wearing her hair pulled back into a simple ponytail and dressed in an oversized tee-shirt and jeans. Now, she was wearing makeup and had squeezed herself into a skin-tight, bright red minidress that accentuated her figure. She was stunning.

I stammered as I tried to find the words to answer her but could not get anything out. She let me stutter for a while but finally asked, "Aren't you happy to see me?"

I wasn't, but I could not bring myself to say that. I was heartbroken to see her. Hannah and I had run into Rafaela while walking through Balboa Park in San Diego months before. She had been begging me to tell naval investigators the real reason that I had nearly beaten her husband to death. Randy Green was facing years in prison for assaulting me, a senior petty officer, and she wanted me to confess that he was acting in self-defense. She wanted me to tell them that we were going to hurt him for breaking the arm of Rafaela's son in a drunken rage. If I didn't, and her husband went to the stockade, she warned me that she would end up back in the Philippines, working as a prostitute.

At the time, I thought she was exaggerating, but seeing her before me proved me wrong. "Rafaela, what are you doing here?"

"What it look like I doing, Murpee? I looking por love!"

I shook my head in sadness. "Why didn't you stay in the US? I know things would be hard for you after Randy was out of the picture, but they would have had to have been easier than this."

Rafaela scoffed. "Stay in da US? What I gonna do in da US widout Randy? I no know how do anything but dis! And I can't do dis in US widout getting arrested. Ip I get arrested, dey deport me anyway. So here I am!"

Trying to swallow the lump in my throat, I told her I was sorry. "Rafaela, that man was…"

"Dat man was my husband, Murpee!"

"He was beating you…"

"So what! You no tink men hurt me now? Sometime, dey beat me por pun. Dey tink dat because dey give me money to puck dem dat dey can do anyt'ing dey want. So dey hit me. Dey…" Rafaela started shaking. She looked around, presumably for her purse. Suspecting that she was seeking a cigarette, I offered her one of mine.

"Randy no was a perpect man, Murpee," she said after I lit her Marlboro. "And I was not bery happy wid him. Still, it was better wid him dere dan it is widout him here. Especially por Manny. He hab a chance to do good in California. Here, he just another poor boy."

"Randy would have eventually killed you, Rafaela. He would have…"

"No!" Rafaela barked at me. "No! Randy no is you daddy, Murpee! He not! He might hit us, but he never going to shoot us like you padder did to you pamily!"

"You don't know that…"

"Neidder do you!" Rafaela's eyes were getting glassy.

I sat there staring at her for a moment, trying to figure out what to tell her. Finally, I just said, "I'm sorry."

Rafaela scoffed. "A lot op good your apology do por me."

"What do you want me to do, Rafaela? What can I do?"

Sliding up close to me, she slipped her hand between my legs. "Pay my bar fine, Murpee. Take me home tonight."

"Rafaela, I can't…"

"I suck you dick, Murpee. I suck you until you dry." With her other hand, Rafaela grabbed me behind my neck and pulled me in until our lips met. She then stuck her tongue between my teeth. I was too shocked to resist.

"Let me puck you, Murpee," Rafaela purred. "I take you between my tits. I pull you deeeep into my pussy and puck you so, so hard. I let you cum in my pace. You can rub it in my eyes. You can piss on me, pull my hair, choke me, punch me. I even take you in my ass, Murpee. Deep into my ass…just like I do to all dese men every single day!" As tears started rolling down her cheeks, she hauled off and slapped me across the face.

"Every day, Murpee!" She struck me again. "You see what you do to me, you son-op-a-bitch! You ruin my lipe!" She balled up her fist and planted it on my nose. "I hate you! I hate you! I hate you!" Each exclamation point came with another punch. I took them all. "You did this to me! You pucking prick!" The last one split my lip and drew blood.

Alerted by the commotion, a young man with arms covered in crude prison tattoos rushed in to separate us. Able to see that Rafaela was hysterical, he grabbed her around the waist and dragged her away to someplace in the back of the bar. Rafaela let out a long, anguished scream and kept hurling curses at me while I paid my tab and left.

As I walked away, I knew that Rafaela Green would now be added to the list of people that would haunt me forever. She was yet another woman I had wholly ruined despite good intentions. I thought about what she was doing, what she was enduring in the Olongapo skin trade. I caught myself wondering if it would have been more humane had I allowed Randy to kill her instead of having beaten the bastard into clinical epilepsy.

*****

I intended to go back to the ship, but I ran into Tony Bard and his girl at the jeepney stop. Telling him about my encounter with Rafaela, he shook his head in disbelief. "Jesus Christ. You know, Doyle, I'm not going to sit here and tell you that you guys did the right thing. You took the law into your own hands. That has consequences. Knowing what I know now about Randy Green, I can honestly say that you saved Rafaela's life, though. Her son's, too. What are you going to do?"

After a shrug and a sigh, I said, "I'm going back to the ship. I don't think the Philippines is agreeing with me."

Bard sighed as well. "I'm not letting you go back sober. Let's go back to the Captain's Mast and at least get you all fucked up."

We never made it. We took a jeepney back into town, where we ran into Dixie and his girl, Darlita. After slamming a few beers on the sidewalk, Kevin pulled me over to a food cart to try a local delicacy. *Belut* is a fertilized duck egg that is hard-boiled just before it is ready to hatch, then allowed to ferment. It was disgusting, but I ate a half-dozen on a dare from Bard. Afterward, I asked if anyone had seen Palazzo after our altercation. Dixie grinned. "I saw him walking into a place called Marylin's."

Anna and Darlita both giggled. "He going to play 'smiles.'"

I heard of that game. It was where a bunch of men sit around a table drinking beer while trying to guess which one of them was being serviced by the girl beneath the tablecloth. It was something Palazzo would do.

Making our way up Magsaysay, our dinner was comprised of various types of street food. We had more monkey meat as well as *lumpia*, a type of delicious spring roll dipped in banana ketchup. At Darlita's insistence, we also tried *isaw*, skewered pig intestines grilled over an open flame. It tasted much better than it sounded. Eventually, we found a kiosk selling a garlic-flavored noodle dish called *palabok* and rounded it off with a serving of shaved ice and fruit.

Finally full, we were way up Magsaysay Drive, well past the places where Americans usually ventured. We stumbled into an open-air tavern to take a load off of our feet and settled down with a couple of San Miguels to watch the locals pass. It was the first bar we had come across that was not a brothel, though I was sure that the table next to us was full of off-duty working girls. "No," Dixie corrected me. "They're Benny Boys."

"No shit?" I asked, spinning my head around to take a closer look. Sure enough, they all had Adam's apples.

We had a few rounds of beer there, and I enjoyed hanging out with Bard, Dixie, and their dates. I did not feel like a third wheel at all. In fact, because of my modest Tagalog skills, I talked with the ladies more than Tony and

Dixie did. Like the little girl I met earlier, they enjoyed teaching me the local lingo once they discovered I was willing to learn. Before I knew it, both Palazzo and Rafaela Green had fallen off of my mind.

Sometime near midnight, I stood up to start making my way back to the ship. As I was stretching, I watched Bard drop his head into his hands and start shaking it in disbelief, laughing.

"What?" I asked, glancing down to see if my fly was open or something.

"Look behind you," Tony told me. "Is that Master Chief?"

I spun around to see Darrow walking down the street. He was heading right for us with his arm around the shoulders of a woman he was obviously having a good time with. He spotted us just after we saw him and rose his arms up into the air in victory. "Hey, guys!" the master chief shouted. He then pulled his girl in tight and planted an enthusiastic kiss on her lips. "I found her! I told you I'd find her if I looked hard enough! This is Lorna, the girl I've been telling you all about!"

We cheered and welcomed the couple into our group, making room for them at our table. Since Darrow ordered a fresh round of drinks, I stayed even though I was flirting with a curfew violation. After a quick toast and a sip of her cocktail, Lorna excused herself to use the restroom. When she was out of earshot, I leaned in toward Darrow and asked, "What happened?"

"You know that grocery store you dropped me off at?"

"Yeah."

"She runs it now."

I burst out laughing. "You've got to be fucking kidding me!"

"Nope," Darrow said while taking a drag off of his cigarette. "I stepped into the store and literally ran into her as she walked out of her little office up front. There was no way to avoid her."

Shaking his head, Kevin said, "That sounds like divine intervention."

"Fuck," Darrow responded, turning to me. "Whatever it is, I had the best of intentions, Doyle. I really did."

"Master Chief," I said. "You can still do the right thing here. Tell her that you're married and…"

Darrow shook his head. "Nope. Too late to do the right thing."

"What?" I gasped. "You already…"

OLONGAPO EARP

"Yep," my master chief told me. "We already did the wrong thing. Did it twice, actually." As he confessed this, Darrow rummaged around his pocket. After pulling out a key, he slid it across the table to me and asked, "You interested in an apartment?"

*****

CHAPTER 12

Dixie, Bard, and I all leapt at Darrow's offer to take over his apartment. For forty American dollars apiece, the price of one night in a cheap Philippine hotel room, we had a place to sleep for the entire month we were in Subic Bay. I very quickly discovered that I might not have thought things through, though.

Bard's girl, Anna, was a screamer. She was also very limber and approached sex like it was some sort of acrobatics competition. She bent Tony into positions that a human body should not be able to twist. By default, this made Tony a screamer, too. The two of them made sexual intercourse sound like a violent home invasion, which set off Dixie's competitive nature. Not wanting to be outdone, Kevin decided to break out the good sex and do everything he could to make Darlita even louder than Anna. My room was between Bard and Dixie, so of course, I was having a hard time sleeping.

When they had all finished, I was the one who needed the cigarette. I got up and felt my way through the dark to the courtyard to light up. About halfway through my smoke, a trike pulled up in front of our building and dropped off a woman so short that, at first, I thought she was a child. Then I saw the way she dressed. She had on a satin Chinese-style *cheongsam*, short-sleeved, form-fitting, and very, very sexy.

After paying her driver, the woman picked up her high heels from the sidecar and walked barefoot right toward me without realizing that I was there. When she saw me in the shadows, she jumped back and screamed bloody murder, begging me not to hurt her.

"*Okay lang! Okay lang!*" I tried to reassure her, telling her everything was good.

"*Ako ang iyong...bagong kapitbahay! Nakatira ...ako dito!*" That was my attempt to convey that I was one of her new neighbors, but I struggled to come up with the right words. My vocabulary in Tagalog was limited. I also had a difficult time figuring out how to put the words in the proper order.

The woman clutched her chest as she tried to decipher what I said through my thick American accent. Once she put it together, though, she breathed a loud sigh of relief. "Oh my god!" she exclaimed in English. "You scare me to death! You must be da man Mari telling me about."

"Mari?" I asked. In the excitement, I forgot the name of the little girl I met in the courtyard earlier.

"My daughter. I tink she see you dis apternoon. She tell me about a white guy who speak Tagalog in da flat across prom us."

We heard the door to my apartment open and watched as Tony and Dixie ran through it in their underwear. "Hey! Who's down there? Is everything all right?" Dixie asked.

"Yeah, Kevin," I answered. "It's fine. I'm just down here scaring the shit out of our neighbors."

Sensing there was no imminent danger, Dixie's girl slid up behind him and looked down at us. As an expression of recognition flashed across her face, she called out, "Tala? Is dat you?"

Tala squinted up the stairs until she figured out who was calling to her. "*Divina! Halo!*"

Divina had introduced herself to me as Darlita. That Tala knew her by a different name did not surprise me. Women working in any facet of the sex industry rarely used their real names. Forgetting that I understood a fair amount of Tagalog, Divina told my neighbor that I seemed like a nice guy and Tala should try sleeping with me.

Tala looked embarrassed. "You understan' dat, right?"

I nodded and grinned. "A little."

She shook her head. Now that she was closer to me, I could see that Tala was absolutely striking, even in poor light. Her skin was flawless, and other than red lipstick, she did not seem to wear, nor need, any other makeup at all. She had long, straight black hair pulled back into a bun, and in a city filled with beautiful girls, she was still a cut above the rest. I imagined that she was in very high demand wherever she worked, and I was ashamed for wondering to myself how many men she had been with that night.

"Now dat you scare me so bad," Tala started, still breathing hard. "Can you gib me a cigarette?"

I passed her one of my Marlboros and lit it. After taking a couple of drags to calm herself down, Tala looked me over a bit and asked, "You no wit anybody?"

"Huh?"

"You no get girl yet?"

I shook my head. "No. I'm not with anybody."

Tala laughed. "Why? You picky?"

I smiled nervously, trying to come up with an answer that would not offend her. "No, I'm just ugly and alcoholic."

Tala laughed but knew firsthand that the economy of Olongapo was based upon getting unattractive drunkards laid. She was not buying my answer. "You married or just you no sleep wit bargirls?"

"No bargirls," I told her.

"Too good por us?" she asked.

"No, I just don't pay for sex," I answered.

"You too cheap?" Tala's eyes lit up like she was relishing a challenge.

"I don't think so," I told her. "Especially considering how much money I spend on liquor."

Tala giggled. "Ip you spending lot of money on booze, sooner or later you gonna be buying a girl in Pilippines. We hard to resist when you sober. When you drunk, you have no chance."

I laughed. "That's why I got an apartment. I can party here without always being tempted by such pretty women."

"Ah! Ah! Ahhhh!" Tala laughed back harder. "Ip you want dat, you should get a new apartment. Two op us live right next door to you."

OLONGAPO EARP

Great. I drew in a deep breath, "Then I guess I can only ask the two of you to have mercy on me."

Tala shook her head. "We no take prisoners. It no good por a man to be wit'out a woman por long time. How you gonna take care op your needs?"

I held up my left hand.

Tala giggled again. "Dat no substitute por a real girl."

"I don't know," I told her. "It's never left me unsatisfied yet."

Tala held her own hand out. "My name is Tala Bono, but I don' know why Divina call me dat. Here in Olongapo, everyone call me Tina."

I took her hand and shook it. "I'm Doyle."

"Dat your last name?"

"No, my first. My last name is Murphy."

"I never meet someone named Doyle bepore."

"You know, I've only heard of one other person named Doyle myself. Doyle Wolfgang von Frankenstein. He was a guitarist in The Misfits. I don't think he was born with that name, though."

"Well, it very nice to meet you, Doyle," Tala said. She then flicked her cigarette toward the street, "But I need to go to bed now. Bye-bye."

"*Magandang gabi,*" I said, wishing Tala a good night as she walked away. She was short but flawlessly proportioned. She had a perfectly rounded backside, curves in all the right places, and ample breasts, something not particularly common in the Far East. I appreciated that there was a full moon that night to allow me to admire her in the dark.

I lit another cigarette and leaned my forearm against the steel security bars separating our courtyard from the street. Seeing Tala reminded me how much I missed my former fiancée. I wondered if Hannah was back home in Australia yet. Had I known that she was waiting for me somewhere, resisting a port town full of Tala Bonos would have been so much easier.

*****

The next morning back aboard the ship, I tried to seek out John Palazzo to apologize for the way I blew up at him the day before. Unfortunately, he had the first watch and was not present at morning roll call. After muster, I strung my hammock up in my radar dome. I then cranked up the air conditioning and passed out for a few hours to catch up on the sleep I had missed the night before. By the time I woke up, packed a bag, and headed back into town, Palazzo had already been relieved from his post. Feeling that I had graver sins to atone for, I promised myself to seek him out the next day. Then I left the ship.

I caught a trike to our apartment and, after dropping off my clothes, spent the next hour trying to get back out to Barrio Barretto via jeepney. Once there, I made my way up Long Beach Road until I found the bar I ran into Randy Green's ex-wife in, The Blue House. It was still early when I arrived, so there were only a couple of girls there milling about with the bartender.

"*Halo*," I said as I stepped up to the bar. "*Kamusta ka?*"

Asking everybody in Tagalog how they were doing worked wonders to warm up a crowd. English was a compulsory course of study in Philippine schools, so nearly everyone spoke it to some extent, especially around Olongapo. The place had been under American influence for so long that the streets all had English names. Still, the locals were more comfortable talking in Tagalog. They appreciated hearing foreigners trying to speak it.

We suffered through a couple of minutes of small talk until everyone realized that I had passed the boundaries of my limited vocabulary. Switching to English, Nino, the bartender, asked, "What can I get you, my friend?"

"I'm looking for a girl."

"Of course, you are," he said, motioning toward the two women seated to my left.

"No, no, not like that," I corrected him. "I'm looking for a particular girl. Rafaela Green."

"Who?"

"Rafaela Green. She works here."

Nino shrugged his shoulders. "I don't think so, friend. I do not know anyone named Rafaela here. Do you?" he asked the two girls. They both shrugged their shoulders and shook their heads.

I did not sense that they were jerking me around. The three of them seemed to legitimately not know who I was talking about. I tried to describe her. "She stands about yay tall," I said, holding my hand up to my chest. "She has mocha skin, black hair, and brown eyes..." I tapered off, realizing that I was describing every woman in the entire country.

"He means Marta," said a man as he stepped out of the doorway leading to the rooms in the back where the girls took their guests. He was the guy with the tattoos that pulled Rafaela off of me the night before. Holding out his paw, he introduced himself. "My name is Danilo."

I shook his hand and told him my name in return. After a sigh, I said, "I should have known she would not be using her actual name at work."

"Yes, dese women need a person dey can go back to being after dey leave this lipe. Da woman named Marta will stay here in Barrio Barretto. Rafaela can go back to be da girl dat does not know anyt'ing about dis place." Danilo looked like the guy who ran the Blue House, but he was no pimp. He was the person the girls depended upon to keep them safe. The prison-needle quality of the ink on his arms suggested he had a past that qualified him to do that very well. Danilo was looking at me as if he were still trying to figure out if I was someone who needed hurting or not. "What you want with Marta?"

"I want to help her."

"How you do dat?" he asked.

It was only then that I realized that I did not have any idea how to better Rafaela's situation. I must have figured I would work one out after I learned what she needed. "Well, for starters, I was hoping to pay her bar fine so we could talk."

Danilo shook his head as he walked up and took a seat next to me. "I no tink she wanna talk to you. What you do to her in California?"

"She didn't tell you?"

The Blue House's bouncer shrugged. "She say you a violent man who no like her husband. She say you beat him very bad. So bad he never get better. You hurt him, frame him por a crime, and make it so he have to divorce her or go to prison por a very long time. She come back to Barrio Barretto because widout husband, she cannot appord to live in America. Dat her side op da story. What yours?"

"Did she tell you that her husband beat them? Did she tell you that her husband broke her son's arm?"

The bruiser looked surprised. "Manny? He break Manny's arm? No, she no say dat. But even ip dat true, dat no your business. Look at where she working now. Is she and Manny better? I no tink so."

"Maybe she is. My father was a lot like Rafaela's husband. The man made our lives a living hell. One day, he walked in drunk and, for some reason that I will never know, pulled out a shotgun and killed my entire family. Randy would have eventually done the same to Rafaela and her son. I'm sure of it."

"So, you beat him to protect dem?"

I sensed that Danilo's intentions were good. Still, I was not going to trust some former prison gangster with my deepest, darkest secrets. Sticking to the script in the NCIS report, I told him, "Randy thought we were going to beat him for what he did to Manny. To get the first punch in, he assaulted me. He got hurt while I was defending myself. It was all caught on the camera located over the ship's well deck. That was why they never charged me, and that was why he was facing a five-year prison sentence."

"Dat what happen?"

I nodded. "That's what happened." Technically, it was the truth. I just left out the part admitting that, yes, we were planning on putting Randy Green in a world of hurt for what he had done to that little boy.

Danilo nodded a few times, taking in what I told him. "It sound like you do right t'ing. Marta no gonna see it dat way, dough. My advice to you to stay away prom her."

I hung my head. "There's got to be something I can do. Something that…"

"What you gonna do? You gonna marry dat girl and take her away prom here? You gonna take care op her and her son in America?"

The two working girls looked over at me in anticipation of my answer. I felt like they had put me on the spot. "I, uh, I don't…"

"Op course you not," Danilo said. "I work in place like dis por pive years. You no kind op guy who marry bargirl. You no ugly enough, and you sound like smart guy. You gonna do somet'ing wit you lipe. You have no problem getting a good girl. You no need whore por wipe."

I looked at the girls apologetically, but they seemed unfazed by the bouncer calling them whores. "Dey okay, man. Dey know what dey are,"

OLONGAPO EARP

Danilo said. "You a good guy. I know you want to help — dere not'ing you can do, dough. Look, you need to leave Marta alone. She blame you por all dis. You never change her mind. Nino!"

The bartender bounced over to answer the call. "Yes, boss!"

"Get dis man a pitcher op Bullfrog. On da house. Make it a good one."

Nino grinned and nodded. "Yes, sir!"

I watched Nino pour a shot of damn near every bottle of booze behind the bar into a blender. He then topped it off with ice cubes, some sort of fruit juice, and what looked like citrus soda. He then blended it up, transferred it to a pitcher, and dropped it in front of me along with a glass. It looked lethal, and I expected it to taste like lemon-flavored battery acid. I was shocked by how smooth it went down, though. It was tart and sweet, with hardly any taste of alcohol to it at all. Cold and refreshing, it was the perfect drink to counter the Philippine heat.

"How you like it?" Danilo asked after I took my first drink.

"I freakin' love it!" I told him before taking another large gulp.

The Blue House's resident bruiser laughed. "Good. You need to be very carepul wid dis stupp, dough. Ip you no carepul, it knock you out quicker dan Mike Tyson."

I nodded, but unable to resist the flavor, I took another sip while Danilo turned the subject back to Rafaela. "Porget about Marta, man. Having you here no gonna make her peel better. It only make t'ings worse por both op you. She do what she hap to do to survive. You no gonna improve her lipe and da harder you try to help her, da more you gonna realize dere not'hing you can do. She have a hard lipe. It no your pault she here no more dan it your pault dat dese other girls work here too. Let it go."

There was little chance that anyone would mistake Danilo as an intellectual. He did not look like a man who had much use for books. Nor did he seem like someone who often sat in meditation pondering the mysteries of the metaphysical. He was no idiot, though. His austere upbringing, his childhood spent running shantytown alleyways, and the hard time he served that earned him the ink on his arms gave him an insight into the human condition that would rival that of any anthropology doctor churned out of Dartmouth. Danilo knew the plight of Olongapo's poor far better than I ever could. It would be folly to ignore his advice.

Still, it was not easy to give up on Rafaela and Manny. I had to think about it for a while. I eventually concluded that Danilo was right, though. Anything less than marrying Rafaela and whisking her away from Barrio Barretto would be little more than an empty gesture. She would still be stuck in the Philippines, renting her body out to anyone wanting to use her. I finished my pitcher of Bullfrog, nodded my head, and told Danilo, "Okay. I'll leave her alone."

I remember Danilo patting me on the shoulder. "Dat's da best decision, my priend. It da only decision. Nino! Get dis man another pitcher of Bullfrog!"

That was about when things started getting a little fuzzy.

*****

I woke up on the couch in my apartment late that night. I was foggy, still insanely drunk, and had a headache so intense that I thought my eyeballs were getting pushed out of my head. Master Chief Darrow and a Filipino man in military fatigues were standing over me. Darrow was shaking his head. "You know, Doyle, you are the luckiest son-of-a-bitch I have ever met."

Feeling like there was a bayonet piercing my skull right between my eyes, I slowly sat up and said, "I don't feel very lucky. What happened?"

Darrow gestured to the Filipino. "Doyle, this is Sergeant Tejada of the Philippine National Police. I told you about him. He and I go way back."

The sergeant held out his hand, and I slowly shook it. "You can call me TJ, Doyle."

"Glad to meet you," I groaned, feeling like I wanted to get sick.

"So," my master chief continued. "I'm in Barrio Barretto riding shotgun on patrol with TJ here when this girl runs up to us and flags us down. She says there's some suspicious characters carrying away a drunk American further down the beach. TJ guns the Jeep, and we roll up on a half dozen Filipino gang bangers dragging your drunk ass across Long Beach Drive."

"Really?" I asked.

"Really," TJ answered. "You know what dey trying to do wit you?"

OLONGAPO EARP

I shook my head, careful not to leak any loose brain matter out of my nostrils. "I was just out having a couple of drinks, and…Jesus Christ, does my fucking head hurt."

"Doyle, it wasn't even five o'clock when we found you. How much did you have to drink?"

Shrugging, I answered, "I don't know, a couple of drinks. No, wait, a couple of pitchers."

"Of beer?" Darrow looked surprised. He knew I could handle my alcohol better than that.

"No, some frozen stuff," I answered, still not quite lucid enough to remember the name.

Darrow and TJ looked at each other and laughed. "Bullfrog?"

I pointed my finger at them. "That's it."

"Doyle," the master chief started. "You have to be careful with some of this stuff here. You probably don't realize it because you can't taste the alcohol, but you might have drunk a dozen shots in just a couple of hours. That shit will mess you up."

"Yeah, and dose boys we saw wit you? Deys really bad guys. I don't know what dey gonna do wit you, but I know it no gonna be good. Deys dangerous people. You very lucky we get you before dey take you away."

"Did you catch any of them?"

"No," TJ told me. "Not yet. I don't know who dey are, but I know what gang work dat part op Barretto. We gonna get dem sooner or later and figure out what dey want wit you. Maybe dey rob you, wait por you to wake up and force you to get money prom ATM. Or maybe dey give you to NPA as hostage."

"NPA?"

"New People's Army," Darrow reminded me. "The communist guerillas that operate in the countryside around here."

"Seriously? They kidnap Americans?"

My master chief shook his head. "Not usually. Oddly enough, they tend to leave us Yankees alone. In fact, they went to such lengths to avoid conflict with us that when I was in the AFPD, we joked that NPA stood for Nicest People Around. Still, every once in a while, some radical group will splinter off and make us a target. Hell, they just assassinated a US Army

Colonel here a few years ago, a Special Forces badass that founded the SERE school." SERE stood for Survival, Evasion, Resistance, and Escape.

"You very lucky," Sergeant Tejada told me once again. "You a very easy target when you alone out here. Do not go out and get dat drunk by yourselp, okay?"

"Okay," I said. That was when the bile in my stomach lurched up my throat, forcing me to rush to vomit in the sink. After that, I did TJ one better by promising him that I would never allow myself to get that drunk ever again. Period.

It was a promise I could not keep, mainly because it would be weeks before I would remember even making it. In fact, it would be quite some time before my first conversation with Sergeant Tejada started coming back to me at all.

*****

CHAPTER 13

The next morning was murder. I spent most of the night vomiting and woke up dehydrated and exhausted. If not for Dixie and Bard, I never would have made it back to the ship on time. I barely got through roll call, earning myself some serious stink-eye from Krause. He had to have known how wasted I still was. I had not consumed an alcoholic beverage in over seventeen hours. Still, had Krause marched me to the master-at-arms and demanded I take a breathalyzer test, I was sure I would have failed it. I never felt so hungover in all my life.

Though I told myself I was going to seek out Palazzo and make nice that morning, I was in no shape to deal with that man. I left muster, caught a few hours of sleep in my radar dome, then once again went back to crash in my apartment. That was when I discovered the extent to which brown-outs were a way of life in the Philippines.

The local utilities were unable to meet Olongapo's demand for power. As a result, they had to cut electricity away from residential areas and divert it to the commercial zones during working hours. That put a severe crimp in my plans of passing out naked in front of our apartment's air-conditioning unit. All I could do was lie in bed and sweat. My bedroom was a sauna. It grew so hot in there that even the geckos running the walls abandoned it for milder climes outside. Before long, I decided to join them.

I dragged the picnic table in the courtyard to the shade offered by the steps to the upstairs apartments. It was a Herculean task in my condition, and I exerted myself enough to doze off again as soon as I lay down on top of it. From there, three hours passed like thirty seconds and I did not stir at all until I felt something sharp jab me in the ribs. When I opened my eyes, I saw Mari Bono, the little girl next door, standing beside me. She was poking me with a stick to figure out if I was still alive. Judging by how far back she jumped when I moved, she was almost as surprised as I to find that I was.

"*Ayos ka lang ba?*" Mari asked as I forced one of my eyes open, wondering if I was okay.

"No, but I think I'm getting better," I answered in the best Tagalog I could muster. "I'm hungry, though." Looking at my watch, I estimated that it had been at least thirty hours since my last meal.

Mari smiled at me. "Do you like *lumpia*?"

"I love *lumpia*," I answered.

"There is a *sari-sari* store down the street that sells *lumpia*. You can get some."

"Do you like *lumpia*?"

Mari's face lit up. "Yes. It is my favorite. After Jollibee spaghetti."

I reached into my pocket and pulled out a handful of crumpled peso notes. Handing it all to the little girl, I told her that I would buy us a *lumpia* dinner if she would go get it. "If you fly, I'll buy," I told her in English, then explained what it meant in Tagalog. She giggled, liking the way it rhymed. "Get us a couple of Coca-Colas, too!" I shouted as she ran out of the courtyard.

When Mari returned, I suspected that I had handed the little girl far more money than I thought. She came back with a LOT of *lumpia*. But nothing to drink. "I have to go back. I could not carry it all!" Mari told me after I asked where our Cokes were.

It was easy to see why when she returned. Bottles were expensive. When you ordered a Coke in a *sari-sari* store, they poured it into a cheap little plastic sandwich bag and put a straw in it. You could only carry one per hand, and you could not set it down. I had to hold Mari's when she got back so she could run up to her apartment and get some banana ketchup to dip our food in.

As the two of us devoured our *lumpia* together, I watched Mari as she ate. I noticed that she winced as she chewed, obviously in pain. "Are you okay?"

"My teeth hurt."

"Really?" I asked. "Do you have a loose tooth?"

Mari shrugged. "Maybe."

"Can I take a look?"

Mari opened her mouth. After I peered inside, I was the one who winced. Her back teeth were a mess of decay. She needed a dentist.

It took me a while because I confused the Tagalog words for lips and teeth, but I managed to ask her how long her mouth had been bothering her. She told me for a long time. "Does your mother know?"

Mari nodded. "She working a lot to get money to fix it."

I let out a long sigh. The thought of what Tala had to do to pay the dentist ran through my head, turning my stomach. I wondered if Mari knew how her mother made her living. I doubted it.

The more Mari and I talked over our plates of *lumpia*, the more I realized how much Tagalog I was learning from her, and how much I was enjoying learning it. I liked Mari. She was smart, spunky, and loved to giggle. And when she giggled, I could not help but erupt into full-blown belly laughs. My stomach was still in a fragile state, however. I had to be careful how hard I laughed to keep myself from bursting out into a Technicolor yawn.

Besides Tagalog, I also learned a lot about Mari and her mother. They chose that apartment for the same reason that my master chief had. It was out of the way, which helped them avoid someone they were having problems with. I assumed it was an ex-boyfriend of the little girl's mother.

Like any other child who did not get as much attention as they needed, Mari talked a lot. She was taking full advantage of having someone around who was willing to listen to her. I only understood about a quarter of what she said, but I enjoyed her company. I had never spent much time around children, so I never realized they could be so funny.

And sad. Mari missed her mother and wanted to spend more time with her. She felt guilty that Tala had to work so much to earn the money they needed to fix her mouth. Like a child would tend to do, Mari thought it was her fault that her mother was gone so much. She believed that if she had only taken better care of her teeth, Tala would be home more. It was sad to hear.

After we finished eating, I went upstairs with Mari to her apartment and knocked on the door. Mahal, the woman sharing the flat with Tala, stuck her head out and allowed me to introduce myself. As a bar girl, Mahal's English was far better than my Tagalog. "Do you know when Tala will be home?" I asked her.

"Late. She work very long shifts."

"On Magsaysay?"

"No," Mahal said, looking at me with disapproval. She shuffled Mari inside and closed the door behind her so that we could speak candidly. "She work at da Pagoda in Barrio Barretto."

Shit. Barrio Barretto again. For some reason, I was hesitant to go back there but not able to recall why. "I don't remember seeing a bar called The Pagoda. Where's it located?"

"Closer to Baloy Beach, at end op da strip." She suggested that I take a trike when I got off the shuttle because it was a long walk.

*****

Mahal was not kidding. I ignored her advice when I got to Barrio Barretto and tried to hoof it to the Pagoda. Even the Blue House, the bar I had gotten so drunk in the night before, was a haul when not stopping for a drink at every third watering hole. I considered popping in there for a rest after Danilo spotted me and tried to wave me back inside. I declined, though, fearing a hard descent into another Bullfrog coma.

The Pagoda did not in any way emulate the traditional east Asian building it was named after. It looked like any other bar and brothel lining Baloy Beach. The only thing that made it seem Chinese was the way that the girls dressed. They all had on short-sleeved, collar-less *cheongsam* dresses with long slits cut from the hemline to the upper thigh. It was a sexy look, and upon seeing it, I found myself confronted with a fetish that I did not even know I had.

OLONGAPO EARP

A bubbly young lady slid up alongside me as soon as I walked in. "Hi, Joe! You come sit wit me?"

I smiled and told her I couldn't. "I'm looking for someone. Is Tala here?"

"Who?"

Bar names, Doyle. Bar names. "Tina. I'm looking for Tina."

"Oh! No, Tina no here now. She very busy. Dere couple op other men looking por her. You can wait por her at da bar, dough. You sure you no want girl who no so busy?"

"I'm not here for that," I told the young lady. "I want to talk to her about her daughter."

"Oh! She okay?"

"Yeah, she has something wrong with her teeth, though."

The young lady nodded. "Okay. I make sure she know."

When I sauntered up to the bar and told the woman tending it that all I wanted was water, she laughed. "Hard night last night?"

"You have no idea," I said. I still could remember almost nothing after my second pitcher of Bullfrog from the day before.

As I drank my water, I sat back and watched what was going on around me. For a place located so far away from Magsaysay, the Pagoda was very busy. A black drape covered the passageway to the "boom-boom" rooms in the back. Every so often, one of the ladies would take a man through that curtain. And every so often, a man would emerge from it by himself, sweaty, disheveled, and smiling. Occasionally, a woman would emerge from it a little while later, cleaned up, hair put back in place, and makeup fixed, ready to go back on the prowl.

Not everyone used the "boom-boom" rooms, though. Those were for what the girls called a "short-time." If a man wanted a woman for a "long-time," he paid her bar fine for the entire night. That got her off of work and freed her to leave. It was a kind of hall pass that allowed a bar girl to be out on the street with her client. I did not understand the system, but I figured it worked to exploit a loophole in the law. It let one of the world's biggest red-light districts thrive in a country where prostitution was technically illegal.

I saw Tala come out from behind the curtain after about half an hour. She was not put together like the other girls I saw walk in from the back when she did. Her hair was still messed up, her lipstick smeared, and beads of sweat popped up all over her forehead. She looked distressed as she scanned the crowd for a familiar face. A Marine stood up and approached her, apparently next in line, but she stuck her index finger up at him to let him know she needed a moment.

When Tala's eyes glided over my part of the bar, I waved. Zeroing in on me, she marched over and asked, "Is Mari okay?"

I nodded. "She's fine. Have you seen her mouth, though? She needs a dentist."

Tala looked at me with disbelief. "Is dat it? You come all dat way here to tell me Mari's mout' hurt? You no tink I know dat? You tink I no take care op my daughter?"

"No, no, no," I told her. "You got it wrong. Mari told me that you're working a lot to earn money to fix her teeth. She misses you and…"

Tala's eyes narrowed. She did not trust me. "Why you talking so much to Mari?"

"She's trying to teach me Tagalog, so…"

Tala stuck her finger in my face. "You stay away prom my dau…"

"Fine. Can I pay for her to have her teeth fixed, though? That way, you don't have to work so much and can spend more time with her."

"What?" Tala asked.

"How much does it cost to get a kid's teeth fixed? If you want, tell me what dentist you take her to, and I'll pay for them to see her. I want to help Mari get her teeth treated."

Tala was still suspicious. "Why? What you want prom us?"

I shrugged. "I don't know. Mari's helping me learn Tagalog. If you'd let her keep talking to me, that'd be nice. I understand why you wouldn't want her hanging around a twenty-two-year-old guy, though. If you want me to stop talking to her, I will. Still, I want to help the two of you with her mouth."

Before Tala could answer, some greasy old fat man came up from behind her. He wrapped his arms around her waist and pulled her body against his. Planting a slobbery wet kiss on the side of Tala's face, he told her, "That was great, honey! You here tomorrow? I'm thinking about coming back for more."

OLONGAPO EARP

I glared at the classless geezer, shooting him a look that suggested he get lost before I knocked him in the chops. He grinned and shot me a look back, daring me to. Tala turned on a fake, uninterested smile. Instead of brushing him off, though, she told him that she would be there by ten in the morning.

From a logical standpoint, I believed that prostitution should be legal, as long as the women engaging in it were doing so of their own accord. In my view, how free could you be if you could not even choose what to do with your own body? On an emotional level, though, I thought it was disgusting. Picturing what that creepy old man had paid Tala to do struck some primal nerve deep inside of me. It made me nauseous. Tala must have seen it on my face because, for an instant, she looked ashamed about me seeing her at work. "Dentist no is cheap. Why you wanna spend so much money on girl you no even know?"

I shrugged. "Because if I don't spend it on Mari's mouth, I'm going to blow it on alcohol. After what I did to myself yesterday, letting me help Mari just might save my life."

*****

A jeep emblazoned with the decals of the Philippine National Police passed me on the opposite side of the street shortly after I left The Pagoda. It slammed on its brakes, did a U-turn, and pulled to a stop right beside me. "Murpee!" I heard the officer shout from inside it. "Murpee! Get da puck over here, you pucking idiot!"

With my memories of the previous night still hazy, the officer only seemed vaguely familiar. The fact that he was calling me by name showed we had met, but I had little recollection of it. I could see his face standing above me through some mental fog but could not put it into any context. The officer saw my confusion and laughed. "Do you even know who I am?"

I glanced at the rank on the lapel of his fatigues. "Sergeant, I have no idea."

Laughing even harder, the officer exclaimed, "You were dat pucked up? You no remember me? I save your pucking lipe last night!"

It was not ringing a bell.

"I'm TJ mudderpucker! Sergeant Tejada! I'm a priend op your master chiep!"

At least those two aspects came together. I suddenly remembered Darrow from the night before, but all the sergeant's talk about saving my life was completely lost on me. Equal parts amused and frustrated, the policeman ordered me to get into the jeep. He then reminded me how he and Master Chief Darrow interrupted a gaggle of Filipino gang members carrying me across the street. Tejada also told me how they were about to take me to the hospital, fearing I had drunk enough to kill myself. They only reconsidered after I started coming around on the couch in my apartment.

When TJ finished, he looked at me again and shook his head. "You no remember any op dis?"

The fractured memories would eventually come back to me, but not until weeks after leaving Subic Bay. At the time, I was clueless. "Jesus Christ," Tejada said as he floored the jeep's accelerator and peeled off toward the other end of the strip. "I tell you again, den. Barrio Barretto is my beat. I patrol all da time here. I know evert'ing about it. Ip you come here wit you priends, it perpectly sape. Ip you come here by youselp and get so drunk you pass out on da beach like you do, you gonna get into trouble. You understan'?"

I nodded.

"What you doing here, anyway? Your master chiep say you no looking por da girls in da bars. Dis long way prom you apartment. What bring you all da way out here?"

I explained the situation with Mari's teeth. I told him I came out to Barrio Barretto to get permission to take the little girl to the dentist. "Are you pucking kidding me?" TJ asked. "You riskin' coming back here by youselp because some kid have a toothache?"

The policeman grinned. "Your master chiep say you a good boy. He say you like a son to him. He say you very smart." Tossing a sideways glance my way, Tejada then said, "I don't see it."

"To be fair, until now, you've only seen me drunk," I told him, trying to stand up for myself.

TJ laughed. He then pulled a pack of cigarettes out of his pocket and offered me one. As I was lighting it, Sergeant Tejada said, "OK. I give you another chance. Because op your master chiep. You know, Brad and I go back long time. Long, long time. I know him more dan twenty years."

"Yeah, I've heard him talk about you." Darrow told me how the two of them once shot the corpse of a child-molesting lieutenant commander to manipulate evidence. I declined to mention that to TJ, though.

"You really gonna pix da teeth op dat little girl next door?"

I nodded. "That's my plan."

"When?"

"I don't know. As soon as possible."

Tejada nodded as he pulled up to the jeepney stop. "I know good dentist. Let me talk to him. Maybe I get you deal. I stop by you place tomorrow; let you know."

"That'd be great!" I held out my hand to the policeman. "Thank you, Sergeant Tejada…"

"You call me TJ."

"I'm not sure if I'm capable of that. Master Chief Darrow told me over a year ago I could call him 'Brad' as long as we're not around anyone else. I've still never done it."

Tejada laughed and shook my hand. "Okay. You go home and be carepul. I see you tomorrow about da dentist. Okay?"

*****

A jeepney left as Tejada and I pulled up, so when I took a seat on the bench to wait for the next one, I was there by myself for almost fifteen minutes. That made me a little nervous. Eventually, a couple showed up and took a seat next to me. They then began passionately mauling one another in a way that suggested either they were too drunk to be aware of my presence or too horny to care. Within twenty minutes after that, three more pairs arrived and started doing the same thing.

At some point, one of the bar girls lifted her eyes and caught me staring at her. It was bound to happen. As the jeepney stop filled up, there was nowhere else for me to look but at people engaging in foreplay. The girl giggled and blew me a kiss, causing me to laugh at the absurdity of my situation. I was in the easiest place on earth for a man to find a woman, yet I was going home alone. That girl must have thought I was either the biggest loser on the planet or had some heinous rash that I did not want to expose the ladies to.

Thirsty and feeling a little awkward, I gave up my seat and walked about a half-block to a nearby *sari-sari* store to get a soft drink. When I turned to go back to the stop, I saw that the jeepney had arrived, loaded up, and was already taking off. I broke into a sprint to catch it, but it was a futile effort. I only succeeded in arriving back at the same bench I started from, out of breath and having to begin the process all over.

It was getting late, so the jeepney stop was filling up quicker. At least this time, it was not all couples. A single Marine, drunk and happy, showed up with the crowd and took a seat across from me. Seeing I was by myself, he said, "I know a smart man when I see one. You doing a 'short-time' tour out here too?"

I shook my head. "Naw, I'm just out here visiting a friend."

The Marine squinted. "Oh yeah! I saw you at the Pagoda! You were talking to Tala!"

I took another look at the leatherneck and recognized him. He was the guy that Tala told to wait a minute when she came out of the back to see me. I nodded to him that he was right.

"Man, is she good or what? You ever have her do that thing where…"

"No, I haven't," I interrupted. "I've never been with her that way."

The Marine looked at me like that did not compute. "Oh. Then how do you know her?"

"We're neigh…" It came out before I realized that Tala would probably not appreciate me telling one of her customers that I knew where she lived. "We've seen each other around."

"You a squid?" the leatherneck asked next. "I've never seen you here. You come in on the *Belleau Wood*?"

I nodded, grateful to change the subject. "How about you?"

"I'm at the barracks here in Subic, attached to A Company. I'm on the security detachment. I'll be leaving with you guys, though. You're dropping us off in Okinawa."

"Cool. You been here a while?"

"More than three years." Leaning forward and sticking out his hand, the Marine introduced himself. "I'm Terry Mulvaney."

"Ah, a fellow Mick," I replied, shaking his hand. "I'm Doyle Murphy."

OLONGAPO EARP

Mulvaney grinned. "Man, you can't get a more Irish name than that."

Subic Bay Marines tended to be a severe lot by nature. Mulvaney was an exception. He was laid back and very talkative. As we waited for the next jeepney to arrive, the lance corporal gave me the rundown on Baloy Beach. He talked about its girls, its gangsters, its heroes, its villains, and all the little peculiarities that gave it its notoriety.

The Marine also told me many stories about an infamous member of the Armed Forces Police Department, a guy they called "Olongapo Earp." To hear Mulvaney tell it, this guy was a cross between Dirty Harry and J Edgar Hoover. I kept the fact that he was talking about my boss to myself, hoping it would keep him from censoring what he said to me.

The leatherneck told me a story about how Olongapo Earp broke a Marine major's jaw for resisting arrest in the 1970s. He recounted it with such detail that I would have suspected he had seen it himself. Considering both of us would have been in elementary school at the time, it was unlikely he would have been an eyewitness. Mulvaney also claimed Earp single-handedly brought down a ring of sailors smuggling heroin out of Vietnam toward the end of the war. He also said it was Earp's contacts in the NPA who tracked down a group of militants that shot four airmen to death outside Clark Air Base in the mid-1980s. Word had it that he persuaded the communists to execute the killers and dump their bodies in front of the main gate as a show of contrition. When it came to my master chief, Terry Mulvaney seemed like a pretty big fan. I wondered if he knew his idol was back in Subic Bay for a few weeks.

Usually, non-stop talkers like Mulvaney drove me crazy, but at least this one never seemed to run out of interesting things to say. He did stop for breath once we reached Magsaysay, though. As we got out of the jeepney, he asked, "You going back to your ship now?"

"Nah, I have to catch the green line," I said, naming the color of the jeepney that would take me home.

"Oh yeah? Me too," the Marine said.

"Really? Where are you going?"

"All the way to the end of the line."

"To the Balanga Bus Terminal?" I asked.

Mulvaney nodded. "Yeah, I got a place on the other side of the Santa Rita River, up in Gordon Heights. I have to catch a bus to get that far up."

J.E. PARK

I had no idea where Gordon Heights was. I had never heard of it. "Sounds like a haul. Why you living so far north?"

"It's not that far. From here, it's no further than Baloy Beach. I live up there because it's cheap. The further away from the base you go, the lower the rents. As a bonus, my old lady is far enough away that she doesn't catch wind of my trips to the Pagoda." The Marine laughed as if cavorting with prostitutes behind his girlfriend's back was hilarious. He cut it short when he noticed that I was not laughing with him. Changing the subject, Mulvaney asked, "So, you're on the *Belleau Wood*, huh? You know anything about that guy that got murdered?"

Even though it was a question that hit me like a slap across the face, I played it cool. "You heard about that?"

Mulvaney looked at me like my IQ had dropped 50 points. "It's been all over the news."

"No shit?" That surprised me. I had not heard a thing about it since it happened. But then again, I had not laid eyes on a television set since we had left Japan.

As we boarded our jeepney, I told my new friend how we interrupted the beating that claimed Miller's life. While doing so, I was flirting with triggering another one of my episodes. As we arrived at my place, I felt myself starting to slip into my underwater world. I shouted at the driver to stop and let me off.

"This where you're staying?" the Marine asked as I stood up to leave.

I nodded my head. "Yeah, this is my stop. I'll catch you later. It was nice meeting you." I was having a hard time concentrating.

"Yeah," Mulvaney answered. "Likewise. I'll see you around."

"Yeah, maybe." I felt my sweat pores open up as I rushed to my building. My hands were trembling so much I could barely get the key in the gate to let myself in. I looked up at my apartment and saw that the lights were all off. I was relieved that I would be able to deal with my breakdown alone.

Had I not been so preoccupied with keeping myself together enough to get off of the street, I might have had more time to think about the conversation I had with Terry Mulvaney. I might have picked up that something was not quite right about the lance corporal.

OLONGAPO EARP

Instead, I forgot the man immediately after stepping off of the jeepney. I spent that night writhing in bed, tortured by images of Miller's open skull ripping through my mind. I was far too preoccupied with that for it to occur to me that I had just been followed home.

*****

CHAPTER 14

Sergeant Rico Tejada came through as only Rico Tejada could. Within forty-eight hours of meeting the officer in Barrio Barretto, Darrow came up to me after roll call and told me that TJ had found a dentist for Mari. My master chief also said that the policeman had gotten me an excellent deal. As an added bonus, both he and TJ would be picking us up to get the little girl's teeth fixed as soon as Mari got home from school.

"Seriously?" I asked Darrow. "I just met the man. Why is he going through all this effort for me?"

Darrow shrugged. "He's seen that you're different than the rest of us. Instead of drinking and whoring, you're out here immersing yourself in the culture and trying to help someone. He's impressed. TJ talked to his superiors, and they agreed to split the cost of fixing Mari's teeth as a community outreach initiative. Congratulations."

Unable to believe my luck, I asked if there was anything I could do for Sergeant Tejada in return. After a moment's thought, Darrow asked, "You used to work in a restaurant, didn't you?"

I nodded. "Yeah. I worked in a barbecue joint in Wyandotte, Michigan."

OLONGAPO EARP

"Perfect," Darrow said. "TJ's a big fan of American-style ribs. I saw a grill in your courtyard. Have him over for some grub this weekend. Invite your neighbors, too. Make it a party."

Grinning, I said, "That sounds like a good idea. I'll do that on Saturday."

Darrow shook his head. "Actually, TJ and I already made plans to scout out Pagsanjan on Saturday. One of the *Belleau Wood* canoe trips is heading that way. I want to be there to make sure none of the guys end up where they're not supposed to be. I was hoping that you were coming too."

"Count me in," I told him.

When I got home, I was disappointed to learn from Mahal that Tala would not be there to go with us to get Mari's teeth fixed. "She working very hard," the woman said, apologizing for her roommate. "When da Americans go, we all no have work. She try to make money so dat she and Mari can no be hungry when da base close."

TJ and Darrow got to my place at about two in the afternoon. A half-hour later, Mari came home and was surprised to see us in the courtyard waiting for her. Despite the pain she was in, my little friend was not very excited about getting her teeth worked on. Like any other kid, Mari knew going to the dentist could hurt. Being eight-years-old, she was also fuzzy about the concept of short-term pain for long-term gain. TJ had to bribe her to get into his Jeep, promising to drive with the lights and siren on, something Mahal seemed to enjoy more than Mari did.

The dentist discovered that Mari needed a lot of work. He pulled a couple of her baby teeth and capped a couple of others. We ended up being there for hours. When we got back home, Mari was miserable. And hungry.

"Don't you think it will hurt to eat?" I asked her, struggling through my Tagalog as she took a seat at the picnic table in the courtyard.

The little girl nodded. "But I think I can eat Jolly Spaghetti."

I looked over at Darrow and TJ. "Jolly Spaghetti?"

My master chief laughed. "Yeah, it's a kid's dish from Jollibee." Jollibee was a local Philippine fast-food chain. It was a cross between Kentucky Fried Chicken and McDonald's. There was one on Magsaysay right across from the Shit River bridge.

"You ply, I buy?" Mari asked in English, remembering the phrase I taught her a couple of days before.

TJ erupted into laughter. "No! No! I buy! You ever try Jollibee, Doyle?" After I shook my head, the policeman said, "You gonna love dey's chicken! I gonna bring us all back some."

After TJ and my master chief left, Mahal excused herself and went to get some rest before work. Once she was gone, I looked down at Mari and asked, "Do you want to go inside and watch TV until our food gets here?"

The little girl shook her head. "No, there's nothing on for kids until Saturday."

"Oh." I thought for a moment. "You want to draw with your chalk?"

"No. Could you sit here and talk with me?"

"Me?" I asked. "Not Mahal? She speaks Tagalog better than I do."

"Mahal and my mother are always tired. They work very late. My mom works all the time and is never home. You are the only one who talks to me."

In Tagalog, it only took eight words to say that last sentence, *Ikaw lang ang talagang nakikipag-usap sa akin.* They had a profound effect on me, though. Despite the nightmare that was my own childhood, at least I had never wondered about my mother's love. She and I took the brunt of my old man's abuse, so she made the effort to ensure that I never doubted how much she cared for me. I always had her attention, right up until the day my father murdered her. When Mari told me that I was the only one she had to talk to, it broke my heart to think she felt neglected.

I wondered about Mari's father, but knowing the line of work her mother was in, I dared not ask. I was curious if Mari and her mother had any other family. I wondered if anyone thought about where they could be or what they were doing. Was there anyone out there who missed them? Could it really have only been the two of them? Mari was such a sweet kid, and she was loved. I saw that in how distressed Tala looked at the Pagoda when she heard something might be wrong with her daughter. I had heard that most of the women working Olongapo's bars sent their children to live with relatives. Why had Tala not? Were they like me and had no family to go back to?

"I'm the only one who talks to you?" I asked Mari. "If that were true, you would be driven crazy with boredom by now."

After correcting all the mistakes I made telling her that, she said, "Tell me about your family. Back in America."

OLONGAPO EARP

I sighed. "I don't have one. They all died when I was thirteen."

Mari gasped. "Your mom too?"

I nodded and saw Mari's eyes well up. I could tell that she was picturing what her life would be like without her own mother. Mari did not see Tala much, but the thought of losing her was too much for her little head to process.

"Hey, Mari," I said, trying to soothe her. "It's okay. That happened a long time ago, and things got better. Things always get better as long as you never give up." I then went on to tell her how, after I lost my family, I worked hard to get through school and made it into the Navy. Then, to answer the question on my mind, I asked Mari about her mother's family.

"She doesn't have anybody either," the little girl told me.

"No parents? No grandparents?"

"I don't know. She never talks about her life before me. Doyle, are you happy being alone?"

I let out another long sigh. "Not really."

"Do you want to have a family someday?"

I nodded. "Someday. You know, a few months ago, I was engaged to be married."

Mari's eyes perked up. "Really? What happened?"

I sugar-coated my answer. I told her that we realized that the two of us had different views on certain things and knew that getting married would be a mistake. So, we decided to go our separate ways. *Well, Hannah decided to, anyway. I would still marry her in a minute if she showed up and told me she changed her mind.*

"Are you sad that you did not get married?" Mari asked.

"Yeah, I am," I confided. "I kind of got my hopes up that I would finally have a family."

"My mom is always sad, too," Mari told me before I could change the topic. "She pretends to be happy when she's around me, but she hides and cries a lot. Especially when she thinks I'm sleeping."

Swallowing hard, I tried to think of something to say but came up short. Of course, eight-year-old girls rarely have a shortage of things to talk about, and Mari immediately came up with the perfect solution to all our problems. "Doyle, why don't you be with my mom? If you don't have anyone and she does not have anyone, we can all get together and have each other!"

My mouth opened, but nothing came out. Mari was sitting there staring at me with so much hope in her eyes that I could not bring myself to dash it. Fortunately, I was saved by the sound of someone pounding on our security gate. Relieved to get out of such an uncomfortable conversation, I excused myself, thinking Darrow and TJ needed to be let in with our food.

The person at my gate was not who I was expecting. Judging by the haircut, I guessed that he was a Marine, but not one as congenial as Mulvaney had been the other night. This guy was all business. He looked like he could bench-press a cow with far less effort than it would take for him to spell it. "Can I help you?" I asked.

"Yeah, you can let me in," the Marine slurred, his breath already heavy with San Miguel beer.

"No, I'm afraid I can't," I told him. "You don't live here."

"I'm visiting someone," he growled.

"Yeah? Who?"

"Tina. Or Tala. Whatever name you know the slut by. Open the fuckin' gate."

"Son-of-a-bitch," I mumbled to myself. The conversation I had with Mulvaney played through my head, and I put together all the warning signs.

"Oh yeah!" I remembered Mulvaney saying. "I saw you at the Pagoda! You're Tala's friend!" *He had referred to her by her real name, not her bar name. He knew her.*

I also remembered his answer when I asked him how far up the green jeepney route he was going. He told me, "All the way to the end of the line." *Of course, he was. He wanted to see where I got off.*

I remembered Mari telling me that they moved so far from Magsaysay to avoid someone. I assumed that the man beating on the gate was that guy, and Mulvaney was the prick who told him where to find his former girlfriend. Mahal opened up her door to see what the racket was, and screamed when she saw who was at the gate. That confirmed my suspicions.

Mahal ran down the steps and grabbed Mari, picking her up and carrying her to their apartment. She then locked the door behind them. This agitated the leatherneck, who began beating on the gate with more urgency, yelling at Mari to come see him. When they were gone, he started screaming at me. "Let me in! Let me in, goddammit!"

"Fuck off."

"You want me to kick this motherfucking gate in? Is that what you want me to do?"

With a shrug and a smile, I dared him to. "Go ahead and try."

The Marine did, and I quickly discovered that the faith I put in our security fence was grossly misplaced. The gate gave way on the third kick, as did my cocksure grin. Not only did the lock disintegrate, but the bar it was latched to broke in half as well, allowing the intruder to march right in.

"Hey! You fucking stop right there, goddammit!" I yelled. "That's an order!"

The jarhead sneered. "Who the fuck do you think you are to give *me* orders, squid?"

"I'm an E-5! Same as a Marine sergeant…" The Corps was full of lance corporals. A man had to have brains to get promoted in the Marines, so I was confident that the knuckle-dragging drooler breaking into our yard was at best an E-3.

The leatherneck threw his arm out and batted me out of his way. "So what? I don't take orders from faggot sailors…"

I leapt up and jumped on the intruder's back, throwing an arm across his throat. I was trying to put him in one of those chokeholds Master Chief Darrow used on me when I got out of control. It didn't work. The Marine bent himself over at the waist and threw me over his head, knocking the wind out of me as I landed on my back. After clocking me in the ribs for good measure, he continued to the stairway that led up to the girls' apartment. "TALA!" he screamed.

"Jesus Christ," I gasped, struggling for air. Oddly enough, I was not thinking about how to stop the Marine at that point. I was wondering how long I had been in the Philippines. It was less than a week at that point. During that time, I nearly got into a fight with Palazzo and was assaulted by the ex-wife of the shipmate I crippled the year before. Then I was almost robbed by a local street gang after passing out on Baloy Beach. Now I found myself in the middle of a domestic dispute between a prostitute and her insane ex-boyfriend. I doubted that I had the stamina to keep that tempo up until the end of the month.

When I got to my feet, the Marine was pounding on the door to Tala's apartment, demanding to be let in. I ran to the trash cans, finding a couple of empty beer bottles that Dixie tossed out, then dashed to the foot of the steps. The first one I threw at the Marine missed. It sailed over his head, cleared the property, and exploded onto the street on the other side of the wall. The second one hit him in the elbow. He did not seem hurt by it at all, but it turned his attention back to me. "You got a death wish, you pansy?"

I laughed. "That supposed to scare me? You think I'm intimidated by pussies who get their rocks off by terrorizing little girls? You're not impressing me."

The Marine turned red and charged down the steps, leaping at me from on high in an attempt to take me to the dirt. He jumped a little early, and I had plenty of time to step out of the way. The jarhead hit the ground hard and, seizing the opportunity, I kicked him in the gut as hard as I could. It had little effect. My second kick had even less. That one I aimed at the Marine's jaw, hoping to put him down. Instead, I missed the mark and watched helplessly as my loafer flew off my foot and launched high into the air. It sailed out of our yard, over the back wall, and into the jungle, never to be seen again. I'm pretty sure the monkeys got it.

While I was watching my footwear fly away, the Marine jumped up and nailed me in the temple, dropping me to the deck before I could block it. I think I blacked out for a moment. When I got around to lifting my head again, the jarhead was already back upstairs, trying to break Tala's door down.

At that point, I was starting to wish that my roommates were home. Tony would have been useless in a fight, but I doubted he would do any worse than I was. Dixie was the man I could have used right then, but he was cruising Magsaysay looking for a new playmate. He did not get home until just before curfew, and there was no way I could hold the Marine off that long. It was up to me to get my ass kicked all by myself.

Tala's ex was pounding on the girls' door so loud that he never heard me sneak up from behind. Knowing I was over-matched, I was not concerned with fighting fair. I cranked back with everything I had and planted my fist right at the base of the Marine's skull. The blow hit him hard enough to send his face bouncing off of the door jamb, drawing blood across the bridge of his nose.

OLONGAPO EARP

Enraged, the goon planted his shoulder into my gut in return. He lifted me right off of my feet and charged across the hall, slamming me up against the door of my apartment. While pinning me there, he got in two hard blows against my sides, one for each kidney, and let me fall to the floor. The leatherneck then planted a kick to my stomach hard enough to make me nearly puke. He was gearing up to hit me again, but being as drunk as he was, he lurched off-balance. This allowed me to jam one of my feet against the inside of his knee.

The cretin's leg bent in an unnatural direction, and I heard something pop as he howled in agony. The Marine immediately went down and rolled over onto his side to nurse the wounded joint. I seized the momentum, jumping onto his back and attempting to put him into another chokehold. Then, in a dazzling array of wrestling moves that would have impressed me had I not been on the receiving end of them, he switched our positions. I found myself face down on the ground and getting choked out from behind. I was helpless, so, with no other option, I sunk my teeth into his arm.

I bit my assailant hard enough to loosen his grip. I then rammed my head backward and smashed it into his nose. Still, the Marine held fast. The second time I did it, it knocked him rearward sufficiently to twist his bum knee again. That resulted in enough pain for him to let me go. Once released, I took several shots to the bruin's face that ultimately drove him onto his back with his legs spread wide open. That was a juicy opportunity. I drove my foot, the one that still had a shoe on it, deep into the intruder's groin. That finally seemed to do the trick.

While he was immobilized, I grabbed the jarhead's feet and dragged him to the stairway. As I pulled him back down to the ground level, I made sure his head bounced off of every concrete step along the way. When we reached the foot, though, the Marine came back to life. He yanked one of his legs free and swept my own out from beneath me. Before I realized what was happening, the goon had me straddled and was throttling me with a furious series of punches thrown about my head and shoulders. I managed to get my arms up to protect my face, but I was getting my ass kicked at that point. There was nothing I could do about it. That was when I heard Mari burst out of her apartment and jump onto the Marine's back, slapping him while screaming, *"Itigil! Itigil! Itigil!"* Stop! Stop! Stop!

147

And then she struck the bastard so hard that he flew off of my chest. At least that was what it looked like from my perspective. I was so busy getting pummeled that I did not see Sergeant Tejada run into the courtyard and ring the Marine's bell with his nightstick.

Once my attacker was off of me, Mari threw her arms around my neck and started bawling. I carried her away from the chaos as my master chief and Tejada got medieval with our guest. They made sure that Tala's ex-boyfriend was not going to jail that night. He was going to the hospital.

Mari was hysterical. To calm her down, I laughed and asked, "You hit that big guy, didn't you?"

"*Oo,*" she answered as tears streamed down her face. Yes.

"You did that for me?"

Mari wiped her eyes and smiled. "Yes."

Despite the beating I took, I had to laugh. "Do you have any idea how brave you are!?! That guy was scary! I don't even think the men I live with would have had the guts to do what you did! You want to know something?"

"What?"

"*Ikaw ang aking bayani,*" I told her. You're my hero. Mari's face twisted up as she started crying again. Her arms wrapped around my neck so hard I was not sure if she was hugging me or trying to choke me out, too.

*****

When Tala got home, she was beside herself, wracked by fear, guilt, anger, and confusion over what had happened. "How he pind me? I move to get away prom him! I change job to get away prom him! How he track me down?"

"One of your customers followed me home," I said to her, right in front of Darrow and Sergeant Tejada. At TJ's insistence, I told them all about how Mulvaney saw me talking to her at the bar, how he used her real name, and how we took the same jeepney back that night. It seemed innocent at the time, but it developed sinister undertones the instant I heard that man pounding on my gate.

Tejada turned to my master chief. "You tink you can pind dis guy?"

OLONGAPO EARP

Darrow shrugged. "I'll make a trip to the A Company barracks and see what I can find out."

Daniel Morris was Tala Bono's ex-boyfriend. He was the man she hoped would get her out of Olongapo, but soon after he moved in with her, it was clear he was more interested in becoming her pimp than her lover. His feelings toward her became crystal clear after he beat her for telling him she wanted to quit work so that she could be with him exclusively. The next time he had duty, she gathered up her daughter, changed jobs and apartments, and left him a note telling him to stay away from the two of them.

He tracked her down to Barrio Barretto and beat her up at work soon afterward. The local hooligans, very likely the same people who tried to rob me a few days before, banged him up pretty bad in return and banned him from Baloy Beach. When the tale of what happened made its way back to the A Company barracks, Morris's command placed Barrio Barretto off-limits to him also.

As LCPL Morris was lying on his side, bleeding out of his broken mouth, Sergeant Tejada barred him from the rest of Olongapo as well. "Unless you want to go to jail," TJ told him. "You tell everybody dat you got jump by gang boys, you hear? And ip I see you out here again, I no gonna send you back to base in handcupps. You goin' back in a pucking casket. Got it?" After getting a nod out of the battered man, the policeman set him free, literally kicking him out of my yard. Using his feet, Tejada savagely throttled Morris in the ribs until he was in the street, lying prone against the curb.

"You're letting him go?" I asked when TJ returned.

"Yeah," Master Chief answered. "We gotta keep this one off the books. After what happened to Miller in Sasebo, the captain has adopted a zero-tolerance policy regarding liberty incidents. If the skipper gets wind of this, we're both going to be on restriction for the rest of the time we're here. Especially in your case."

Darrow thought for a moment. "Jesus, Doyle, why does this stuff always happen to you? You seem to have a knack for being in the wrong place at the wrong time."

After everyone left, I went to look for Tala and Mari. I found them sitting in an old metal rocking chair in the courtyard. Tala held her daughter in her lap, both of them crying to themselves as they slowly rocked back and forth. I wanted to talk to them and make sure that they were all right, but I sensed that they were having a moment. That was something they rarely got together, so I decided to let them be.

*****

Several hours later, after the sun went down and I was drinking with my roommates, we were interrupted by a knock on the door. I got up to answer it since I was pretty sure that it was Tala Bono, and I was right.

For the first time, I saw Mari's mother dressed for comfort instead of seduction. She wore loose jeans, a t-shirt that fit her like a dress, and flip-flops instead of high-heels. She let her hair down and removed her makeup. She was still gorgeous, but without all her bargirl armor on, she looked vulnerable. Tina, the woman who worked at the Pagoda, was formidable, confident, and tough. Tala, the woman with a little girl to feed, was just winging it

"Can I speak wit you?" Tala asked after I opened the door.

Nodding, I welcomed her inside. "Can I get you something to drink?"

Tala stood fast, shaking her head. "Can we speak outside, maybe downstairs in da courtyard?"

"Okay," I said, grabbing my beer and following her to the picnic table, now back at the far end of the yard.

Once seated, Tala's tears started flowing. "Doyle, t'ank you por what you do por my daughter. Everyt'ing. Buying her pood, pixing her teeth, protecting her prom Danny. I don't know how to repay you por all dis."

"Hey Tala, you don't have to do anything for me. Hanging out with Mari is keeping me out of trouble. Well, at least it was until Danny showed up."

"Doyle, I...I...we already so par in debt to you por everyt'ing you do por Mari. I need to ask a pavor prom you, dough, and I no t'ink I know how..."

"For Mari?" I asked. "Tell me what she needs. I..."

Tala heaved, noisily drawing in a deep breath of air while doing so. "She need you to stop doing all dese t'ings por her! Please! You have to stop!"

Unsure of how to answer that, I stammered. "I don't understand..."

OLONGAPO EARP

Sobbing, Mari's mother cried, "Dat right! You no understand! You no understand what you doing to her!"

"Tala, did I do something wrong?"

Shaking her head, she answered, "No! No! You doing everyt'ing right! She just a little girl, Doyle. She have little girl pantasies and..." Tala paused to get herself together. "Doyle, I born on Leyte Island. My pamily very poor. Dere lot of bad boys in da place where I grow up. Dey in trouble all time, in gangs, dey always doing bad t'ings. When dey want somet'ing, dey take it and everyone apraid op dem, so no one ever stop dem. When I was thirteen, dey take me. I have Mari when I only pourteen.

"I never tell my parents what dem boys do to me, I very ashamed. So, when dey see I am having Mari, dey ask who da pather is and I tell dem I don't know. Dat make dem ashamed too, and scared. Dey can no appord to feed another baby and dey very upset dat dey daughter give her body to boy she no know. So dey kick me out op my house."

Tala winced at the memory, discarded like trash by her own parents. "Dem boys, dey kill me when dey make Mari. Dey kill who I was and who I dream I become. I had to go to missionaries to take care op me until I have my daughter. But dey want to take Mari away prom me because dey say I too young to take care op her. She da only person I got, dough, so I run away to keep her. I come to Olongapo to work, but I know dere only one type op job I can do here. It scare me, and I no want to do it, but it only way I can take care op my little girl. But I only pourteen, I too young to work in Olongapo. I pind people dough dat tell me to go to Pagsanjan. I can work dere. So, I do. Dat horrible place, but I stay dere two years until I get job here in Olongapo."

After taking a moment to wipe her eyes, Tala continued. "Doyle, da girl I was when dose boys take me, she died. She gone now, replaced by Mari. Dis body you see, dis body dat used to be Tala? Dis body now Tina. Tina only have one job in dis lipe. Tina here to protect Mari. Tina feed Mari, Tina clothe Mari, Tina keep roop over Mari head, and Tina work hard, very hard, to send Mari to good school. It very expensive. Tina only live to see Mari do what she want to do when she grow up and be happy. Tina protect Mari prom having to live a lipe like Tina. Mari never have to sell herselp to keep pood in her belly. She be a nurse. Or a teacher. Or a journalist. She no gonna supper through her lipe like me."

I felt like it was my turn to speak, but I had nothing to say. The best I could come up with was, "Tala, how does me staying away from Mari help her?"

"Mari never have man in her lipe dat she connect wit," Tala answered. "You dough, she t'ink you really nice. She surprised by a white guy dat can speak her language a little and is good to her wid-out wanting not'ing prom her mot'er. She like you a lot an' talks to me all da time about you since you here. Dere no kids in our barrio, and da other kids at her school no play wit her because dey mothers know what I do. You da only priend she t'ink she has.

"Like I tell you, she a little girl wit little girl dream. She tinks ip we nice to you dat you marry me and take care op us. She tinks you take us wit you to America and..."

"I...I...hey, look, Tala," I stuttered. "I barely know..."

Tala let out the saddest laugh I ever heard. "You can relax, Doyle. I no proposing to you. I telling you way dat a little girl mind work sometime. I don't know you good, but I tell you smart man. You kind man. Plenty op girls see dat, and you make a nice lipe wit one op dem. I know what I am too. I know how I make my living. I know I damaged and..."

"Hey, Tala, one day, you're going to find someone who..."

Mari's mother suddenly looked angry. "Stop it! Ip I have to hear dat again..." Standing up to leave, Tala said, "Look. In pew weeks, you ship leave Philippines porever. When it goes, da base close too. I don't know what me and Mari going to do. I do know dat da higher you get my daughter's hope up, da more you allow her to have pantasies, da more her heart break when you leave. Please, Doyle. Please. Leave my little girl alone."

Tala sobbed, then rushed up to run back to her apartment. I stood to try to comfort her but stopped myself after a couple of steps. In the moment, my heart was breaking for her. She did not deserve the lot she had drawn in life. Neither did Rafaela. I wanted to rescue them both, but there was nothing I could do about either.

For an instant, I wondered what it would be like being with someone like Tala. She was so beautiful, and with Mari, they would be an instant family, something I never had. Would we have dinners together, play board games on weekends, and go on picnics in the park? Or would we end up like the Greens? Would Tala and I drink away our demons and ignore Mari while our relationship deteriorated into violence?

What Tala did for a living disgusted me, yet I could not help but be impressed with the sacrifices she made for Mari. She endured unimaginable violations every night to give her daughter a fighting chance in an unspeakably harsh place to live. That was love at its fiercest, in its most primal form. I sensed she was sincere when she spoke to me and thought it sad that few men would ever consider her as anything other than a commodity to be bought and used. She deserved a chance at a better life. It was a shame that she would probably never get it.

But what if I gave her a chance? I shook my head to force the thought from my mind.

You've had a few beers, I thought to myself. *And you haven't been laid since Hawaii. You're thinking with your dick. Don't be an idiot. She's playing you, and you're taking the bait.*

I lit myself a cigarette and looked up the steps to Tala's door as the angel on my shoulder tried putting thoughts into my head. *But that woman is so gorgeous. If you just let her in a little bit…*

My inner devil was having none of it. *What's the matter with you? Of course, she's gorgeous! That's why you keep your guard up! You let it down with a woman like that and she'll destroy you, you fucking imbecile.*

I wondered if bar girls were really so bad. If I did ever let Tala in, would I ever be able to trust her? Would I always be suspicious of what she was doing whenever she went somewhere without me? Tala would have been so far out of my league had she not been a hooker. If I ever did give her a chance, would she be grateful for it? Or would she stay with me just long enough to get a better offer?

Moron, why are you even thinking about this? Your mind is getting away from you here. You need to reel it back in a little.

How would I react if I was with a woman like that, and she did try to leave me? What if we ever had children together, and she wanted to take them with her? Would it drive me mad like Randy Green? Could it push me to do to Tala and Mari what he had done to Rafaela and Manny?

Or could they push me even further? Could they force me to do to them what my father did to…?

I cringed, hearing the shotgun blasts that cut my family down.

You fucking idiot. You did it now.

My eyes clenched shut, and I saw Tala and Mari holding each other, pleading for me to stop. They were begging for their lives like I imagined my mother and sister did with my father. Unable to bear that thought, I forced my eyes open again, fighting to keep from falling into one of my episodes. I took several deep breaths and did what I could to wrangle the thoughts racing through my mind. My eyes then focused upon a palm frond silhouetted before a full moon. I concentrated on that until I relaxed enough to be out of danger. Then I collapsed onto the picnic table and wiped the cold sweat from my brow.

Tala was right. She and Mari were not my responsibility. If seeing Rafaela in Barrio Barretto taught me anything, it was that my attempts to help people like them only made things worse. If I really wanted to help, I needed to stay as far away from them as possible.

*****

CHAPTER 15

As soon as we stepped off the bus in Pagsanjan, a group of young men started working the foreigners in the crowd. "Hey, Joe!" one of them called out to me. "Welcome to Pagsanjan! You wanna see da wattapalls? I take you see da wattapalls! Dey just like Niagara Palls in New York!"

"No, thank you," Master Chief Darrow told him, keeping his eyes focused straight ahead as he walked. He was doing his best to look as disinterested as possible.

"How 'bout boat ride! You wanna ride da rapids? Huh? You wanna ride on the river?"

"There's rapids here?" I asked my master chief. "Can we take a ride on the river?"

Darrow reached down and took my hand, pulling me closer to him as he shuffled the duffle bag he was carrying to the opposite shoulder. He then put his arm around my waist and guided me to his other side so that he was between the street urchin and me. I knew it was an act, but it still made me very uncomfortable. I was praying that no one from the ship saw that. "We're not here to play in the water."

The young man smiled knowingly. "You looking for *pom-pom*? I find you a *pom-pom*!"

Darrow stopped. "No, we want something different. How about a *pam-pam*?"

"A girl? Okay. I pind you a young girl! How old?"

My stomach tied itself into knots. That was how easy it was. One minute after stepping off the bus, my master chief was negotiating with some derelict over the price of defiling a child. I had to look away. Not wanting to blow our cover, I stepped over to a kiosk selling souvenir tee shirts and started browsing. It was an excuse to keep my back turned to the man bartering with my master chief. I did not want him to see the look of disgust on my face.

As I pulled out a shirt that falsely advertised a "Hard Rock Café – Pagsanjan," I realized that I was not cut out for police work. I was far better suited as a vigilante, beating miscreants like Randy Green into epilepsy rather than this stuff Darrow was trying to do now. I regretted what I did to Rafaela's husband, but only because of what happened to her as a result. That kid my master chief was talking to, though? That shit stain, I could beat to death, slowly and methodically, and not lose a wink of sleep over it.

"Doyle," Master Chief Darrow called out to me. "What are you doing? Come on, this guy's going to hook us up."

If there was a red-light district in Pagsanjan, I never saw it. Things were done differently there. Pagsanjan was a resort town, a legitimate vacation spot for people who wanted to take advantage of the Bumbungan River. People did not want to take their families on holiday to places where the sex trade was as in your face as it was in Olongapo. You told someone what you were looking for, and they discreetly delivered it to your room.

My master chief's inquiry was handled with even more discretion. Once our contact knew what we were in the market for, we had to follow him to where we could find it. He led us off the main avenues and into a winding maze of slums in the district's shantytown. There were no streets there, only narrow alleyways full of smoke, trash, and, surprisingly, people. It was a busy area, teeming with pedestrian traffic. Most of the folks there were Filipino, usually aged north of fifty years by the look of them. The few natives I saw closer to my age looked surly and tough. They seemed to size us up as we passed, wondering how best to separate us from our money. Offer us sex? Sell us *shabu*? Or just stick us in the ribs with something sharp and grab our wallets while we bled out?

Darrow and I were not the only foreigners walking those alleys that day. We were, however, the only ones led by a guide. The others looked like they knew where they were going. I studied them as we walked and was relieved to see that none of them looked like servicemen. Their hair was way too long, they lacked purpose in the way that they walked, and their faces indicated that they were obviously too old.

We eventually arrived at a bloc of cabanas somewhere in the heart of the shantytown. They were put together with whatever the residents could find: bamboo, corrugated tin, rotten plywood, and discarded tarp material. The interiors of these cabanas were much nicer, though. These were places that generated money, so they contained actual beds. The people who lived there usually slept on some sort of pad thrown on the floor. There were also a couple of chairs, ratty but clean, and a jug of water to clean ourselves up with.

"Is okay?" our contact asked after he finished showing us the place.

"Good enough," Darrow told him as he handed the kid some peso notes to take care of the rest of our business. After our guy left, the master chief turned to me and asked, "You alright?"

I shook my head. "It's taking everything I have to keep myself from killing that fucker."

That was not what my master chief wanted to hear. He pointed his index finger at me. "Keep your shit together, Murphy! I mean it! We're not fucking around here!"

"I will but…"

"No 'buts,' goddammit! Shut your trap and focus on what we need to do! I don't want to hear another word out of you until he comes back!"

Our silence did not make anything better. In fact, it made things worse. The cabanas were not built with soundproofing in mind, and I could hear what was going on in the rooms around us. It was disgusting. Darrow heard it too and glared at me, trying to determine my state of mind by the look on my face. I was going to tell him I was alright, but he put his index finger to his lips, reminding me to be quiet.

Our guide was not gone long. Within fifteen minutes, he opened our door and strolled right in with a girl in tow. I guessed her to be little more than ten or eleven. She was older, but with her hairstyle and the shape of her face, she looked way too much like Mari. Darrow saw it also and tensed up as if he was preparing to take me down in case the resemblance made me do something stupid. I did not have the chance to, however.

No sooner had the door swung shut behind our guide than Sergeant Tejada pushed it back open again. Stepping inside, TJ pulled a pistol from the small of his back and pointed it at the kid who brought the girl to us. The guide tried to duck, but before he could move, I had him by the throat, squeezing tight enough to keep him from screaming. He was not breathing well, either. I then slammed him up against the wall hard enough to snap a couple of the bamboo rods.

Tejada took a couple of steps forward so that he could put the barrel of his weapon right up against the cretin's forehead. In Tagalog, he then asked, "You gonna be quiet when this man lets go of you?"

Unable to speak, our guide nodded, and TJ told me to let him go. He had to say it twice, though, before I finally did. After I stepped away, the policeman asked the kid what his name was.

"Dado."

"Dado what?"

"Dado Afuang."

TJ nodded. "Well, Dado, I give you a choice today. You wanna go to jail, or you wanna do what dese guys want you to do?"

Dado's look hardened. "I no telling you about my priends. I go to jail."

"Dey no lookin' por you priends, Dado. Dey looking por some Yankee sailors."

"Americans?" You could see Dado relax. He would not be tainted as an informer if he was just giving up foreigners. "What Americans dey lookin' por?"

"Military Americans. All of them." Darrow opened up the duffel bag he was carrying and showed him the disposable cameras he brought. "You can pass these out to your friends. If any American military men come back here and mess with these kids, you get a picture of them with the *pam-pam* or *pom-pom* they're with, okay? If I can identify them, I'll pay you twenty American dollars. Okay?"

OLONGAPO EARP

Dado nodded. "Okay. No many military guys out here. Dey have to stay in Olongapo now. You guys da pirst I see dat I t'ink in da Navy por a long time."

"It should be easy then." Darrow pulled out a stack of photographs of Lieutenant Krause. "You get pictures of this guy with a *pam-pam* out here, I pay you five hundred dollars. Do you understand?" The kid's eyes lit up greedily.

I reached into the pocket of my cargo shorts and pulled out some pictures I had of Palazzo. Handing them to Dado, I added, "I'm offering a hundred bucks if you get this guy."

Darrow looked over at me. He had no idea I was adding Spanky to our mission. "Do you really think that Palazzo is capable of this?"

I shrugged. "I don't know. If he is, though, I want to find out."

My master chief nodded. "Fair enough. Look, I'm going to work out some details with this dirtbag. We're also going to inform him of what we're going to do to him if he screws us over on this, too. Why don't you get that little girl out of here and take care of her?"

"Sure," I said. "No problem." Before we went outside, I reached in my pocket and handed her a wad of peso notes. It was probably three times more than what she would have earned doing what Dado brought her to us for.

Once outside, I then asked her in Tagalog, "Do you like *lumpia*?"

*****

Knowing that Darrow and Tejada would be a while giving Dado his instructions, I bought the little girl some dinner and a couple of soft drinks. I then had her point me in the direction of the cabanas and spent the next half hour lost in the alleys trying to get back to where I came from. When I finally found Darrow and TJ, both were a little miffed.

"Where the hell were you?" Darrow growled.

"Lost," I answered. "This place is a labyrinth."

"You gotta be carepul inna place like dis, Murppey," TJ said. "You get inna lot op trouble out here ip you no know what you doing."

"I know, Sergeant. I've seen more of this place than I think I can handle. You mind if we get the hell out of here now?"

It had been a long time since Darrow had been in this part of Pagsanjan. Tejada made it there a couple of times a year for the government's semi-annual crackdown on the place, so he led the way out. When we were finally walking, Darrow turned to me and said, "I wish you would have talked to me first before throwing Palazzo's picture at that guy."

"Really?" I asked. "Why?"

Darrow shrugged. "I have a sense for this kind of stuff, Doyle. Palazzo's not tripping any of my switches."

"Seriously? He's tripping all of mine," I countered. "The man's addicted to porn. Christ, you saw him before we left San Diego. The guy couldn't stop playing with himself. The bastard was getting caught red-handed jerking off every other day."

"I'm not saying the guy doesn't have issues. I'm saying that I don't think he has this particular kind. Doyle, a hundred dollars is a lot of money to these people out here. You put that kind of bounty on a man's head in these parts, and they can do some pretty shady stuff to collect it. Say these guys make Palazzo if he does end up out here? There are hookers all over this country that are of age but look young. Man, even with all the time I spent in this country, I have a hard time telling if a woman is fourteen or forty. They could honey trap the poor bastard, get him thinking he's with an eighteen-year-old when he's actually with someone who isn't even in high school yet."

"And you're not worried about them doing that to Krause?"

Darrow shook his head. "Palazzo isn't lying in bed at night obsessing about how he can ruin the two of us. Krause is. I didn't ask that Dado guy to frame the lieutenant, but to be honest, I ain't going to be looking a gift horse in the mouth if he comes through for me. Unlike Palazzo, Krause did trip a couple of alarms that have me thinking that he's hiding something out here. He was a little too forceful in his warning to us to stay away from the place, you know?"

"So, it's a gut thing with…"

A rickety door opened up before us and I watched as a white guy stepped out into the alley in front of Tejada. Before the door closed, I caught a quick look inside. The man left a young boy behind that looked to be twelve or thirteen and obviously a *pom-pom*.

OLONGAPO EARP

Sickened, I took another look at the man who exited the cabana. At the same time, he turned his head toward me. When our eyes met, there was a mutual flash of recognition that made both of us gasp.

*****

I was hit with a jolt of panic. The man I spotted in the Pagsanjan alley was Michael, the missionary I pointed my shotgun at during my first night in Subic Bay. In a flash, all the reasons this chance encounter was not in our best interests ripped through my mind. Michael was a missionary with Hope's Children Ministries, the same organization where our division officer once worked. He could connect me to the *Belleau Wood,* not to mention to Krause, and blow our chances of catching our lieutenant in Pagsanjan.

Besides the threat he posed to our operational security, it appeared that Michael was also scum. He was someone in desperate need of a beating in the flavor of the one I had delivered to Randy Green. Guessing what I was capable of doing to him, the missionary broke off eye contact and bolted through the crowd. That triggered some predatory instinct deep within my brain, and I took off after him. I was so focused on my prey that I never heard Darrow or TJ calling after me to stop.

I do not know if Michael was an athlete or just fueled by terror, but I discovered that the man could run. He was also lithe and agile, able to effortlessly dodge and cut around the mass of people that filled the alley. I was much larger and clumsier. Despite my best efforts, I plowed gracelessly through the crowd, bowling people out of my way. That was not making me any friends among the locals.

Michael should have lost me in no time. Early in the chase, though, he tripped over a stack of wicker baskets and wiped out in a spectacular fashion. He had a half-block advantage at that point, but by the time he got back on his feet, I was close enough to reach out for him. My fingers just grazed the back of his shirt before he started putting distance between us again. Being so close to my quarry gave me a bit of a boost. That allowed me to keep up for about another block. After that, my pack-a-day cigarette habit caught up to me, and I started losing him once more.

I tried to keep pushing, but Michael increased his lead to a few yards, then to a few shacks. I reached in deep and tried to fire my adrenaline afterburners, but I was gassed. Tripping over my own feet, I ended up crashing into the dirt while watching my prey turn a corner and pass out of sight.

It took me forever to get back up. Once I did, I was out of air, fighting for breath. Intoxicated by oxygen deprivation, I stumbled around a bit, trying to balance myself. I attempted to jog to the corner that Michael had disappeared around, but even that was too much effort. An angry crowd of people, many of whom I had probably knocked over, began to gather around me. Though I did not speak the local dialect, I had no problem understanding the threats and insults they hurled my way.

Ignoring the mob as best as I could, I limped toward where I lost my missionary. I knew the chase was futile at that point, but my choices were to keep trying to catch my man or face the crowd behind me. I kept going.

Shantytown alleys are ad hoc and helter-skelter. They are not laid out in gridlines by civil engineers the way streets are. They formed as new places were built. The passageways twisted and turned, few of them leading to anywhere with a purpose. Many came to unexpected dead ends. At some point, Michael must have gotten himself turned around and run into something like that. Even over the din of the crowd, I heard the sound of sprinting, sneaker-clad footsteps heading right for me. I squatted down to get my head beneath the throng and waited until the runner was almost upon me before I sprang.

My victim never saw it coming. He was running full bore right at me when I emerged above the mob and planted my fist in his face. I caught him beneath the eye so hard, it took him off of his feet. Inertia spun him around, lifting his legs into the air while his head careened back toward Earth. He hit the ground even harder than I hit him. When he landed, he was completely still.

I, on the other hand, felt like I had shattered my wrist. I hollered out in pain and tucked my paw into my armpit, jumping around as fresh bolts of agony shot up my forearm. With my attention focused on my hand, I was too distracted to notice that a half dozen tattooed young men had joined the crowd around me. Hooligans like that tended to like watching a good fight, but these guys were eyeing me with severe disapproval. "Wadda puck, mayn," one of them called out to me in a thick accent. "Wha you tink you do-een?"

"What?" I asked, unable to decipher the accent.

"You hear me! I say wha you tink you do? Wha you problem?" The young punk took a step toward me, and I pulled my right hand out from under my armpit. I tried to shake out the remaining discomfort before I needed to use it again.

I stole a glance down at Michael. He was out cold and not going anywhere. That allowed me the opportunity to size up the kid in front of me. The street hoodlum was short and wiry. Had I faced off against him back in the States, I would never have given him a second thought. This guy grew up mean in the Pagsanjan ghetto, though. His eyes were full of "I just don't give a fuck." His need for street cred far outweighed any instinct he had for self-preservation. I still thought I could take him, but it was going to hurt.

"Hey! Muddapukka!" the kid called out once more. "You an'sa me?"

Pointing at the man I put on the ground, I said, "That piece of shit was molesting a boy back there and…"

"I don't gib a puck! Dis no you bidness! You tink you go here and start trouble? We pix trouble here!" With bunched fists, the kid took a step toward me. To show him I was not backing down, I stepped toward him in return. Then his gang stepped up to back their leader, and I began to realize how screwed I was.

There were six of them. Two were holding knives, handles in hands, the blades resting up against their wrists to make them inconspicuous. To my back, there was a crowd in which I had not made any friends. I also suspected that they were none too pleased with me interfering with the local racket. It was looking like I was going to get messed up.

Then I heard a commotion rise from behind the crowd to my rear. "Hey! Hey! Get out of the way! Now!" That was followed up with a bunch of orders shouted in Tagalog that I did not understand. I did not dare turn to look at them. Taking my eyes off of those boys would have been begging one of them to poke holes in my gut. Besides, I recognized the voices anyway.

The gangsters before me may not have known Sergeant Tejada, but they knew what the authoritative voice of a policeman sounded like. They made their weapons disappear with a sleight of hand that would have impressed Houdini himself.

Before long, I had both Darrow and Tejada by my side, panting and cursing, contemplating cutting back on cigarettes even more than I was. Directing his attention to the gang's apparent leader, TJ pointed his finger at the young man. "You gotta problem here?"

The punk answered the sergeant in angry Tagalog. TJ's tone of voice was even angrier. Within moments, both of them were shouting at each other. All I could make out was that the gangsters were not thrilled about having a *poutie* running amok in their neighborhood. They liked me assaulting the tourists (or rather, their customers) even less.

The longer their arguing went on, the more frustrated I sensed Tejada was getting. He was losing patience with the lack of respect the kid had for his authority. When the hoodlum crossed one point of etiquette too many, TJ hauled off and smacked him across the chops.

All conversation around us went quiet. Foolish expressions crept across the gangsters' faces, suggesting that they were wondering whether they could rush Tejada before he could draw his weapon. One of them seemed to like his odds and made a sudden move in that direction. Master Chief Darrow shut that down with a haymaker planted in the thug's temple. That dropped him writhing into the dirt right next to the missionary. At that, I saw the punks getting ready to charge as Tejada drew his weapon. Darrow took a single step back to pull himself from TJ's line of fire, and I froze, unsure of what to do next.

Once the crowd saw a firearm introduced to the fray, it split and scattered. The three of us and the half dozen gang members stood fast. I looked at the leader's face and sensed that this was not going to end well. He was not intimidated by the gun pointed at his face and he sneered at Sergeant Tejada. It was as if he was daring him to pull the trigger. When it looked as if TJ was on the verge of doing exactly that, a gravelly voice behind us called out to him in Tagalog. If I understood correctly, it said, "Tito, what are you doing?"

The gang leader immediately relaxed in deference to the approaching senior, who strolled into the no man's land between us. After stopping in front of Sergeant Tejada's pistol, he faced the young men and told them all to go home.

OLONGAPO EARP

This did not sit well with Tejada. "I give the orders around here, old man," he snarled.

"Do you?" the elder asked in flawless English, turning around to face TJ. His eyes stared down the barrel of the sergeant's weapon for a moment before glancing back up to meet Tejada's gaze. "Or are you letting yourself be bossed around by Olongapo Earp, here? Officer, I suggest you let these boys go one way, and you go the other. Get this thing over with before someone gets hurt."

The elderly man looked like he belonged in the Pagsanjan slum that surrounded us. He was unkempt and dirty, had a mouthful of rotting teeth and a nose that had been broken more than once. On the other hand, he spoke English without any trace of an accent and carried himself with a fearless sense of importance that was out of place among such disenfranchised people.

As in most Asian societies, the elderly in the Philippines enjoy a certain amount of reverence. I suspected that that was the only thing keeping Tejada from knocking the man's teeth out. Even the younger hoodlums would never dare imply that TJ was Master Chief Darrow's lapdog. "Who da puck you tink you are?" the sergeant asked.

"I'm the *punong barangay*." The old man looked at me, guessing that I had no idea what a *punong barangay* was. He was right. "I'm the neighborhood leader here—the *kapitan*. My name is Paulino Favila. Do you remember me, Earp?"

It took a moment, but my master chief nodded. The expression on his face suggested that this was not a happy reunion. "I remember the name," my master chief said. "You look a lot different now than the last time we met."

Favila shrugged. "I got a little older. And I haven't recently been beaten half to death by a mob of liquored up Blue Shirts acting on your behalf." Blue Shirts were the armed guards that watched over the businesses in the Philippines. Darrow once told me they had much of the same power and privileges as police officers. He also said that they brought a certain mercenary flavor to the local law enforcement community. They were more reminiscent of the Pinkerton detectives of the Old West than they were of the mall cops of American suburbia.

"The Blue Shirts beat you *half* to death?" Darrow snickered. "I should have paid them *half* their fuckin' wages then."

Tejada lowered his weapon. Despite the unpleasant history Darrow and Favila shared, TJ was not going to gun down a *barangay kapitan*. Not in broad daylight on a crowded shantytown street, anyway. There were too many witnesses. "Who da puck dis guy, Brad?"

"Paulino is a little bit of everything," my master chief answered. "He's a pimp, a pusher, a thief, a murderer. And now he's a *kapitan*. How did you get this gig, Paulino? You tell everybody around here about how much of a war hero you were? How you practically kicked the Japs off of Luzon single-handedly before you got sent to the camps?"

Paulino raised his arms. "The Philippine people remember our sacrifices. They appreciate what we did. They showed their appreciation by asking me to continue to serve them as *barangay kapitan*. They asked me to use my wisdom and experience to keep the peace around here. That is what I'm trying to do, Olongapo Earp. Keep the peace. If I let these young men kill a policeman right here in our neighborhood, well, the cops'll storm this place. They'll burn it right to the ground. That's why I'm letting you walk out of here. For my people. Make no mistake, if I caught you in here by yourself, well, I'd be settling a debt that I've been dreaming about repaying for many years now. Many years."

Favila directed a steely gaze at Master Chief Darrow and then another at Sergeant Tejada. When neither of them challenged him, the *kapitan* turned back to his boys and told them to go home once again. Tejada was about to counter the old man's orders, but Darrow stopped him. "Let them go, TJ. Let's cut our losses."

"What?"

Darrow nodded sympathetically. "Let them go and let's get the hell out of here."

I pointed down at Michael, who was just now starting to come to, squirming in the dirt. "What about him?"

"Leave him," Favila told me. "You're lucky I don't have my boys do to you what you did to this guy. He's a man of God."

"Man of God?" I scoffed. "He's a fucking perv…"

"You're a fucking imbecile," the *kapitan* interrupted, his ire now focused at me. "That man is one of the few sources of comfort the kids around here have. I know what goes on in my *barangay,* young man. I know there's much evil that happens here, and I know who carries it out. This man is no evil-doer."

I took a step toward Favila, sticking my finger in his face. "Yeah? You know what happens here? Then why don't you fucking stop it?!?"

Darrow grabbed me by the neck, swung me around, and sent me stumbling in the direction we needed to start walking to get out of the slums. "Get going, Doyle! Now!"

"But…"

"But nothing! Go!" For the first time since I had met him, Darrow appeared as if he did not have control of the situation. More disconcerting was the fact that he was unable to hide it. He looked scared. I saw it, Tejada saw it, and no doubt, the gangsters saw it too. He kept pushing me forward, walking at a gait that was practically a jog. Calling back to Favila, Darrow said, "We'll see you later."

The old man laughed. "You'd better hope not, Olongapo Earp."

*****

Once we were out of Favila's sight, Darrow broke into a trot. Tejada and I followed suit. From above us, the shantytown's residents saw us beating a hasty retreat and started taunting us from the rooftops. When they started throwing things, we sprinted. For the last block before we broke out of the shantytown, it felt like we were running for our lives. It was a half-mile before we slowed down again, coming to a halt before a local *sari-sari* store. While gasping for air, Darrow smiled wide and ordered us a round of San Miguel beers. He then toasted, "To yet another successful mission!" His demeanor had changed entirely.

"Successpul?" Tejada gasped, still trying to catch his breath. "How da puck you call dat a success?"

"I got that son-of-a-bitch right where I want him!"

"What are you talking about?" I thought Darrow had lost his mind.

"Fucking war hero," my master chief laughed. "I remember that prick. His gang supplied dope to sailors who sold it on base during the '70s. One of the Americans working with them shorted them some cash, so they kidnapped this guy's kids until he could cough up the dough. The sailor

J.E. PARK

came to us to get his children back. Now, Favila wasn't directly involved with the kidnapping, but he knew who was. That's why I hired some Blue Shirts to bring him in. We worked Paulino over until he gave them up and got the kids back. Then we sent their father to the stockade for a few years."

Darrow took a long drink of his beer and smiled like he was recalling a favorite memory. "I had them let Favila go. I thought I could cultivate him into an informant but he disappeared as soon as he was released. To be honest, I thought his own guys snuffed him out for ratting on the kidnappers. To appease my curiosity, though, I dug into him. I found out that though he was born here on Luzon, he was raised in Seattle when his parents moved there in the '20s."

"So, he wasn't even here when the Japanese invaded?" I asked.

Darrow shook his head. "No, he was here in the Philippines during the war. During the Great Depression, his old man turned to burglary to feed his family and got himself arrested. Since none of them were citizens, they all ended up getting deported back here to PI. No one knows what Favila did during the Japanese invasion, but during the occupation, he collaborated with the Japs. He offered to pose as a camp laborer to spy on the American prisoners since he spoke fluent English. He wasn't a war hero. He was a fucking traitor."

Tejada's jaw dropped open. "And now he da pucking *punong barangay*! And da crime boss? Ip dey pind out 'bout dat shit wid da Japanese, dey gonna pucking kill him! Dey gonna pucking kill him slow!"

"Yeah, well, we need to get him someplace where we can safely make him aware of what we know. We gotta keep up the facade that he has the upper hand on us, too. If his boys suspect we're pulling his strings, they'll turn on the guy. Despite that little cock-of-the-walk act he pulled on us back there, the man's a fucking weasel. I'm sure he'll do anything to make sure that little secret of his stays secret. He'll be able to give us the picture of any military man that steps foot in that place better than the guy we already got. We've got this in the bag. You think we can get to him tomorrow?"

"Puck, Brad. I got men who can get to dis guy tonight!" TJ assured us.

OLONGAPO EARP

"Great! The file on him is in one of those boxes I gave your old boss, Chico Acosta, back in 1977 or '78. It'll be in archive because when I turned it over, we thought this prick was dead."

Tejada nodded. "Okay. I have da guys at da station go get 'em and drive dem over here right away." TJ stood up and slammed the rest of his beer. "I gonna go pind a telepone. I be back."

After Tejada left, a thought occurred to me. I turned to Darrow and asked, "Master Chief, do you really think this guy is so desperate to keep his secret that he'd work for you?"

Darrow pulled out his pack of cigarettes and lit one. "Absolutely. The stuff the Japanese did here was unspeakable, Doyle. Brutal. Horrific. To this day, you still get the occasional story of someone settling some wartime grudge around these parts. It doesn't matter that this shit happened fifty years ago. To many of these folks, it was just like yesterday. If Favila is outed as a collaborator, these people will eat that fucker alive. That's no joke."

"So, you think he'd do anything he could to keep it quiet?"

"Yeah. It'd not only ruin his life; it'd end it. It'll undo his legacy, too. People would do what they could to erase all memory of him, to make it seem like he never even existed."

"You think that he'd kill to keep it secret?"

"Fuck yeah," Darrow said without hesitation. "He most certainly would."

"You think that maybe he'd try to kill *you*?"

"Kill me himself? Naw. He doesn't have the balls." Darrow paused, losing himself in thought for a little while. "But there are plenty of others around here who do, though. Now that you mention it, I would bet that he's wasting no time getting the word out to the bastards that I'm back in town again."

After a nervous pull out of his beer bottle and a quick peek at the people milling about around us, Darrow let out a sigh. Looking at me a little more uneasily, he then told me, "Keep your eyes peeled, Doyle."

*****

CHAPTER 16

Master Chief Darrow and I were pretty happy with ourselves after we left Pagsanjan. With Favila's boys looking for military men sneaking into their neighborhood, we were confident that we would catch Krause. At least we would if Darrow's suspicions about the man were correct. The only open-end we had was Michael. After I told Tejada everything I knew about the guy, he was confident he could close that loop as well.

It was a long bus ride back to Olongapo. Darrow killed time by telling me all about the things he and Tejada had done together back when he was on the AFPD. The two of them were brutes and had taken a lot of very nasty people out of circulation. They also saw to it that many innocent victims got the justice they would never have received from the country's notoriously corrupt court system. Darrow was proud of what they had accomplished, and the more I heard, the prouder I was of what my master chief had done, too.

We arrived back in town at about twenty-two hundred, then drank until just after midnight. It was about then that Tejada tracked us down and let us know that Favila folded as Darrow guessed he would. Turning to me, though, TJ got very cross. He did some investigating into Michael out in Pagsanjan. The man was apparently a saint. I did not catch him red-handed molesting a boy in Pagsanjan. The sergeant told me I caught him trying to save one.

"Then why did he run?" I asked, trying to justify what I did.

"Because he see da look on you pace and know you gonna puckin' kill him!" The sergeant shook his head. "You no mo' goin' to Pagsanjan, Doyle. You done! Brad, you no go back to dat place either. You know where da Monkey Hut is?"

"The Monkey Hut?" Darrow repeated. "Near the river? That place is still around?"

Tejada nodded his head. "Yeah, it still dere. Favila gonna get word to me ip he get pictures of military guys in da barrio. When he do, you gonna meet one op his people at da Monkey Hut. I have a local PNP guy in plain clothes dere watching to make sure you okay. You go straight dere and come straight back. Okay? Everyone know now dat Olongapo Earp back in town." TJ slapped me in the back of the head. "Danks to dis maddapukka."

The sergeant was furious with me. Granted, I had scored a coup by attracting the attention of Paulino Favila. I had also robbed some very vulnerable Pagsanjan kids of one of the few resources they had to get out of the sex trade, though. TJ had to tell Michael that he was under investigation for child abuse. He ordered the ministry to keep him confined in their Manila compound until the PNP cleared him, and Tejada was fit to be tied about that.

"Man, is there a way I can make this up to TJ?" I asked Darrow as we left the bar to make our way home.

My master chief shrugged. "Don't worry about it. It'll blow over. If you want to do something for the guy though, do that barbecue I told you about. Grill up some ribs for the man."

Darrow and I parted ways after a half dozen blocks. While I walked back home, I thought about what I would need to make up some American-style barbecue sauce. I wondered if I could find it in the Philippines. I needed ketchup, steak sauce, honey, apple juice, and…

"*Halo*, Doyle!"

Mari scared me out of my skin when I walked through the broken gate to our apartment building. "Jesus! Mari!" I gasped. I then stole a quick look at my watch and, in my best Tagalog, exclaimed, "It's almost one in the morning! What are you still doing up?"

"I was waiting for you."

"Me? Why?"

"I want to show you my teeth! They're all good now! I wanted to thank you!" Mari ran up and threw her arms around my waist, hugging me tightly.

"Mari, you need to show me during the day!" Remembering Tala pleading with me to keep my distance from her daughter, I peeled the little girl's arms from around me. I tried to lead her back to her place. "You should be in bed now!"

"Doyle," Mari asked as we walked up the stairs. "Did I do something wrong?"

"No, of course not. Why would you ask that?"

"I've been trying to see you for three days, and you keep staying away. Mommy also told me I need to stop bugging you."

"Mari, I'm a grown man. I have things to do. I can't sit around here all day playing with little girls. Don't you have any friends to play with?"

Mari hung her head. "No."

"What? Why don't you..." I stopped myself from probing further. I remembered Tala telling me why the little girl did not have any friends. I would have liked to have had a heart-to-heart with Mari about that but reminded myself that her mother did not want me to make her my problem. "Look, we'll talk about this some other time. Right now, you need to go to sleep."

"Can we talk tomorrow?"

"We'll see."

I watched Mari's shoulders slump as she hung her head even lower. "We'll see. That means no." Mari let go of my hand and started running up the stairway toward the door to her place. "I'm sorry, Doyle."

"Sorry?" I asked as my little friend reached the top of the steps. "Sorry for what?"

"Whatever I did to make you not want to hang out with me anymore."

Before I could tell her that she did not do anything wrong, Mari burst through her door, slamming it behind her.

OLONGAPO EARP

Tala got home at three, and I was lying in wait. Trying not to scare her, I paced about inside the gate, smoking, so that she saw me well before she tried to let herself in. "*Halo*, Doyle. What you do up so late?"

"Waiting for you," I answered.

"Por me?" Tala asked. "What you want wid me?"

"Within the next couple of days, I'm having a barbecue for Sergeant Tejada, the policeman who helped me fix Mari's teeth and took care of your ex-boyfriend."

"Okay?"

"Well, it wouldn't be right if Mari wasn't there to help us thank him," I told her. "Do you mind if she hangs out with us for a little while? If you want, I'll pay your bar fine that day so that you can be here too to watch her around…"

Tala grimaced and held her hand up to make me stop talking. "You no pay my bar pine, Doyle. No one hab to pay me to spend time with my daughter." Tala then buried her face in her hands. "Dat what you t'ink? You have to pay me to be wit Mari?"

"Hey, Tala," I pled. "I didn't mean to make you feel bad."

Shaking her head, Mari's mother said, "I tell Mari to stay away prom you, Doyle. And now she hate me. She hate me. She no believe I trying to keep her prom breaking her heart."

"Tala, I know that you're trying to protect her. One day, she will too."

"She never have anybody to take care op her but me," Tala cried. "It no pair dat I have to keep her away prom people who be nice to her to protect her! I no know when she get dat chance again to meet someone who nice to her like you."

Tala looked around for a place to get off of her feet, sitting herself down on the bench of our picnic table. I took a seat next to her and awkwardly put my arm around her shoulder, trying to comfort her. "She's a special kid, Tala. She'll be alright."

After a long sigh, Tala took a moment to compose herself and then wiped the tears out of her eyes. "She be alright. Everyt'ing will be alright. Americans always say t'ings like dat. Maybe t'ings always work out in da US. Dey never work out por people like me and Mari. Not here. Doyle, when you leave da Philippines, ip Mari write you letters, you t'ink you can write her back?"

I flinched in surprise. "Of course, I would. Tala, I'd love that!" Despite my best efforts, my voice cracked. "I've been in the Navy for four years. I've never gotten mail before. Well, mail that wasn't some sort of bill or official document, anyway. I never got a letter."

"You never got a letter?" Tala asked. "Why not?"

I shrugged. "Well, I'm kind of an asshole and nobody likes me."

Tala busted out laughing. "No, seriously, how come you no get mail?"

"I'm a foster child. I don't have any family and my friends from back home, well, they're not into things like literacy. They're into punk rock."

"What happen to you pamily?"

"That's a long story and it's too late to get into it now. Can I tell you all about it in a couple of days when we have our barbecue?"

Tala smiled and patted my knee. "Okay. I tired too. I gonna go to bed. I make you tell me everyt'ing at da party. Alright?"

"Okay. I'll see you then."

Tala stood up to walk back to her place. After a couple of steps, though, she turned to face me again. "Doyle, porget what I say you about Mari. Ip you want to see her again, it okay."

That made me much happier than I would have expected it to. "Thank you, Tala. Good night."

Waving at me, Mari's mother wished me sweet dreams before walking away. As she ascended the steps, I found that I could not take my eyes off of her. It defied belief that a woman subjected to so much hardship could be so stunning. I wanted her, but I worried about the potential I had to hurt Tala and Mari.

I needed somebody, though. I thought about Yukiko back in Japan. She might not have been as heart-stopping as Tala was, but she was certainly no slouch. She was exotic and sophisticated. My physical attraction to her aside, I could see the two of us enjoying long, meaningful conversations together. Yukiko and I had more in common, not to mention we shared a traumatic experience, having both witnessed the murder of David Miller. The two of us would be far more compatible than Tala and I would be.

Mari's mother was no idiot, but she never had anything other than a rudimentary education. As intensely as my body longed for her, I had a hard time imagining us ever connecting on an intellectual level. I feared that once the sexual novelty wore off, she would end up more a servant than a partner.

I could not imagine Yukiko ever falling into a role like that and wished I had a way to get in touch with her. I remembered her reaching out to me as she was led out of the park the night Miller died. I asked if she would meet me when we got back. "Yes! I will!" she said. "We'll go see the monkeys!"

Playing that memory over again in my mind, I felt that maybe there was something else there. The two of us saw something horrific that night, but I also thought we made a connection. Perhaps she saw something in the way I handled myself that made her reconsider how she felt about me. I was not sure, but I wanted to get back to Japan soon and find out.

I doubted that I could wait that long, though. That became crystal clear as I caught the silhouette of Tala's body as she ducked into her apartment.

*****

J.E. PARK

CHAPTER 17

I suspected that things were going to go sideways when Anna, Tony Bard's girlfriend, dragged a plastic kiddie pool into our living room. I knew it for sure when Dixie's girl *du jour*, Elena, started filling it with booze. They must have poured six bottles of rum in there. Then they added another half dozen fifths of cherry brandy, at least twelve cans each of Red Horse Beer, Coca-Cola, orange soda, and 7-Up. Finally, they finished it up with a couple of jugs of pineapple juice and ice. It was delicious, though a bit reminiscent of the Bullfrog that knocked me comatose during my first night in town.

"That's good," I told the girls, complimenting them as I licked my lips after my first sip. "What is it?"

"Mojo," Elena told me, giggling. "You betta be carepul wid dis stupp dough! It get you bery drunk, bery quick!"

She did not have to tell me twice. I had one cup and spent an hour on the couch, content to watch the geckos running the walls until our guests started showing up. That was my reminder to start cooking Tejada's ribs.

The turnout for our party was incredible. Lorna, our master chief's girlfriend, was able to get us a great deal on meat from the grocery she managed. We were not only able to feed our entire division, but every resident of the four apartments in our building as well. In addition to Sergeant Tejada, his wife, Mayte, and his three kids, we also hosted a few of his PNP colleagues. A pair of them were in uniform and on duty. We even had a troop of *matsing*, the local species of Philippine macaque, show up and take seats upon the wall in the rear of the complex.

Claude Metaire, who I had not seen much of since landing in the Philippines, saw them first and got very excited. "Doyle! Doyle! Look ovair zhere!" he exclaimed in his thick Guianan accent. "Monkays!"

"Monkeys!" I said as I spun around. "No shit?" Up to that point, I had heard them chattering but had never actually seen them.

I grew up near Detroit, Michigan. Because of that, some things would always seem exotic to me, no matter how often I saw them. One of them was palm trees. The other was monkeys. I was grilling when Claude told me about our visitors, but I could not stop myself from dropping everything to look at the *matsing* with him.

"*Mon Dieu,*" Metaire said as he took a couple of steps to get a closer look at the animals.

"Be careful, Claude," I tried to warn him. "Don't get too close. And whatever you do, don't look them in the eye."

"What?" Metaire asked. "Why you no look zhem in zee eye?"

"It's a sign of aggression," I had seen that on National Geographic once. "It means you're challenging their position in the group's social hierarchy."

"Wha? Zhat sounds like *merde*." To prove me wrong, Metaire went as close as he dared to the biggest monkey on the wall. He then made the goofiest face he could and looked the animal right in the eye, barking like a seal to get its attention.

All of us had, at one time or another, heard the term "going ape-shit." Until Claude Metaire accidentally challenged an alpha macaque's mating privileges, however, none of us had ever seen it in a literal sense. We were impressed. With an ear-splitting shriek that stopped all conversation, the creature leapt from the wall. It then bared its teeth and charged what it understood to be a six-foot-tall romantic rival. Metaire shrieked too, though at an octave that was far higher than the monkey's. He then ran for his life.

What followed next was pure pandemonium. People were screaming and running in all directions. They were not that afraid of the monkey but had to move fast to keep from being plowed over by Claude. The children sought shelter beneath the picnic table. The adults ran up the stairs and through the gates into the street. Metaire ran everywhere else.

Claude was an athletic man. I watched him circle the courtyard three times in mere seconds. He then got halfway up the steps before leaping back to the ground when he saw his little beast gaining on him. There was no way that Claude could outrun the monkey, but I suspected that the monkey did not really want to capture Metaire, either. The *matsing* had the upper hand, but looking at it from the monkey's point of view, Claude Metaire was four times the creature's size. He was also ten times its weight. It seemed wise enough to know how much damage it could sustain if it actually caught his quarry.

After several laps around the courtyard, Claude decided that he needed out. He dashed for the gate leading to the street, but the monkey cut him off and forced him in the other direction. With a running start, Metaire then demonstrated an amazing feat of parkour. He stepped on a chair, pushed off against the side of our building, and landed atop the back wall of our yard. As the rest of the monkeys scattered out of his way, Claude then bounded up into one of the trees for safety.

Like the *matsing*, humans are primates. We instinctively know that when something is chasing us, our safest course is to seek higher ground. We rush for the treetops. This makes sense when you're being chased by a saber-toothed tiger, a Shi-Tzu with attitude issues, or your girlfriend's irate husband. It makes less sense when you are being attacked by a long-tailed macaque, however. They live in trees.

By the time Claude stabilized himself on a branch big enough to support his weight, his pint-sized assailant was waiting for him. It gave my man a second good look at his fangs, let out another shriek, and charged once more. Metaire lost his grip and fell on his back atop the wall. He screamed out in agony, then let gravity make him its bitch, dropping violently onto the turf head-first. It was a brutal fall and I thought for sure that Claude had killed himself. The females of the monkey troop then decided to add insult to injury. Screaming a chorus of simian insults at Metaire, they celebrated his defeat by tossing feces at the guy. It was one of the harshest rejections I had ever born witness to.

OLONGAPO EARP

Claude should have been dead, but aside from a few scratches on his back and shoulders, he was otherwise unharmed. Once we saw that he was alright, the party roared with laughter.

None more so than Tala. She usually had a smile on her face. That was part of her job. There was never any genuine merriment behind it, though. This time, however, she laughed like she meant it. She was gasping for air with her arms around her belly, trying to contain herself, but failing spectacularly. She was gorgeous, and I found myself unable to look away from her.

When Tala could catch her breath again, she caught me staring at her. Seeming not to care, she wiped the tears from her eyes, gave me a little wave, then walked over to the picnic table to share the laugh with her daughter. She had dressed down, wearing denim shorts, a simple tee shirt, and no makeup, but never had I seen her more desirable. I started to walk over to talk to her but stopped myself. I remembered what getting involved with a bar girl did to Randy Green. I turned around and forced myself to go back to cooking my ribs.

Decomposing manatees.
Eyeballs pierced with darts.
Richard Nixon naked blowing bloody liquid farts.

*****

Claude Metaire's fight with the monkey set the stage for the rest of the day. The music went loud and the bar girls in attendance called their friends. Before we knew it, our little place on Harris Street was livelier than the nightclubs on Magsaysay.

Defying belief, we drained the pool full of Mojo in two hours. It was quickly refilled, though not at all to the recipe. It seemed that everyone that arrived brought something to add to it: vodka, whiskey, soda, beer, or some sort of fruit juice. At times, what was in the pool tasted better than the Mojo. At other times it could, and did, induce vomiting.

At about seven, when the punch was at one of its low-water marks, Rick Hammond noticed a dead lizard lying in the bottom of the pool. Our best guess was that one of the geckos had fallen off the ceiling and drowned in it. Our party came to a screeching halt as we fished the reptile from our beverage and put it in a makeshift casket repurposed from a discarded matchbox. We then wrapped it in an American flag bandana we stole from Clay Fordson and took it outside on a funeral procession around the block. The PNP officers at the party rode in front of us with their lights on while we marched. Holding the tiny little coffin over our heads during the procession, we beat our chests, tore at our clothes, and pulled our hair to show our grief.

When we got back, we brought our cold-blooded comrade to the bathroom and held him over the toilet. Dixie then played "Taps" for him on a kazoo that Mari lent us before rendering the creature a crisp salute and flushing it down the commode. It was a proper burial at sea. After that, we spent forty-five minutes figuring out how to unclog the toilet without a plunger when the matchbox got lodged in the pipes.

Once we had a successful flush, we went back to drinking. In honor of our dearly departed guest, we rechristened the living room hooch "Gecko Stew." That pool full of booze stayed on the living room floor for almost the rest of the time we were in Olongapo. It was replenished continuously by nearly everyone who walked through our door.

Despite teetering on the edge of alcoholic psychosis for much of that day, I did spend some quality time with Mari and a couple of Tejada's kids. I bought my little friend a board game the day Tala told me I could see her again. At a point when the antics of our guests started exceeding the bounds of what was appropriate for children's eyes, I snuck the youngsters up to Tala's apartment and played *Sorry!* with them a few times.

When I emerged from Tala's place, I spotted Master Chief Darrow and Tony Bard arguing over the merits of the submarine versus surface fleets. Bard was a former submariner. The *USS Belleau Wood* was the first vessel he served upon that traveled above the waves. Our master chief had spent three decades attached to the surface fleet. It started as good-natured ribbing. As often happens when highly intoxicated people kid, though, someone crossed a line and it stopped being fun.

After Darrow made a comment about 100 sailors descending to the depths only to come up as fifty couples, Bard turned red. Tony was not a fighter, so he decided to end the discussion by turning around and walking away. Before our LPO took two steps, though, Darrow dropped to his knees, grabbed Bard's shorts, and ripped them right down to his ankles, underwear and all. Tony was mid-step when it happened, so his feet got tangled up, and he fell to the ground. This allowed Darrow to rip his shorts completely off, which he then tossed over the gate and into the street.

At first, Tony looked mortified as the party once again erupted into laughter. After a moment, though, he just shrugged and started dancing his way to the street to get his clothes back. Adding to the hilarity, Bard would wave his pecker threateningly at anyone who got too close. When he came back, Tony was dressed and laughing with the rest of us. He strolled right up to Master Chief Darrow with his hand outstretched. "That was a good one," Bard admitted. "No hard feelings."

"No hard feelings," Darrow said back, reaching out to shake hands. Before he could stop it, though, Bard dodged and went to pants the master chief.

Tony did not get the full article as Darrow did. He just got his outerwear. Still, he took the master chief's shorts right down to his ankles, leaving him standing there in a pair of pink Hello Kitty boxer shorts. Again, the crowd melted down, roaring at Darrow's choice in underwear.

Lorna, the master chief's girlfriend, was gasping for air. "Oh my god," she cried, trying to explain things to Tala. "He gonna kill me! I bought dem por him por joke and I tell him por days, 'Why you no wear dose underwear I buy you?' He pinally wear dem por da pirst time today!" She was laughing so hard that we could not understand the rest of what she said.

*****

Nearly everyone had left the party by midnight so that they could make it back before the one o'clock curfew. A half dozen of our men were too drunk to go anywhere, though, so we let them stay. Most of them passed out on the living room floor next to the pool of Gecko Stew.

Bard and Dixie eventually retired to their rooms with their girls. I made my way back down to the courtyard to relax with a final cigarette before going to bed. As I lay back on top of the picnic table, Tala snuck up to me and took a seat at my side. "Can I borrow a cigarette prom you?" she asked.

"Sure," I said, smiling as I handed her the pack.

"It be a bery busy day por you, no?" Tala asked as she lit her smoke. "You look bery tired."

"I am," I told her. "It was worth it, though. I had a good time. How about you?"

Tala returned my smile, crossed her arms upon the table, and rested her head upon them. "I did. I hab bery good time. Mari too. She say dat you sneak away prom da party and play dat game wit her and da udder kids. She say dat was a lot op pun por her."

"It was fun for me too. That's kind of what I thought having a family was supposed to be like, you know? It was nice."

"Do you remember da udder day? When you say you tell me what happen to your pamily?"

I nodded, my smile disappearing. It had been a good day and I did not want to ruin it by going back there. Still, I had promised. Since I did not see Tala that often, this would be one of the few opportunities I would have to ease her curiosity. "My dad killed my family. My mother, my sister, and my little brother."

Tala gasped and brought her hand to her mouth. "Oh my god! Why?"

I admitted that I did not know the exact thing that had set it off. "I wasn't there when it happened. I guess that it was the natural culmination of the abuse he'd been dishing out on us for years."

"Where you go apter dat? Da Navy?"

"No, I was only 13. I spent five years with a foster family."

"Poster Pamily. A pamily take care of you? Were dey nice?"

I shrugged. "Better than living with my father. They fostered me because they needed the money. It was actually a good arrangement. I had been through a lot by that time, so I was pretty mature for my age. I did everything they expected me to do to earn my keep, and they didn't take advantage of the situation. We were roommates. They kept the money the state gave them to take care of me, and they let me keep whatever I earned on my own. For the most part, I stayed out of their way, and they let me do whatever I wanted as long as I didn't get into any trouble."

"Dey no write you letters?"

"Nope," I told her, shaking my head. "I haven't spoken to them since I left for boot camp."

"You no like each udder?"

"Naw, it's not like that," I said. "They're a little odd, you know? It's like they're emotionally stunted. They never went anywhere, they never did anything, and both of their families were just like them. My foster parents did not even connect to each other, so it was nothing personal. You know, when I think back to my high school years, the two of them hardly register. All my memories are of friends, classmates, and co-workers. I didn't dislike my foster parents; we just had nothing in common."

That was not the first time I told someone of my foster family. Usually, they told me it was sad that I went through that period of my life without parents that loved me, but Tala did not. I bet she would have rather gone through what I did than deal with what she had to at that age. I know that I would not have wanted to trade places with her.

"How about your family?" I asked her. "Have you seen them since they kicked you out?"

Tala shook her head as I rolled over onto my side to face her. We were now a little closer than was comfortable, but neither of us made any effort to move. "No. When dey get rid op me, I neber want see dem again. Ever. When I child, dey okay, but lipe bery hard por us. We all work bery hard to survive. There was neber time por us to enjoy each udder, to be happy together like udder people. So, it no like when I leave, dat I leaving much behind."

I understood. "So you don't have any happy childhood memories either, eh?"

"Nah, I remember being hungry, always have mud on my peet, on my hands. I remember I always scared op da gang boys. Scared op da police, or op da soldiers, too. We at da bottom op da ladder in my home. We da garbage. Everyone do to us what dey want. No happy memories op being a child. As much as I hate my lipe, it better now dan it be den."

"What about since you left? Do you have happy memories of now?"

Tala pursed her lips as she thought for a moment. "Well, I no hungry all da time anymore. And I remember having Mari, someone I love more dan anyt'ing." Even in the dark, I could see tears welling up in Tala's eyes as a particularly good memory came to her. "I remember da first time Mari told me she love me too. I just get here in Olongapo. We hab not'ing to eat, nowhere to sleep, and no place to go. I was sitting wit her on da beach, Baloy Beach, crying and wondering what we gonna do. Mari look up to me and say, '*Mahal kita, Inay. Mahal kita.*' I spend da whole night under da stars wit her, rocking Mari back and fort.' Da two op us tell how much we love each udder all night long."

That sounded like Mari. I smiled. "Were there any more good times?"

"Yeah, anytime I get to do somet'ing wit Mari is a good memory. The first time she go to da good school, I bery happy. I happy when I take her to Jollibee. I happy when I come home, and she tell me all about how nice to her you are. I happy today at da party. I bery happy now, talking to you."

Tala leaned in, moving her lips a little closer to mine. I reciprocated, inching my face closer to hers to see what she would do. She moved forward a little more, then both of us surrendered and went in for the kiss. Right before our lips met, though, my mind raced to what Randy Green told me the day that I nearly killed him.

"...she made me this way! If only she'd not go out when I was on duty! If only she looked at me as something more than a ticket to the United States! I know! I know! Some of it's my fault! I should've never married a whore but..."

Rafaela had not made Green into the monster that he was. She was just the key that let all his demons out. Randy loved her. He could not bear the thought of her cheating on him even though her acts of infidelity existed only in his mind. It drove him mad. It could drive me mad, too, if I got emotionally invested with a bar girl.

I pulled back from Tala just as a vision of my father popped into my head. His face twisted in rage as he searched for my mother. Clenching my eyes closed to try to force him away before a full-blown episode came on, I backed up. "I'm sorry, Tala, I'm so sorry. I can't do this."

Tala pulled back also, nervously bobbing her head in understanding. "I know, Doyle. I know. I sorry. I know better, but..." Tala choked, trying to collect herself as she stood up from the picnic table. "It okay. You no owe me anyt'ing. I..."

Running away back to her apartment, she turned back to me and said, "No, it okay. It late, and time por us to go to bed. I see you some udder time, Doyle."

"No, look, Tala, please. Listen to me for a moment," I pled as I rolled off of the picnic table to go after her. "Please!"

OLONGAPO EARP

It was too late. By the time I reached the stairs, Tala was already inside her apartment. Still calling for her, I bounded up the steps to the second floor. I was ready to pound on her door to explain, but I stopped myself.

I realized that there was nothing I could say that would make Tala feel better. The best thing I could do for her was to have the decency to walk away and not make everything worse.

*****

CHAPTER 18

I did not sleep that evening. Under a great deal of stress and no small amount of sexual tension, I feared that I might have an episode coming on. That was something I did not want to deal with when I had several shipmates passed out on my living room floor. I was able to control my breakdowns, but at great personal expense. It was exhausting to repress my issues and the longer I pushed them off, the worse they got when they did eventually break through. When the sun finally rose after a very long night, I made the rounds, waking people up. Then I went outside to summon a small fleet of trikes to get us all back to base on time.

At morning quarters, Lieutenant Krause knew that most of us had been through an epic bender the night before. If word had not gotten back to him about what had happened at my place, he could see it during muster. Thirty men of the CSE Division stood before him, sweating the rancid remnants of Gecko Stew through their pores. They were all rubbing red, sleep-deprived eyes, and a few of them had not yet gotten enough alcohol out of their systems to stand up straight at roll call. Our lieutenant thought it the perfect time to announce a field day to present the spaces for his inspection by ten hundred. This cut into the sleep I was planning on getting that morning, but it did not affect me much otherwise since I was on duty that day anyway.

I found that the Radar Repair Shop's spaces were already in excellent shape when I got to my office. I asked Palazzo and Kent, who had been on duty the previous day, if they had cleaned up our areas.

Palazzo nodded. "Krause was the Officer of the Deck yesterday when some of the drunks started pouring in from your party. I overheard him telling the Petty Officer of the Watch that he was going to do this to mess with you guys. Steve and I want to get out of here early so we can try to get to Manila. We know none of us are leaving until we're all cleared by the lieutenant, so we thought we'd get a head start on this stuff."

I nodded my head. "Smart move. Manila, eh?"

Kent grinned. "Yeah, they've got four entertainment districts. My god, the girls are smoking up there!"

"You know that Manila is outside of the quarantine area, right?"

"Yeah, well, there was a curfew in Tijuana too that you guys always ignored," Palazzo said. "I figure it's not wrong if you don't get caught."

"So, the two of you have been hitting every red-light district on Luzon?" I asked. "Is that your plan?"

Kent laughed. "That's the plan. We've done two of the districts in Manila. We did Angeles City…"

"I thought Pinatubo blew that place off of the map."

Palazzo shook his head. "No, it's pretty messed up from the eruption, but there's still a few bikini bars open over that way."

"And those places are off of the charts!" Kent exclaimed, his exuberance getting the best of him. "You would not believe the stuff the girls do to you up there!"

"Yeah? Like what?" I asked. Kent was excited. He was also young and wanted to fit in with the rest of the CSE veterans. Steve had heard the stories of our exploits, and I sensed that he wanted to earn one of the Tequila Viking tattoos that some of us had on our arms. He wanted in so bad and was desperate to show me that he could be just as crazy as the other guys. I wondered if he was naïve enough to walk into a trap if I set it right. "What'd the girls do to you in Angeles?" I asked.

Kent looked back at Palazzo as if checking to see if this was something he should be talking about. This made John burst out laughing and get up from his seat to leave the shop. "Dude," Palazzo said to Kent. "Tell him whatever you want. I can't listen to it again, though."

I was genuinely interested now. Palazzo was one of the most sex-obsessed men I had ever met. If Kent had done something outlandish enough to make him leave the room, I had to hear what it was. Once Palazzo was gone, Steve lowered his voice to a conspiratorial tone and asked, "Doyle, you ever been cuffed to a bed?"

"You forget what I told you about Hawaii?"

"Oh yeah," Steve said, laughing. "So anyway, this girl takes me back to her room, right? We get undressed, and she starts working me all over. Anyway, I blow my wad, but she's not done with me yet. She's trying to get me going again, but I'm drunk and tired, and all I want to do is take a nap. So, I doze off for a few, and the next thing I know, I wake up handcuffed to the headboard. This chick is sitting on my stomach, showing me this big long length of steel balls on a string. Dude, there was nothing I could do about it. I tried to fight her off, but even while I'm struggling, she shoves these things up my fuckin' ass."

I was taking a drink of coffee when Kent said that last part, and I shot it out of my nose. "She did what?!?"

"She shoved them right up my ass! I know this sounds gay, but, man, I did NOT consent to this shit! So anyway, she jumps back on me and starts rubbing herself on my junk while working this string coming out of my butt. Next thing I know, I'm hard as a rock! And lasting forever! This girl's going crazy on me, too! The bed's jumping all over the place, shit's falling off the nightstand, and this chick's screaming bloody murder! Man, it had to sound like someone was getting murdered in there!"

I was laughing now, howling as Kent told me what had happened. Steve completely let his guard down and started really getting into his story. "Now, once she was satisfied, this girl sets to finishing me off. She clenched herself tight around me, working herself up and down my dick. While she's doing this, she starts pulling these steel balls out of my ass, one by one. Every one of these things coming out sets off this sensation like I ain't ever felt before! Then, when she senses that I'm getting ready to cum, she rips the rest of them out all at once. Pulls the cord like she's trying to start a fuckin' lawnmower!"

"Oh my God," I laughed, gasping for air. "What'd that do to you?"

OLONGAPO EARP

Kent's eyes were wide open as if he was having a hard time believing his own story. "Dude, I thought I had a stroke. It's like I started convulsing and lost control of every bodily function all at once. Cum, piss, shit, snot, sweat, tears…everything started flying out everywhere! I'm pretty sure I passed out. The next thing I know, the cuffs are off, and she's trying to get me to quit crying so we could go clean up."

Roaring with laughter, I asked, "She made you cry?"

"Yeah, but not like you're thinking. I wasn't sad or hurt; it was like I'd just seen the face of God or something. I was overwhelmed with this sense of spiritual ecstasy, yet I knew that I'd never experience that sort of thing ever again. You can't if you know it's coming."

It took a couple of minutes for me to collect myself. "Dude, that is some of the most twisted shit I've ever heard! You're a fuckin' animal! Man, Kent, you've earned your Tequila Viking tattoo."

Kent's eyes lit up. "Seriously?!? I earned my ink?"

Wiping the tears from my eyes, I nodded and said, "Yeah. You did. Oh my god, that was hilarious. That shit happened in Manila?"

"No, Angeles City."

"Oh yeah, that's right. Can you get shit like that in Manila?"

"I don't know," Kent answered. "It's not as if it's written on a menu. Hell, even if it was, I don't even know what you'd call it."

"You guys been anywhere else?" I asked, dangling the bait.

Kent nodded. "We heard about a place up in Baguio. Couldn't find anything there, though. We came back."

"Barrio Barretto?"

"Of course."

"Quezon?"

"You heard about somewhere in Quezon?" Kent asked. "We pass through there going to Manila."

"Pagsanjan?"

"Ha! Yeah, we…" Kent caught himself just before he sprung my trap. The expression on his face went from levity and bravado to fear. "I…uh…no, we didn't…"

"Bullshit." I was not laughing anymore. "You fuckers went to Pagsanjan, didn't you?"

"Hey, Doyle, you got it all wrong. We…"

I remembered Tala telling me about how when she was too young to work in Olongapo, people took her to Pagsanjan. I bet she had to service fat, disgusting fucks like Steve Kent and John Palazzo. I stood up and grabbed Kent by his shirt, ripping him out of his seat and throwing him up hard against the workbench. I was careful to keep my voice down so I did not attract the attention of anyone passing by our office door. "You fucking went to Pagsanjan, didn't you? You like kids, Kent?"

"N-n-n-n-no, Doyle! We went rafting! On the river out there! We signed up for that trip here on the ship!"

"And you didn't mess with any of the girls out there?"

"No! Christ! No! Well, we met a couple of girls in the bar, but we didn't mess with any of those kids! I swear, Doyle! I swear! We didn't even see anything like that!"

"What about Palazzo? Did he do anything out there?"

"Just the same thing I did!"

"Were you together the whole time?" I snarled.

"Yes! Yes! I fucking swear it!"

"Did he talk about wanting to check out anything like that? Ask around for anything? Mention the word *pam-pam*?"

"*Pam-pam*? What the fuck's a *pam-pam*?" Kent cried. "No! No! Christ, even if he did want to check out something like that, there's no way he'd dare after seeing Krause patrolling the place!"

I released my grip on Kent's shirt. "You saw Krause in Pagsanjan?"

Steve nodded energetically. "Yeah! He was around the bus stop!"

"Did he see you?"

Kent shook his head with equal enthusiasm. "No, I don't think so. Once he saw everyone was coming off in an organized group, he walked away. I think he was looking for people coming out there on their own."

I stared at Kent for a moment, watching him shake. I was convinced that he had no desire to see the seedier side of Pagsanjan, but he had given me nothing that would exonerate Palazzo. John could have convinced Kent to go out there with him to scope out the place and gotten spooked when he saw Krause. Kent and Palazzo were in the same duty section as our division officer. If Palazzo had wanted to get out there without the danger of running into the lieutenant, he would have to trade duty days with someone. As the first step in Palazzo's chain of command, I would have to approve the chit allowing the swap. At least I knew to put my guard up if Palazzo tried to get out of a duty day.

It was time to calm Kent down before somebody walked in on us. I gently slapped him on the cheek, *mafiosi* style. "Okay, Steve, relax. I believe you."

Kent exhaled a long breath, signaling his relief. "Thanks, Doyle. Please, I would never…"

"You hear about what I did to Randy Green, Steve?"

My new guy swallowed hard. "Yeah, I heard a few things."

"I want you to keep that in mind as I tell you that I don't want you talking about this conversation we had with anyone. You got that?"

"Yeah, Doyle, I got it,"

"Good. And if Palazzo suggests going to Pagsanjan for some younger entertainment, I want you to go along with it. As long as you tell me first, I'll make sure you come out of everything alright. Now, I don't want *you* suggesting the two of you go out there thinking you'll score brownie points with me. That ain't the way this shit works. I'm not looking to frame him. Palazzo's a pervert; that's no secret. I just want to make sure I don't have a fucking pederast in my shop, Steve. If he never brings it up, that's great. If he does, though, I'm going to see to it that he suffers. Any questions?"

"Can I still get my Tequila Viking ink?" Kent asked.

"Yeah, Speedy," I assured him. "You're demented enough to wear it." I then told him that he could go.

"Hey, Steve, one more thing," I said to him as I picked up the IC phone to call Master Chief Darrow. "What day was it that you saw Krause out in Pagsanjan?"

*****

I had had an exhausting duty day and a late watch. When we were relieved Thursday morning, I strolled down to the berthing area and collapsed into my rack. When I woke up, it was already after lunch.

With the ship's galley closed, I left and made myself a meal from the street vendors lined up across the Shit River bridge. Then, instead of taking a trike back to my place, I walked there just to take in the sights. I met a very cute young lady selling newspapers about a third of the way home. We talked for a little while and, encouraged by her effort in improving my Tagalog, I asked if she would let me buy her dinner later. She laughed and then suggested that the girls working Magsaysay Drive would be better able to serve my needs.

The girl who sold me a soft drink a few blocks from my house told me the same thing. So did another young woman who walked past me on the sidewalk when I tried to strike up a conversation. It was not my day.

I got to my apartment before two in the afternoon. Tala walked out of our broken security gate as I was stepping up. "Hi," I said to her as she turned her head my way. She was in her work dress, the Chinese-styled red one with the slit up the side of her leg. She had pulled her hair up into a bun and applied her makeup expertly. She looked like a supermodel. I had no doubt the night would be profitable for her. "Are you okay?" I asked her as we passed each other.

"Yes, I pine," Tala said. "Same as I always am." She was not smiling, not even in her usual fake way.

"Are you sure?" I asked.

Tala looked impatiently at the ground. "What you want me to say to you? Yes, Doyle. Everyt'ing good por me. Lipe never be better. Da puture is bright, and dere is not'ing but milk and honey por me and Mari por da rest op our lives. Dat make you peel better?"

I did not know how to respond. I just stood there looking dumb until Tala's trike pulled up in front of us and the driver asked her to step inside. "You hab what you want to know now? I need to go to work, Doyle."

Unless you can tell me something to convince me to stay home. Please, Doyle. I don't want to do this. Please don't let me do this. I don't know how much longer I can keep this up.

It was in her eyes. She was pleading for me to help her, to save her and her daughter. I wanted to reach out to her, to take her hand and do something for them, but what was I going to do? Make my life even more of a wreck for a prostitute that I had not even known for two weeks? Their lot in life was not fair, but it was also not fair that I seemed to be their last chance to escape it at the moment. They were not my responsibility.

So, I did nothing. I stood there mute as Tala stepped into the bike's sidecar and drove away to let herself be used over and over again. It broke my heart and turned my stomach, but there was nothing I could do about it.

OLONGAPO EARP

When she was finally out of sight, I turned to take the last few steps to my place, only to be stopped by Mari blocking my path. "*Halo*, Doyle."

"*Halo*, Mari," I said, forcing myself to smile.

"Can we play a game today?"

"Hmm," I answered as I thought for a moment. "How about we do something different and try the beach instead?"

*****

CHAPTER 19

Darrow was not pleased. He threw the pictures on the table and downed half a glass of straight vodka. "Look, anywhere in the world we go, no one ever has any trouble picking American servicemen out of a crowd. We all have the same haircuts. We have tattoos, sideburns, and mustaches. We all walk with the same swagger."

"Yeah. And all you guys dress like dorks," Sergeant Tejada said while looking directly at me.

"What?" I asked TJ while glancing over myself. I had on my usual liberty attire. I was wearing a bright Hawaiian shirt worn over a Billabong tee, cargo shorts, and deck shoes *sans* socks. "I spent years perfecting this look."

If Master Chief Darrow heard our exchange, he ignored it. "The perverts in these pictures aren't even military! Most of them are too fuckin' old! Hey! Look at this guy!" Darrow pointed at a picture of a man whose hair fell past his shoulders. "Who the fuck is this hippy? Huh? In what Navy does this guy serve? Greenpeace's?"

I picked up the picture and gave it a closer look. "Could be. He looks like he'd fit in as a deck ape on the *Rainbow Warrior*."

OLONGAPO EARP

"And these people," Darrow said as he grabbed another handful of photos. "These guys aren't even American, I bet! Those punks work the crowds in that area. They know the difference between an American and a goddamn Swede! I'm telling you, TJ, Favila's fucking with us!"

Letting out a long, tired sigh, I took a drink out of my beer. "Master Chief, don't you think it's a good thing that these guys aren't catching any of our people back in that shithole? It could mean the guys we serve with aren't fucking creeps."

Darrow slammed his palm on the table hard enough to make Lorna jump all the way over on the living room couch. "There's almost a thousand men on the *Belleau Wood*, Doyle. You can't get a thousand people from anywhere and not have at least five or ten of them not be worth a shit. You, of all people, should know that. I've never had a ship this size pull into this place and not caught a couple of assholes out in Pagsanjan. They're out there, Doyle. That fucker Favila's playing us."

Turning to Tejada, I asked, "That what you think, TJ?"

The policeman thought for a moment and then nodded his head. "Yeah, I tink so. Favila is protecting his bidness. He giving us pictures of people he know we can't touch and no taking picture op anyone he even tink may be in da Navy. Dat way we no bodder any op his customer."

I sighed. "So, what can we do about it?"

Tejada stood up from Lorna's table and adjusted his gun belt. "Tomorrow, I go back dere wit some op my boys and we gonna show dose guys dat dey not poolin' us. Make sure dat Paulino know dat da next time we come, we comin' por him ip he no come tru por us."

"That's not good enough," Darrow said. "I gotta go out there and see for myself. Krause was there four days ago. It's possible that we've already missed our opportunity with that son-of-a-bitch. I don't want to miss it on anyone else."

TJ shook his head. "You no goin' out dere, Brad. Dere people out dat way gonna cut you t'roat."

"I'll go with him," I said to Tejada. "I'll watch his back."

Darrow and TJ both protested that at the same time. "You can't fuckin' control yourself," my master chief told me. "I'm going in low key, watching the bus stop, seeing if I can find anyone heading in that direction."

Tejada again told Darrow to stay away from Pagsanjan, sparking an argument between the two men. Tired of the noise, Lorna turned off the television and went to bed. I stood up from the table, got myself another beer, then went outside to smoke in the street. I was on my second cigarette when Tejada stormed out of the door. "Good night, Sergeant," I said to him as he passed.

"Puck both you maddapukkas!"

Darrow came out a couple of minutes later. "C'mon, Doyle," he said. "Let's go get fucked up."

I shook my head. "I'm going to take a pass. Me and Mari went to the beach today and I'm all wiped out. Besides, I'm already pretty fucked up."

Master Chief glowered at me. "What's the matter with you?"

"What? What do you mean?"

"What do I mean? You've been mopin' around all night. What's bothering you?"

I shrugged. "I'm fine. Look, I just don't want…"

"It's that little girl's mother, isn't it? Tala?"

My face told Darrow everything he needed to know. "Jesus Christ, Doyle!" my master chief exclaimed. "What's your goddamn problem here? If you like her, go for it!"

"I don't pay for sex, Master Chief."

"Then don't! For Christ's sake, I saw her giving you those googly eyes the whole time we were at the party, Doyle! Ask her to hang back with you the rest of the time we're here. I bet she'd leap at the chance to stay with you for a while. When we leave, give her some cash to help them out. Not as payment for her services, but because you want to."

"Master Chief, I don't want to get attached to her."

Darrow smacked the side of my head. "Dipshit, you already are. You're spending time with that little girl like she's your own kid. That's not a bad thing, man. Hell, it's the reason we like you so goddamn much. You care about shit like this."

"But Master Chief, if I cross that line, if I let Tala and Mari all the way in, how the hell do I leave them when we're done here? We're gone in a couple of weeks!"

Darrow took his index finger and jabbed it hard into my chest. "That's the easy part because you don't have any say in the matter. When the

OLONGAPO EARP

Belleau Wood pulls away from that pier, your ass is on it no matter what you want to do. You know that. Hell, Doyle, she knows that."

"But…"

My master chief reached out and put his hand around my neck. "Look, we've only got a little more time left here. You can spend it tearing yourself apart the rest of the time we're in Olongapo. Or, you can just give in and see to it that you, Tala, and that little girl have the time of your lives while we're in port. Can you imagine how happy Mari would be to have both you and her mother spending time with her from now until we leave?"

I turned around and leaned up against the wall as I finished off my beer. Master Chief Darrow was an insanely persuasive human being. Especially when I was drunk. "Fuck it. Fine. Let's go to Barrio Barretto."

*****

Before setting out for the Pagoda Bar, Master Chief Darrow had the trike we hired take us in the opposite direction. "Where are we going?" I asked.

"To see a *manananggut*."

"A what?"

"A *manananggut*."

That word was not in my vocabulary. "What the hell is a *manananggut*?"

"You'll see. You're going to love this."

I discovered that a *manananggut* was a type of Filipino moonshiner. Master Chief Darrow's guy was in his fifties. He lived closer to the coast in a bamboo shack tucked in amongst a small forest of coconut trees. His name was Datu, and every day he climbed atop the palms, which was an impressive feat for a man his age. Three stories above the ground, he cut the fruit stalks with a curved knife, collecting the sap in a bamboo container overnight. By the time morning came around, the palm juice had already fermented to the same level as a strong beer. It was then sold to the locals as something called *tuba*.

"How do you like it?" Darrow asked me as I took my first pull from a plastic gallon jug. We bought it for less than the cost of a single beer in town.

"It's sweet," I answered, handing the jug back to my master chief. "And fizzy. It's good, though. How come I never heard of this stuff before?"

"You don't see it much around here. It's more common on Cebu. Still, they can't serve it in bars or restaurants, so that's why foreigners never hear about it."

"Really? Why can't they serve it? It doesn't seem all that strong. It's illegal?"

Darrow shook his head. "No, it's not against the law; they just can't make it stay *tuba*. After a few days, it turns into something called *suka bisaya*, a type of vinegar. What we're drinking now is the fresh stuff."

Having loaded ourselves up with palm wine, we got back into the trike. On our way to Barrio Barretto, we guzzled *tuba* as if we expected it to go bad before we passed Magsaysay. Neither Darrow nor I were sober when we left Lorna's place, but by the time we got to the Pagoda Bar, the two of us were smashed. As I fell out of the trike's sidecar, I forgot where we were going or what I was going to do there. My master chief had to point me toward the door of the Pagoda and remind me of my mission.

"What am I supposed to do?" I asked Darrow. "Go in there and kidnap her? Throw her over my shoulder and walk out? I mean, I'm sure Tala would love to see me walk in drunk and make a scene where she works. Chicks dig that kind of thing, right?"

Darrow put his hand on my shoulder, more to steady himself than to make a point. "Just talk to her. Let her know that you don't know how things will work out, but you want to give this thing with her a try. If she says yes, walk out of that place with Tala on your arm. If she asks you to pay her bar fine, run out of there without her."

"Okay," I said, turning around and stumbling into the Pagoda. Before I took two steps, though, I asked myself, *What the hell do I think I'm doing?*

From a physical standpoint, I wanted Tala even more than I wanted Yukiko. Could I get past her line of work, though? I understood that she was only doing it to provide for her daughter, but she was still a prostitute. Was I capable of putting that aside? As I walked through the door, even in my alcoholic fog, I suddenly decided that I was not.

Before I could leave, though, I took a good look around the bar. It was getting late, and business was dying down. There were a half dozen girls working the floor and about eight customers. I caught sight of the bubbly young girl who first approached me the last time I was there. She was tucked away in a back corner, getting mauled by some greasy old loser. He was sucking on her neck while she stared off into space. She looked impatient for the geezer to pay her bar fine and get everything over with. It was obvious that she wanted to be somewhere else. Anywhere else.

I tried to wrap my head around what it must have been like for these women to rent their bodies out to men that they would not have dared touch otherwise. Day in, day out, over and over and over again. I could not think of a more dehumanizing existence.

Cursing to myself, I started walking to the bar. I still had no desire to get myself mixed up with a bar girl, but Tala was Mari's mother. I could not stand the thought of her having to go through what she did to take care of her daughter. I needed to get her out of that place.

As I approached the bar, the tender looked at me and smiled seductively. "Hi, Joe! Can I help you?"

"Yeah," I answered. "Can I talk to Tala?"

"Who?"

Bar names, dammit! Bar names. "Tina. The short girl."

"Tina? No, I so sorry. She no here."

I cursed again. "Do you know where she is?" I doubted the barmaid knew. Someone probably paid her "long-time" fee.

"No, I no know. She no work here no more."

That gave me pause. I saw her dressed for the Pagoda just hours before. "Are you sure?"

The barmaid nodded. "Yeah, she quit today. She come into work and say she no do dis anymore. She say she goin' home."

*****

"Hey! Hey, you! Squid!" I was through the Pagoda's door when I heard someone calling to me, but since I was already outside, I kept going. Before I got down the front steps, though, the door burst open, and whoever it was shouted, "Hey! I'm talking to you, goddammit!"

I intended to ignore him, but the voice sounded familiar. It was the Marine I had met the last time I was at the Pagoda. Too drunk for his name to roll off my tongue, I had to mine it out of my memory. When it came to me, I pointed my finger at him, "Mulvaney, right?"

"Yeah, that's right," the Marine said as he stepped into my personal space. "I heard you and a couple of your buddies fucked up a friend of mine."

I grinned. "That's right. We messed him up pretty bad. I guess your boy ain't shit unless he's beating up little girls."

"Is there a problem here?" Master Chief Darrow asked, stepping up to us.

"There's no problem here, old man," the leatherneck growled. "Mind your own fuckin' business."

"Murphy, who the hell is this?"

"A big fan of yours, Master Chief. He was talking about you the whole way back to Olongapo. This is Terry Mulvaney, the cocksucker that followed me home and told Tala's ex where to find her."

"A big fan of who?" Mulvaney asked, a little bit perplexed. Looking at Darrow, he then asked, "Who the fuck are you?"

I could not help but laugh. "That's Olongapo Earp, dick spit."

What the Marine did next was entirely inexplicable. I could only imagine that the stories he heard about Olongapo Earp spooked him. Sensing what my master chief might do to him, he must have decided to hit Darrow before the master chief could hit him first. When Darrow got close enough, Mulvaney tried to take a swing at him.

He did not even come close to hitting his target, though. The Marine bunched his fist and cocked his arm back, but before he could fire, I hooked my own arm under his and stopped him from throwing the punch. Darrow then dealt out a brutal blow to the jaw that knocked Mulvaney back into me. That allowed me to get around his other arm and put him in a full nelson. Then Darrow shattered the Marine's nose.

My master chief hit the man twice more in the face, splitting his lip wide open. He then nailed him in the gut with everything he had. Mulvaney retched, throwing up all over his feet. "Let him go now, Doyle."

When I released Mulvaney, the Marine dropped to the ground into his own vomit. Right about then, a trio of local toughs who had stumbled upon the fight stepped up and started goading us. I had a feeling of *déjà vu*, as the situation I got us into in Pagsanjan threatened to replay itself in Barrio

OLONGAPO EARP

Barreto. It looked as if hoodlums all over the Philippines took their roles as shantytown peacekeepers very seriously. "You t'ink you tough guys? Two boys against one? Dat chickenshit! Who you t'ink you are?"

My master chief laughed. "Who do I think I am? Weren't you listening? I'M OLONGAPO MOTHERFUCKIN' EARP!!"

"Olongapo Earp? Dat bullshi…" Before the punk could finish his sentence, Darrow hit him so hard that a bloody wad of snot flew out of his nose. It passed through three feet of air before landing on one of his buddies' faces. With the odds now three against two, I followed my master chief's lead. I grabbed the closest guy to me and let him have it.

Darrow and I made short work of the first three hoods, but things got trickier when four of their buddies showed up. They started getting the upper hand quickly, and the two of us got into trouble. I was taking more punches than I was throwing. My master chief got kicked over a fifty-five-gallon drum being used as a garbage can and spun out all over the gravel. When he jumped back up, he brought the drum with him. Raising it over his head, he whipped it at a couple of the street punks that were stupid enough to bunch up together. He then grabbed the bar stool from off the Pagoda's porch. Swinging it with one hand, he took out another one of the thugs and started laughing. He was having the time of his life.

I was not. Though I could hit my adversaries much harder than they could hit me, they were quicker. I was having a tough time getting my punches to connect. When one of them got close enough for me to grab, I wrapped my arm around his neck and attempted to choke him out. That blocked the front of me from his comrade. From that point on, I could only be hit in the back, where I was not particularly vulnerable. That was the position I was in when my ears detected a "click" that I had only heard before in movies. I looked up in time to see another tattooed hooligan coming right at me with a switchblade knife in his hand.

The only thing I could do when the guy wielding the blade lunged was to turn as fast as I could. That put the man I was choking between us. It worked once, but it looked like his second try was going to hit the mark. Fortunately, Darrow saw what was going on. Before the knife slid between my ribs, my master chief broke away from the men he was grappling with and grabbed the thug's forearm. He then snapped the hooligan's wrist with a move he had learned while in the AFPD.

The gang banger howled in pain, screaming loud enough to grab his friends' attention. At the same time, a Jeep sped up to us and flipped on its lights and sirens. That was the cue for the street punks to scatter. By instinct alone, I was taking off to join them. Before I took two steps, though, Darrow grabbed me by the collar and asked, "Where do you think you're going? Stand fast and put your hands in the air."

*****

Of course, Master Chief Darrow knew the two officers who rolled up on us. It turned out that I did too. They had been at the party I threw for Tejada and escorted the funeral procession for the lizard that drowned in our punch. The locals got away like they usually did, but another responding unit caught the Marine we beat up. They took him to jail while the master chief and I were given a ride back to Lorna's place. When we got there, Sergeant Tejada was waiting for us.

"Waddapuck da matter wit you two?" TJ asked, shaking his head. "Are you pucking stupid?"

"We got jumped," Darrow told his friend. "There was nothing we could do."

"Jump my ass. You puck up dat Marine boy pretty good."

"Do you know who he is?" I asked.

"Yeah, I know who he is. I don't care 'bout dat—puck dat guy. Did you have to announce to da whole Barrio Barretto dat you Olongapo Earp, dough?"

"Oh my god," Darrow gasped, sounding genuinely surprised. "Did I say that out loud?"

I nodded my head. "Yeah, you couldn't have been less discreet about it if you'd had a fucking bullhorn."

Tejada dropped his face into the palm of his hand. "Bradley, what I gonna do wit you? You not a cop here anymore, so dese guys know you not carrying a gun now. I told you when you get here, you need to lay low! You gonna get yourselp killed!"

"You're right, TJ," the master chief said with an adequate amount of contrition. "It won't happen again. That's it, I'm staying close to home."

OLONGAPO EARP

"Close to home? Bradley, you just told all dose gang boys dat Olongapo Earp is back here in Subic Bay! Dey now know dat you here wit da ship and not wit da AFPD! You got more people who no like you here den anywhere else in dis whole country!"

Shaking his head one more time, the sergeant let out a long, frustrated sigh. "Jesus Christ, Bradley! Is dis da way you make it so you go back to Pagsanjan?!? You plan to make Olongapo more dangerous to you dan Favila's people?!? Puck! Go to Pagsanjan den! Go puck wit Paulino!"

I nodded at Darrow, expressing my willingness to go with him if he needed me to. TJ dashed that plan out of hand. "You no go to Pagsanjan, dough, Doyle! You stay da puck here! I bet you started dis shit, didn't you?"

Though Darrow did most of the damage, it was I who had started everything. Flashing TJ a sheepish grin, I shrugged my shoulders.

"Oops."

*****

CHAPTER 20

Since we were dropped off after curfew, I stayed that night at Lorna's place, sleeping on the couch. When I woke up the following day, I was relieved to see that neither the master chief nor I had any cuts or bruises on us that could not be covered up with a long-sleeved shirt. We did not want anything alerting Krause of the fight we had gotten into the night before. We made it through roll call, and after getting dismissed, Darrow split for Pagsanjan. I went home.

I did not go to my apartment first, though. I went to Mari's and knocked on the door. Mahal answered, looking tired and unhappy. "Mari no here, Doyle. She at school."

"I'm not here for Mari. Is Tala home?"

Mahal nodded and let me in, waving her hand toward the direction to Tala's bedroom. Her door was already open, and I could see her moving about inside, packing. "Hello, Tala," I said, trying not to startle her.

When Tala looked up at me, I could see that she had been crying. She wiped her eyes and said, "*Halo*, Doyle. Mari at school."

"I know. I didn't come here to see her. I came to see you. We went to the Pagoda last night looking for you. You quit?"

Tala nodded. "I quit."

"Why?"

Tala looked at me like I was a complete moron because, well, I was. "Why you t'ink? When I go to work, I pretend it not me dere doing dose t'ings. It Tina doing dat stupp." Tala stifled a sob. "I can't do it anymore, Doyle! I hope Mari porgive me, but I can't! It killing me!"

As Tala broke down, I stepped into the room and wrapped my arms around her, trying to calm her down. "Shhhhh. Tala, breaking out of that life is nothing that needs forgiveness. She's going to love you no matter what."

As she bawled into my chest, Tala cried, "I keep t'inking dat one day, someone gonna rescue me prom all dis. I see girls meeting men and getting taken away somewhere else where dey can start a new lipe. Dey leave dis all behind, but no one coming por me and Mari, Doyle! Nobody! And now da base is closing and I can't even do dis job anymore. Whether I want or not, I have no way to feed Mari when you ship leave da Philippines. I porced to pind a new way to live, so I need to just do it. I gotta get me and Mari out op dis place!"

"Where are the two of you going to go?"

"I don't know. I t'ink we go to Manila. Maybe I can work as da maid or be a waitress or somet'ing. Anyt'ing but a whore."

"Tala, Tala, don't say that. You did what you had to do to take care of Mari. If you think of yourself as a whore, that's all you'll ever be. You're a good woman. Don't let anyone tell you otherwise."

Tala stopped crying and pushed herself away from me, her emotions turning from despair to anger. "Dey don't have to tell me dey t'ink I am a whore! I know what people t'ink op me by da way dey treat me! By da way *you* treat me! You very nice to me, Doyle, but I see da way you look at me! I know you want me, but you no gonna ever try to be wit me because you t'ink I dirty and no worthy op you."

"You're wrong…"

"I not!" Tala yelled. "I try to kiss you, and you jump back like I have disease! You no t'ink I good enough por you and you know what, Doyle? You right! I dirt! I piece op garbage! I never gonna get clean, Doyle! I never gonna get dis scum opp op me!"

I reached out and grabbed Tala hard by the shoulders. "Tala! I couldn't kiss you because I don't want to abandon you when we leave! Look, I'll admit it. I have feelings for you, but I've only known you for a couple of weeks. I don't know if I can do this. Yes, you're a bar girl and, Tala, I don't have time to figure out which kind of bar girl you are. Are you someone who actually has feelings for me, or are you someone who only sees me as a way to get into the United States? I can't figure that out in two weeks!"

Tala sniffled and squinted her eyes at me. "Dat da excuse you usin' to make yourselp stay away prom me? You no want to admit it, but you no get over what I do por a living!"

I groaned and sat myself down on Tala's bed. "If I'm going to be completely honest, yeah, I don't know if I can or not. There was a guy in my division, Randy Green. He came over here and married a girl from Olongapo that was working the bars. Tala, she was a sweetheart and from what I know, devoted to her husband and son. Her husband could not get over her past, though. It drove him crazy, and he began imagining that she was cheating on him. She stuck with the guy, even after he started beating her. Even after he broke her son's arm to get her to unlock the door she was hiding behind."

"Dis guy a priend op yours?"

I shook my head. "No. I beat him so badly after he hurt his stepson that he almost died. I came very close to going to prison over it. Look, Green was a piece of shit. I could not imagine what could drive men like him and my father to do what they did to their wives and children. After I met you, though, I put some thought into it. I realized that neither of those men were well to begin with. Both of them were already messed up in the head; they only needed something to pull the trigger to set them off.

"Tala, because of what my father put me through, among other things, I've got issues myself. I like to think that I could never hurt a woman or a child, but I get these rages, too. I get rages like the one that I went into when I almost killed Randy. I never know what I'm going to do when I fly into one of those things."

I paused for a moment to collect my thoughts, wondering if I could smoke in Tala's bedroom. I decided against it. "I'll never know what it was that set my father off. That guy was always mean as far back as I can remember. Randy, though, was driven off the deep end by the knowledge that Rafaela was way out of his league. Deep down, he probably believed it was just a matter of time before she realized that she could do better and left. In his twisted mind, I think he resented her because of something he thought she would someday do to him. He needed to hurt her before she hurt him."

"You t'ink you a brain doctor por crazy people or somet'ing?"

I laughed. "No, but as much as I hated my old man and Randy Green for what they did, I'm coming to understand how they came to do it. Both of those guys had rage issues. They could get themselves so worked up that they couldn't help themselves. When they snapped, they did heinous things that they never imagined themselves capable of."

"How you know dat?" Tala asked.

"Because I've been there. I've done it too. When I crippled Randy, I was in one of those states. I didn't realize what I was doing. Hell, I don't even remember most of it. I couldn't imagine ever hurting a woman, a child, or someone that I cared about. Still, if there was anything that someone could do to trigger that kind of outburst, it would be destroying a family that I've finally built."

Crossing her arms, Tala asked, "Have you ever hit your girlpriend, Doyle?"

I shook my head. Just having someone ask me a question like that made me sick to my stomach. "No. Never. And if I ever do, I hope someone puts me down like a rabid dog. I'd deserve it. But Tala, my old man messed me up bad. I get these breakdowns that, while they suck, only really affect me. If I'm confronted with an extreme event though, it's something else entirely. I lash out. Once my rage is triggered, I don't even know what I'm doing.

"Tala, when you went to kiss me the other night and I pulled away, it was not because I worried about what you could do to me. It was because I was worried about what I could do to Mari and you."

Tala stood there staring at me, trying to decide how sincere I was being. "You go to da Pagoda last night? What you going to do dere?"

For some reason, her question embarrassed me. I felt my face getting red. My voice was barely audible when I said, "I wanted to pull you out of there and ask you if you would stay with me instead."

Again, Tala stood there staring at me. Forever. "You t'ink you a danger to me, Doyle? In you heart?"

I shook my head. "I don't think so, but I don't know. I don't think my father married my mother thinking that one day he would kill her. I don't think Randy Green dreamed of torturing Rafaela and her son when he asked her to marry him. I'm terrified that I may have more in common with those two pricks than I realize, though."

Shaking her head, Tala took a step back from me and pushed her door closed. "I no t'ink a man dat spend so much time and help Mari like you do could ever hurt a woman, Doyle."

Tala then removed her shirt and joined me on the bed. Taking my face in her hands, she pulled me in, kissing me gently on the lips. "I take my chances."

*****

CHAPTER 21

The first thing that piqued Sergeant Tejada's suspicions about Rickie Ibay was that the man did not recognize him. Everyone who spent time in the bars along Magsaysay Drive or in Barrio Barretto knew Rico Tejada. The American sailors knew him, the working girls knew him, and so did their pimps and pushers. Rickie Ibay did not, though, and that raised a flag. It told TJ that the gaunt, sickly little man with the twitchy gait of a *shabu* addict was an outsider. He did not belong there.

Tejada was off duty and in street clothes, but that should not have mattered. Danny Paduano, one of Barrio Barretto's notorious enforcers, recognized the policeman right away. He stepped out of the Scooby Booze bar before Ibay and almost ran right into the officer as TJ was trying to buy his newspaper. Showing Tejada the proper amount of deference, the hooligan nodded his head and wished the sergeant a good morning as he passed.

Rickie Ibay did not, though. He stepped out of Scooby Booze and looked Tejada right in the eye without any flash of recognition at all. He then turned his back on the policeman, walking up the street with his face pointed at the signs above. He appeared to be looking for someplace in particular. Tejada flipped the newsgirl a couple of peso coins for his paper and then began tailing Rickie to see what he was up to.

Olongapo may have virtually industrialized prostitution, but Magsaysay was something of a safe zone when it came to street crime. The city's livelihood was dependent upon sailors spending money there. All it took was one mugging, one injured American, for the base to put the town off-limits. It had happened before, and the pain it caused was immediate and unrelenting. With only a couple more weeks of American cash flow left, Tejada could not afford for there to be an incident now. The longer TJ followed Ibay, the more he felt that the man was about to create one.

Shabu addicts do not move in straight lines. They tend to wander aimlessly, but with mania and speed. The only time tweakers look like they knew where they are going was when they are on their way to get a fix. Or when trying to earn the cash they needed to score it. As *shabu* was not sold on the street along Magsaysay, Tejada doubted that Ibay was in town to buy dope. He was there to score cash. With the way he looked at the signs above the businesses he passed, TJ guessed that Rickie knew where to find some.

Suspecting a robbery, Tejada pulled his pistol from the small of his back and deftly put it in his pocket. He could pull it out quicker from there. He then picked up his pace to close the gap between them.

Rickie Ibay stopped when he got to the Dirty Crow. He looked up at the sign twice, making sure that he was at the right place. The low life then stepped into the doorway to study the people inside. Tejada saw the expression on Ibay's face change as he appeared to have found what he was looking for.

As the addict pulled something out of his pocket and stepped inside the bar, Tejada cursed. He drew his weapon, disengaged the safety, and took off after his quarry at a dead sprint.

*****

"Palazzo got his ass kicked by a girl?" Master Chief asked, cracking up.

I was leaning against the bar, laughing so hard at the fight I had seen that morning that I could barely answer. Though it was not even noon yet, I was already pretty boozy. When Darrow found out that Tala and I had slept together the night before, he whisked me off of the ship after roll call and insisted on buying me a few drinks before he went to Pagsanjan.

"Oh yeah," I told him. "We were getting out of our trikes in front of the Shit River bridge. Palazzo was walking in from Magsaysay Drive. Suddenly, this other trike comes barreling up and screeches to a halt right beside him. Then this little chick, who's like four feet tall, jumps out and starts beating the shit out of the guy. She's screaming bloody murder the whole time, chasing him all around the intersection. It was like watching that monkey attack Claude!"

Remembering the *matsing* incident had the master chief giggling. "What'd Spanky do to deserve it?"

"Oh man," I said, wiping the tears from my eyes. "You gotta hear it like I did. I'm sitting on the bus with the guy on our way back to the ship. I ask him, 'What the hell was that all about?' He looks at me and says, 'I got pretty drunk yesterday. I got up in the middle of the night to use the bathroom, and I kinda missed the toilet.'"

I struggled to keep from busting up again. "So, I'm looking at this guy, his shirt's all ripped, and he's got fingernail marks gouged into his cheeks, right? I ask him, 'She got that mad at you for missing the toilet?'"

We laughed so hard that the barmaid and a couple of the girls came in closer to hear the story. "So John says, 'Yeah, I missed the toilet and accidentally peed in her purse.'" I then imitated that nervous laugh Palazzo always punctuated his sentences with.

"What?" Darrow exclaimed while the girls groaned in disgust. "He pissed in her purse?"

"Wait! Wait!" I pled. "It gets better! I asked him, 'Why the hell does she keep her purse on the floor in the goddamn bathroom?' So you know what John tells me? He goes, 'She doesn't. She left it on the couch in the living room.'"

We all lost our shit. Darrow buckled over in tears, the girls roared in hilarity, and I was laughing so hard that no sound was coming out. Then everything went silent. Our laughter was replaced with a ringing in my ears that drowned out the noise of everything else. Disoriented, I glanced over at the girl standing at my right elbow. Though I could not hear her, her face was contorted as if she were screaming and her cheek was covered in blood. I then turned toward my master chief, who looked shocked and in disbelief. After that, I caught sight of a man standing in the doorway, pointing a gun right at us.

Things were moving in slow motion. In fact, it was so slow that everything appeared to have stopped entirely. The only movement was a lone knife twirling in the air above us, seemingly suspended there all by itself. As I watched it, it crept by in an arc over our heads. Eventually it landed on the bar, bounced, and then sailed across the aisle to disappear against the bottles of booze lined up against the wall. As if on cue, that was when the ringing stopped. Everyone began moving in real time, and all hell broke loose.

Moving to push my master chief out of the line of fire, I jumped off my stool, tripping over someone lying at my feet. After regaining my balance, I watched the man on the floor writhe around for a second. Both his hands clutched at his throat as blood pumped out from between his fingers. He did not look familiar. When I looked up, though, some of the smoke had cleared, and I recognized the man in the doorway. It was Sergeant Tejada.

"Jesus Christ," Darrow gasped, looking toward the door at his friend. "Wha…wh...wha?"

"He gonna put dat knipe in you back, Brad!" Tejada shouted. He was shaking.

My master chief looked down at Ibay, stepping back to avoid the puddle of blood pooling beneath his head. "You know that guy?" I asked him.

Darrow shook his head. I could see he was rattled. "Nope."

Tejada scanned the small crowd inside the Dirty Crow. Luckily, it was still early, and we were the only Americans there. "You two need to get da puck out op here now! Go!"

Still not able to fully process what the sergeant was telling him, Darrow turned to TJ and asked, "Do you have any idea who this is?".

Tejada shook his head. "No. I no tink he prom around here. He know you, dough. He going right por you."

"You think he's a hired man?" the master chief asked.

Sergeant Tejada nodded. "Yeah, he a hired guy. Someone want to kill you, but no can pay much to do it. Guy like dis, he kill por cheap. You need to go, Brad! Get out back door and go to Doyle place. I meet you dere."

"So, we're not going to Pagsanjan?" Darrow asked, obviously not thinking clearly.

OLONGAPO EARP

TJ shook his head. "No, I no tink we gonna go to Pagsanjan today. Or ever. It look like Pagsanjan coming here."

*****

The Shore Patrol arrived at my apartment long before Tejada did. I barely had time to explain what had happened to Tala, take a shower, and change clothes before they were knocking on my door. Master Chief Darrow answered it, wearing a tee-shirt he had borrowed from me. "Can I help you?"

"Hello, Master Chief," said MA1 Trevor Carlton, looking a bit nervous. He was not expecting to find Darrow there. "I'm here under orders to escort you and Petty Officer Murphy back to the ship."

"Under whose orders?" Darrow asked.

"Lieutenant Krause."

My master chief nodded. "Of course. Does the captain know about this?"

Shaking his head, the master-at-arms told him, "I have no idea."

"Can you do me a favor and make sure that he does? Let him know what time we're going to arrive on the quarterdeck?"

"Sure. I can do that," Carlton answered.

"Now?" Darrow sounded a little irritated.

Flustered, Carlton grabbed his radio. He then stepped out of the apartment to make Darrow's call, leaving his Shore Patrol escorts to get us to the Jeep.

When we arrived at the quarterdeck, there was no captain there to greet us. Nor was there any division officer. Instead, there was only a set of instructions to go to the EMO office and call Lieutenant Krause when we got there. While we changed into our uniforms, Darrow left a message with the captain's office to let him know where we would be.

"What did you not understand about zero tolerance for liberty incidents, Darrow?" Krause roared when he finally barged into the EMO office.

"Are you implying that I was involved in one?" my master chief asked.

"Are you telling me that you were not involved in a shooting out in town, Master Chief?"

"Is this a game where we can only speak in questions?" I asked. I was still a little drunk. Both Krause and Darrow shot me a look to let me know that I would be better served by keeping my mouth shut.

"There was a shooting on Magsaysay and I've got reports by my people who saw both you and Murphy at the bar where it happened!"

"Really?" Darrow laughed. "You have people? Who the fuck are *your* people?"

"None of your business!" Krause snapped.

"Like hell, it isn't!" Darrow shouted back. "Who the hell told you that I was at a bar where a shooting happened? Huh? Who was it?"

Before Krause could answer, the captain walked through the door of the EMO. "Attention on deck!" I yelled, snapping to attention.

Fleming put us at ease as he stepped into the space. "What's going on in here? I can hear the yelling all the way down the passageway!"

"Sir," Krause started. "There was a shooting at the Dirty Crow this morning. I have reports that Murphy and Darrow were involved."

The captain turned to the master chief with a look of complete shock on his face. "You shot someone?" he gasped. I found it amusing that the conclusion the skipper leapt to was that Darrow would have been the man behind the trigger. I thought it revealed just how dangerous the captain thought our master chief was.

Darrow scoffed. "Of course not. From what I understand, and I could be wrong, there was an attempted robbery of the bar we were at. The suspect was shot by an off-duty police officer."

"You were at the bar where there was a shooting, and you don't know what happened?" Fleming did not sound like he was buying that.

"Well, sir, that's why I would hesitate to say that we were 'involved' in a shooting. We didn't even see what happened. We only saw the aftermath."

"That's a lie!" Krause shouted, forgetting himself. "You're going on liberty risk! Both of you are confined to the ship for the rest of the time we're in the Philippines! No liberty! The two of you are walking time bombs! You sow chaos and destruction everywhere you go! You're criminals! Deviants! Disgraces to the uniform! And if it's the last thing I do, I'm going to see that both of you hang from…!"

OLONGAPO EARP

"Master Chief," the captain quietly interrupted. "Would you take Murphy outside for a moment while I speak with the lieutenant in private?"

"Aye aye, sir," Darrow responded as he led me out of the room.

Once we were outside of the EMO office and out of earshot, I turned to Darrow and saw that he was ready to explode. "What's up?"

"You don't see it?" my master chief snapped. "I thought you were supposed to be the smart guy."

I shrugged. "See what?"

Darrow shook his head. "I'm not getting into it here in the passageway."

The man was fuming. Surprisingly, I was not. The severity of what had happened had not sunk in yet, but I suspected an episode of epic proportions was on my horizon. I sighed at the prospect of having one more thing to add to my retinue of psychological horrors. They were piling up. "You know, Master Chief, I'm beginning to think the lieutenant's right."

"About what?" he spat.

"Sowing chaos and destruction everywhere I go."

"What the fuck are you talking about?"

I shrugged. "I was talking to Bard the other day. You know that he's never seen a dead body? He's still got two parents, four grandparents, and all his aunts and uncles. I buried four of my people when I was thirteen and got a girl killed in El Salvador six years later. Master Chief, I've watched three people get killed in just the last four months. This isn't normal."

Darrow looked at me. "The guy at the bar was alive when we left."

"Well," I countered. "I'll bet you my next paycheck that the son-of-a-bitch ain't sucking air now."

It took ten minutes for Captain Fleming to say his piece to our division officer. He never raised his voice enough for me to hear what they discussed, though. Judging by the way Krause stormed out of his office, it must have been scathing. We waited for him to get out of sight before Darrow and I walked back into the EMO.

"What happened, Darrow?" Fleming asked as he sat on the master chief's desk. He knew that what my master chief had said before was only for the lieutenant's benefit. The captain now expected to hear the real story.

"What happened, sir, was fucking amateur hour."

"I don't have time for this, Master Chief. Spell it out for me. What's going on here?"

"We're getting to him," Darrow said. "That son-of-a-bitch knows we're on to him, and he made a move to take me out. That's what happened."

"Are you serious?" the captain asked.

"Sir, I was on the AFPD for eight years. I have a head for this kind of thing. He knows that we've been looking for him in Pagsanjan. He doesn't know what I've found out so far, so he hired some degenerate to take me out to cover his ass."

"That's a pretty wild hunch," Fleming said.

Darrow shook his head. "No, think about it. He calls me in here to tell me he received some report 'by his people' that we were involved in a shooting out in town? What 'people' does he have reporting to him out there? He ain't got no fucking people! Krause knew someone was coming after me and whoever he arranged it with told him they fucked up! That's how he knew what happened and that we were there! We got to the Crow early, and the place was still dead when this shit went down. There wasn't anybody that saw us there."

"Then how did this guy that came after you know where to find you?"

Darrow shrugged. "Sir, everyone on Magsaysay knows who I am. The people who can hire a tweaker to do this know how to put the word out for someone to call them if they see me pop up. It's not hard. It's not expensive either."

The captain shook his head. He was having a hard time digesting what Darrow was telling him. So was I. "How do you think he found out you were on to him about Pagsanjan?"

"We had a run-in with someone from those missionaries Krause worked with. Hope's Children Ministry. Maybe he got word out to the lieutenant that we were out there. The guys we have out in Pagsanjan looking for pervs have proven to be less than trustworthy also. They might have sold us out. The *barangay* captain out there in the slum is no fan of mine. I've got some dirt on him from way back in World War II. He might be inclined to help Krause to make sure it doesn't get out. That prick also knew me and Tejada were headed that way today. He could have sent word to Krause to be on the lookout for us."

Fleming stared at Master Chief Darrow for a long while before speaking. "Do you have any evidence at all to back this up?"

OLONGAPO EARP

"No, sir. I'm pretty sure my evidence died at the Dirty Crow. I know I'm right, though, skipper! Look, there's plenty of people out there all over the island of Luzon that would like to see me dead, sir. The difference between them and whoever did this was that those other guys know how to get a man iced. They would have hired a proper villain, not a junkie. Whoever arranged this had no idea what the fuck they were doing! It was hasty, unplanned, and reeks of someone taking advantage of an opportunity. It was like they just found out I was there and had to scrounge up somebody quick willing to take the shot. The fucker who stepped up probably had no idea who I was. He was just handed a knife, told to go to the Crow and stick it in the back of the old man with the flat top."

Captain Fleming turned around and sat in my master chief's seat. "You're sure of this?"

"I'm as close to positive as I can be without whoever hired the tweaker. My man Tejada will get to the bottom of that, though. I'll get him, sir."

"No, Master Chief. You won't," the captain said.

Darrow looked like he'd been smacked. "What?"

"This is out of control. You're backing off the lieutenant, and I'm calling in the Naval Investigative Service to figure this out. No more hunches. I'm making this official."

"Sir, I can handle…"

"I'm sure you can, Master Chief," the captain said, cutting him off. "If you were acting in your old capacity on the AFPD, there is no one else I'd rather have on the case than you. You're not a cop anymore, though. If that man tried to have you killed, I aim to make sure that he does hard time for it."

Focusing his gaze directly upon me, the captain added, "I also aim to make sure you two don't end up under investigation yourselves. Especially if Krause's battered body ends up washing ashore somewhere near Cubi Point. The two of you are finished with this stuff. That's an order. You're going to give the man some space and let him do whatever it is the NCIS can catch him for."

"Like try to kill us?" I asked.

"That ain't happening again," the master chief growled. "TJ's going to go ballistic on those fuckers in Pagsanjan. In fact, if Krause shows his face out there again to arrange another attempt, I'd put even money on those guys slitting his throat to cover their asses."

The captain stood up. "That would certainly tidy things up nicely, wouldn't it? I hope for your sake that's not how this ends. If anything happens to that man outside of official channels, I'm sicking the NIS on you two, also. Got it?"

"Yes, sir," Darrow and I answered simultaneously.

After the captain took his leave, I plopped down into the lieutenant's chair while Darrow took a seat in his. "So, what are we going to do now?" I asked.

"You up for a road trip?"

I shrugged. "To Pagsanjan?"

"No, Doyle," the master chief said, shaking his head. "Didn't you hear the captain? We've got to stay away from there. That's fine with me, too. Fuckin' place makes my skin crawl."

"Then where?" I asked.

"Lorna wants to take me back to her village to see her folks again," Darrow told me. "It's been years. She's from a tiny place near Porac, close to Mount Pinatubo. Bring Tala and Mari. We'll ask Bard and Dixie if they want to come, too. We'll make it a day trip."

"What about Krause?" I did not understand how a road trip to Porac would solve our problem with the lieutenant.

"What about him?"

"Are we going to just let him get away with that shit?"

Darrow smiled at me. "Krause ain't getting away with nothing. The captain's getting the NIS involved now."

"And you're okay with that? What if they don't find anything?"

My master chief laughed. "What if they don't find anything? Doyle, that man tried to kill me. The gloves are fucking off. If the NIS comes snooping around the *USS Belleau Wood* looking for dirt on our lieutenant, I'm going to make sure that they fucking find it."

*****

OLONGAPO EARP

CHAPTER 22

I was sitting at the picnic table in our courtyard, discussing the attack with Tejada and Darrow. That was when I began to realize how close the master chief had come to being killed at the Dirty Crow. I felt that old anxiety start to take hold and noticed how hard it was for me to concentrate. I had an episode coming. When my sweat pores opened up, I made my excuses to turn in for the night and escorted my guests to our broken gate.

TJ did not believe that Krause was behind the attack. After they identified Rickie Ibay, they found that he had no ties to Pagsanjan that they knew of. Darrow would not waver, however, and countered that the lieutenant must have hired the killer himself. The men were still arguing about it as I hustled the two of them onto the sidewalk. When I left, I had every intention of locking myself in my room to ride out my breakdown, but Tala was waiting for me as soon as I reached the top of the stairs. "Are you okay, Doyle?"

Shaking my head, I said, "No, I'm not. I need to go to bed."

"Alone?"

I nodded sadly. "Yes, Tala, alone."

"I no t'ink it good por you be alone tonight."

My hands were starting to shake now. Things were happening fast. "Trust me, Tala, I need to be by myself. Please. You don't understand, but I have these things that get triggered by…"

Tala reached out and put her hand on my cheek. She then leaned forward and pressed her lips up against mine. It was hard to explain, but it was a kiss almost devoid of sexual desire. It was just a connection. Through her lips, Tala was making me see that she knew something was deeply wrong with me, but she understood. Whatever was coming, she was going to help me through it. She was going to stay, no matter how damaged I may be. I was suddenly awash in this alien sensation of comfort, and I noticed that I was no longer shaking as I returned her kiss.

With the thought of what had happened that day purged from my mind, I guided Tala into my apartment. Embracing each other and ignoring my roommates, we made our way into my bedroom. Then, once the door closed behind us, we made love. For hours.

When we finished, Tala drifted off to sleep. I did not. I had never been so at peace than I was at that moment, and I needed to savor it. I realized that, as much as I had loved Hannah, there were things about myself that I had to keep hidden from her. If I ever showed her the violence I was capable of, the rages that allowed me to cripple monsters like Randy Green, I knew that she would leave me. And I was right. After watching me destroy the man that nearly got Macklemore and me killed in Mexico, she broke off our engagement and left, never to be seen again. She knew that she was better than me.

Tala did not. In her mind, she was more tainted and ruined than I could ever hope to be. She was willing to accept any fault of mine unconditionally. All she asked in return was that I give her a chance and try to look past what she had to do to put food in her daughter's belly.

At that moment, I could. Tala was a good woman, and at least for that night, I did not think about what she had done before. I was able to see her as she was now, beautiful, nurturing, safe, and content.

I was exhausted when I got back to the ship the next morning. After roll call, I went to my radar dome to get more sleep and confront the episode that Tala delayed, needing to get it out of the way. It never came, though. I slept hard for four solid hours. When I woke up, I went back to my apartment, made love to Tala again while Mari was at school, then slept for four more.

When Mari got home, I treated us all to Jollibee. After that, we played board games until the sun went down and Mari went to bed. Then Tala and I went back to my room for the night. Again, there was no episode. The following day I had duty, but Tala and Mari stayed in my head the whole time I was on the ship. I went yet another day with no flashbacks or nightmares. The next day, we took Mari to the beach, and once more, there was nothing.

I fell into this routine, where all I did, and all I wanted to do, was get home from work to spend time with Tala and her daughter. Krause became Darrow's problem, and I could not have cared less about how he dealt with it. I stayed out of the bars and remained sober, save for a couple of beers at night. And the occasional drink pulled from the kiddie pool of gecko stew that still occupied our living room floor.

For the first time in nine years, I went an entire week without thinking of my father and my murdered family. I even purged the thought of the girl in El Salvador from my mind. I forgot about Randy Green and what had happened to Macklemore and me in Mexico a few months before. I forgot about watching Hulagu get dumped into the ocean and the murder of David Miller. Even what happened at the Dirty Crow got pushed out of my head. I just saw a man bleeding out from a hole shot through his throat, yet I felt like it had never even happened.

I was experiencing something that I had never known before: normalcy. I was finally doing something that most people did every day and getting a taste of what it was like to be ordinary.

It was euphoric, but as the days ticked by bringing us closer to our time of departure, I grew uneasy. I wondered if the cosmos was giving me this gift only to make the pain I would feel when I left Tala and Mari as visceral as it could possibly be.

*****

Master Chief Darrow was standing up in the hired jeepney, trying to keep his balance as it bounced around atop the rough mountain road. "A couple of rules, gentlemen. I want you to keep in mind that not only are we going

WAY outside of the quarantine area, but we are also going into a part of Luzon that is known for NPA activity."

"The communists?" Dixie asked.

"Yeah, the communists," Darrow answered.

"Wait," Bard started. "Are you telling us we're going to a place that's overrun with communists? You sure this is a good idea?"

"It's fine. Look, I used to come out here all the time. I'm pretty sure the NPA only calls themselves communist so that the Russians will give them weapons. I had contacts in the NPA that I used all the time when I was in the AFPD. They're not very anti-American. They're mainly anti-corruption, so as long as you're not a crooked politician or a policeman, you're pretty safe."

I looked around at us all seated in the jeepney. Besides Darrow and Lorna, there were Tony Bard and Anna, Dixie and Elena, myself, Tala, and Mari headed to the province of Pampanga. After Darrow commented about the NPA targeting corrupt police officers, I wondered if that was why Sergeant Tejada was conspicuously absent.

The village Lorna was taking us to was somewhere near the town of Porac. It was so far out in the boonies that it was not even mentioned on a map. To hear her describe it, my master chief's girlfriend grew up in a few wooden shacks built around the only electrical outlet within ten miles. As of 1992, they were still without running water. They drew it out of the ground with a hand-pump like in the American Old West.

Master Chief Darrow continued. "I've never had trouble with the NPA out where we're headed. That doesn't mean they'll hesitate to put a bullet in our heads and dump us in a ditch if we're not on our best behavior, though. Mind your manners. Don't discuss politics or religion. Don't touch anybody on the head. Don't shake with your left hand. If you're offered food, you make sure you eat it no matter how gross it is. Actually, devour it with relish and compliment your host on her cooking. Men, these people are very poor out where we're going. They don't have much to offer, so refusing their hospitality is very insulting."

"Have you ever been to this place?" I asked Tala.

She shook her head while combing her fingers through her daughter's hair. "I no t'ink Mari ever be out in da country before. I never take her. I grow up in area like dat. I no want to go back."

OLONGAPO EARP

I suddenly felt bad for asking her to come. "I'm sorry, Tala. If you don't want to go, we can stop and…"

"No, no, no. I go wit you. It pun when you no have to live dere. It be good por Mari too. She only know city and concrete. She can breathe good air. Presh air."

Switching to Tagalog, I asked Mari if she was happy to see Lorna's village. She smiled and gave me a thumbs up. It seemed to me that she got excited about any change of scenery.

Once out of the city and driving through the mountains, I was surprised by how green things were getting. It had been just over a year since Mount Pinatubo blew up. I had been under the impression that the surrounding area had been devastated. For most of our ride, though, there was still plenty of lush scenery to be seen. The only real evidence I saw of the eruption was in the rivers we passed. It appeared that the rain washed all the volcanic ash into the waterways and turned it into concrete. It made the jungle look crisscrossed with newly paved roads.

It was a long drive. Mari got tired and dozed off in my lap. As I was so transfixed by the landscape flying by, Tala passed time by talking with Lorna. I tried to eavesdrop, mainly to improve my Tagalog rather than any desire to be nosy. Even with my poor grasp of the language, I learned much about Darrow listening to the two women talk.

I heard that Lorna's father had hurt himself in the late 1970s, and she left her village to help support her family. With a great deal of naivete about how girls earned good money in Subic Bay, she was persuaded to work as a singer in one of the bars on Magsaysay Drive.

Tala nodded knowingly. It was the way some of the girls got lured into the business. They first got jobs, such as singers, that paid virtually nothing. While they starved, the girls watched women pulling in more cash in a week servicing military men than what their parents could earn in a year on the family farm. Lorna was there for two days before she received her first tip. That was when ET1 Darrow slipped her enough cash to rent a room for a month. He told her that if she wanted to avoid a life of sorrow and violence, she needed to find another way to make a living. When Lorna confessed that she had no skills, Darrow pulled some strings and got her work bagging groceries.

Lorna shined a light on what was one of the more obscure aspects of the Olongapo Earp mythos. Brad Darrow regularly intervened to save young country girls from getting sucked into the Magsaysay skin trade. It was low-key, but the man had an eye for picking out vulnerable young women on the brink of destroying themselves. He pulled them from the vortex and often redirected them toward legitimate work. If they were old enough, Darrow could even occasionally get them coveted, high-paying jobs on the military base. Most often, though, he accumulated favors among the locals and cashed them in when he saw someone in need.

Grateful to Darrow for what he had done for her, Lorna reached out to him after she was settled. She wanted to see if she could help him help others. They began working together, discreetly to avoid the ire of the bar owners, to put young women at risk into a better situation than renting out their bodies to put rooves over their heads.

Darrow's girlfriend admitted that the man was no saint. When she met him, he was married to his high school sweetheart and had two young daughters who lived on base. Still, he had several regular girls in town that he would see. The bar girls all wanted to be with Olongapo Earp. If they had his attention, they enjoyed his protection. The bar owners, the gang boys, and especially their customers would not dare lay a hand on them if they were with him.

Eventually, Lorna and my master chief became involved as well. Their relationship was the last straw for Darrow's wife, who tolerated her husband's other dalliances as meaningless trysts. When it became evident that there was more to what Lorna and Darrow had than just physical attraction, Mrs. Darrow packed up their children and left. Their divorce was brutal. After it was over, Darrow never had any contact with his children again.

Olongapo Earp left the Philippines for the second time in 1980. He returned a few years later with a new wife but old habits. Lorna was not responsible for wrecking that marriage. Once it was over, though, she wasted no time rekindling their relationship. They had three years together before Darrow left again to report aboard the *USS Belleau Wood*.

"All that time together, and he never married you?" Tala asked.

Lorna shrugged. "There is no sense to marry a man like Bradley. I love him and will always love him, but I know what he is. He will never settle down. The best I can do is take all the time he is willing to give me."

I was still looking over the scenery, pretending that I could not understand what they were saying, when I saw Tala turn to look at me. She did not ask it, but in her eyes, I saw the question she longed for me to answer. "How much time are you willing to give *me*?"

*****

Driving into Lorna's village, I began taking the threat that the New People's Army posed much more seriously. The area looked almost identical to the scenery I saw in every Vietnam movie I ever watched in high school. There were rice paddies everywhere, green mountains in the background, and palm trees lining the dirt roads. Everywhere I looked, people clad in black pajamas and cone-shaped *salakot* hats worked the fields. Even the water buffalo looked the same. I would not have been surprised at all if someone pulled out a Kalashnikov and opened fire on us as we passed.

Darrow must have seen the expression on my face. "Does it remind you of 'Nam, Doyle?"

"Doesn't it remind you?" I answered.

My master chief shook his head. "Not particularly. I was there. The people don't look anything alike to me. This place probably reminds you of Vietnam because you've only ever seen it in the movies. And most of those movies were filmed somewhere around here. Or in Thailand."

When we finally arrived at the half dozen huts that Lorna grew up in, they were almost deserted. "Where is everybody?" Dixie asked as he jumped out of our jeepney. "Didn't they know we were coming?"

Darrow waved his arm toward the rice fields that surrounded us. "They're around. They're just out there at work, keeping their distance for a little while."

"Keeping their distance? From us?" Bard asked. "Do they think we're a threat?"

"No, not us. The NPA is a threat, though, and they don't want to be seen getting too friendly with us until they know it's okay."

I felt Mari squeeze my hand and point at one of the huts. She had spotted another little girl looking out of one of them who seemed to be her age. "Can I go see her?" Mari asked her mother.

Tala looked at Lorna. "Of course!" Darrow's girlfriend told Mari. "That is my niece, Clara! Go play with her." Lorna waved at the little girl. "*Halo, Clara!*"

"*Halo, Tiya!*"

While Mari deserted me to play with her new friend, the rest of us got comfortable around the jeepney. We broke open some of the beer that we brought while Lorna told us all about the place she grew up in. At some point, an ancient Toyota pulled up to let an even more ancient man out of it. "Olongapo Earp!" the man called out in flawless English. "It's good to see you again!"

Darrow walked over and embraced the new arrival. "Paco!" The two men talked for a few moments between themselves before the master chief led him our way. "Guys, this man is one of the village elders around here, so to speak. He'll never admit it, but the word in these parts is that he was quite a prolific bandit when the Japanese occupied this area. I tend to believe the rumors. For an old peasant farmer who never had two nickels to rub together, he boasts the biggest collection of samurai swords that I have ever seen. That's why we call him Paco Villa."

"Ah, whatever," Paco said, brushing off the master chief's flattery. "We all did what we had to in the war. I did alright after it too. I'm just poor because everything I got, I passed down to my people."

I grinned. That sounded Marxist enough for me to wager that Paco was the NPA man, showing up to check us out.

"What brings you back, Bradley? It's been a long time since you've been here."

"I know. I wanted to see what's changed since I left."

Paco looked around as I handed him a beer I pulled from one of our coolers. He seemed surprised by the offer but accepted it. "Why, thank you, young man! Well, as you can see, the place hasn't changed much, just the people. When's the last time you were here?"

Darrow thought for a moment. "It's been five or six years, for sure."

OLONGAPO EARP

"Five or six years! Yeah, I remember that now! Things were getting crazy back then. You were out here when Colonel Honasan tried to overthrow Aquino. You had to go back. How come you didn't return?"

Darrow shrugged. "We weren't allowed to. After that coup attempt, Aquino let General Ramos have his way with the NPA out here. Our command didn't want us getting caught in the crossfire."

Paco sighed. "General Ramos. Now President Ramos. That son-of-a-bitch sent cutthroats against the people out here. Murderers. Rapists. Gangsters. And now he's in charge of the whole goddamn country. Gahh! That man was a Marcos stooge. He hid in the north during the war, making up stories while we were down here making Japanese corpses!"

Master Chief Darrow smiled but stayed silent. Sensing that he was not going to draw Darrow into any political discussions, Paco changed the subject. "The place hasn't changed much, Bradley, but we have new people here now that you haven't met!" Smiling, Paco turned to his driver. "Mariano! Why don't you go tell Lorna's people that their daughter is here with guests!"

That seemed to be the cue that we were alright as far as the NPA was concerned. As soon as Mariano pulled away to collect people from the fields, a middle-aged woman emerged from one of the huts. She beckoned us to take seats at a long communal table out in the yard. Paco asked the woman, another aunt of Lorna's, if there was anything she could get us to snack on. "*Bagoong*?" the woman asked.

"Perfect!" Paco told her. "Do you and your boys like *bagoong*?"

"Yes. We love it!" The slight crack in Darrow's voice as he answered was a clue that we probably would not.

Bagoong is a Philippine condiment made, as far as I can tell, with pulverized fish meat mixed with insane amounts of salt before being left to ferment. It smells like rotten fish and tastes like, well, very salty rotten fish. I learned that it is a staple in local cuisine. The Filipinos utilized it in the same way as aromatics would be in the West, but it could be used as a spread as well. In Lorna's village, it was served to us heaped upon slices of mango.

Our girlfriends went after the *bagoong* like it was any run-of-the-mill chip dip. We Americans were much more tentative. Still, we had all heard Darrow's warning about how rude it was to refuse food. We gave it a try, suppressed our gag reflexes, and made sure that we did not deprive our girlfriends of their share. Rushing to get the ordeal over with, we got through the entire bowl in pretty good time. We tried washing the horrid taste out of our mouths with our beer. It didn't work.

Surprised at how quickly the local delicacy had been devoured, Lorna's aunt looked us over in amazement. "You like our *bagoong*?" she asked.

Aware that we were probably dining with the leader of a communist guerilla group, we all nodded in tandem. We faked sounds of delight while telling Lorna's aunt various versions of, "Delicious! Top Rate! Unique! Incredible! I've never eaten anything quite like it before!"

We might have overdone it. Delighted with our reactions and beaming with pride, Lorna's aunt said, "I make it myselp! You sit dere! I bring you more!"

By the time the villagers began filing in to see Lorna and her friends, we were on our third serving. We were grateful for the excuse to leave the table, introduce ourselves, and pass out some of the beer we brought to the thirsty farmers. We met Lorna's aunties and most of her uncles. There were also friends from neighboring fields and a mob of kids from all around. They were all curious to see the foreigners since Americans rarely made it out that far into the countryside. Mari was delighted by that and disappeared among them.

One little guy stole the show, though. Crying out, *"Nanay! Nanay!"* a little boy of about four years of age emerged from the gaggle of children and ran for Lorna as fast as he could. When he reached her, he threw his arms around Lorna's neck and peppered her with kisses, which she returned with enthusiasm.

We were blindsided. I had been to Lorna's place. There were pictures there of her parents, friends, and relatives, but no sign at all that she had a son somewhere. She never spoke of him, and never did she hint that she might have been a mother. She stayed quiet about it even when Tala and Anna spoke of their babies. It was not the fact that Lorna had a son that gobsmacked us, though.

It was how much that little Filipino boy looked just like Master Chief Darrow.

*****

OLONGAPO EARP

We all saw it. Tala looked at me aghast, and I turned my head toward Bard and Dixie to gauge their reactions. Both of them were stunned. Like me, they were doing the math in their heads to figure out if Darrow was still in the country when that little boy was conceived. He was. Anna brought her hands up to cover her mouth, and Elena buried her head into Dixie's shoulder to hide her face. Then we all looked toward our master chief.

Olongapo Earp was speechless. He was standing there with his mouth agape, trying to say something but unable to get the words out. He looked lost and, for the first time since I had known him, vulnerable. When he could finally speak, Darrow stammered for several seconds before he said, "Wh…wh…why didn't you tell me?"

"I no gonna trap you, Bradley. I no was gonna tell you at all, but I t'inking to myselp no is pair por you to no know about dis. I no know how to tell you. I try but can't. So, I show you. Is best way, I t'ink."

"Why now?" Darrow choked back a sob, but the tear that rolled down his face broadcast what he was feeling anyway. "Why didn't you tell me sooner? We had all this…all this time…I could have been with him. I could have…" My master chief's face twisted up in regret, and he finally let it out. It was now Tala's turn to bury her face in my chest, and I saw that Anna had to turn away too to hide her tears.

"I don't know, Bradley. I apraid I no know how you react. Maybe I selpish, but I apraid maybe you avoid me, and I want all da time prom you I can get." Lorna was crying now too.

"*Ano ang mali, Mama?*" the little boy asked, wondering what was wrong with his mother.

After telling her son that everything was fine, Lorna turned back to Darrow. "I sorry, Bradley. I so sorry. I know I wait too long, but I no know you coming here to Olongapo again. I t'ink you gone porever. When you come back, I surprised and no know how to do dis. I do da best I can."

Master Chief Darrow took a couple of steps toward Lorna and his son, then got down on his knees. "Can I see him?"

Lorna nodded. "*Nais mo bang makilala ang iyong tatay?*" she asked the little boy. Do you want to meet your father?

The boy's eyes opened very wide as his mother released him from her hug and set him free. "*Ang lalaking iyon ang tatay ko?*" the boy asked back, wondering if the big tattooed American man in front of him was really his dad.

"*Oo,* Bradley. *Siya talaga,*" she assured him, revealing to us that she had even named him after the master chief.

Darrow held out his arms, beckoning the little boy to give him a hug. Little Bradley took a couple of tentative steps toward his old man but then reconsidered and ran back to his hut, screaming in terror.

Paco Villa laughed and got up from the table, walking toward Master Chief Darrow. The elder then placed his hand upon my boss's shoulder and said, "He'll come around, Olongapo Earp. It will just take a little while for him to get used to you. He's a good little boy."

As the old man walked toward his beat-up Toyota, he turned to Darrow one last time and smiled. "I knew you would do the right thing, Bradley. I'm glad you accepted that little boy. It would have made me very sad if I had to kill you."

We all laughed at Villa's little joke, but as the elder drove away, I found myself wondering if he was actually kidding.

*****

It took a road trip to the closest *sari-sari* store to load up on candy and soft drinks, but Darrow won over his son. We passed out the sweets *en mass* to most of the children to lure them away from the huts. Our master chief coaxed his little boy back outside with a melting chocolate bar. After that, Darrow pressed a wad of peso banknotes into the palm of one of the locals, who returned a short time later with large strips of pork. We grilled that up and served it to everyone, allowing our master chief to give his son his very first lesson in barbecue.

After our meal, we hiked through the rice paddies. It was harvest time, so they were dry. That allowed Lorna to walk down in the fields instead of on the dikes like the rest of us. At one point, she crossed paths with an *ulupong,* a native species of cobra. She was startled so badly that she made what we estimated to be a four-foot vertical jump to join us back atop the dike. We were all impressed, both with Lorna's athleticism as well as the size of the snake.

OLONGAPO EARP

"They get bigger," Darrow told us. "I got a call one time from base housing telling me a python was on the grounds making a meal out of some Marine sergeant's pit bull. When I got there, I saw this thing was a fuckin' monster! I had to shoot it because it could have swallowed a kid. When we measured the thing, it was more than twenty feet long. We preserved its skin and had it hanging back at the station for the longest time."

Along our walk, we came across a little patch of jungle that we ducked into. Elena and Anna, both island girls, showed us how they could climb to the top of the coconut trees and throw down their fruit. None of the Americans could get more than five feet off the ground.

When we returned to the village, Dixie, Bard, and I went for a ride with our girls in a cart pulled by a water buffalo. Darrow and Lorna stayed behind and had a heart-to-heart talk. After the *carabao* returned us to where we started, we loaded up the jeepney. We then pulled Mari away from her new friends and took off back toward Olongapo. With us was Bradley Junior, sitting in his father's lap and chattering away non-stop in a language that his father did not understand. Not that it mattered.

We did not go straight home. Not wanting to waste any daylight, we drove past Olongapo. We found ourselves a deserted stretch of Luzon's western coast somewhere around Pundaquit and played in the surf as the sun went down.

Having gone swimming in my street clothes, I got out of the water a little early to drip dry in the sand. Dixie fell onto the beach to my right and handed me one of the last cold beers left in the cooler. "I'm not going home," he told me.

"What?" I asked.

"I'm not going home. Ever. I've never had a day like this. We drove through the most beautiful piece of earth I've ever seen. We drank beer with communist guerillas. I watched the toughest man I know cry like a bitch after finding out about a son he never knew he had. Now I'm watching the most gorgeous girls I've ever known play in the ocean together, silhouetted before a sunset that I've only seen on postcards. I can't go back to Ohio after this. I'm going to reenlist."

"You poor bastard," I said.

"C'mon, Doyle! Do it with me."

I laughed. "I can't. The captain told me after the Mexico fiasco that my career in the Navy is finished. I'm getting out."

"And doing what?"

I had to think for a moment about that. "I have no idea," I sighed. I wondered how far the $50,000 I had in a Panamanian bank account would go toward setting me up in a place like Olongapo. "Maybe I could come back here."

Dixie grinned. "Me too. That's what I'm going to do. I'm doing my twenty years, then retire right here on my pension. Then you and me are going to spend the rest of our days on a beach like this. We'll watch beautiful bronze-skinned girls bouncing in the waves. We'll make every day play out exactly like this one."

I took a drink out of my beer and watched a wave crest over Mari's head, knocking her down, laughing into the water. Tala was giggling herself as she helped her daughter up. A few feet away, Darrow was sitting in the surf. Bradley Junior was standing on his lap, looking around in wonderment, taking in the first time he had ever set foot in the ocean. Lorna was ankle-deep in the water, unable to take her eyes off of the master chief and her son. Tony Bard and Anna were further out, up to their necks, embracing each other and enjoying long, passionate kisses beneath an orange sky.

"Yeah," I said to Dixie as I leaned back into the sand. "It has been damn near a perfect day, hasn't it?"

It was a perfect day up to that point. I was still several hours away from knowing how imperfect it would unexpectedly become.

*****

CHAPTER 23

At first, I thought I had been stabbed. I was jolted awake by a piercing pain deep within my bowels, forcing me to bolt upright and cry out in pain. Then the second wave hit. It was so intense that my entire body went rigid as I fell back to the bed on my side, curled up in misery. "Doyle!" Tala cried, startled awake. "Are you okay?"

"I don't know," I gasped through clenched teeth. Then a third wave hit, the one that felt like a large piece of broken glass tearing its way through my intestines. That was followed by some alarming gurgling noises bubbling up through my stomach. They were loud enough for Tala to hear.

"Is dat gas?" she asked, sounding dismayed and surprised.

"Oh, Christ," I groaned. "Maybe, but it hurts!"

"Do you need help? Do you need to go to bathroom?"

"Aaaaarggh!" I snapped, growing irritated by Tala's interrogation. "I don't know what I need! Just let me…"

Suddenly it felt like that piece of glass in my gut found a ride on a bullet train down my large intestine. It was moving through me fast toward the exit, and before I knew it, it was pounding on the back door, screaming to get out.

I was hoping that Tala was right about it being gas, but there was no way that I was going to trust it. I rolled out of bed as fast as I could and bolted for the door, doubled over in agony.

Once I escaped the bedroom, I was surprised to find myself already a half-lap behind Dixie in a furious race to the toilet. "No!" I shouted out. "No! Kevin! Please…"

Dixie was in no position to negotiate. He was buck naked. With one hand clasped over his mouth and the other clutching his backside, he was holding on for dear life to keep himself from blowing out of both ends. There was no time for courtesy. He knew before I did that this was an every-man-for-himself situation. He ran for the head like his life depended on it, his wee white willy waving wildly in the wind as there was no time for modesty either. In as much distress as I was in, I had to let him go. When you cross paths with that flavor of desperado on a midnight trip to the loo, your instincts tell you to stay the hell out of the man's way.

Before I could take two steps, Dixie was in the bathroom with the door closed behind him. I fell to my knees and pounded on the barrier between us. "Come on, Kevin!" I cried out. "Please let me in!"

My ears then registered two sounds together that should never be heard coming out of a single person at the same time. I instantly knew that our bathroom had just been rendered unusable. As I writhed on the floor outside of the head, I thought of every position I could reasonably expect the human body to contort into. There was no scenario I could come up with where Dixie could twist enough to purge himself from both ends simultaneously and make everything into the toilet. I knew I needed another option but was unable to come up with one. Frankly, I did not think that I could move any further than I already had without catastrophic consequences.

"DIXIE!" I yelled, pounding on the door one more time. "PLEASE! I'm begging you! I need in there now!"

Kevin tried to answer, but he sounded like a laryngitic wharf seal throwing up a flounder. It punctuated how hopeless my situation was. There were two very sick men in an apartment with only one toilet. All I could do was laugh, which turned out to be a horrible move. My intestines twisted up around themselves, constricting to expel everything inside of me. I doubled over again, grunting as I fought to keep everything in for a few moments longer. With my desperation overpowering my instincts, I had to go in. If I could not use the toilet, I had no choice but to go for the shower. I could just keep the water running and waffle stomp whatever came out of me down the drain. I reached out for the handle above me, twisted it, and pushed opened the bathroom door.

I immediately wished I hadn't. Kevin was on his knees with his head heaving into the toilet bowl. It appeared that his melon had only recently made it in there as the entire commode was covered in vomit. His left hand appeared glued to the handle, flushing to get the contents of his stomach out of his face. Dixie's right hand gripped the lip of a little garbage can that he was holding to his backside as tight as he could. He should not have bothered with that, though. The damage had already been done.

While Kevin was struggling to decide which end he needed to stick into the toilet first, his bowels made the choice for him. His posterior blew like canon shot. *Bagoong*-fueled waste blasted across the decorative towels and all over the shower curtain. The bathroom was destroyed. There was no way that I could use it. I had no time to find alternative accommodations, though. If I did not figure out something soon, we would all be spending the next day cleaning far more of the apartment than we ever intended.

By this time, Tala had thrown on a nightshirt before running out of our bedroom to help. She rushed to my side to get me off of the floor but screamed when she saw how Dixie had redecorated the bathroom. This woke up the rest of the apartment, with Elena emerging from the bedroom to check on her man.

Seeing the condition I was in, Tala knew that I needed to get to another bathroom fast. With strength I never expected to come out of someone so tiny, she lifted me back onto my feet. "WE NEED GO TO MY APARTMENT!" she screamed at me. "GET UP, DOYLE! RUN!"

But I couldn't run—even the act of standing put more stress on my intestines than I could bear. By the time I hopped twice, I knew the battle was lost. I was ripping off my tighty-whities as Bard and Anna were stepping out of their room.

"Jesus, Doyle!" Tony yelled. "What the fuck are you doing?!?"

Anna figured it out. She saw where I was headed and screamed out in horror. "NO, DOYLE! NOT IN DA KITCHEN! NOT IN DA…"

I hopped again, but my underwear got tangled around my ankles, tripping me up and sending me crashing to the floor. Somehow, I still managed to keep everything contained. I rolled over and leapt to my feet with my back to the counter. Leaning back, I put my hands on the edge of the sink and lifted myself over it. The floodgates opened while I was still in the air, but I managed to keep everything off the floor. I also missed the area where we stacked the wet dishes. I was praying to God that I had at least picked the side of the sink with the garbage disposal, though.

"Noooooooooo!" Anna screamed as she watched me defile the kitchen. Elena screamed too, having finally seen what Dixie did to the bathroom. At this point, everything deteriorated into pure bedlam. Anna started yelling at Tony to do something about his shipmates. After finally tearing her eyes off of Kevin to see what I was doing, Elena began laying into me. Tala came to my defense and, in return, started yelling at both Anna and Elena.

The shouting was so loud that it woke up Mahal next door, who groggily stumbled over to our place. She let herself in to see what was happening. At this point, I was pleading for someone to bring me toilet paper. No one could hear me, though, so I turned on the water faucet and tried to run it over my backside while throwing up into the other side of the sink. "Oh my God!" Mahal yelled. "Doyle! Are you okay?"

After being reduced to dry heaves, I looked over at my neighbor and asked, "Is that a trick question?"

Tala's roommate did not understand and took a couple of steps toward me. "We need get you to da bathroom! Why you no go use da bathroom?"

"Go look at it," I told her before retching again.

"No! Mahal!" Tala pleaded. "Don't! Don't look into da bathroom!"

Mahal screamed. It was too late. She looked.

In a weird way, I was kind of proud of myself. I was constipated all through basic training because there were no stalls around the toilets. I could never drop a deuce with an audience. That night, though, I had five people in my living room screaming at each other and at me. Yet there I was, in the throes of a *bagoong* cleanse like I did not have a care in the world. At least I had nothing to care about until I saw Tony Bard start turning green.

OLONGAPO EARP

"Hey!" I shouted out, trying to get everyone's attention. "We're out of plumbing fixtures! Someone's going to have to do something with Tony!"

The girls fell silent and looked over at our leading petty officer. He nodded at Anna. "Yeah, I'm not feeling very good. Tala, can I use your bathroom?"

The faces of both Tala and Mahal contorted in terror as they ran screaming from our apartment. "Noooooo! No! No! No! NOOOOOOOOOO!"

Elena ran too, locking herself into her room while Anna did the same. Tony tried to enter after his girlfriend, but she wedged herself between the bed and the door to keep him out. "Anna! Please! Let me in!"

"Let you in?" Anna yelled back. "What you t'ink you gonna do in here! Shit in you bed?!? No! I no lettin' you in!"

She had a point. Since I had the sink and Dixie had the bathroom, there was only one option left. Ripping off his shorts, Bard dove into the kiddie pool in the middle of our living room and, while purging his bowels, earned his Tequila Viking tattoo.

Despite everything going on, I started to laugh. It was all I could do. I could not see him at all, but I heard Dixie begin cracking up as well. His laughter echoed off the sides of the toilet bowl, making everything even funnier. After a little while, probably because Dixie and I could not stop, Tony busted up too. Before we knew it, the three of us were roaring between dry heaves and explosive bowel movements. "IT NO PUNNY!" Elena screamed from behind the door, making us laugh even more.

"Hey sweetie," I called over to her. "Can you please bring us some toilet paper?"

"And something to read!" Dixie yelled. "I'm going to be here a while!"

We were stuck like that for hours. We thought we were done a couple of times, but any attempt to move was met with near disaster. At dawn, we were just well enough to clean up as best we could to get back to the ship. The apartment was such a mess that we seriously discussed abandoning it.

*****

"How was your night?" I asked Master Chief Darrow after quarters.

He looked pale and exhausted. "Pretty rough," he said. "You guys get sick?"

Bard could barely stand; he was so wiped out. "Oh my god, did we ever. You should see our apartment."

"You should see my fuckin' bed," Darrow countered.

"Oh no, don't tell me you shit the bed," Dixie said.

"Shit the bed? Fuck, guys! I shit all over Lorna!"

I busted out laughing, pissing Darrow off since he was trying to keep his voice down. "It's not funny, Doyle! I was lying on my side, naked, my ass facing her way, and there was no fucking warning! I thought I was dealing with a runaway fart, but I lost complete control. Shit went flying everywhere!"

By now, Dixie and Bard were dying too, so even Master Chief Darrow caught himself giggling under his breath. "Okay. Maybe it's a little bit funny. For Christ's sake, though! I met my son for the very first time yesterday, and the kid couldn't even look me in the eye this morning after seeing what I did! You think he was afraid of me when we first met? You should see him now!"

*****

If the trip to Lorna's village was the best day of our time in the Philippines, the day after was among the worst. Dixie, Bard, and I spent the morning on the ship trying to recuperate, which turned out to be a good move. After we ate lunch, we were struck with a second wave. Fortunately, our ship's heads were far better equipped to deal with it.

Once we were sure everything had passed, the three of us made our way back to the apartment to try to tidy up what we could. When we got there, though, we saw that Tala had nearly finished cleaning it all by herself. Elena and Anna packed up and left. The USS Belleau Wood only had a little over a week left in port anyway, and the two girls figured that now was a good time to cut their losses and split. Both Tony and Dixie seemed almost relieved. It saved them the trouble of telling them goodbye later.

Tala was determined not to let me off the hook so easily. We were all amazed by how much she had accomplished. The only big job left for us was to get rid of the rancid kiddie pool with the defiled remains of our

OLONGAPO EARP

gecko stew still sloshing around inside of it. We drained it as best we could with a bucket. Ultimately, though, we still had to carry it outside like three pallbearers mourning the demise of a favored beverage. We threw it over the courtyard's back wall into the jungle, doing our best to place it where the monkeys congregated. It was a final "fuck you" from our friend Claude Metaire.

*****

As bad as our morning was, Master Chief Darrow's was far worse. Dixie, Bard, and I were on the ship when the second wave of *bagoong* belly struck us down. The master chief was at a local fish market, wearing a pair of white shorts, when it hit him.

He was in the middle of a crowded street, shoulder to shoulder with a mob of humanity when the sensation crept up on him. It happened so fast that all he could do was look at Lorna and say, "God help us," before undoing his belt and dropping trou straight to his knees.

At first, the crowd looked at him in surprise and disapproval, trying to figure out what he was doing. When he fired off a warning shot though, people began pushing to get out of the way. It was as if they just heard the second horn heralding the arrival of the apocalypse. After Darrow's bowels cleared themselves the first time, they broke into a full stampede.

Knowing that the cops would be getting there soon, Darrow tried to run away with them. He could not gain much speed with his shorts around his knees, though. He knew that he could not pull his pants back up before running, either. With white shorts on, everyone would be able to tell exactly who had desecrated the fish market.

Lorna knew this and swooped in to help. Yelling at her son to stay close, she ran to one of the ice tables and grabbed a bucket of water from off the ground. She then bolted back to the master chief and started splashing it on his bare behind to clean him up. As Lorna did this, Darrow skipped over to one of the vendor tables, where he saw rows of tuna wrapped in old newspaper. Tearing off a large piece of yesterday's headlines from one of the fish, my master chief was able to finish the job. He then got his pants back up, scooped up his son, and ran for home.

It was a story that earned an honorable mention on Olongapo's nightly news broadcast. The reporters stated that the authorities were close to identifying a suspect, but they never did. That was once again thanks to the interference run by Sergeant Rico Tejada of the Philippine National Police. Master Chief Darrow did not get so much as an indecent exposure ticket.

Now, it was obvious that men like Darrow were not in the habit of seeking validation from their subordinates, but, regardless, we were all in awe that the man unleashed a bowel movement sensational enough to be mentioned on TV. We doubted that our master chief wanted to join our little club, but we made a point of letting him know that he had done more than enough to earn the coveted Tequila Viking tattoo.

I also cannot express how honored we were when he told us that he intended to get it inked on his back the next time we pulled into Hong Kong.

*****

CHAPTER 24

Bill Kramer, the former nemesis of Warren Macklemore, was a drooling idiot. After his part in getting Macklemore thrown out of the Navy, Kramer ended up something of a pariah. Despite being married, Bill spent his time in the Philippines accompanying one of his few friends, Mike Deaver, through every whorehouse in Olongapo while still claiming to be faithful to his wife. This became a source of great hilarity when he picked up a scorching case of gonorrhea.

The general rule in the US Navy was that whatever happened in the Philippines stayed in the Philippines. As despised as Kramer was, nobody considered telling his wife what he had been up to. Well, nobody considered it besides Kramer, anyway. Painfully aware of how disliked he was, Bill was sure that someone would rat him out. To get ahead of the problem, he thought it would be a good idea to call his wife and confess. It wasn't.

Donna was furious. She called her husband a long list of names to make sure that he knew exactly how big a scumbag he was. At some point in that conversation, Kramer thought he would look better if he told his wife that he was not the only errant husband in Olongapo. He dropped the names of several married men in the department that he saw cavorting with Filipina prostitutes, too. He also dropped the names of a couple that didn't, among them my guy, Rick Hammond, and Stu Pulaski, who worked for Bard in Comm Repair.

The men were livid with Kramer, to say the least. Even Deaver, Bill's stalwart drinking buddy, abandoned him. He did not want to be anywhere near the guy when the men decided to take their pound of flesh.

Accused of whoring around on liberty, Hammond stopped going out into town and offered to take my last duty day in the Philippines for me. I wanted to accept his offer, but I discovered that tension with Kramer had reached a boiling point. I got word that several men were planning to escort the son-of-a-bitch to the Nixie Room for a "bo'sun locker counseling session." In other words, they were going to kick the living shit out of him.

It was almost a year to the day since I beat Randy Green into epilepsy in that very space. I was not about to let good men, especially ET3 Pulaski, make that same mistake. When they opened the door to the Nixie to see if their stolen key worked, they found me inside waiting for them.

"You all know that this is a secured space, right?" I asked the surprised men. I then pointed to the small torpedo-shaped devices secured against the aft wall. "See those fish over there? The electromagnetic frequencies they transmit are classified. Do you have any idea how much trouble you'll be in if you got caught stealing the key to this room?"

The men all looked at each other in shock, but no one offered to guess. I had to answer my own question for them. "You'd be in a lot of trouble, *but*, not nearly as much as you'll get into for beating Kramer's ass."

"Look, Doyle!" Airman Clepper shouted at me, "That man ruined my fucking marriage!"

"No, Joe," I countered. "You ruined your own marriage. All Kramer did was out you for it. Look, I'm not condoning what the dickhead did. It was a punk move. I'm not going to let you all make a bad situation irretrievably worse, though. Trust me, guys. Think about what I went through with Randy Green. That man nearly died and I almost spent the best years of my life in the stockade for it. The captain was very clear to me after that. If he hears of crew members taking matters into their own hands again, he's going to make sure that they do hard time for it. There isn't going to be any reduction in rate, sixty days restriction, and forfeiture of a half month's pay times two. You're going to prison."

Cleveland was not persuaded. "That son-of-a-bitch is getting me divorced!"

"Then you're getting divorced," I told him. "Would you rather go through a divorce as a free man or as a federal prisoner?"

When nobody answered, I nodded my head in understanding. "I'm sorry this happened. I can assure you that nobody wants to see Bill Kramer get his ass beat more than me. I'm not willing to lose a single one of you to have it done, though." Holding out my hand, I ordered Pulaski to turn over the keys.

After the men had left, I locked up the Nixie Winch Room and then returned the stolen key to the EMO office. I was a little disappointed to discover that Lieutenant Krause was not there. As much as I hated that man, I had doubts about whether he was responsible for the attempted hit on Darrow. I thought some resentful *shabu* dealer or a gangster with a grudge was a far more likely suspect. I wanted a little more interaction with the lieutenant to get a better read on the guy but would not be getting it that day.

I let myself out of the EMO through the porthole and climbed the ladder to the SPN-35 platform. I intended to string my hammock up to do some serious thinking. However, when I got to the door, I discovered it was already open and full of cigarette smoke. Master Chief Darrow was sitting on the deck with his back up against the aft wall. He looked like hell.

"Are you okay?" I asked as I walked inside. I was going to light a cigarette myself, but the air in the dome was already so thick that I did not need to. Reaching behind the radar, I turned on the air conditioning to filter out some of the smoke.

"Not really," Darrow told me while shaking his head. "I have a big decision to make and I'm really struggling with it. I'm wondering if you're struggling with the same one. Do you know what you're going to do about Tala and the kid?"

I let out a long sigh. "That's what I was coming here to think about."

"She's good for you, Doyle," my master chief told me.

I nodded. "Do you know that I've not had a single episode since we've been together? No flashbacks, no nightmares, nothing? Not even after watching that prick get shot at the Dirty Crow. Everything I've ever been through, my family, the girl in El Salvador, Hulagu, even Randy Green, it's like it's all gone. I think it's because I know that no matter what I do, Tala and Mari will be there for me if I want them to be. As fucked up as I am, I'm the best option they got."

"Are you going to be there for them?"

I dropped my head into my hands. "Fuck! I don't know, Master Chief! I just don't know! I want to, but for Christ's sake! She was a whore. I can take the girl out of the bar, but can I get the bar out of the girl? I keep going back to those goofy-looking fuckers I always saw walking 32nd Street with gorgeous Filipina girls on their arms. I was always thinking, 'Ha! That loser had to marry himself a hooker!' Am I big enough to have people look at me and Tala that way and not care? I'm not sure I am."

I put my back up against the dome and slid down to the deck to put myself at my master chief's level. After lighting myself a smoke anyway, I asked, "Do you remember Space Kate from Ocean Beach? You met her the night I got engaged to Hannah."

Darrow shook his head. "Not really."

"Well, she was a good friend of ours. After Hannah dumped my ass, she told me that there was no way that we would have made it anyway. She said it was better things got broken off before we got married. She said she loved Hannah, but she'd led something of a sheltered life. Without having been through a lot of adversity, Kate said that Hannah'd never be able to relate to all the shit I'd gone through. She just wouldn't be able to understand."

I paused as I tried to remember the exact words that Kate had said to me. "She told me something like, 'One day, you're going to meet someone that can handle you. You'll meet a girl who's been through a lot of shit herself. The two of you will make each other very happy.' I'm sitting here wondering if Tala may be that girl."

Darrow nodded. "She might be."

"And she might be like any one of the chicks you come across at the Trophy Lounge on any given night. Maybe she's just manipulating me into taking her and her kid back to the States so that she can dump me and find someone better. I've barely known her a month, Master Chief. I haven't had the time to figure out exactly what I'm dealing with here."

OLONGAPO EARP

Master Chief Darrow thought for several moments before asking me a question. "Would you like more time?"

"Here? In Olongapo? Sure," I answered. "You can manage that?"

Darrow shrugged. "Eventually. Doyle, I've got a year until I retire. Twelve months. After that, I'm coming back."

I winced. "Are you serious? What about your wife? What about Jung?"

Letting out yet another long sigh, Darrow said, "I'm going to ask for a divorce. Doyle, I've got a son here in the Philippines. A mixed-race son. Do you know what the phrase '*pekeng tisoy*' means?"

"I know that '*pekeng*' means 'fake.' I've never heard the word '*tisoy*' before, though."

"It means white boy. *Pekeng tisoy* means something like 'fake American.' It's what Filipinos call the Amer-Asian kids around here, the children of prostitutes. It's like calling a black man a nigger back home. That's the kind of shit my boy's going to be up against growing up here on his own."

"Jesus," I said.

"Yeah, but if his old man's around to protect him, get him educated, and set him up with a livelihood, well, he'll be fine. Hell, the mayor of Olongapo, Dick Gordon, is the son of a half-breed. He's even a quarter Jewish in a very Catholic country. His old man, Jimmy Gordon, was the guy who got Olongapo returned to the Philippines. Before him, the city was run by the base commander, an American military officer. If I stay, my boy has a fighting chance at being somebody. If I leave, he's going to end up an outcast, like the *shabu* junkie that tried to kill me at the Dirty Crow."

I shook my head. "I don't blame you, Master Chief, but it doesn't seem very fair to Jung."

"It's not," Darrow groaned. "She's a grown, industrious woman, though. She can take care of herself. My son can't."

After taking a drag off of my cigarette, I asked, "You think Tala can take care of herself?"

My master chief did not even hesitate. "Not really. She'll try. She'll get out of Olongapo, try to find work. She's a peasant girl, though. She doesn't have any skills. Sooner or later, Mari will get hungry. The temptation for Tala to start selling herself again will prove too hard to resist. Tala's done a remarkable job so far, Doyle, but these women eventually break. They start using dope to dull the pain, and then there's no going back. Odds are that Mari will end up following her mother into the same line of work."

"Fuck you, Master Chief."

"What?" My insult caught Darrow off guard.

"How stupid do you think I am?" I asked. "You think I'm too dumb not to realize when I'm being played? You're trying to guilt me into staying with Tala, aren't you? Why? You're playing some sort of angle here. What do you want?"

"What are you talking about?" Darrow tried to claim innocence, but he sounded disingenuous.

"What. Do. You. Want?"

My master chief sighed and gave in. He knew I wanted him to get to the point. "I want to help, Doyle. I want to help you. And me."

"How?"

"You said that you didn't know if you could handle people wondering if you were with a whore. What about if you were here? In the Philippines? It's different here, especially around Olongapo. People look at a person like Tala on your arm, and they're almost rooting for her. 'Hey! Look at her! Homegirl did good! Married herself a rich American! She's moving up in the world!' Things like that are so common in these parts; people don't even think twice about it."

"And what would I do here?"

Darrow dropped his cigarette into the soda can he was using as an ashtray. "You got any plans tomorrow?"

"Not particularly," I said. "No."

"Good," my master chief replied. "I got something to show you. I'll swing by your place when I leave the ship. Have Tala keep Mari home from school. We're going to take another road trip. It's not too far away, but I think it might be right up your alley."

*****

Staying in the Philippines…

It sounded like a good idea at the time, but I had to wonder if it was what I wanted. Was Tala what I wanted? She was gorgeous, and I enjoyed spending time with her, but the truth was that my desire to be with her had more to do with Mari than it did with Tala. I did not want that little girl following her mother into the sex trade. I wanted to give her a fighting chance at a better life. I did not see Tala and me spending nights under the stars discussing philosophy like Hannah and I once did.

As I walked into the radar repair shop, Rick Hammond was there playing video games. "Hey Doyle," he said. "You got a letter. It's on your desk."

That surprised me. After four years in the Navy, I had never received mail before. Looking down, I spotted an envelope with blue and red stripes along the edges, indicating it was international post. Picking it up and flipping it over, I saw that it was from Yukiko Fukuyama back in Japan. My heart started to race. Yukiko *was* someone I could lie on the beach and discuss the cosmos with. "Jesus Christ," I muttered under my breath.

It was not the reaction Rick expected to hear from me. "I figured that of all people, you would be thrilled to get a letter," Hammond said. "Is something wrong?"

"I don't know." I tore open the envelope and sat down at my desk to read the note inside.

Dear Doyle,

I am so sorry it took me so long to write to you. It was tough to get your address. Steve Morgan at Shooter's Bar helped me a lot. I hate to admit this, but we figured out how to write you from a couple of angry American ladies who were in his place. They were looking to get back at their husbands for cheating on them in the Philippines.

I wanted you to know that I have not been able to stop thinking about the day that poor boy was killed in the park. I was so proud of you for what you did to save his life. I am so sorry that it did not work. I have been thinking about you a lot since that day, and I wonder if you are thinking of me too.

Doyle, I am looking forward to seeing you when you get back to Japan. I pass the base every day when I come home from work, and I always look to see if your ship is here yet. When I see your ship come in, I will wait at the Albuquerque Bridge at 6 pm for a little while. If you want to see me, meet me there.

I hope you are having fun in the Philippines, but not as much fun as the husbands of the ladies I met at Shooters.

I miss you and hope to see you soon!
With Love,
Yukiko

"Son-of-a-bitch," I growled as I leaned back in my seat, reaching to light another cigarette.

"What's wrong?" Hammond asked, keeping his eyes riveted to his game on TV. "What was in the letter?"

"An option that really complicates my life right now."

*****

When Master Chief Darrow and I crossed the bridge over Shit River the following morning, a hired jeepney was already waiting for us. In it were Lorna and little Bradley, Tala, and Mari. A half-hour later, we were on the coast in the general vicinity of a sleepy little village called San Felipe. There was nothing in sight but a pair of fishing catamarans further up the coast.

It was a beautiful place with a spacious sugar sand beach. The row of coconut palms at the end of it was so thick we could not even see the road from the water. Traffic was sparse, and the entire area seemed deserted. With lush, verdant mountains behind us and nothing but blue ocean before us, we were standing on an unspoiled parcel of paradise.

I was still admiring the view when Sergeant Tejada arrived with his wife and kids in his marked patrol vehicle. "Hey, Doyle!" TJ called to me as they got out of the Jeep. "What you t'ink about dis place?"

"It's beautiful!" I answered, shouting to be heard above the wind. "The water's a bit rough, though! I wish I had a surfboard!"

TJ and Darrow grinned at me. Tejada reached into the back of his Jeep and pulled out a six-foot board, throwing it in my direction. "You've got to be kidding me!" I exclaimed. "Where the hell did you find this?"

"It be in da station por a long time. I t'ink it recovered in theft investigation or somet'ing. Da owner probably a tourist who go home long bepore we pind dis t'ing. No one ever claim it, so we use it prom time to time."

I was like a kid at Christmas, grabbing the board and running out into the surf. Once I got out a bit, the breaks were quite respectable, coming in at the highest end of my skill level. Still, as clumsy as I knew I was out there, I was a point break superhero to all the kids on the beach. They cheered and applauded every time I caught a wave and laughed their little butts off every time I wiped out.

After a couple of hours of surfing, we moved down to a calmer stretch of ocean, and I tried to teach a couple of TJ's kids how to ride. When they gave up, I took the younger ones out bodyboarding. We eventually broke for lunch and drifted into the village. San Felipe was just large enough to serve street food, but rural enough that we could still feed six adults and five children for less than twenty dollars.

When we finished eating, we drove the kids to a spot where they could swim without clinging to an adult for dear life. The women and children went right for the water while the three of us men hung back. Opening a beer apiece and passing them around, Darrow asked, "So, what do you think, Doyle? How's the surfing?"

I took a drink of San Miguel and shrugged. "Well, it's not going to attract any international competitions or anything, but it's plenty enough to have some fun in."

"Even for experienced surfers?"

I looked over the waves and nodded. "Yeah, it's just challenging enough to have a good time while you're partying. It's a bit light for someone serious about it, though. Are the waves always like this?"

Tejada shrugged. "Sometime bigger. Sometime smaller. Depend on time op da year."

Nodding, I said, "It usually does."

"You think it has what it takes to be a destination? For surfing?" Darrow asked.

I scanned the area and pressed my lips together. "It's really beautiful here, but it's a bit light on infrastructure. There's nowhere for anyone to stay. Not much in the way of nightlife. You guys thinking of building something here?"

My master chief grinned. "It's for sale. What do you think it would take to get surfers out this way?"

I shrugged. "As far as infrastructure? Less than you would think. I've heard some of the surf gypsies in Ocean Beach rave about going to Central America. There they stay in bamboo shacks right on the sand on the Pacific coast of Nicaragua. Give them a thatch roof with a single light bulb, a mattress with mosquito netting, a fan, and access to a freshwater shower and you'll about have it covered. Hell, even in California, they'll party until they pass out in the sand, and let me tell you, the nights get pretty goddamn cold in OB."

"What else you t'ink we need?" asked Sergeant Tejada.

"Well, a bar, for sure. Something to eat. The bank of food carts like we had lunch at would do just fine." I looked at Sergeant Tejada. "And you would need a somewhat relaxed attitude when it came to certain recreational substances. Look, these people aren't usually coke heads and they certainly aren't putting needles in their arms. If surfers don't have easy access to marijuana, though, they aren't going to bother coming. Letting them get their hands on the occasional magic mushroom wouldn't hurt either. You think you could get your buddies on the force to keep their distance from these guys, Sergeant?"

Tejada smiled and pulled a pack of Marlboros out of his pants pocket. He then withdrew something out of it that most certainly was not a cigarette. Lighting it up, he took a massive drag off of it and passed it over to Master Chief Darrow while holding the smoke in. "I no t'ink I get any problem prom da police, Doyle."

Darrow took a long hit off of the joint, too, before passing it to me. "You want in on this?"

"The pot or the business you guys are talking about?"

"Both."

I took the blunt and looked at it for a moment. "It's been an awful long time since I did this shit. What if I get popped on a piss test?"

My master chief shrugged. "Then I'll cover your share to get into our business. They'll throw you out of the Navy, and you'll have to get started here a little earlier than planned."

I looked at the joint and then back at my master chief. "Fuck it," I said as I took my first spliff hit in more than five years. "How much is this plan of yours going to cost?"

"A lot," the master chief said.

"You have enough?"

Darrow shook his head. "Not yet, but TJ and I have something in the works."

OLONGAPO EARP

My spidey-senses started to tingle. "What?"

"You've got to tell me you're in with us before I get into that. And I want you to think about it for a while first. This isn't something you're going to want to rush into."

I looked the two men over as I passed Tejada the weed. Having been in the Philippines for a month now, I realized that TJ and my master chief were hitting far above my weight class. It was no secret that both of them bent the rules with little hesitation. They had been doing it for decades and, as far as I knew, had never been called to the carpet for it. They seemed to know what they were doing. The question was, did I?

My instincts were screaming at me to run away and refuse outright, but I looked over at Mari playing in the surf with her mother. I pictured her ending up desperate enough one day to accept a job singing for tips in a Barrio Barretto bikini bar.

When the joint made its way back to me again, I took an even bigger hit off of it than I did the first time. "Say I did tell you that I wanted in. What would it take?"

"Well, for starters, it would take that fifty grand you have in Panama," Darrow told me. "That should get a couple of cabanas built and buy you a share in the bar that we need to set up. You would also need to travel a bit to spread the word about this place. Thailand. Bali. Australia. Wherever it is those surf gypsies you were talking about go. That's as much as I'm willing to say until I get your decision."

It might have been the weed, but I saw Darrow let his guard down and flash Tejada a very large grin when they thought I was not looking. The sergeant smiled back. They knew that I was already in. Even if I didn't.

*****

CHAPTER 25

San Felipe was the high-water mark of my time in the Philippines. It was another perfect day, but after that, every ticking second was a reminder of how soon we would be leaving. Elena and Anna had already moved out, making our apartment seem much emptier. With Dixie and Bard on duty the day after my trip to the ocean, I hosted Darrow and Tejada for a quiet night in to talk. After a few beers, we were taking stock of our time in Subic Bay.

Lorna was sitting on the living room couch, speaking with Tala. Mari was keeping Little Bradley occupied on the floor. I saw Lorna steal a peek at Master Chief Darrow with glassy eyes. The look on her face betrayed that she wondered if her boy's father would be coming back as he promised. I had not made Tala any such assurances, but I had been sensing that she was hoping for one, too. I wondered if she knew what Darrow had offered me.

"I sorry we no catch your boss in Pagsanjan," TJ told my master chief as we sat at my kitchen table.

OLONGAPO EARP

Darrow grimaced. "I'm not done with that son-of-a-bitch yet. You ever straighten out those fuckers over there, TJ?"

The sergeant nodded. "Yep. We still get not'ing, dough. We pucked up a couple op da gang boys pretty bad. Dey keep saying dat dere no military guys going to Pagsanjan por da kids. Dey snapping pictures op anybody dey pind dat look American. Dey try to give us somet'ing, anyt'ing, to keep us prom coming back. Dey just come up empty."

"You believe them?" Darrow asked.

Tejada nodded. "I do."

"Maybe you were wrong, Master Chief," I said. "Maybe Krause isn't as depraved as you think." I, for one, was relieved that American military men were not visiting that vile place.

Darrow shook his head. "No, I'm positive he got tipped off. I know he's spending time with that missionary group. I'm almost certain that the prick you knocked out in the alley somehow got word to him that we were out there. He knows I'm on to his particular flavor of kink. That's why he's so desperate to shut me up. Why else would he send someone to snuff me out?"

Tejada pointed his finger at my master chief. "You don't know it was him dat do dat, Bradley. You got a lot op enemies in Olongapo. I can t'ink op so many people who like to hurt you dat I can't even investigate dem all. It too bad Rickie Ibay died. I never know who behind dat now."

"I'm telling you, TJ, that prick Krause did it. That man has a hard-on for me like you would not believe. It's been driving me nuts trying to figure out why, but I'm convinced that this guy thinks I wronged him in some way. He's trying to get me to pay for it."

"But to da point op trying to kill you, Bradley? C'mon! He an oppicer in da United States Navy! He not some crime boss out dere putting contracts on da people who work por him!"

"You remember Wayne Pomeroy, TJ?"

"Who?"

"Chief Pomeroy. He was the guy who found out his wife was fucking a Marine major out of Cubi Point. You could not have found a more model sailor, TJ. This guy was a Mormon. He didn't drink, he didn't smoke, and even while we were arresting him, he couldn't even bring himself to swear. The guy was in church every Sunday. This man went through his entire life and never even got himself a traffic ticket. Four hours after discovering his wife is getting some on the side, though, he found some barrio rat to slit her throat from ear to ear. All it took was three hundred dollars. During his interrogation, we found out that he was waiting for payday to hire someone to take care of the major, too. That would have been five hundred."

Darrow took a sip of San Miguel. "TJ, that mama's boy had no street smarts whatsoever. Even he found a junkie derelict to snuff a woman and an American military officer for less than a thousand bucks, though. I'm sure Krause could, too."

Sergeant Tejada nodded. "Yeah, I remember dat guy now. I peel sorry por dey kids. Still, Bradley, dis no peel right. My instinct telling me you wrong."

"My instincts are telling me I'm right! Do you know Lieutenant Krause, TJ?"

The sergeant shook his head. "No. I never meet him."

"Well, I sit next to the son-of-a-bitch every goddamn day. Do you trust my instincts?"

The sergeant looked at Darrow for a long moment, remembering all the time he had spent with him. The AFPD and the PNP worked hand in glove with each other. They had been through a lot together. Tejada knew that there were few policemen whose instincts were more reliable than Darrow's. "Yes, Bradley. I trust your instincts."

"Then put your back into working this angle, Rico. We need to get this cocksucker before he gets me. Understand?"

*****

As much as I enjoyed the company of Sergeant Tejada and my master chief, I wanted to spend time with Tala and Mari. I tried easing my guests out of the apartment by nine. When everybody got to the door, however, Tala and Lorna suddenly discovered that they had so much more to talk about. Instead of standing there staring at them, we made our way outside for some fresh air. Once on the other side of the gate, standing on the sidewalk, we lit cigarettes while we waited for my master chief's girlfriend.

We were three days from departure. Darrow and Tejada were making plans to meet each other one last time the following afternoon. As they talked, I caught myself impatiently staring up and down the road, wondering what was taking Lorna so long. As my gaze glanced across the street, I noticed movement in the narrow space between the *sari-sari* store opposite our apartment and the house standing next to it. At first, I thought it was monkeys getting into the garbage again. When I stepped forward to get a better look, however, I did not find a renegade macaque scrounging for a late-night meal. Instead, I made eye contact with a young boy hiding in the shadows. As I tried to figure out what he was doing there, I saw him panic. He rushed to lift a bandana up over his nose and then pulled a revolver from his waist. When he lifted the weapon and pointed it in our direction, it was my turn to panic.

"MASTER CHIEF!" I screamed, leaping at Darrow and tackling him to the ground. As we hit the sidewalk, the boy's weapon roared from the far side of the road. The stucco wall exploded above our heads as it absorbed the bullets, showering the three of us below with dust and chips of plaster. Tejada dropped to his knees and went for his own gun to return fire. Caught completely off-guard and having had a little too much to drink, he fumbled to get his weapon out of its holster. As shots continued to ring out, he had to give up for a moment and roll toward the curb to get to better cover behind one of the parked cars. The master chief and I followed him.

The kid was coming at us gangster-style, holding his weapon one-handed and aiming sideways. That saved our lives. Firing a revolver that way may have looked cool in the movies, but in reality, it was awkward and offered no muzzle control. It made it very difficult for a boy that small to pull the trigger on a gun that big. It also made hitting a moving target damn near impossible.

Despite being in shock, I was able to understand the shouting in Tagalog breaking out down the street. "Bong! What are you doing?!?" one of the kid's accomplices exclaimed. "You were supposed to wait!"

"I couldn't!" the boy screamed back as he fired off a couple more rounds. "They saw me!"

"The girls and kids are still upstairs!" I yelled at Darrow. "We've got to get these guys away from the house!"

My master chief nodded and looked around. His training and instincts allowed him to assess the situation in a fraction of a second. He spotted two men up the street running toward us with guns drawn to our left. The master chief did not like the odds of going that way. He decided it safer to take our chances with the kid wasting his ammunition. Grabbing me by the shirt, Darrow lifted me to my feet and we bolted toward a fork in the road ahead of us.

Tejada did not follow. With his weapon finally out, he took aim at the men on our left. When they pointed their guns at Darrow and me, TJ squeezed off a round, catching one of our assailants at center mass and killing him instantly. In response, the other shooter shifted targets. He fired three quick shots at the policeman, hitting the sergeant at least once. The last thing I saw before running off of Harris Street was Rico Tejada spinning violently around before hitting the sidewalk. His pistol flew out of his hands and into the street. I then heard my girlfriend run out of our apartment after us, screaming my name.

I wanted to yell at Tala to stay back, but as Darrow and I ducked into the alleys, I was too preoccupied. Not only was the kid and the man who shot Sergeant Tejada on our heels, but two new gunmen appeared out of nowhere to join the chase. Screaming at Tala to stay put would have wasted my breath and since the shooters were all following Darrow and me anyway, there was no real need to. As heavy smokers running uphill, both my master chief and I needed all the oxygen we could get.

The trigger-happy youngster behind us squeezed off three more rounds as we bolted away from the scene. None of them came close to hitting the mark, but they were plenty enough to strike terror in us all the same. "We need to split up, to divide them," Darrow gasped. We were running toward a fork in the alley made up of a narrow row of storage sheds. "You go left."

I nodded, unable to suck enough wind to answer Darrow out loud. When we hit the fork, I went one way, and my master chief went the other. I sprinted as hard as I could and worked on throwing garbage cans over behind me to slow the gunmen down. When it sounded like I put some distance between us, I dared to steal a glance behind me to see what I was up against. I was expecting to see two men chasing me but was shocked to find I had all four of them on my tail. That was when I realized that Olongapo Earp was not the hooligans' intended target. I was.

As I was trying to figure out what I had done to these people, the kid raised his revolver again and fired. After hearing a hollow click instead of another roaring gunshot, the boy cursed and stopped to clumsily reload his weapon. Two of the others fired, but I was already back on the move. Their shots went wide. Tala screamed loudly in the background, sounding as if she had watched me get my head blown off.

I soon realized that I would not escape my attackers in a straight-up foot race. Speed was not one of my strong points. I knew that I had only made it this far because of the adrenaline coursing through my veins, and that was starting to wear off. I needed some instant strategy.

As one of the men squeezed off another round, I spotted a narrow gap between two buildings and ducked into it, immediately regretting my decision. It led straight to the street but was full of trash and construction scraps that tangled around my feet and tripped me up. I landed on my face and had to scurry forward on all fours, clumsily trying to get to my feet again. When I did, I took only two steps before I rammed my head into something that knocked me right back onto my ass. With no time to recover and knowing how close the street assassins were, I had to keep moving. Fueled now by hysteria, I forced myself to push through the mess to get to the road.

The advantage of moving through such a dark, congested passage was that I did not present a very identifiable target. That did not stop the people chasing me from taking their shots anyway. The first guy to reach the opening took aim and waited for me to rise. When he saw my silhouetted head poke up against the relative light of the street before us, he squeezed the trigger. Fortunately, there was a beam in the line of fire between the two of us. The bullet struck the wood instead of me, and I dove for the ground again, breaking forward with a renewed sense of urgency. Once more, I heard Tala scream out from somewhere that was far too close to be comfortable.

When I finally broke out of the space between the houses, it was by barreling through a fifty-five-gallon drum full of metal scrap. I fell over it, dumping its contents out onto the sidewalk along with me. Between fear and exertion, I could barely breathe at all. I no longer had the energy to follow my flight instincts. I had to fight. Turning my head to the side, I spotted a heavy metal pipe among the refuse I had spilled. It was no match for a firearm, but it was better than nothing. With the club in hand, I used my last reserves of energy to bolt across the street, ducking between two houses and making my way into a brand-new alley.

It took the men some time to follow me as they tripped, cursed, and cleared trash to continue their pursuit. Still, they knew I had dashed across the road. The houses on the other side of the street were built on top of each other. There was only one opening that I could have disappeared into, so the gangsters had little difficulty figuring out where I had gone. The first man across rushed into the same space I had with no hesitation at all. I made him pay for that when he came out the other end.

I swung my pipe with every intention of killing whoever emerged from that space. Unfortunately, the close confines of where we were fighting prevented me from following through with the blow. The end of my club caught the cinderblocks of the far building before I completed my swing, absorbing most of the impact. Still, the punk I was aiming for got hit hard enough to fall right to the ground, cupping his bleeding face in his hands. More importantly, he dropped his gun.

The second gangster was almost through the opening as I scooped up the revolver. The third was entering it. I caught them both in very cramped quarters as I squeezed the trigger. The man closest to me threw himself against the wall in time to avoid getting hit. The man farther back dove to the ground the instant he saw I was armed. The boy who fired on us back at the apartment was just coming into view from between the two buildings. I did not even see him when I fired, but it was the kid that got hit.

The bullet struck him high upon the head. It split his crown from front to back and sent his brains erupting from the opening like some sort of macabre grey matter mohawk. He was under a streetlamp when it happened, and I could see the light go out of his eyes even from where I was at. That boy was the first person I had ever killed. Even in the heat of combat, I was struck dumb by it. He was young, no more than twelve or thirteen. He was still gangly and awkward, a skinny stick figure adorned with a mop-top of straight black hair.

For a moment, I was paralyzed with shock over what I had done. The hooligan on the ground was not and fired from the prone position. His bullet let out a deafening crack as it passed by my ear, breaking me out of my reverie and startling me back into flight. This time I back-tracked, sprinting in the direction of my apartment. I looked back when I heard another shot ring out and saw one of the thugs get blown from his cover. When he landed on the ground, he was screaming bloody murder. It looked like someone misidentified his target in the dark and blasted a bullet into his buddy instead of into me.

That could have presented me with an opportunity to go on the offensive, but I was not able to capitalize upon it. I was still too starved for oxygen, having never gotten the chance to catch my breath. My feet got away from me as I fled and I ended up wiping out across the gravel. Rolling over and surprised to find that I still had the revolver in my hand, I sat up and aimed at the opening into the alley.

The remaining hoodlum was expecting as much and must have gotten a running start. He passed through my line of sight far too fast for me to react. By the time I fired, he was already hidden behind a stack of wooden pallets on the other side of the alley. That was when we heard sirens approaching in the distance and realized that the momentum had shifted. Time was no longer on the side of the street punks. It was on mine. All I had to do now was hold out.

The wounded gangster decided that the game was over and got up to flee. I let him go. I did not know how many bullets I had left and the last thing I wanted to do was waste ammo trying to hit someone who could not shoot back. The cops could deal with him. Still gasping for air, I forced myself back up to see if I could get a shot at the other thug. I came up empty. The man whose skull I cracked with the pipe was coming to life at that point. He was shaking and holding his hands up, begging me not to shoot him. Saving my ammunition for the bigger threat, I screamed at him in English to shut up, too scared to remember any Tagalog.

Finally, my target emerged, but with his gun blazing. He was not attempting to hit me so much as force me to eat dirt, in which he easily succeeded. With me trying to get as low as I could, the hooligan made his getaway, firing wildly as he fled. I should have let him go. With anger overriding reason, though, I took a shot as soon as I got back to my feet and missed again.

I stumbled forward. The guy I almost knocked out rolled into the fetal position and screamed out in fear as I passed, but I ignored him. When my target turned to see where I was, I fired again, missing once more. For my fourth shot at the man, I took my time. I went into a textbook firing stance with two hands on the revolver. I pulled the hammer back, lined up my sights against the target's center, and squeezed the trigger.

J.E. PARK

Click.

My eyes went wide. In panic, I turned toward the remaining gang banger and found him already in motion. The instant he heard I was out of ammo, he was on his feet with my pipe in hand, looking to return a favor. With nothing else at my disposal, I heaved my spent revolver at him. It was a futile gesture. The hoodlum batted the weapon away with a power that was impressive for a man unlikely to have ever heard of Ty Cobb.

The punk tried to knock my block off with his next swing, but I was able to duck in time. I then scrambled about the ground looking for something, anything, that I could use as a weapon. The alley was strewn with garbage, various odds and ends of every size, shape, and material. There was nothing, though, that was particularly lethal, or for that matter, even intimidating. What little was there was difficult to collect. Every time I paused, a large piece of heavy pipe came barreling at my head. Eventually, I did grab a jagged piece of wood near the stack of pallets the escaped gunman hid behind. Trying to brandish it, though, was laughably inadequate.

I needed some relief. If I could have gotten an opportunity to catch my breath I could have escaped, but the hood trying to knock my block off would not give me that chance. I decided that if I could throw my adversary off of his feet, I might stand a better chance at running away again. I waited for him to swing one more time, and while he was off-balance, I charged.

It was a desperate move and did not work out the way that I planned. Instead of bowling him over, all I did was push my attacker up against the wall. To make things worse, I also lost my balance and fell to my knees, putting myself in a fatally vulnerable position. My adversary now had the high ground. He raised the pipe above his head, and there was little I could do to keep him from bashing my skull in with it. But I had to try.

I still had the jagged piece of wood in my hand. As the punk tensed up to bludgeon me to death, I used every bit of strength I had to thrust it into his left leg, below the back of his knee. It worked much better than I thought it would. The point punctured through his jeans and penetrated deep into his calf. The hooligan howled out in agony, but it did not keep him from bringing the pipe down. In fact, the adrenaline surge forced him to swing it even harder, but with a life-sparing lack of precision.

OLONGAPO EARP

My head avoided a direct hit. Fortunately for me, my shoulders and back stepped up to share some of the punishment. Still, that son-of-a-bitch nearly put me out. My vision started jumping all over the place, my ears rang, and I was suddenly too woozy to flee. I could not even get to my feet. All I could do was crawl away from the hoodlum and try to keep from losing consciousness.

The gangster had no such issues. He was injured, but enraged. He was also no longer able to run. Having nothing to lose now, he wanted to finish me off before the police arrived.

I had put a couple of houses between us before the derelict got the wood out of his leg. When he came after me again, he was limping hard and unable to put any weight on his injured limb. Even hobbled, the punk was moving twice as fast as I could, screaming curses at the top of his lungs. As I crawled through the alley, I hoped that the police, or at least Darrow, could use his voice as a beacon to find me. The last thing I was expecting was Tala to.

My vision was blurry, and I was unable to focus anywhere but on the ground I crawled over. My ears were filled with the shrieking of the street hood. I never saw Tala coming. She was just suddenly at my side, almost as if by magic. "Get up, Doyle!" she cried hysterically. "Get up! Please!"

I attempted to push her out of the way. "Get out of here!" I screamed at her. "Go find Master Chief! Now!"

"No, Doyle! You need come wit' me! You need come now!" Tala started crying harder as the gangster limped closer. "Please! Doyle! Please!"

"I can't!" By now, I was pleading with her. "You have to go! Go!"

"No!" she sobbed. "No! No, no, no!" Tala paused for a second, and I felt her entire body tense up before she shrieked, "NOOOOOOOOOOOOO!"

I knew that the thug must have been on top of us. I pushed Tala out of the way and rolled over onto my back to face my attacker. Tala then leapt back on top of me, offering herself to the hooligan's pipe, determined not to let him get to me. I was struggling to throw her off, but she was furiously resisting me. I ended up in the surreal position of fighting a woman who was hysterically trying to save my life. "GODDAMMIT TALA!" I screamed at her. "GET OFF OF ME! HE'S GOING TO KILL YOU!"

He was. The gangster did not care if Tala was between us or not. He could bludgeon us both to death just as easily as he could one of us. He raised the pipe high into the air, intent on splitting both our skulls wide open. When he went to deliver the fatal blow, however, the pipe would not move. Master Chief Darrow was behind him, holding it from the other end.

*****

When I saw Darrow, my entire body went limp. It felt like I had fallen into my underwater world again, descending into one of my episodes. Tala had her arms wrapped around my head tight, though. She refused to let me go there. As police officers flooded the alley to stop Darrow from viciously pummeling my assailant, I was strangely calm. When I finally caught my breath, I was so relaxed that it felt like I was only falling asleep as I finally passed out.

I was brought back by Master Chief Darrow lightly slapping me across my face. "Hey! Doyle! You with us?"

I shot upright, very confused. As far as I knew, Tala had been there a split second before. Somehow, though, she had vaporized into thin air and was replaced by my boss. It was like dreaming I was being kissed by Marilyn Monroe only to wake up finding myself swapping spit with Marilyn Manson. "Jesus Christ!" I exclaimed. "Where's Tala?"

"Home," Darrow answered. "Mari's probably beside herself worried about the two of you, so I sent Tala back to let the girls know we're alright. I told her to stay there. I don't want her mixed up in any of this shit."

My memory started flooding back to me, and I recalled what had happened in front of the apartment. "TJ!" I exclaimed. "TJ got shot! Is he...?"

"Oh, man," Darrow laughed. "He's not alright. He's pissed!"

"But he got shot!"

"Yeah, he got shot, all right. Right through the collarbone and out the back of his shoulder by the looks of it. He's in a lot of pain, but I can guarantee you that he's feeling a lot better than the fuckers that did this."

I looked around, trying to get my bearings. "Was I out?"

Darrow shrugged. "Not all the way, but spaced out in some sort of twilight zone for a half hour or so. You should check out the size of the goose egg on the back of your head. You took a pretty good hit to the noggin. You feeling okay?"

I nodded. "I think so. I'm just a little foggy. I've got a killer headache."

"I bet," the master chief laughed. "Hey man, we need to get out of here. As far as these cops are concerned, this was a street gang hit against Tejada. They're going to turn this whole city upside down, and if we want to keep our names out of it, we need to bounce."

That was confusing me even more. "Wait, keep our names out of it? How are our names not all over it already? Those guys weren't after TJ. They were after me."

"Yeah, it certainly looks that way. Look, man, in a few days, the Navy will cease to be an entity in Olongapo for the first time in a century. Things are going to change big around here, and when things change that radically, there's usually a reckoning."

Darrow waved his arm over the policemen working the scene. "You know, up until now, a lot of these guys were on the fence, not knowing which way the wind was going to blow. Some figured that with the Navy leaving, gangsters would fill the vacuum and turn this place into another Patpong, like in Bangkok. Whores galore. Others think Olongapo is going to go legit and pull in some real money by turning the base into a shipping hub. The cops weren't sure which way to bend."

My master chief grinned. "Then this shit happened. The police identified these pricks as gang members from Barrio Barretto and they're fucking pissed that they shot a sergeant in the Philippine National Police. It doesn't matter that he wasn't the target. This place ain't like Mexico, Doyle. Most of these guys take money from the goons to turn a blind eye to their little rackets, but there is never any question about who's in charge around here. Those poor bastards really fucked up. Even the guys leaning the gangsters' way are heading over to Barrio Barretto to tear those punks apart."

Nothing was any clearer. "Master Chief, I don't get where I fit in to all this. Why aren't they interested in figuring out why those guys were trying to kill me?"

"Trust me, Doyle, they're going to get to the bottom of this very quickly. They got two of the shooters alive, and they didn't take them to jail. They took them to an old shack up in the hills and are making them sing as we speak. If I had to guess, we're going to know everything by tomorrow. As far as these guys here are concerned, though, you're irrelevant. The crooks shot a cop! The police faction that wants this place to go legit, a faction that includes TJ by the way, has the excuse they need to declare war. They want to dismantle the gangs right here and now. Even the cops on the Barretto payroll are turning on them. My guess is that a lot of these punks are going to die before they can implicate the police that they were paying off."

Darrow put his hand on my shoulder. "We have two things going for us. First, the fact that these guys were after you complicates the narrative that Tejada was the intended target. That's why we need to get out of here before the reporters show up. They want this kept on the down-low. Second, these guys know we're considering going into business with TJ. Some of them are also. That means we're all on the same side. They don't want this interfering with that. Understand?"

I nodded, rubbing the knot on the back of my head. "Can you help me up so we can get out of here, then?"

Darrow stood and offered me his hand. He had to steady me when I got to my feet, holding me upright until my light-headedness passed. As I was led out of the alley, I asked, "Does anyone know why these guys were after me?"

Darrow shook his head. "No, that's the big mystery at the moment. Whatever it is, I'm pretty sure it's personal, not business."

"Krause?"

Rolling his eyes, my master chief said, "Possibly, but I don't know. I'd believe it if he sent these guys after me, but not you. You're not nearly as much of a threat to him as I am."

A thought occurred to me. "You think it could be related to that fight we got into outside of the Pagoda?"

We were walking out of the alley through the same opening I had entered when Darrow answered. "That's a possibility, I guess. It could have been a matter of these gang bangers trying to save face. Did any of them look familiar to you?"

I was shaking my head as we emerged onto the street. "Not really, but truth be told, I was pretty drunk that night. I wouldn't have recognized anybody if they'd…" I froze as I saw the body of the kid I shot lying in the middle of the street. He looked even younger as a corpse. Without taking my eyes off of the boy, I said, "Master Chief, I killed someone."

OLONGAPO EARP

Darrow nodded. "You did. Congratulations. You're in the big leagues now. The cops are impressed, by the way. Those motherfuckers sent five gunmen after you. Two of them are dead, a third is dying, and you're standing here with a little bump on your head. The guys have already given you a nickname."

"Yeah? What're they calling me?"

Darrow grinned. "Duck Holliday, after Wyatt Earp's trusty sidekick."

"Am I supposed to be flattered by that?" I asked. "Why the hell are they calling me a duck?"

My master chief shrugged. "Because of their accent. They can't pronounce 'Doc' right."

Once we were out of sight of the police officers, Darrow reached into the small of his back and pulled out an old revolver. He stuck it down the front of my shorts and covered it up with my shirt. "What the fuck is that?!?" I gasped.

"I found it in the alley by a pile of pallets," Darrow told me. "I picked it up before the cops got there. Look, I don't know what's going on here. I don't know who the hell those people were. If they come back, though, you should have something more effective than your swinging dick to fend them off with. If you do end up needing it, be frugal, though. There's only two rounds left in it."

*****

CHAPTER 26

Mari was hysterical when I got home. She threw her arms around my waist and completely broke down. The little girl was babbling so fast that I could not understand a word she said. After everything I had gone through, my mind was spent. I could not even try to decipher Tagalog at that point. All I could do was spend a couple of hours rocking Mari on the couch. After she finally drifted off, I carried her to bed.

When I returned to my apartment, I was pretty cross. I went to the refrigerator, opened up a beer, and then tried to ease my shaking hands with another Marlboro. I broke into a coughing fit when I inhaled the smoke. My lungs were still raw from the hell I had put them through while running amok through Olongapo's alleys. After I finished hacking, I turned to Tala, who was still sitting on the couch. "What the fuck were you doing tonight? That guy was going to kill us. If Master Chief had not gotten there when he did, you'd be dead. So would I. Your daughter would have been left here all alone."

OLONGAPO EARP

Tala hung her head. "I trying to save you, Doyle," she told me as a tear ran down her cheek.

"Wha-wha-why?"

"Because I...I..." Tala was on the verge of saying something, and I was pretty sure of what it was. At the same time, I was hoping she would change her mind and keep it to herself. She did, probably because she was too afraid that I would not be able to return the sentiment. "I no know, Doyle," she finally said. "I no t'inking, I worry dat you going to be hurt and I apraid op what dat do to Mari."

"What do you think you getting killed would have done to her? What do you think would have become of her if that happened?"

Tala sobbed. "She be better off. Doyle, I know you good man. You no let anyt'ing bad happen to Mari ip I die por you. I just a whore. You gonna be somebody. You do da right t'ing."

I did not know how to respond. Flabbergasted, I asked, "Is that what you were thinking? That if you get yourself killed that I would feel obligated to take care of Mari? Jesus Christ, Tala! I can't even get my own shit together! What makes you think I can take care of your daughter?"

Standing up with tears now pouring down her face, Tala screamed, "I no t'inking anyt'ing out dere, Doyle! I only t'inking I can't let anyt'ing happen to you! I want to protect you! Like you protect me and Mari when Danny come here dat day! I want to do por you what you do por us!"

Sighing, I put my cigarette out in the ashtray. I then walked over to Tala and took her hands in mine. "Okay. You can't do that ever again. We're even now."

Tala yanked her hands out of mine and slapped me across the face. "Puck you! I don't want to be even! You t'ink I do dat out dere because I t'ink I owe you somet'ing? You son-op-a-bitch! I do dat because I care about you! I do dat because...because...oh, porget it! I can't do dis!"

Tala turned to run out of the apartment. Before she could go anywhere, though, I dropped to my knees, grabbing her around the waist. "Please, Tala. Please. Don't go. I'm sorry. I don't mean to sound ungrateful for what you did, but if you got hurt on my account...Tala...I don't think that I would be able to live with it. Please don't leave. Stay with me."

"Stay wit you?" Tala cried. "Por how long?"

"As long as you want. As long as you can."

Turning around, Tala looked down at me and took my face in her hands. "I can spend a long time wit you, Doyle. How long you t'ink you able to spend wit Mari and me?"

Suddenly I was not feeling very good about myself. Tala Bono proved that she was willing to give her very life for me that night. In return, I could not even give her an honest answer.

*****

When I left the ship the next day, I did not take a trike home like I usually did. I walked. I had a lot of stuff to work out before I got back to my apartment and spending fifteen minutes in a motorcycle sidecar with a chatty driver was no way to do it.

I was still having a hard time wrapping my head around the events of the previous night. In particular, I struggled with Tala throwing herself between me and a street assassin. "You no let anyt'ing bad happen to Mari ip I die por you," she said. It had me wondering if she was trying to sacrifice herself because she thought I would take care of Mari if she died.

Would I have taken care of Mari if Tala had been killed? I meditated on that as I strolled down Gordon Avenue. At least I tried to. Gordon Avenue was a noisy thoroughfare, and it was hard to think listening to the never-ending parade of trikes and jeepneys flying by. Passersby had to almost shout to be heard over the traffic. It was nearly as loud as the alarming hum of electrical cables strung haphazardly above my head. I had never heard them previously as I usually traveled by trike. From the sidewalk that day, though, they made enough noise to break my concentration. Being an electrician in Olongapo must have been scarier than being a police officer.

Would I have taken care of Mari? I pondered that again once I recovered from my distraction. After walking two blocks and risking my life crossing two intersections with no traffic control devices, I decided that I would have.

Could I have taken care of her, though? Absolutely not. I lived on a ship. There was no conceivable avenue open for me to stay behind and provide for an orphan that I was not even related to. Mari did not speak English, and I could just barely get by in Tagalog. No matter what my intentions might have been, had Tala been killed, there was no way that I could have followed through on them. I would have left her behind. She would be forced to face the unforgiving realities of shantytown life all by herself. I shuddered as I thought of her ending up another nameless Pagsanjan *pam-pam*.

Could I take care of Mari now? I could. I could marry her mother and get them out of this place.

Would I be happy that way? I doubted it. I had no idea why I was even considering it. How could I be in love with Tala when I barely even knew her? We had been together a little over two weeks. As much as I tried to convince myself that I was not judging her for having to rent out her body for money, I knew I would never get over it. I would end up like Randy Green, driven insane with distrust and jealousy if I tried to pretend she never did it, no matter what feelings I eventually developed for her.

Feelings. What feelings do I have for Tala, anyway? Not love. I've only known her for a month. I keep telling myself that. I've only known her for a month. We've only been sleeping together for a couple of weeks. That's all the time it took for her to decide that I was worth throwing herself between me and an aspiring murderer for.

Would Yukiko have done that? No. *Would any other woman in the world?* No.

Passing by a *sari-sari* store, I stopped and bought myself a bottle of San Miguel. I then took a seat on a rickety folding chair on the sidewalk and lit a cigarette. Watching the people go by, I took a drink of beer and admitted to myself that, despite my best efforts, I cared deeply for Tala. And I needed to leave her.

If I gave myself to that woman, I knew that I would destroy us both. At some point, I would develop suspicions about her fidelity, and the more I fell for her, the more it would kill me if she ever betrayed me. I was terrified that it could send me into one of my rages, like the one I fell into when I beat Randy Green. Or the one that made me bludgeon the Hockey Mullet Frat Guy for what he did to us in Mexico. I would not want to hurt her, but I was terrified that I would not be able to control myself.

But what about Mari? What about her? I loved her to death, but she was not my responsibility. *You could help her.* I could. And I would. Just not by marrying her mother. I could send them money to help Mari get what she needed to grow up without following her mother's fate.

You could accept Darrow's offer and see to it she's taken care of yourself. You could also spend more time with Tala, get to know her better. You'd be able to make a better decision.

Going into business with my master chief...

When that thought popped into my head, my instincts tried to suppress it. After what happened the night before, there were warning flags all over that offer.

I finished my cigarette and slammed the rest of my beer. After giving the bottle back to the woman running the shop, I started walking again. I was likely dealing with a pretty bad concussion after I got hit the night before. Something that Darrow said to me did not resonate then, but it was starting to now.

"Congratulations. You're in the big leagues now."

What did he mean by that? It seemed like he was welcoming me into the club. I had killed somebody, a kid nonetheless, and my master chief was treating it as if I had completed some rite of passage. Not a single officer came to question me about what had happened. In fact, they seemed to be working to erase my involvement in the incident entirely. It took either fear or money to pull off something like that. I was confident that neither TJ nor Darrow had that kind of cash. That meant they were feared. The police officers were doing what they did because they thought I was one of them.

I was almost home. Approaching the bridge where Gordon Avenue ended and E 20th Street began, I stopped to look at the drainage canal it spanned one last time. It was not a scenic view. Dozens of those humming cables spanned the little river, intersecting the sight of filthy gray water. It smelled worse than Shit River. The banks were steep and lined with stone, strewn over with trash, fallen branches, and the occasional rotting fish. At the bend, where it curved out of sight toward Subic Bay, were a half dozen women washing clothes in the stream. I wondered how dirty someone's laundry had to be before dunking them in water that nasty would be considered an improvement.

Watching those women do their laundry, I began to appreciate how powerless some people were. Especially in a place like Olongapo. I lived less than three blocks from that bridge and rode by it every day. I never even realized that people lived down the river because there was no road leading that way. The buildings were built right to the banks. Just to get home, the people who lived there had to balance along what would have been a curb in the United States, not a sidewalk. And all those humming wires? Not a single one of them led to any of the hovels built around the bend. I doubted any running water or sewage pipes did either.

The people that lived there were, for all practical purposes, invisible. As long as I could physically overpower them, be it through brute strength, numbers, or with a firearm, I knew I could do anything I wanted to them. I would get away with it. Robbery, rape, or murder, it was unlikely that my crime would even be reported. Why bother if it was not going to be investigated anyway? That was the kind of place Tala grew up in. They were all prey.

And who were the predators? The thugs that tried to kill me the night before were some, for sure. So were the pimps that owned the Magsaysay bordellos. So were the blue shirt security guards who could blow the peasants away for stealing bread in a moment of desperation. There were also their employers, who could work them from sunrise to sunset without paying them enough to feed their families. They could even take liberties with the women in exchange for keeping a job open for them.

Tala told me all about the injustices facing people that were that destitute. It was what motivated her to do what she could to keep Mari from ever ending up there. There was a system in place that worked hard to keep them down. It was one that forced a mother to sacrifice herself so that her daughter stood a fighting chance, and even then, success was by no means assured.

As I stood there, a police vehicle sped past me. The cops never stopped to look at the people washing clothes at the river's bend, either. I spent a lot of time with Sergeant Tejada. He did it when he had to, but I did not see him as a man who got his jollies off by terrorizing the slums for fun. Still, he, the people he worked with, the men I would be going into business with if I accepted Darrow's offer, were charged with maintaining the *status quo.* They upheld the system working to keep people like Tala and Mari vulnerable. So, in a way, they were the predators as well. Though I did not want to live among the lambs in Olongapo, I did not relish the idea of running with the wolves either.

When I started walking again, I kept going when I reached my apartment. I retraced my steps from the night before and eventually found myself standing at the spot where I had killed that boy. The blood was still visible in the street. I did not regret what I had done. I had been in a situation where it was them or me. I knew that I never wanted to be in a position where I had to do something like that ever again, though.

But why did I have to do it in the first place?

That was driving me crazy. Five people tried to kill me sixteen hours before, and I had no idea why. Was it a case of mistaken identity? Did Tala's ex have something to do with it? Or did his buddy Mulvaney put them up to it for kicking his ass in front of the Pagoda? Hell, somebody almost stabbed me then. That brawl was just two weeks ago, but it seemed like a distant memory. The realization that I was nearly killed twice in one month began sinking in.

I thought about all the violence in my life. I thought about my family, the high school fights, the bar brawls in San Diego, the girl in El Salvador, and the errant sailors in the Nixie Room. I remembered Randy Green, Hulagu in Mexico, David Miller in Japan, and the Marines in Olongapo. I felt as if I was perpetuating a vicious cycle that I could not break free of. Hannah Baxter, my estranged fiancée, had it right. I had to stop it or stuff like this would keep coming back to haunt me. One day, I would end up doing something that I could not take back. Like shooting a young boy dead in the middle of a Philippine street.

It was an epiphany. I was a violent man among violent men. It needed to end, and I was certain that I could never do that while living in the Philippines. I could not work alongside Olongapo Earp and the officers who were probably still torturing confessions from my would-be assassins up in the hills.

"Congratulations. You're in the big leagues now."

No. People tried to kill me. I had to shoot a kid in the head to defend my own life.

"… the big leagues…"

It's all escalating. It's already gone way too far and is only getting worse. I'm done. I need to put some distance between Darrow and me. I need to cut ties with Sergeant Tejada and the Philippines. That means with Tala. And Mari, too. It's for their own good as well as mine.

"… the big…"

Goddammit! Stop it! I don't want to be in any 'big leagues!'

OLONGAPO EARP

"Petty Officer Murphy," I heard an unwelcome voice from behind me say. "What are you doing here?"

*****

Startled, I spun around and found myself facing Lieutenant Krause. "What am I doing here? I'm staying out this way. What are *you* doing here?"

My lieutenant glowered at me. "Confirming my suspicions. What do you know about what happened here last night?"

"I heard a cop got shot."

"Quit talking to me like I'm an idiot, Murphy!" Krause barked. For a man who prided himself on being a church-going teetotaller, I noticed that he was awfully unsteady on his feet. "It was not 'a' cop that got shot! It was Darrow's buddy! The same guy who was with you two in Pagsanjan!"

"Oh yeah?" I took a menacing step toward the officer. "And how would you know about that?"

"It's in the newspaper!"

"No, not who got shot. How did you know that we were in Pagsanjan...sir?" I spat out the "sir" not in deference to Krause's rank, but in contempt of it. "Did you see us out there, you sick son-of-a-bitch?"

"You better watch yourself, petty officer," the lieutenant growled. "Or..."

"Or what? What do you think you're going to do? Run and tell the captain we almost caught you with your *pam-pam*? Or is it a *pom-pom*? You got yourself a little boy, Lieutenant?"

I was well within my division officer's personal space now. I stood a full head taller than he did, and all things being equal, I could have broken him in pieces if I wanted to. The only thing that would have stopped me was the difference in rank between us. Hitting him would have been fatal for me. Getting him to hit me would have solved a lot of our problems, though.

For a moment, I thought that Krause might take the bait, but he didn't. It was not out of cowardice, either. Not this time. The man leaned forward to meet me and snarled, "You think you know what you're doing here, Murphy? Do ya? Well, let me tell you something, you dumb fucker. You don't know a damn thing! Men like Master Chief Darrow, well, they know how to spot a sucker, and they'll reel you right in. Getcha to do whatever they want, stick your neck out so that when things go bad, you're left holding a bag of shit while they come out of it smelling like roses. Like that boy in the Nixie Room that you beat up so bad. Darrow put you up to that, didn't he?"

"That was self-defense. He came at me with a spanner wrench."

Krause shook his head, "I don't care how you doctored it all up; it only matters that you had to face the NIS alone."

I almost told the lieutenant that it was Darrow who saved my ass, but I bit my tongue in the nick of time. "There was no bag of shit to hold there," I told him instead.

"Have it your way," Krause sneered. "Mark my words, Murphy, you're in a pretty unique position here. You're working for a master chief who's practically the Navy's version of J. Edgar Hoover, and he's got the protection of the captain somehow. Kid, that ain't normal. I've been in the Navy for more than two decades, and I ain't never seen shit like this." The lieutenant's piety seemed to have flown out of the window. He was swearing like the rest of us now.

Krause looked down at the bloodstains on the pavement. "Son, people are actually dying around you and Darrow now. How long do you think you can keep that up? This captain seems to believe all the bullshit the master chief feeds him, but what happens if he's gone? Do you think the next guy's going to tolerate stuff like this? People dropping dead around two of his men?"

"The next guy?" I laughed. "Sir, we've been over this. The captain extended his tour to take the *Belleau Wood* to Japan. He's going to be here a while. If you don't make full lieutenant on the next advancement cycle, you'll be forced into retirement. My enlistment is up in twenty-one months. I don't have to worry about outlasting the captain on this ship. I just have to make it through the next year and outlast you."

My lieutenant flashed an evil smile. "I take it that you haven't seen the news back home in a while, have you? You haven't heard what they're saying about us?"

"No, I don't even think I've turned on a television since we got here. Why?"

Krause grinned even wider, swaying again as he relaxed and backed up. I could have sworn the man was drinking, but I smelled nothing on his breath. Of course, his eyes were hidden behind his sunglasses, so I could not tell by looking at them, either. Chuckling, the lieutenant refused to answer my question. "Never mind. You'll find out soon enough."

As Krause walked away, staggering down Elicano Street back toward the base, he turned and called out, "So! Darrow told you that I was a child molester, eh? Thanks. It helps to know what angle he's going to try to play."

*****

When I got back to my apartment, Master Chief Darrow and TJ were already there. Dixie and Bard were not, having been asked to spend a couple of hours in town. They were advised to steer clear of Barrio Barretto, though, where a lot of stuff was going down. "Where were you?" Darrow asked.

"Walking," I answered. "Thinking. Talking to Krause."

"Krause?" my master chief asked, sounding concerned. "Where'd you see him at?"

"Up the block. Looking over the crime scene."

"What for?"

I glared at Darrow. "What do you think? He read TJ got shot and thought it had something to do with you. He knows you and Tejada are tight." Turning to the sergeant, I asked, "How are you doing, TJ? Are you alright?"

Rico had his right arm in a sling, was doped up on pain pills, and looked like he was ignoring sound medical advice by being there. Still, he said, "I gonna be okay. How 'bout you?"

"In better shape than you are, I guess. You guys find anything out about last night?"

Tejada nodded. "We pind out pretty much everyt'ing. You know a guy wit da name Danny Paduano?"

I shook my head. "Should I?"

"Unless you dealing drugs, pimping girls, or robbing grocery stores, no. Still, he know all about you. He know you name, where you live, who your girlfriend is, he know a lot about you. You sure you no know dis guy? He got a lot op muscles and a lot op tattoos. He hang around da Blue Shack in Barrio Barretto."

Now, Tejada was ringing a bell. "The Blue Shack? Danilo? The bouncer?"

TJ chuckled. "Yeah! Danilo Paduano. Everybody call him Danny, dough. You know him?"

"I met him, yeah. He's the guy that got me all fucked up that night you found me. He introduced me to that drink, Bullfrog."

"Yep. He did. He had da bartender, another prick named Nino, drug it too. You weren't drunk when I pind you, Doyle. You was doped up! Dey was takin' you to da slums and dey's gonna slit your throat! You know why?"

My mind was spinning, but I figured it out. I remembered the other unpleasant encounter I had at the Blue Shack. "Because of someone named Rafaela?"

TJ looked at Master Chief Darrow and said, "You right, Bradley. Dis maddapukka is smart!"

"Let me guess," I said to Tejada. "Rafaela Green's related to him somehow."

"She sure is," Master Chief Darrow chimed in. "Her maiden name is Rafaela Paduano. She's his sister. I filled TJ in on what you did to her husband."

My stomach turned. "That fucker was pimping his sister?"

Tejada shook his head. "No. He no her pimp. He work as muscle to keep da peace in da bars. Dey both barrio rats dough, Danny and Rafaela. Dey always desperate people. Danny happy when she marry an American and get da hell out op dis place. He very angry and sad when she forced to come back and return to her old lipe as bar girl. My boys hurting him very bad to make him talk. He tell us he drug you. He tell us how dey almost stab you in da fight outside da Pagoda."

"That was a hit?" I asked, incredulous.

Master Chief Darrow raised his eyebrows. "Yeah, I was surprised by that one, too. They saw us going to the Pagoda and had one of their boys tail us. When we got into that fight, their man saw an opportunity to stick a knife in you. He took it. Paduano was also behind what happened at the Dirty Crow. He was on Magsaysay that morning conducting business and saw you walk by. He had someone fetch a junkie that owed him a lot of cash and offered to erase his debt if he croaked you. Ricky Ibay was trying to kill *you* that day. Not me."

Tejada nodded. "Dat right. I see Danny on da street. He walk out op da Scooby Booze bar before Rickie Ibay. I no realize dat dey dere together."

"Jesus Christ," I said, pulling out a cigarette. "I survived four attempts on my life? Two of them I didn't even know about?"

"Yeah, you pretty pucking lucky," TJ told me. "And good. Last night, dese guys t'inking it may be da last chance to get you. Danny send pive guys wit guns, and you kill two op dem! Shit, I only get one op da puckers, and I started with a gun!"

I shook my head. "I only killed one."

"Dere t'ree bodies last night."

I laughed humorlessly. "Yeah, well, the third guy walked into his buddy's line of fire and got shot by his own man. He must have bled out after he ran away. I can't claim credit for that one. TJ, was Rafaela in on this?"

Tejada nodded. "Yeah, dis mostly her idea. She begging Danny to kill you."

I did not really want to know the answer, but I asked the question anyway. "TJ, what did you guys do to Rafaela?"

The sergeant shook his head. "Not'ing yet. We no know where she is. Danny Paduano love his sister very much, Doyle. We hurt him very bad por a very long time. She gone and he die wit no telling us where she go."

"Is there any chance you could do me a favor, TJ?"

"What?" the sergeant asked.

"Could you guys just let her get away?"

*****

CHAPTER 27

When Tejada and Master Chief Darrow left, I went for a walk in the jungle behind the house. Confident that the threat to me had passed, I marched up the hill with a small gardening shovel I found in the courtyard. I needed to get rid of the revolver that my master chief handed to me the night before. Somewhere in the back of my mind, I wondered if Darrow or TJ might need it one day, so I treated it like buried treasure.

For the first time, I took a good look at the weapon. It was an old M1917 .45 revolver with the initials "A.J." carved into the wooden handle. The pistol was a genuine antique. I imagined it had been liberated from the American arsenal when the Japanese overran Luzon in 1942. It had probably been used by everyone from the US Army to the Philippine underworld for decades. Still, it seemed to work just fine and was likely untraceable. I wrapped it in a rag, put it in a plastic bag inside of a cookie tin, then buried it next to a Banaba tree, marking its resting place with a large rock. I made sure it would be easy for me to tell someone where to find it later.

OLONGAPO EARP

When I got back to our building, I walked across the hall and knocked on Tala's door. Knowing that I needed to cut ties with the Philippines, I intended to tell her that I was returning to the ship. Continuing to see her after deciding to sever my connections to Olongapo would be unfair. It would be using her for the last couple of days before we pulled out. It would only prolong the pain.

When Tala answered my knock, I started to tell her that I was leaving that night. She dropped her shaking head for a moment, then cut me off before I had a chance to finish. "No, Doyle," she told me. "You no need to say not'ing more. I know. Dese past days, I very happy. Mari very happy. What we have to do, it going to hurt. It hurt today or it hurt Priday. It no sense to make t'ings hurt now when you still here. Can we go on like we do por two more days? Por Mari? Den hurt apter you ship leave da Philippines?"

After nodding my head, Tala reached out and took my hand. She then led me back to my place, to my bedroom, where we stayed until Mari got home.

The next couple of days were bittersweet. Tala and I stayed in bed while Mari was at school. Both of us tried to wring every last drop out of pretending that we actually had a future. When Tala's daughter got home, we rallied around her. We treated her to Jollibee, played board games, and did all the silly stuff you do to keep an eight-year-old girl in smiles.

On my last night in Olongapo, after Tala announced that it was time for Mari to go to bed, the little girl looked up at the two of us with glassy eyes. "Can I sleep with you tonight?"

Tala and I looked at each other, and I nodded.

The plan was for us to wait out Mari and carry her back to her room after she fell asleep. That way, Tala and I could enjoy our last night together. Mari outlasted her mother, though, and the two of us ended up whispering to each other until the early hours of the morning. The little girl fell asleep on my right shoulder; her tiny legs draped over my stomach.

I had Tala on one arm, sound asleep, and Mari on the other, snoring softly. It was hot and uncomfortable, yet soothing in a way that I had never experienced before. I spent the entire night that way. Taking it all in, I wondered what it would be like to have something like that every single day.

My eyes never closed. I watched the geckos run the walls and listened to the sounds of the jungle filter in through my bedroom window. I spent the night reflecting on the month that had been. I could not believe what I had seen and done. I got to be a part of history, a crew member of the last US Navy warship to dock in Subic Bay. I saw some of the most beautiful girls in the world. I celebrated with policemen and had my past come back to haunt me in a way that nearly cost me my life.

As I thought of that, I wondered where Rafaela Green and her son were that night. Even though that woman wanted me dead, I hoped they were safe. I wanted nothing more than for her and Manny to be able to get past what I had done to them and somehow find peace. I wondered if they could escape into the countryside. There they could disappear under the protection of some old bandit like Paco Villa.

I caught myself smiling as I thought of Paco and of Master Chief Darrow discovering that he had a son. Never in a million years would I have ever seen myself breaking bread with communist revolutionaries. Nor being the target of underworld gunmen in the alleys of a Third World country. Christ, the Philippines was a trip.

Eventually, the sky outside became a little less dark, and I caught myself staring at Tala beside me. I was cognizant once again, and grateful, that I had not experienced one of my episodes since we had gotten together. In the past two weeks, I saw a man get shot through the throat and I killed a boy who might not even have become a teenager yet. Either one of those events was plenty to keep me up for weeks in nervous meltdowns. Lying there with Tala and her daughter, though, it was as if I had only seen it happen in a movie. I had little connection to it. Tala had some sort of power over me that could keep all those demons at bay. I was going to miss that.

Poor Tala. I doubted I had the same effect on her and wondered what would happen to her after I left. I wondered if I would ever find out, if I would ever hear from them again.

Inevitably, the sun broke through my window and put down the sounds of the nocturnal rainforest. As much as I wanted to stay right where I was, I had to get back to the ship for the morning muster. I turned my face and kissed Mari on the top of her head. "Hey, little one," I whispered to her. "I need you to give me my arm back. I have to go check in."

OLONGAPO EARP

Mari shot upright as if propelled by a bolt of electricity. Her eyes were wide open and full of distress. "It's morning?" she gasped, looking surprised.

"Yes, it's morning."

The little girl's face contorted in grief. She then fell onto my chest, wrapping her arms around my neck and crying out, "Oh no! No! Nonononono! Noooo!"

*****

Our liberty expired at 19:00. I was packed up and settled with the rent by noon. Dixie and Bard left to embark upon one last blowout before returning to the ship. I stayed behind to be with Tala and Mari. At four o'clock, I took one last look around the courtyard and told the girls that I had to leave. Mari broke down again and threw her arms around my neck, not letting me go until almost five. When she finally did, she kissed me on the cheek, told me that she would write to me, then ran to her room sobbing.

When Tala and I were alone, I reached into my pocket and pulled out an envelope containing more than seven hundred dollars. Handing it to Mari's mother, I said, "I emptied out my bank account back on the ship this morning. That's everything I have. Please use it to…"

Tala stepped back and rubbed her arms as if she felt dirty, shaking her head. "No. No, Doyle. Not prom you. I no take you money. I no want it. All I ever want prom you is time."

I was going to insist that she take it, but I could see by the look on Tala's face that she never would. By accepting my cash, it would make me another one of her customers. It seemed like she needed to see me differently. I put the envelope back in my pocket and looked at my watch again. "Time," I choked. "Tala, I'm out of it. I have to go."

Reaching up to grab the sides of my head, Tala pulled me in and kissed me harder than she ever had before. When she let me go, she said, "I write you, too." She then turned her back on me, running up the steps to comfort her daughter. I hoped that Mari would be able to comfort her back.

We agreed that Tala and Mari would not go with me to the base. Every bar girl working in Olongapo was sure to be there, as would a lot of

J.E. PARK

American military men hoping for one last hurrah before departing. Neither of us wanted Mari exposed to that, so I was going back to Subic Bay alone. Or so I thought.

Sergeant Tejada was waiting for me when I stepped out of the gate. "You need a ride?"

I threw my bag in the back of TJ's patrol vehicle and jumped into the passenger seat. Before I could thank him for his offer, he sped off and said, "You no worry 'bout Tala and Mari. Dey gonna be okay. I take care op dem. Apter you ship leave, da city hire private security to protect da port."

"Blue shirts?" I asked.

"Yeah," Tejada said, grinning at me. "You very observant, aren't you? I know da guy who doing da hiring, and I get Tala to work dere. It good job. Pay very good. I get Lorna job dere, too. It much better dan da grocery she workin' at now."

That was a load off of my shoulders. Changing topics, I asked, "You getting everything straightened out in Barrio Barretto?"

"Oh yeah," TJ answered, smiling like he was having a lot of fun with that. "Da new order op t'ings around here already beginning, Doyle. Da Barretto boys, dey pinished. All gone. Most op dem dead. Da pew dat lept, dey run away to Manila or Angeles. Dey get da message dey no welcome here no more. I hope Pagsanjan next. I gonna go dat way and spread da word about what dat prick Paulino Favila did during da war next week. Den, we gonna be getting us some op dose sick poreigners going dere por our kids."

Tejada asked me to light him a cigarette. He could not do it himself and drive at the same time with his arm in a sling. "You know, I gonna miss da Americans, but in da long run, dis gonna be better por my country. It sad to live in a giant whorehouse. Dere gonna be a lot op new money comin' in, a lot op new opportunity por my people. Ip we do dis right, girls no having to come here and sell dey bodies to get somet'ing to eat. Dey pind real jobs in Olongapo. We just gotta keep new bad guys prom pilling in da vacuum lept by da old bad guys."

"Yeah, I guess that'll be the challenge, won't it?" I said as I passed the sergeant his smoke.

"It sure will. Dere is already a lot op gang boys coming down prom da barrios up nort'. Dey in town now, watchin' you guys leaving, making trouble. We watching dem, dough, taking pictures. Da streets here be empty tomorrow. Ip dey show dey paces again, we gonna make dem wish dey stay north."

"You think you can actually do it? Clean this place up?" I asked.

TJ shrugged. "No, we no gonna ever end da crime. Dere too many poor people here. We no gonna stop da girls selling demselves either. Most op da girls, dey gonna go to Manila, or dey go home. Dose dat stay, we gonna move to Barrio Barretto. Da guys who run good sape places on Magsaysay, who take care op dey girls, we gonna let dem buy da Barretto bars. Olongapo por business, Barretto for girls, San Felipe por our surfing resort, right?"

I laughed, but did not commit. This caused Tejada to ask, "You in wit us or what?"

"Still thinking about it, TJ," I lied.

"What dere to t'ink about?"

"For Christ's sake," I started. "It might be a little much for me here. TJ, I was only here for a month. I nearly got killed four times. Then almost died by eating *bagoong*. We didn't shit the bed; we practically shit the entire apartment!"

The sergeant roared in laughter. "Yeah, I hear about dat! You guys shit da pish market too! Dat pucking punny! You no almost die prom *bagoong*, dough."

"I sure wished I was dead."

"Ha! I bet you did! I bet da girls who clean your apartment wish you dead too!" When he stopped laughing, Tejada looked at me and said, "Hey, dose guys who go apter you? Dat shit all over. We got dem all. Dere no one lept por you to worry about."

"What about the Master Chief? Is there anyone left that he needs to worry about?"

"You no have to worry about anyone goin' apter da master chiep." I noticed that TJ did not bother looking me in the eye when he said that. He knew it was a lie as much as I did. It would be a long time before the Philippines became a place where Olongapo Earp did not have to look over his shoulder again.

That was why I was not coming back with him. Ever.

J.E. PARK

*****

As expected, the streets in front of the base were complete chaos. Every American military man not on duty was out there, as was every one of their girlfriends. A throng of pickpocket street urchins added to the unruly mob. So did the broadcast journalists of a dozen different countries. There were also several conspicuous groups of young delinquents walking the crowd, looking to stir up trouble.

Tejada and I met the rest of my division at the Captain's Mast. Tony Bard, who had a new girl on his arm, shoved a glass of Bullfrog into my hands. "Last chance to drink, Doyle! Bottoms Up!"

Looking to dull my separation from Tala and Mari, I did as asked and then ordered another. I looked around and, not seeing my other roommate, asked, "Where's Dixie?"

Bard grinned and pointed his thumb up in the air. "Upstairs. In one of the boom-boom rooms."

Of course he was. I scanned the crowd. Claude Metaire was at the Mast with a couple of his girls, as was Clay Fordson with his. Steve Kent was further back into the bar, in a dark corner, with another. John Palazzo was closer to me, sitting by himself. I walked over to him while collecting my third drink. "You alone here?"

Palazzo grinned. "Yeah."

"How did that happen?"

"I'm on the Injured Reserve List," he laughed. Palazzo was sloppy drunk, unable to even sit upright. "I got friction burn. Bad."

After getting a drink for Tejada and me, I walked back outside to find him speaking with Master Chief Darrow and Lorna. My boss was a mess. He was even drunker than Palazzo, pressing his face up against his son's as he held him up high, crying like a baby in plain sight of everyone. It was too much for me to take in, so I took a few steps up the block and lit myself a cigarette.

As I smoked, I saw a woman walking toward us in the street, bawling even harder than Darrow. She was pulling a boy about Little Bradley's age behind her. It was evident that his father was American. "Mama, where is daddy going?" I heard him ask in Tagalog.

"Away," she sobbed.

OLONGAPO EARP

"Where?"

"He's going home."

The little boy looked confused. "Then why is he not with us?"

"He's not going to our home, Micky. He's going to his home."

I could see the look of confusion flash across the boy's face. His little head was trying to reconcile that his father's home was now in a different place than his was. Before he had a chance for it to sink in, though, a group of young toughs called out to his mother. "Hey, whore! Whose dick are you going to have to suck to feed your little monkey man now!"

As the punks busted out in laughter, I took a step to go after them, but Tejada reached out and stopped me. "What? You no have enough trouble here, Doyle?" the sergeant asked. "Don't worry about it, we gonna get to dose maddapukkas tomorrow."

He was right. What was I going to do anyway? As they passed, I glared at them. One of the hoods spotted me staring and shouted out in Tagalog, "What, tough guy? You have something to say to me?" He had no idea that I understood every word he said.

"*Oo!*" I called out to him. "*Halika sa tabi ng kalye na ito! Mag-uusap tayo!*" I was inviting him over to my side of the street so that we could talk.

Except for Sergeant Tejada, none of my friends within earshot understood what I had said. They recognized my tone of voice, though. One after one, they set their drinks down and stepped up beside me to let the thugs know that I was not there by myself. When the punks saw the odds were about nine-to-four, they reconsidered taking me up on my offer. After realizing that Tejada was with us, they gave up completely and sauntered off in another direction.

When Dixie joined us fifteen minutes later, we ordered a final round of drinks, toasting Olongapo one more time. We then guzzled them dry. After the last glass was drained, Tony Bard looked at his watch and announced, "It's seventeen forty-five, boys! Time!" We said our goodbyes to Sergeant Tejada and set to herding our men toward the Shit River Bridge.

We were only a couple of blocks away from the base, but getting there was not easy. The sidewalks were so packed that the mob spilled into the street, gridlocking the traffic enough to bring it to a complete stop. All around us, women were bawling. They wept not so much for sweethearts gone, but for the realization that their last hope of starting a new life was leaving with us. As the ladies cried, the roving bands of young men taunted them. The derelicts mocked their tears and made lewd comments about what they were going to do to them after we left.

A reporter from the BBC stuck a microphone in my face as I pushed my way through the crowd. "Sir! Sir! Do you have any thoughts you'd like to share about the American military leaving the Philippines after nearly a century?"

"Sure," I answered. "This is a beautiful country and, aside from this stuff you see here, it's full of beautiful people. They deserve the right to determine their own path. I'll miss this place, though, and I wish them the best."

"Thank you," the pretty young English reporter told me. "Can I ask you another question? What do you think of President-Elect Bill Clinton's plans to allow homosexuals into the American military?"

The question caught me completely off-guard. The status of homosexuals in the Navy had nothing to do with the closure of Subic Bay. The inquiry was out of place, but what floored me was something else entirely. "What? Did you say 'President-Elect Bill Clinton?' Clinton won the election?" George Bush just won the Gulf War the year before. I figured that he would ride the wave of post-victory patriotism right into a second term. I never even considered the possibility that he could lose.

The reporter laughed at me. "Yes, Bill Clinton won the election."

"Holy shit," I said, ruining the chances of the footage ever making the airwaves. "When did that happen?"

"About a month ago. Where have you been?"

Shaking my head, I looked at her and said, "Lady, you have no idea."

Delayed by the reporter, I was one of the last of us to cross Columban Road. Finding Bard, Dixie, and Metaire huddled in a group at the foot of the bridge, I asked, "Have we got everybody?"

"All except one," Dixie said, staring across the street back at the crowd, his mouth agape.

"Who are we missing?"

"Zhe mastair cheef," Claude answered, staring off in the same direction as Kevin.

I tried to see what they were looking at, scanning the crowd.

OLONGAPO EARP

"Doesn't Master Chief's wife watch a lot of CNN?" I heard Tony Bard ask.

"Yeah," I answered. "She uses it to learn English. Why?"

Tony didn't have to answer. I found what they were looking at. On the edge of the mob, illuminated by a camera crew, Master Chief Darrow was talking to a CNN correspondent. Those reporters hit the jackpot with that guy. He was a hulking man, standing over six-feet-tall and covered collar bone to ankles in old school Sailor Jerry tattoos. They knew he was as tough as he looked, and they had him on record, howling like a baby. With his Filipina girlfriend crying on one shoulder and his son sobbing into the other, they could not have found a more touching visual.

After seeing that, I was pretty confident that Jung Darrow would have divorce papers filed before the *USS Belleau Wood* even left the pier.

*****

The following morning was a lot like leaving San Diego. There were bands and there were speeches. One flag was lowered and a different one was raised. There were more speeches and handshakes, more photo opportunities, and several rounds of accolades. Then we were called to man the rails, the mooring lines were lifted, and the tugboats arrived to push us away from the pier.

It was a somber occasion, and the sailors manning the rails were pensive and silent. Hearts were very heavy. Most of the men had fallen into lust for a few weeks, but many genuinely believed that they were in love. Some of us were somewhere in between and had not had enough time to decide. We were losing forever the opportunity to come back and figure it out.

Most of the crew felt like they were going to miss someone in Olongapo, but Master Chief and I had people there that we were abandoning. He was leaving behind a little boy of mixed race, thus vulnerable to harsh ostracism as long as his father was not there to shield him from it. Mari was not my flesh and blood, but I feared for her future as if she were. Tala had a new job for now, but what if it did not work out? What if she had to go back to working the bars? How long could she keep a path open for Mari to escape that life if she could not escape it herself?

J.E. PARK

As the city of Olongapo faded into the distance, my heart sank. I realized that I had missed an opportunity to make a big difference in a little girl's life. I could have saved her from a grim future, but I blew it. I blew it because, deep down inside, I simply knew that I would never get over the things her mother did to survive. Now that it was too late, it was occurring to me that what Tala did for Mari did not make her unworthy of me at all.

It was I who was unworthy of them.

*****

CHAPTER 28

We were somewhere between Luzon and Taiwan when we heard the boatswain's whistle pipe through the 1MC. That was our signal that the captain was about to make an announcement. After a pause to give the crew a chance to give him their attention, Captain Fleming's voice filled the air.

"Good evening Devil Dogs. This is your captain speaking. First and foremost, I want to thank you for a successful mission in providing support to personnel shutting down the Subic Bay Naval Station. We completed our task far ahead of schedule. It was a historic moment where you were under the eyes of the nation, and you carried yourselves accordingly. I know everyone also enjoyed some great liberty and acquired some memories that will last you a lifetime. I am also proud to say that liberty incidents were minimal, and I want to thank all you Devil Dogs for your good work." I managed to keep myself from laughing out loud at the part where he praised our conduct out in town.

Before continuing, the captain cleared his throat. "Men, with the mission to Subic Bay now behind us, I want all of you who are not on watch to get in front of a television set within the next fifteen minutes. It's important that you see firsthand what is being said about us back home. The eyes of the country are always upon us, every day and every minute. We must always remember that and act with professionalism, courage, and kindness. That is all I am going to say for now. I want everyone to see the tape we are playing at 18:30. We will play it again on Channel 5 every two hours to ensure everyone has the chance to watch it. I will address you again tomorrow. Good evening, Devil Dogs."

I was in the hangar bay when the announcement sounded. The EMO was the closest CSE division space that had a television in it, so that's where I went. It was dinner time, so most everyone else was in their berthing areas or eating in the galley. Lieutenant Krause, Darrow, and I were the only ones in the division's office. "You know what this is about?" I asked my master chief.

"Not a clue," he answered. "What about you, Lieutenant?"

Krause looked at both of us and grinned. "I've got an idea. You'll see." With that, he reached up and turned on the TV.

As advertised, the show started right on time. It was the tape of an American news program made with a low-quality VHS recorder back in the US. The first thing it showed was footage of our ship leaving San Diego on our way to Sasebo. I guessed it was pulled from one of the network's Southern California affiliates.

A familiar female reporter's voice was narrating. "The USS *Belleau Wood* has a reputation as being the Pacific Fleet's floating 'Animal House'…"

The rest of her sentence was drowned out by the entire ship erupting into cheers and applause at once. The radio room next door was so loud that I could not hear what was being said, but I did not have to. The scene they were broadcasting showed Macklemore punching GM2 Crowley out on the pier as we were getting ready to leave San Diego. Darrow and I both buried our faces in our hands. I recently wondered if I would ever get to see that footage, and there it was.

As the noise subsided, we heard the reporter continue. "…sparking a massive melee in Tijuana, Mexico, a few months before leaving California. The crew was also involved in a bar brawl at the Enlisted Man's Club in Japan shortly after their arrival that caused extensive damage. The antics of the *Belleau Wood's* crew took a deadly turn on October 27th, however, when two sailors brutally assaulted one of their own, beating him to death in the public restroom of a Japanese park."

The cheering stopped abruptly. The story on the television was about David Miller's murder.

The report was hard to watch. I could not point out anything in it that was factually incorrect, but its viewpoints were biased against us to an enraging extent. For instance, we later heard from friends in San Diego that the crew went to a sports bar frequented by 32nd Street sailors. They interviewed scores of them about what they thought of Clinton's plans to allow homosexuals in the military. The response to that question was almost universally along the lines of, "We don't like it, but we're in the Navy. We follow orders and will have no choice but to accept it."

None of that was broadcast, however. What they showed was footage of two inebriated knuckle-draggers stupid enough to go on camera and say, "I guess I'll have to start killing fags."

The reporters then trotted out a *Belleau Wood* fireman I had never seen before. He spoke at length of the abuse he suffered at the hands of his fellow engineers after he had fallen under suspicion of being gay aboard our ship. The reporter then interviewed another former sailor who left the military years before after being outed. That man expressed some pretty outrageous claims. He made it sound as if murdering gay men by throwing them overboard was an everyday occurrence.

The longer I watched, the more furious I got. Miller was brutally murdered. There was no doubt about that. Knowing Pruitt, I was not going to contest that Miller died because he was gay, either. What I was upset about was the reporters implying that the entire ship had a hand in his death. The report regularly replaced the names of Pruitt and Decker with "the *Belleau Wood's* crew." It was as if those of us who did everything we could to save Miller's life murdered him as well.

I was getting ready to walk away when the screen filled with a shot of Deborah Miller, David's mother. She was sitting on her couch somewhere in Connecticut, staring into the camera. You could see that she had done all the crying that she was capable of and was now reduced to an empty shell. The woman looked broken. Her husband had passed away when her son was three. She never remarried and never had any other children. Her parents were long gone, and she had been an only child as well. David Miller was all that that woman had.

"I…I…I just don't understand," she told the reporter. "I…I saw his body when it came home, and what they did to him…I just don't…I don't understand. They did that to him because of who he loved? Not because he killed somebody. Not because he hurt somebody. Not because he stole something, not because he was a spy or a traitor…but because of who he loved? I…I don't understand."

It was hard to watch. You could see that this woman was experiencing a loss so visceral that you could not help but hurt with her. It was particularly difficult to watch her describe David as a child. I wondered what she had to look forward to during the years she had ahead of her. To her, Miller was the one bright spot in an otherwise hard life. For an instant, I saw her son's body on the floor in front of me, as vividly as I had seen it in the restroom, and I cringed.

As the show ended, Krause stood up and turned off the TV, smiling at Darrow and me. "You like that?" he gloated.

"What's the matter with you?" Darrow growled at our division officer. "Petty Officer Murphy was there that night. What do you think is so funny about a young man getting murdered like he did?"

"Oh, there's nothing funny about Miller's murder. Especially seeing as he was killed before he had the chance to repent for his disgusting, sinful ways and get right with Jesus Christ," Krause said. "I'm just happy to see that God has finally found us worthy of His blessing! He has reached out to save this ship, and the Navy, from the wickedness that has infested it."

"What the fuck are you talking about?" Darrow asked, losing patience with our division officer.

Krause pointed at the television. "You don't get it? That was national news, gentlemen. That was seen all over the country. Even in Washington DC. Men, what do you think our new president's going to do in light of this when he takes office in January? You think he's going to reward Captain Fleming for commanding a 'floating Animal House' that murders its own? Or do you think he's going to take our captain away from us?"

Shocked, I looked at Darrow. With a look of genuine concern on his face, my master chief nodded at me, telling me that our skipper getting removed was a real possibility.

OLONGAPO EARP

We were in serious danger of losing our patron, the man who had been protecting us since I beat Randy Green into epilepsy the year before.

*****

A week later, I came out of my episode to find Yukiko naked and cowering in the corner, screaming at me to stay away from her. I was unable to figure out where I was or what had happened. One second, I was fighting my father, the next, El Salvadoran soldiers. I snapped out of it when I was back in Olongapo, shooting at the gang punks in the alley off of Harris Street.

I couldn't understand how it happened. There were no triggers, no stressors; there was nothing that could have set me off. Yukiko and I had finished making love. We were lying on the futon on the floor of her apartment. She had fallen asleep and I was watching her, marveling at her porcelain skin. When she shifted her position to get comfortable, the expression on her face changed ever so slightly. It made me remember how she looked the evening that David Miller was killed.

After that, everything happened at once. Whisked back to that night, I relived running across the Albuquerque Bridge, trying to keep Miller's life from falling out of his head. Then it was that boy in the Philippines, but this time in slow motion. I watched the bullet pierce his skull high above his eyes, forcing its contents to erupt from the top of it in a grotesque geyser of gory gray matter. And then came the rest.

Things between Yukiko and I went way too fast. I never had the chance to confide in her about my episodes. She had no idea of what my father had done to my family. Nor was she aware of any of the sordid events I had experienced since joining the Navy. My episode came at her out of nowhere, and she was not even close to being prepared for it.

Not that I was. I nearly got stabbed outside the Pagoda. I watched a man get shot through the throat. I even killed someone myself. I did that all without ever triggering a flashback. I had convinced myself that I was cured.

"Yukiko," I said, reaching out to her. "Are you okay? Are you hurt? Did I…"

"Get away from me!" A streetlamp shining in from her window cast a shard of light across the corner where she sought refuge. It illuminated her neck, and I thought it looked reddened as if my fingers had been wrapped around it.

I swallowed hard, feeling like I was going to vomit. I needed to get out of there. As I searched around for my clothes, I tried to apologize. "Yukiko, I'm sorry. I should have explained, but there was just no time. It seemed like we came right from the bridge to here and…I don't know. I get these dreams, well they're not exactly dreams, they're more like flashbacks where I relive some stuff that happened to me and…"

Looking over at Yukiko, I could see that she was having none of it. Her eyes were wide in terror and I could tell that she could not understand a word that I said. Explaining it to her now was futile. Instead, I kept apologizing as I got dressed. Then I ran out of the door.

There were no cabs out that late and my bearings were all off. It took me forever to determine which direction the base was in. As I walked, I tried to figure out what had happened. Yukiko was everything I wanted. She was beautiful, smart, sophisticated, and exotic. She was also independent and successful. The two of us together could have accomplished so much. When I thought about it, though, that could have been what triggered me.

Yukiko did not have to put up with my episodes if she did not want to. She could do better, and she should. There was no reason for her to latch on to someone as damaged as I was. The realization hurt, but it was what it was.

Space Kate's words once more echoed around my head:

One day you're going to meet someone that can handle you, a great girl who's probably been through some shit herself, and the two of you are going to make each other very happy.

More than ever, I now believed that that 'someone' was Tala.

Yukiko did not need me. Tala did. As I walked back to my ship that night, I finally realized that I needed her too. If I brought her back to the United States, I would still fear losing her. If I was in the Philippines with her, though, I was the best offer that she was going to get.

By the time I crossed the quarterdeck, it was four in the morning and I was out of cigarettes. Knowing that Master Chief Darrow kept a carton in his desk, I walked straight up to the EMO office to grab a pack. When I opened the door, I was surprised to find my master chief in civilian clothes, drunk, and sitting at his desk. Then again, I wasn't. "Jung threw you out, didn't she?"

Darrow nodded. "Yep. She saw me on CNN the day we left Subic. She bought her plane ticket back to San Diego within an hour but stayed long enough to kick me square in the balls before she left."

I grinned. "Sorry, Master Chief. It happens to the best of us. In high school, a swift kick to the crotch and a blast of mace to my eyes was the way my girlfriends let me know that we should start seeing other people. You okay?"

My master chief shrugged. "I'm okay as can be, I guess. It sucked, but it had to happen. It's better this way than if I'd dragged it out. So, what are you doing here, anyway?"

"I need to bum a pack of smokes off of you."

Darrow reached into his drawer and tossed me a pack. After I lit one, I took a seat in the lieutenant's chair. "Hey Master Chief, this thing you and TJ are working on in San Felipe. Is it legit, or is it cover for something else?"

The master chief's eyes narrowed at me. "What do you mean by 'cover?'"

"Exactly what I said. Look, you and Tejada go way back, and by your own admission, you've not exactly spent your career doing things by the book. Before I make a decision, I need to know if I'm getting into a legitimate business or getting sucked into something darker. 'The big leagues,' as you put it."

Darrow stubbed out his cigarette. "Yeah, Tejada and I have a history. Olongapo is a complicated machine with a lot of moving parts. You had the interests of the military on one side, the interests of the Philippine economy on the other. You had the safety of the sailors you had to protect, and the bar girls you had to protect from the sailors."

Even while drinking, Master Chief Darrow was able to articulate Olongapo's complexities in a way I could understand. "You know, prostitution is illegal in the Philippines, yet Subic Bay is one of the biggest red-light districts in the world, right? Some loopholes are exploited to let it operate in the open. Because of that, we call it a 'gray market.' The gray market depends on the black market to keep it running. If we crack down too hard on the black market, we create a vacuum. When we do that, the criminal elements start fighting each other to fill the void. That leads to violence, which nobody wants. So, Tejada and I worked to promote stability. Is that clear?"

I took a drag off of my cigarette and nodded. "Yeah, that makes sense."

"If you have a group working the black market that can stay out of the headlines and not stir things up, it can work very well. They can get the girls what they need to get through their lives and even help us keep undesirables out before they become a problem. The danger is in letting them get too powerful. You don't want them running the show like they do in Mexico. With this in mind, the cops will let them do their thing, but not for free. They pay a hefty premium for the police to look the other way while these gangsters conduct their business. If the crooks get out of line, though, the cops do not hesitate to put them back into their place, no matter how much they're paying."

My master chief chuckled. "Like when those dipshits shot Tejada. Oh my god, was that ever a colossal clusterfuck! Four hours after that happened, damn near the entire gang running Barrio Barretto was assuming room temperature.

"Anyway, Tejada's been doing this stuff forever. It's time for him to get out. That happens to coincide with me getting out of this racket here in the Navy. We thought about opening a small beach resort, but the prime spots with nice calm water are way out of our price range. The only one that is attainable to us has water that's a little too rough for little children to be swimming in. According to you, it has some potential for surfing, though. We don't know shit about surfing. You do. We need you for this. It's a legit business that's going to allow us to avoid doing things like we had in the past."

"And you're going to let me buy in for $50,000?"

Darrow nodded. "That and your help in putting together a deal for Tejada here in Japan that's a little less legit. He's got something in the Philippines that he needs to sell. He wants us to find the right buyer."

I sank into my chair. "Drugs?"

Darrow looked at me like I was an idiot. "Of course not."

"People?"

"For Christ's sake, no."

"Is it something I'm going to have to smuggle into Japan?"

OLONGAPO EARP

Darrow shook his head. "No, none of that. There's some risks that have to be taken, but I'm assuming those. In fact, that part's already done. All we want from you is to find the proper person and set up a meeting. Not even here in Japan. We want you to convince them to meet with Tejada in Olongapo. Once that deal is finished, you'll have a third share in our San Felipe venture."

"Set up a meeting? That's it?"

My master chief glowered at me. "Look, Doyle, there is no 'that's it.' When I told you 'Welcome to the big leagues,' this is what I meant. It ain't going to be easy. It's going to be work. Tejada and I have done stuff like this before, so we know how to cut the risk. We've done everything we need to for this to go as best it can. Make no mistake, though, if we have a weak link here, it's you. If you fuck this up, everything falls apart. I think you can do it, though. In fact, you're a far better person to play the part we have planned for you than either me or TJ."

"What's the merchandise that Tejada's trying to peddle?" I asked.

"Are you in, or are you out?"

"I need to know what…"

"Are you in? Or are you out?"

I thought about Tala. I thought about Mari. I thought about spending the rest of my life on the beach in a tropical paradise, hanging out with people like Space Kate and Dreadlock John. It would be just like Ocean Beach.

When I considered it, I never had much of a future. My father made sure of that. If this worked out, though, I could make myself happy for a very long time. If it didn't, well, maybe that was just my destiny. I escaped a lengthy prison sentence for what I had done to Randy Green, one I probably deserved for what happened to Rafaela and Manny in the process. If I lost this gamble and landed behind bars for whatever Darrow and Tejada wanted me to do, maybe it was just karma.

Resigning myself to whatever fate wanted to do with me, I looked Darrow in the eye and said, "I'm in."

*****

J.E. PARK

EPILOGUE

By the end of December, Tala was walking the former Subic Bay Naval Station with a shotgun in her hands and the sun on her face. She asked Lorna to take a picture of her, which she sent to me in a letter. Tala barely cleared five feet in height but did her best to look as fierce as she could in her uniform, holding her weapon. It was adorable. She reminded me of a cute little attack bunny.

In her letter, Tala told me that she was grateful for the opportunity Sergeant Tejada offered her. She put Mari into a new school, a better one, where all the other mothers knew her only as a security guard. Nobody considered her a whore any longer.

She also told me that Mari was wonderful. Her daughter finally had friends and was doing great in school. English was her favorite subject. She seemed to study it during every waking moment, hoping to speak to me in my native tongue one day. She had grown tired of my awful Tagalog.

Tala said Mari talked about me all the time and often told her friends about how I saved her from an American Marine. Apparently, she forgot how bad I got my ass kicked that day. Mari was also a bit confused about the shooting that had happened at our apartment. According to her, the bad guys shot a policeman, and I saved his life by luring them away. Then I beat them all up before they were arrested. Sergeant Tejada confirmed her version of events when he stopped by to check on them. In Mari's eyes, I was larger than life.

OLONGAPO EARP

Tala's letter described a lot of changes happening in Olongapo since we left. There was a bloodbath in Barrio Barreto, and the gang members had cleared out. The brothels along Magsaysay closed as soon as the American flag was lowered over the base. Many of the working girls flocked to Barrio Barretto, but business was so light that most left after a week or two. Baloy Beach was so tame now that Tala told me she was taking Mari there to swim when she got home from work.

Not all the change in Olongapo was good, though. Tala told me how she was heartbroken to see so many more children on the street now. Most were the result of relationships between Filipina women and American men. With their fathers gone and their mothers working long hours, these kids were on their own. They were hungry, neglected, and shunned by other children.

Tala remembered what it was like for her to be on her own at such a young age. Wanting to help, Tala volunteered with a local organization, Children's Hope Ministries, to get the street kids into shelters. She told me it was tough for her to work there, as it often was like reliving her own painful childhood. Having a child who was half-American was a heavy burden for a single woman to bear in the Philippines. It was a scarlet letter, suggesting to everyone that she once worked in the sex industry, whether she had or not. It was impossible to start anew that way. Some women could not handle it. After the pullout, there was a rash of suicides and drug overdoses. That resulted in a lot of orphans. Others simply abandoned their kids and went home.

That was the case the week before, Tala wrote to me. They were called to pick up a six-year-old found living on his own by his landlord. The boy told them that his mother dressed him one morning and sent him to school. She kissed him on the cheek and told him she would be waiting right there for him when he got back. When he returned that afternoon, though, she was gone.

Tala was with them when they processed the little boy into the shelter. They were surprised that, though he was not Amer-Asian, the boy was not very comfortable speaking Tagalog. "Where did you learn to speak English?" the American missionary asked.

"California," the little boy answered.

"Did you live there?"

The little boy nodded.

"Do you have family there?"

The boy shook his head.

The missionary looked at the notes the officers had written. "Your name is Manuel?"

"Yes."

The man wrote that down. "And your mother's name?"

"Rafaela," Manny told them. "Rafaela Green."

Tala struggled to maintain her poker face. She had never heard of Manny before, but after I was nearly killed outside of my apartment, she certainly knew who Rafaela was.

"Do you have any idea where your mother is, Manuel?" one of the missionaries asked.

The little boy shook his head. "No, but I don't think she's coming back."

Tala was pretty sure that Rafaela was not returning, also. In her letter, Tala wondered if Manny's mother was the type of woman who would abandon her son to go into hiding. I did not wonder that at all. I knew that there was no way that Rafaela would leave Manny alone on her own. The only thing I was wondering about was if anyone would ever find her body.

And what I was getting myself into with Tejada and Darrow.

End

Next in the Tequila Vikings Series: Neptune's Martyrs (Aug 2021)

Author's Note –   Did you enjoy this story? If so, I invite you to *please* leave a review on Amazon.com! Good reviews not only raise the visibility of an author's work; they massage our fragile egos. It keeps us from priming our muses with absinthe and psychosis.

OLONGAPO EARP

Acknowledgments

No great task is ever undertaken alone, and this was certainly no exception. There were plenty of people who offered me their encouragement and support in getting this, and the subsequent books of this series, written.

The first people I have to thank is my family. This has been a LONG effort, three years in the making, and there was a lot of time taken away from my wife and children to get this done. To Patrina, Regan, Mason, Carson, Fairen, and Linden, I love you and thank you for your patience, enthusiasm, and support.

Second, I have to thank the men I served with aboard the *USS Belleau Wood* in the early 1990s. The *Tequila Viking* series is absolutely a work of fiction, but it was inspired by the diverse cast of colorful characters I was in the Navy with. I would like to acknowledge those who invited me into NPA territory while we were closing the base down in 1992 and supplied me with enough anecdotes to keep *Olongapo Earp* interesting.

As usual, I also need to thank the Grand Blanc Authors Meetup who have continually read, critiqued, and listened to my work for three years now. THANK YOU!

I would also like to thank Jim Goodman, the admin of the Subic Bay Olongapo & Angeles City Memories (For Vets) Facebook group, for his support of the Tequila Vikings release. If you were stationed in the Philippines, check out his group! If you were not, you could also learn more about Olongapo at The Subic Bay Project group he also runs. That one's a bit more family-friendly. I also need to shout out to Steve Morgan, the world's best bartender in Sasebo, Japan, for his invaluable advice that helped me navigate my misadventures in the Far East during my gloriously misspent youth. I sincerely thank you. Not going to lie, though. My liver's still pissed.

And, of course, my beta readers! Rich Sorgenfrei and Tim Geniac, thank you so much for your help and invaluable assistance in helping me get this done.

OLONGAPO EARP

And, of course, to you, the reader, thank you so much for continuing through the second book in the Tequila Viking saga. I hope I earned the opportunity to have you continue on and read Book 3 – *Neptune's Martyrs*.

Appendix I
Slang and Abbreviations

1MC -	The ship's public address system.
Aft -	In the direction of the stern of a ship.
AFPD	Armed Forces Police Department – An American military law enforcement organization tasked with keeping order in Olongapo, Philippines
Airedales -	Sailors assigned in roles to support air operations.
A School -	Navy school that teaches a recruit how to do their job.
BCD	Bad Conduct Discharge. Also known as the "Big Chicken Dinner."
BE/E School -	Basic Electricity and Electronics School. This is the first phase of training for US Navy electronics rates for ET, FC, ST.
Blanket Party -	(or "Bosun Locker Counseling Session" or "Fan Room Counseling Session") Unauthorized, and illegal, disciplinary action involving violence to adjust a crew member's behavior or mete out revenge if a man could not be held accountable through normal channels.
Booter –	Green, new sailor. Fresh out of boot camp or A School.
Brig -	The ship's jail.

OLONGAPO EARP

Bow -   The front of a ship.

Bulkhead -   Wall on a ship.

Captain's Mast -   Non-judicial punishment for relatively minor (misdemeanor) offenses. Sentences can range from restriction, loss of pay, confinement with bread and water, or discharge from service (known as Article 15 in other services).

C School -   Technical school that teaches a sailor how to perform a specific task or repair a particular piece of equipment. Training that allows a sailor to become a specialist within their rate.

CIC -   Combat Information Center. The place on a ship where the crew monitors the radar, sonar, and other detection systems. It is a dark room with a lot of electronics gear.

CSE -   Combat Systems (Electronics). A division of the Combat Systems Department in charge of maintaining radar and communications equipment.

CSO -   Combat Systems Office -or- Combat Systems Officer. Is used interchangeably as a space or a person. The CSO person is located in the CSO location.

CO -   Commanding Officer.

Deck -   The floor or the ground on a ship.

Deck Apes -   Boatswain's Mates, sailors assigned to the Deck Department charged with maintaining the appearance and working order of ship's surfaces.

EMO -   Electronics Materials Office -or- Electronics Materials Officer. Is used interchangeably as a space or a person. The EMO person is located in the EMO location.

Field Day -   Deep cleaning of a ship's spaces.

Fore -   In the direction of the bow of a ship.

Gedunk -   Junk food.

GI Shower -	(or "The Scrub") When the sailors pull a crew member with hygiene issues into the shower to clean him up with wire brushes, scalding water, and industrial abrasives.
Gundecking -	Signing off work as complete despite not actually doing it.
Head -	Bathroom.
Helm -	The wheel used to steer the ship.
IC Line -	Ship's internal telephone system.
JAG	Judge Advocate General – A Navy lawyer
Ladder -	Stairs.
LBFM -	Little Brown Fucking Machine. Slang for Filipina bar girls (not derogatory. It is a complimentary, if vulgar, term – bar girls would often refer to themselves as an LBFM).
Liberty Drip -	Venereal Disease.
Master-at-Arms -	Navy version of an MP (Military Policeman).
NIS -	Naval Investigative Service. The US Navy's version of the FBI. At the time of this story, the NIS had just been renamed as the NCIS (Naval Criminal Investigative Service), but the change was new, and the sailors of the fleet still usually referred to it by its old name.
OOD -	Officer of the Deck. This is the watch that controls access to the ship and is in charge of the quarterdeck while in port.
Overhead -	The ceiling on a ship.
Passageways -	Hallways on a ship.
Pecker Checkers -	Hospital Corpsmen, the ship's medical personnel.
PI -	The Philippines.
PMS -	Preventative Maintenance Schedule. This dictates the frequency and timing of equipment maintenance tasks.
POOW -	Petty Officer of the Watch. Mans the podium on the quarterdeck while in port, armed with a

	pistol. Makes the announcements over the 1MC, logs activity about the ship.
Port -	The left side of a ship when facing forward.
Rank -	Paygrade of a sailor, his place in the command hierarchy.
Rate -	The job a sailor is trained to perform aboard a ship.
RPPO	Repair Parts Petty Officer – the technician on temporary duty to requisition parts for the division.
Sand Dog -	San Diego
Scuttlebutt -	A rumor or a drinking fountain.
Shellback -	A sailor that has gone through the Shellback initiation ritual while crossing the equator – a tradition hundreds of years old.
Skating -	Avoiding work, goofing off (also skylarking).
Space -	A room or a compartment on a ship.
Snipes -	Engineers. Sailors charged with the propulsion of ship and essential services such as electricity, water, and fuel.
SP –	Shore Patrol. US Navy version of MP, but composed of duty personnel, not professional military police personnel.
Starboard -	The right side of a ship when facing forward.
Stern -	The back end of a ship.
TJ -	Tijuana, Mexico
Trons -	Electronics
Twidgets -	Technicians, sailors working in technical rates.
UCMJ -	Uniform Code of Military Justice. This is the list of laws and regulations that apply to military personnel, violations of which can be punished under a Captain's Mast or court-martial.
Wog -	A sailor who has never crossed the equator and has not taken part in the Shellback initiation.
XO -	Executive Officer (ship's second in command).

J.E. PARK

Appendix II
Rates and Rank

Officers

Naval officer ranks are straightforward, progressing from the lowest officer paygrade (O-1) to the highest (O-10).

O-1	Ensign (ENS)
O-2	Lieutenant Junior Grade (LTJG)
O-3	Lieutenant (LT)
O-4	Lieutenant Commander (LCDR)
O-5	Commander (CDR)
O-6	Captain (CAP)
O-7	Rear Admiral Lower Half (RADM)
O-8	Rear Admiral Upper Half (RADM)
O-9	Vice Admiral (VADM)
O-10	Admiral (ADM)

Enlisted Rates and Rank

Rank

Enlisted ranks are among the most complicated of any US military branch. A typical enlisted rank consists of a two or three letter rate designation followed by letters or numbers that identify a sailor's paygrade. For instance, the rank "ET2" means that a sailor is an E-5, a second-class electronics technician. The "ET" signifies that the sailor is an Electronics

Technician. The "2" indicates that their paygrade is E-5. An ETSN would be a junior Electronics Technician whose paygrade was E-3. An ETCM would be a Master Chief Electronics Technician (paygrade E-9).

Junior enlisted ranks are identified by hash marks on the right arm, the color of which designates which general function of the ship's contingent they work for.

Seaman (White Hash Marks) – General seamanship duties
Airman (Green Hash Marks) – General aviation duties
Fireman (Red Hash Marks) – General engineering duties

E-1	Seaman / Airman / Fireman Recruit (SR, AR, FR)
E-2	Seaman / Airman / Fireman Apprentice (SA, AA, FA)
E-3	Seaman / Airman / Fireman (SN, AN, FN)
E-4	Petty Officer Third Class (PO3)
E-5	Petty Officer Second Class (PO2)
E-6	Petty Officer First Class (PO1)
E-7	Chief Petty Officer (POC)
E-8	Senior Chief Petty Officer (POCS)
E-9	Master Chief Petty Officer (POCM)

Rates

AC	Air Traffic Controller
AG	Aerographer's Mate
AO	Aviation Ordinanceman
BM	Boatswain's Mate
DS	Data Systems Technician
ET	Electronics Technician
FC	Fire Control Technician
GM	Gunner's Mate
HM	Hospital Corpsman
MA	Master-at-Arms
MS	Mess Specialist
OS	Operations Specialist

OLONGAPO EARP

QM	Quartermaster
RM	Radioman
SK	Storekeeper
ST	Sonar Technician
SM	Signalman
YN	Yeoman

Author's Note –

The Engineering Department is grossly underrepresented in this story. This is only because it is told from the viewpoint of an Electronics Technician. ETs tended to work near the top of the island structure on an amphibious assault ship, several stories above the waterline. The snipes worked deep within the ship's bowels, well below the surface of the ocean. The two groups did not mix much, served different duties and watches, and rarely crossed paths anywhere but on the mess decks. On the occasions I did run into an engineer shipmate out in town, ninety-five percent of the time they did not even look familiar to me, nor I to them. Mad props to the snipes, though – they worked insanely hard at a dirty, demanding job. Without them, a navy ship goes nowhere. - JEP

About the Tequila Vikings Series

The *Tequila Vikings Saga* is a four-part series chronicling the story of Doyle Murphy as he seeks his place in the world and a way to overcome the trauma of his childhood while serving aboard the *USS Belleau Wood*.

Book One – Tequila Vikings
Book Two – Olongapo Earp
Book Three –Neptune's Martyrs
Book Four – Darien Gap

Next in Series – Neptune's Martyrs

Longing to return to the Philippines, Doyle Murphy embarks upon a risky venture with Master Chief Darrow and Rico Tejada that can set them up for life. Or destroy them all forever.

About the Author

J.E. Park grew up near Detroit, MI, where he spent much of his gloriously misspent youth seeking misadventure within the Motor City's punk rock scene. After high school, he joined the Navy and spent several years bar brawling his way across the Far East, the experiences that formed the bedrock of the *Tequila Vikings* novels.

SNEAK PEEK
NEPTUNE'S MARTYRS

Prologue

S taff Sergeant Emilio Payan laughed at the Pampanga Aeta when they fled their homes in April. More often known as *negritos,* Payan always thought the Aeta were a funny people. They were short, very dark, and the hair on their heads was coarse and kinky. They looked more like African pygmies than Filipinos. They lived more like them too. They dressed in rags and slept in bamboo huts without electricity or running water. The Aeta also prayed to the spirits of nature, which Payan considered an affront to the tradition of Philippine Catholicism.

Their animistic religions, along with their ways as hunters and gatherers, made the Aeta seem primitive. Emilio Payan was far from being the only Filipino to regard them as unsophisticated and prone to the whimsy of superstition. It was why the sergeant ridiculed them when they abandoned their homes on the slopes of Pinatubo. All it took was a few minor earthquakes around the mountain's summit, and the runts went running for the lowlands.

On June 15th, 1991, ten weeks after the start of the Aeta exodus, Sergeant Payan realized that the *negritos* had been on to something, and he wished that he had fled with them.

By then, it looked like the world was about to end. Pinatubo erupted on June 12th, spewing a column of ash more than twelve miles into the

313

heavens. Payan saw it happen firsthand. Stationed at the Cesar Basa Air Base, he was less than fifteen miles from the volcano. From the porch of his barracks, it looked as if he was standing right in the middle of it. A massive ash cloud blotted out the sky and once the sun set that night, it would not rise again for two days.

Like everywhere else within a hundred miles of Pinatubo, the base descended into chaos. The facility never received any warning about an impending eruption. Because of that, they never got its squadron of F-8 Crusaders off of the ground. Most of Basa's airmen had to be dispatched to the hangars to do whatever they could to save the jets. The commander of the base sent others to secure the food and water supplies. Some rushed to maintain communications and coordinate the base's response to the disaster. Payan ended up on a detail ordered to secure the armory on the other side of the facility. This gave the sergeant pause. Payan's objective was located that much closer to the source of the commotion that he wanted to get away from.

The airbase's arsenal was housed in a large, square cinderblock building. It had a flat roof perfectly designed to capture all the ash spewed by an erupting volcano and hold it in place until it collapsed under the weight. When Payan stepped inside, the rafters were already creaking with an ominous warning that they were not going to hold up for long. Within thirty seconds of their arrival, half of the detail was urgently ordered to find shovels to clear the roof. The other half was sent scrounging for materials to shore it up.

The shovel squad was first to find success, ransacking a nearby groundskeeping shack. It does not snow much in the Philippines, so the scavenged shovels were not quite the right tool for the job. Still, they were better than nothing. Upon their return, Payan's men tied bandanas around their mouths to keep ash out of their lungs. They then climbed atop the building and started shoveling feverishly to save it.

Despite their obstacles, the frantic digging of the Philippine airmen gave the roof a fighting chance. None of Payan's men had construction experience, so the scaffolding the other half rigged up was worthless. The sergeant ended up sending them for shovels, also. Trying to reinforce the roof at that point was proving little more than an exercise in futility.

OLONGAPO EARP

Digging was an exhausting effort. The airmen were working in a blizzard of ash that was accumulating quicker than Yukon snow. Still, the troops' efforts were paying off, and they could get ahead of the crisis. Eventually, they even earned brief periods of rest after the girders stopped groaning. Then the rain started.

June is the beginning of the monsoon season in the Philippines, and torrential rainfall at that time was the norm. At that point, any moisture at all added to the volcano's ash would have been devastating to the men trying to save the armory. What the airmen had to deal with the day Pinatubo blew defied comprehension. While at the peak of a historic volcanic eruption, the island of Luzon had to contend with the added catastrophe of getting slammed by Typhoon Yunya as well.

The battle for the armory was lost. Payan ordered his men down off of the roof. "Airman Zubiri!" the sergeant screamed, trying to get the attention of a mechanic in the motor pool.

"Yes, Sergeant!" Sonny Zubiri answered.

"Do you know how to hotwire a truck?"

Sonny grinned. He was from Olongapo. He knew how to hotwire a car long before the Philippine Air Force trained him to be a mechanic. "Of course I do, Sergeant!"

"Good," Payan said, placing his hand on the young man's shoulder. "I need you to go out on base and steal me every truck you can! Bring them back here. We need to move these weapons before we lose them."

"Where are you going to move them to?" the airman asked.

Payan shook his head. "I don't know! One problem at a time! Go get me my trucks!"

Another airman, Ronaldo Dela Rosa, approached the sergeant once Sonny Zubiri left. "There's an Aglipayan Church a few kilometers from here. It's been empty a while, but the building is still good. It has a pointed roof, so the ash should fall off instead of building up like it is here. The weapons should be safer there." A blast of wind shook the armory and started the roof supports protesting again. After hearing that, Airman Dela Rosa added, "And so will we."

Payan nodded in agreement. He looked at his watch and then out the door that Zubiri had used, shaking his head in disbelief. It was one in the afternoon, yet it was dark as midnight outside. The wind was screaming, it was raining concrete, and the volcano was making the ground shake. Turning to the airman, Sergeant Payan sighed. "Yes, I would feel much better sheltered in a house built by God than one built by a relative of Ferdinand Marcos. Even if it's not Catholic."

Emilio Payan tried to radio his plans back to the command center, but there was no answer. When Airman Zubiri returned with the first transport, a Kia-built M35, he tried again with the truck's CB. Still, he came up with nothing. "I think the main base is out of power," the airman said. "The road to it is cut off, and I couldn't see any lights at all ahead of me."

"You can't see anything in this shit," Payan answered. "Not even the sun."

Zubiri turned a dial on the console, and the men heard a local news announcer come over the truck's speakers. "At least the regular radio is working."

"What have they been saying?" Payan asked.

Zubiri looked at the sergeant. "They're saying it's bad out there. Very bad. Bridges are washed out, and landslides are happening all over Pampanga and Zambales. There are reports that a couple of villages were completely swept away."

That concerned Sergeant Payan. The base was close to the Gumain River, which originated somewhere up on Pinatubo's slopes. He feared that the ash could form dams in some of the highland streams. If that happened, they could burst and send lahars, towering waves of mud, barrelling down the sides of the volcano, burying them all alive. "We need to get these weapons the hell out of here."

"Fuck the weapons, Sergeant," Airman Zubiri said. "We need to get the hell out of here ourselves!"

The sergeant shook his head. "This base is going to take some severe damage. It's going to be very compromised when this is all over. You know as well as I do that the New People's Army is all over these mountains. If we don't secure this armory, the communists are going to march right in here and take…"

It was 13:42 military time. Mount Pinatubo roared with the second most powerful volcanic explosion of the twentieth century. It was exceeded only by Alaska's Novarupta in 1912. The shockwave rocked the truck Payan and

OLONGAPO EARP

Zubiri were sheltering in and blasted them from the M35's cockpit and into the mud.

Nine hundred feet of mountain top was blown high into the sky, some of it landing as far away as the South China Sea, twenty-five miles away. Much more of it poured into where Payan and his men were struggling to hold their ground. Besides the wind, the ash, and the water, Payan's detail now had to contend with volcanic rocks raining down upon them like mortar fire.

"GO GET ME MORE TRUCKS!" the sergeant screamed as they both dove back into the deuce-and-a-half for cover. Zubiri could not hear him, however. Temporarily deafened by the explosion, the only thing the airman registered was the ringing in his ears. Still, he was able to read Payan's lips beneath the vehicle's dome light. Leaving the truck, Zubiri scrambled to carry out his orders. He figured that the faster they completed their mission, the sooner they could get the hell out of there.

The next truck Airman Zubiri got to the armory broke down as soon as it arrived. The other vehicle was already gone, delivering its first load of weaponry to the church. The mechanic discovered that the ash had plugged up the air filters and, starved of oxygen, the engine stalled. It was not a difficult situation to rectify in a closed garage, but trying to fix it in the midst of a cement storm was something else entirely. It took far more time to get the second truck running than it should have, yet the first M35 did not return before Zubiri finished. Worried that it could have stalled too, the airman rode with the men on the second gun run instead of looking for another vehicle.

As the airman suspected, the first team had broken down on the way back to base in Pabanlag, short of the bridge to Apalit. Zubiri disembarked to get their transport running again while the crew doubled up to unload back at the church. They at least passed the airman on the return trip before breaking down again.

Staff Sergeant Payan decided that was the best that they could do. They would run two trucks back and forth while keeping Zubiri on the road to get them running again when they broke down. In three hours, the sergeant's men made five trips. They dropped a considerable amount of weaponry on hallowed ground but barely made a dent in the cache still left in the armory.

J.E. PARK

*****

Airman Zubiri was finishing up the seventh repair of the exercise when a loud crash went off behind him. He was in Apalit, about a half kilometer from the bridge. Judging by the sound, Zubiri suspected that the span over the Gumain River had just been obliterated. At first, he wanted to run up the road to confirm his suspicions, but the racket was loud enough to be heard over the ringing that still filled his ears. That alone was enough to convince him to drive in the opposite direction as fast as possible.

Sonny cursed. If the men were to be stranded, it was better to be at the church where the roof was less likely to collapse. The armory was a death trap. Zubiri already knew that they were cut off from the rest of the base, so there was no option to retreat to the command center. "What the hell are we going to do?" the airman asked himself as he raced back to Sergeant Payan to give him the news. *Stay in those flimsy houses outside the perimeter? They can't survive this any better than the armory. Nothing can.*

As the airman approached the base's fence, he sensed that things were beginning to lighten up. He could see the headlights of the other truck from the far side of the guard post. Zubiri was using them to guide himself to the armory when he heard another roar rising in front of him. Then the lights suddenly went out. The truck, along with the buildings, weapons, and men, were swept away by a massive lahar that swallowed them from the west. They vanished right before Zubiri's eyes. Instinctively, Sonny threw the M35 into reverse and stomped on the gas, but it was a futile gesture. He did not make it twenty-five yards before the wall of mud slammed into him too.

The M35 weighed more than two tons, but it was thrown to its side as if it were a toy. The lahar pushed the vehicle off the road and into a field, relentlessly forcing it forward until it slammed into a row of trees. The impact snapped the palms like toothpicks and blew the truck's side windows out. The Kia then flipped onto its back, allowing the mud to pour in with no way for Zubiri to escape.

"SERGEANT PAYAN!" the airman screamed. He knew no one could answer his cries, but it was all that he could do. The mud was rising fast inside the cab, and Zubiri could sense that drowning in it seemed inevitable. Near tears, the airman cried out again. "SERGEANT PAYAN!

OLONGAPO EARP

PLEASE!" When the sergeant failed to answer, Zubiri appealed to someone higher up in the chain of command. "JESUS CHRIST! HELP ME! JESUS, SAVE ME!"

Nothing. The mud crept up the cab, engulfing Sonny to his waist. At that point, he gave up trying to call on his sergeant and his savior. He started crying for his mother instead.

Of all the names the airman invoked to save his life, only Imelda Zubiri proved powerful enough to intervene. As if guided by her divine hand, the overturned truck struck something solid enough to flip it over onto its side again. The mud within the cab lurched up and slammed Zubiri into the dashboard hard enough to force all the air out of his lungs, then it buried him. But only for a moment. When the airman fought his way to the surface, he not only caught a breath of precious oxygen; he found a path of escape through the window of the passenger door as well. Sonny was able to climb up the seat and pull himself from the M35.

Once out of the truck, Zubiri discovered that he was much higher off the ground than he realized. The Kia was riding atop a lahar that was at least twenty feet high. It stopped moving with the wave of mud only after becoming entangled within a clutch of trees a kilometer from where the airman had started. Sonny was among the upper limbs, balancing upon a massive vehicle being sucked into the muck. From the cab, Zubiri raced along the side of the transport until he could reach branches thick enough to support his weight. The airman then scrambled as high up into the canopy as he dared. As Sonny held on for dear life against the wind, he watched the mud engulf his truck beneath him until it completely disappeared.

The eruptions of Mount Pinatubo ceased at about 10:30 that night. Typhoon Yunya, by then a tropical depression, ended a short time later, pushing out into the South China Sea. Airman Zubiri remained stuck in the trees, wet and freezing, while the winds lashed at him through the night. Morning brought little relief. When the sun finally rose for the first time in thirty-six hours, it baked him without mercy. There was no cover. The leaves had been ripped off the trees by wind shear that often exceeded ninety miles an hour.

By the time he was discovered by an American helicopter surveying the damage to Clark Air Base nearby, Zubiri was delirious. Driven mad with thirst and ravaged by both hypo- and hyperthermia, he was hallucinating and hysterical. The airman had stripped down to his underwear and was shrieking for his mother to save him once more. When a rescue chopper from the Philippine Air Force finally plucked Sonny from his perch, he collapsed from exhaustion. He passed out the moment the medics placed him on a stretcher and did not wake up again for more than three days.

*****

A week later, Zubiri was in a hospital on the outskirts of Manila. Lieutenant Carlos Enverga from the Basa Air Base told him that he was the only survivor of the twelve-man detail sent to secure the armory. The search and rescue teams located two bodies, but hopes were not high that they would find any more. There was little left of that part of the base. The only thing that remained of the armory was the foundation, and even that sat beneath fifteen feet of hardening sludge.

"What about the weapons?" Zubiri asked.

The lieutenant shrugged. "Lost. We found a few that were salvageable, but most of what we recovered was ruined."

Since the officer did not mention anything about what they had stashed at the church, neither did Zubiri. "Payan was worried about the NPA getting hold of them."

Enverga laughed. "Good luck to them. It's like trying to find pencils in quicksand. We can't even locate the truck you said you were swept away in. I don't see how they would ever come across the odd rifle in that stuff."

Sonny nodded. "What a waste. Eleven men gone, and we lost the armory anyway. It hardly seems worth it."

"It wasn't." Lieutenant Enverga thought for a moment, then asked, "You don't blame yourself for this at all, do you? For not getting to them with the truck in time to evacuate?"

Zubiri flinched as a realization struck him. *The lieutenant thinks the truck was for the men, not the weapons. He has no idea what we were doing.* Airman Zubiri shrugged, running with the lieutenant's assumption. "I failed. How can I not?"

"Stop it. You men were up against the fury of God that night. Your opinion of yourself must be very high to think you had any chance of holding back that kind of power. Is there anything I can do for you, airman? Have you heard from your family?"

Zubiri shook his head. "They're all displaced, too. Phones are down. We don't know where they're at."

"You know anyone else we can get in touch with who may be able to track them down?"

Sonny thought for a moment. "I have a cousin in the Philippine National Police. It might help if you somehow got in touch with him."

The lieutenant pulled a small notebook and a pencil out of his shirt pocket. "Do you have a name?"

Zubiri nodded. "Sergeant Tejada. Rico Tejada. He works in Olongapo." *He'll know what to do with the weapons we saved.*

*****

"…and now TJ's sitting on five truckloads of M-16s, hand grenades, MP5s, 9mm pistols, and a bunch of ammo." Master Chief Darrow stubbed out his cigarette as he finished the story. Leaning back in his chair and putting his feet up on his desk, he added, "As far as the Philippine government is concerned, it's gone. It's buried beneath a couple dozen feet of volcanic concrete. The only people he can sell it to in PI are drug runners, communists, mutineers, or Moro separatists. The kind of people most likely to use the weapons against him. He's willing to unload the cache at a bargain to someone who can get it out of the country."

"And he thinks we can find someone like that in Japan?" I asked.

Darrow shrugged. "I do too. The *yakuza* are a pretty sophisticated group with international contacts. They could unload them to the Burmese or someone else in the Golden Triangle. Or even the Chinese triads. The trick is going to be finding someone to talk to."

"And you think I can do that?"

My master chief shrugged. "You speak a little Japanese. You're pretty knowledgeable about the culture. You'd be better doing it than I would. That also happens to be the least risky part of this too. The way I see it is we split the operation to keep our exposure down. I'll handle the merchandise, the samples, and never be seen with our contacts. You manage the connections so you'll never be seen with the merchandise. If I get pinched, I'm fucked, but I can't give up our *yakuza* guys. If you get pinched, they can't tie you to the guns."

I had to trust Darrow on the operational side of what he was proposing. It was too far out of my area of expertise. "What's our cut on this?" I asked him.

"Ten percent."

"Of what?"

Darrow grinned. "TJ thinks he's sitting on roughly eight million of product. He might be overestimating a bit, though."

My jaw dropped as I did the calculation in my head. "That'd be $400,000 apiece."

"It would," my master chief agreed. "Not bad for simply arranging a meeting, is it?"

*****

www.ingramcontent.com/pod-product-compliance
Lightning Source LLC
Chambersburg PA
CBHW020907200626
46814CB00001BA/220

* 9 7 8 1 7 3 5 0 9 4 0 3 8 *